Critical Acclaim for

THE EX

"A horror story for all midnights."

—*The Boston Globe*

"There are not many readers who will be unmoved. Written in a literate style, *The Exorcist* is to most other novels of its kind as an Einstein equation is to an accountant's column of figures."

—*New York Times Book Review*

"Immensely satisfying, it holds its readers in a vise-like grip worthy of Poe."

—*Los Angeles Times*

"Wonderfully exciting."

—*Newsweek*

"Absolutely superb. Blatty makes you think this scary tale really might have happened."

—*Cleveland Plain Dealer*

"Up till dawn, I was, with *The Exorcist*. A shocker . . . driving to a violent conclusion."

—*Cosmopolitan*

"A page-turner par excellence. Poe and Mary Shelley would recognize [Blatty] as working in their ambiguous limbo between the natural and the supernatural . . . hair-raising."

—*Life*

"A tremendous novel . . . fast, powerful, and completely gripping, a hypnotic combination of morality tale and supernatural detective story. A parable for our times, a stunning achievement."

—*The London Sunday Express*

"*The Exorcist* should be read twice; the first time for the passion and horrifying intensity of the story, with a second reading to savor the subtleties of language and phrasing. . . . It's an experience you will never forget."

—*St. Louis Post-Dispatch*

"Suspense that never lets up!"

—*Publishers Weekly*

"A fantastic and deeply religious novel that will touch the reader to his very soul as it touches on things in this world that cannot be explained away rationally."

—*Texas Abilene Reporter-News*

THE EXORCIST

Also by William Peter Blatty

Fiction

Which Way to Mecca, Jack?
John Goldfarb, Please Come Home
I, Billy Shakespeare!
Twinkle, Twinkle, "Killer" Kane
The Exorcist
The Ninth Configuration
Legion
Demons Five, Exorcists Nothing
Elsewhere
Dimiter
Crazy

Nonfiction

I'll Tell Them I Remember You
William Peter Blatty on 'The Exorcist': From Novel to Film

40th ANNIVERSARY EDITION

WILLIAM PETER BLATTY

HARPER

NEW YORK . LONDON . TORONTO . SYDNEY

HARPER

A hardcover edition of this book was published in 2011 by HarperCollins Publishers.

First Harper paperback published 2011.

Designed by William Ruoto

Library of Congress Cataloging-in-Publication Data is available upon request.

ISBN 978-0-06-209435-3 (hardcover)
ISBN 978-0-06-209436-0 (pbk.)

22 OV/LSC 20 19

For Julie

And as [Jesus] stepped ashore, there met him a man from the city who was possessed by demons . . . Many times it had laid hold of him and he was bound with chains . . . but he would break the bonds asunder . . . And Jesus asked him, "What is your name?" And he answered, "Legion."

—Luke 8:27–30

JAMES TORELLO: Jackson was hung up on that meat hook. He was so heavy he bent it. He was on that thing three days before he croaked.

FRANK BUCCIERI (giggling): Jackie, you shoulda seen the guy. Like an elephant, he was, and when Jimmy hit him with that electric prod. . .

TORELLO (excitedly): He was floppin' around on that hook, Jackie. We tossed water on him to give the prod a better charge, and he's screamin'. . .

—EXCERPT FROM FBI WIRETAP OF COSA NOSTRA TELEPHONE CONVERSATION RELATING TO MURDER OF WILLIAM JACKSON

There's no other explanation for some of the things the Communists did. Like the priest who had eight nails driven into his skull . . . And there were the seven little boys and their teacher. They were praying the Our Father when soldiers came upon them. One soldier whipped out his bayonet and sliced off the teacher's tongue. The other took chopsticks and drove them into the ears of the seven little boys. How do you treat cases like that?

—DR. TOM DOOLEY

Dachau
Auschwitz
Buchenwald

Contents

THE EXORCIST

Prologue

Northern Iraq . . .

The blaze of sun wrung pops of sweat from the old man's brow, yet he cupped his hands around the glass of hot sweet tea as if to warm them. He could not shake the premonition. It clung to his back like chill wet leaves.

The dig was over. The tell had been sifted, stratum by stratum, its entrails examined, tagged and shipped: the beads and pendants; glyptics; phalli; ground-stone mortars stained with ocher; burnished pots. Nothing exceptional. An Assyrian ivory toilet box. And man. The bones of man. The brittle remnants of cosmic torment that once made him wonder if matter was Lucifer upward-groping back to his God. And yet now he knew better. The fragrance of licorice plant and tamarisk tugged his gaze to poppied hills; to reeded plains; to the ragged, rock-strewn bolt of road that flung itself headlong into dread. Northwest was Mosul; east, Erbil; south was Baghdad and Kirkuk and the fiery furnace of Nebuchadnezzar. He shifted his legs underneath the table in front of the lonely roadside chaykhana and stared at the grass stains on his boots and khaki pants. He sipped at his tea. The dig was over. What was beginning? He dusted the thought like a clay-fresh find but he could not tag it.

Someone wheezed from within the chaykhana: the withered

proprietor shuffling toward him, kicking up dust in Russian-made shoes that he wore like slippers, groaning backs pressed under his heels. The dark of his shadow slipped over the table.

"Kaman chay, chawaga?"

The man in khaki shook his head, staring down at the lace-less, crusted shoes caked thick with debris of the pain of living. The stuff of the cosmos, he softly reflected: matter; yet somehow finally spirit. Spirit and the shoes were to him but aspects of a stuff more fundamental, a stuff that was primal and totally other.

The shadow shifted. The Kurd stood waiting like an ancient debt. The old man in khaki looked up into eyes that were damply bleached as if the membrane of an eggshell had been pasted over the irises. Glaucoma. Once he could not have loved this man. He slipped out his wallet and probed for a coin among its tattered, crumpled tenants: a few dinars; an Iraqi driver's license; a faded plastic Catholic calendar card that was twelve years out of date. It bore an inscription on the reverse: WHAT WE GIVE TO THE POOR IS WHAT WE TAKE WITH US WHEN WE DIE. He paid for his tea and left a tip of fifty fils on a splintered table the color of sadness.

He walked to his jeep. The rippling click of key sliding into ignition was crisp in the silence. For a moment he paused and stared off broodingly. In the distance, shimmering in heat haze that made it look afloat like an island in the sky, loomed the flat-topped, towering mound city of Erbil, its fractured rooftops poised in the clouds like a rubbled, mud-stained benediction.

The leaves clutched tighter at the flesh of his back.

Something was waiting.

"Allah ma'ak, chawaga."

Rotted teeth. The Kurd was grinning, waving farewell. The man in khaki groped for a warmth in the pit of his being and came up with a wave and a mustered smile. It dimmed as he looked away. He started the engine, turned in a narrow, eccentric U and headed toward Mosul. The Kurd stood watching, puzzled by a heart-dropping sense of loss as the jeep gathered speed. What was it that was gone? What was it he had felt in the stranger's presence? Something like safety, he remembered; a sense of protection and deep well-being. Now it dwindled in the distance with the fast-moving jeep. He felt strangely alone.

By ten after six the painstaking inventory was finished. The Mosul curator of antiquities, an Arab with sagging cheeks, was carefully penning a final entry into the ledger on his desk. For a moment he paused, looking up at his friend as he dipped his penpoint into an inkpot. The man in khaki seemed lost in thought. He was standing by a table, hands in his pockets, staring down at some dry, tagged whisper of the past. Curious, unmoving, for moments the curator watched him, then returned to the entry, writing in a firm, very small neat script until at last he sighed, setting down the pen as he noted the time. The train to Baghdad left at eight. He blotted the page and offered tea.

His eyes still fixed upon something on the table, the man in khaki shook his head. The Arab watched him, vaguely troubled. What was in the air? There was something in the air. He stood up and moved closer; then felt a vague prickling at the back of his neck as his friend at last moved, reaching down for an amulet and cradling it pensively in his hand. It was a green stone head of the demon Pazuzu, personification of the southwest wind. Its dominion was sickness and disease. The head was pierced. The amulet's owner had worn it as a shield.

"Evil against evil," breathed the curator, languidly fanning himself with a French scientific periodical, an olive-oil thumbprint smudged on its cover.

His friend did not move; he did not comment. The curator tilted his head to the side. "Is something wrong?" he asked.

No answer.

"Father Merrin?"

The man in khaki still appeared not to hear, absorbed in the amulet, the last of his finds. After a moment he set it down, then lifted a questioning look to the Arab. Had he said something?

"No, Father. Nothing."

They murmured farewells.

At the door, the curator took the old man's hand with an extra firmness.

"My heart has a wish: that you would not go."

His friend answered softly in terms of tea; of time; of something to be done.

"No, no, no! I meant home!"

The man in khaki fixed his gaze on a speck of boiled chickpea nestled in a corner of the Arab's mouth; yet his eyes were distant. "Home," he repeated.

The word had the sound of an ending.

"The States," the Arab curator added, instantly wondering why he had.

The man in khaki looked into the dark of the other's concern. He had never found it difficult to love this man. "Goodbye," he said quietly; then quickly turned and stepped out into the gathering gloom of the streets and a journey home whose length seemed somehow undetermined.

"I will see you in a year!" the curator called after him from the doorway. But the man in khaki never looked back. The Arab watched his dwindling form as he crossed a narrow street at an angle, almost colliding with a swiftly moving droshky. Its cab bore a corpulent old Arab woman, her face a shadow behind the black lace veil draped loosely over her like a shroud. He guessed she was rushing to some appointment. He soon lost sight of his hurrying friend.

The man in khaki walked, compelled. Shrugging loose of the city, he breached the outskirts, crossing the Tigris with hurrying steps, but nearing the ruins, he slowed his pace, for with every step the inchoate presentiment took firmer, more terrible form.

Yet he had to know. He would have to prepare.

A wooden plank that bridged the Khosr, a muddy stream, creaked under his weight. And then he was there, standing on the mound where once gleamed fifteen-gated Nineveh, feared nest of Assyrian hordes. Now the city lay sprawled in the bloody dust of its predestination. And yet he was here, the air was still thick with him, that Other who ravaged his dreams.

The man in khaki prowled the ruins. The Temple of Nabu. The Temple of Ishtar. He sifted vibrations. At the palace of Ashurbanipal he stopped and looked up at a limestone statue hulking *in situ*. Ragged wings and taloned feet. A bulbous, jutting, stubby penis and a mouth stretched taut in feral grin. The demon Pazuzu.

Abruptly the man in khaki sagged.

He bowed his head.

He knew.

It was coming.

He stared at the dust and the quickening shadows. The orb of the sun was beginning to slip beneath the rim of the world and he could hear the dim yappings of savage dog packs prowling the fringes of the city. He rolled his shirtsleeves down and buttoned them as a shivering breeze sprang up. Its source was southwest.

He hastened toward Mosul and his train, his heart encased in the icy conviction that soon he would be hunted by an ancient enemy whose face he had never seen.

But he knew his name.

Part I

The Beginning

Chapter One

Like the brief doomed flare of exploding suns that registers dimly on blind men's eyes, the beginning of the horror passed almost unnoticed; in the shriek of what followed, in fact, was forgotten and perhaps not connected to the horror at all. It was difficult to judge.

The house was a rental. Brooding. Tight. A brick colonial gripped by ivy in the Georgetown section of Washington, D.C. Across the street was a fringe of campus belonging to Georgetown University; to the rear, a sheer embankment plummeting steep to busy M Street and, just beyond it, the River Potomac. Early on the morning of April 1, the house was quiet. Chris MacNeil was propped in bed, going over her lines for the next day's filming; Regan, her daughter, was sleeping down the hall; and asleep downstairs in a room off the pantry were the middle-aged housekeepers, Willie and Karl. At approximately 12:25 A.M., Chris looked up from her script with a frown of puzzlement. She heard rapping sounds. They were odd. Muffled. Profound. Rhythmically clustered. Alien code tapped out by a dead man.

Funny.

For a moment she listened, then dismissed it; but as the rappings persisted she could not concentrate. She slapped down the script on the bed.

Jesus, that bugs me!

She got up to investigate.

She went out to the hallway and looked around. The rappings seemed to be coming from Regan's bedroom.

What is she doing?

She padded down the hall and the rappings grew suddenly louder, much faster, and as she pushed on the door and stepped into the room, they abruptly ceased.

What the freak's going on?

Her pretty eleven-year-old was asleep, cuddled tight to a large stuffed round-eyed panda. Pookey. Faded from years of smothering; years of smacking, warm, wet kisses.

Chris moved softly to her bedside, leaned over and whispered. "Rags? You awake?"

Regular breathing. Heavy. Deep.

Chris shifted her glance around the room. Dim light from the hall fell pale and splintery on Regan's paintings and sculptures; on more stuffed animals.

Okay, Rags. Your old mother's ass is draggin'. Come on, say it! Say "April Fool!"

And yet Chris knew well that such games weren't like her. The child had a shy and diffident nature. Then who was the trickster? A somnolent mind imposing order on the rattlings of heating or plumbing pipes? Once, in the mountains of Bhutan, she had stared for hours at a Buddhist monk who was squatting on the ground in meditation. Finally, she thought she had seen him levitate, though when recounting the story to someone, she invariably added "Maybe." And maybe now her mind, she thought, that untiring raconteur of illusion, had embellished the rappings.

Bullshit! I heard it!

Abruptly, she flicked a quick glance to the ceiling.

There! Faint scratchings.

Rats in the attic, for pete's sake! Rats!

She sighed. *That's it. Big tails. Thump, thump!* She felt oddly relieved. And then noticed the cold. The room. It was icy.

Chris padded to the window and checked it. Closed. Then she felt the radiator. Hot.

Oh, really?

Puzzled, she moved to the bedside and touched her hand to Regan's cheek. It was smooth as thought and lightly perspiring.

I must be sick!

Chris looked at her daughter, at the turned-up nose and freckled face, and on a quick, warm impulse leaned over the bed and kissed her cheek. "I sure do love you," she whispered. After that she returned to her room and her bed and her script.

For a while, Chris studied. The film was a musical comedy remake of *Mr. Smith Goes to Washington.* A subplot had been added that dealt with campus insurrections. Chris was starring. She played a psychology teacher who sided with the rebels. And she hated it. *This scene is the pits!* she thought. *It's dumb!* Her mind, though untutored, never took slogans for the truth, and like a curious bluejay she would peck relentlessly through verbiage to find the glistening, hidden fact. And so the rebel cause didn't make any sense to her. *But how come?* she now wondered. *Generation gap? That's a crock; I'm thirty-two. It's just stupid, that's all, it's a . . . !*

Cool it. Only one more week.

They'd completed the interiors in Hollywood and all that remained to be filmed were a few exterior scenes on the campus of Georgetown University, starting tomorrow.

Heavy lids. She was getting drowsy. She turned to a page that was curiously ragged. Her British director, Burke Dennings. When especially tense, he would tear, with quivering, fluttering hands, a narrow strip from the edge of the handiest page of the script and then slowly chew it, inch by inch, until it was all in a wet ball in his mouth.

Crazy Burke, Chris thought.

She covered a yawn, then fondly glanced at the side of her script. The pages looked gnawed. She remembered the rats. *The little bastards sure got rhythm*, she thought. She made a mental note to have Karl set traps for them in the morning.

Fingers relaxing. Script slipping loose. She let it drop. *Dumb*, she thought. *It's dumb.* A fumbling hand groping out to the light switch. *There.* She sighed, and for a time she was motionless, almost asleep; and then she kicked off her covers with a lazy leg.

Too hot! Too freaking hot! She thought again about the puzzling coldness of Regan's room and into her mind flashed a recollection of working in a film with Edward G. Robinson, the legendary gangster movie star of the 1940s, and wondering why in every scene they did together she was always close to shivering from the cold until she realized that the wily old veteran had been managing to stand in her key light. A faint smile of bemusement now, and as a mist of dew clung gently to the windowpanes. Chris slept. And dreamed about death in the staggering particular, death as if death were still never yet heard of while something was ringing, she gasping, dissolving, slipping off into void while thinking over and over, I am not going to be, I will die, I won't be, and forever and ever, oh, Papa, don't let them, oh, don't let them do it, don't let me be nothing forever and melting, unraveling, ringing, the ringing—

The phone!

She leaped up with her heart pounding, hand to the phone and no weight in her stomach; a core with no weight and her telephone ringing.

She answered. The assistant director.

"In makeup at six, honey."

"Right."

"How ya feelin'?"

"Like I just went to bed."

The AD chuckled. "I'll see you."

"Yeah, right."

Chris hung up the phone and for moments sat motionless, thinking of the dream. A dream? More like thought in the half life of waking: That terrible clarity. Gleam of the skull. Nonbeing. Irreversible. She could not imagine it.

God, it can't be!

Dejected, she bowed her head.

But it is.

She padded to the bathroom, put on a robe, then quickly pattered down old pine steps to the kitchen, down to life in sputtering bacon.

"Ah, good morning, Mrs. MacNeil!"

Gray, drooping Willie, squeezing oranges, blue sacs beneath her eyes. A trace of accent. Swiss. Like Karl's. She wiped her hands on a paper towel and started moving toward the stove.

"I'll get it, Willie." Chris, ever sensitive, had seen the housekeeper's weary look, and as Willie now grunted and turned back to the sink, the actress poured coffee, then sat down in the breakfast nook, where, looking down at her plate, she smiled fondly at a blush-red rose against its whiteness. *Regan. That angel.* Many a morning, when Chris was working, Regan would quietly slip out of bed, come down to the kitchen to place a flower on her mother's empty plate and then grope her way crusty-eyed back to her sleep. On this particular morning, Chris ruefully shook her head as she recalled that she had contemplated naming her Goneril. *Sure. Right on. Get ready for the worst.* Chris faintly smiled at the memory. She sipped at her coffee and as her gaze caught the rose again, her expression turned briefly sad, her green eyes grieving in a waiflike face. She'd recalled another flower. A son. Jamie. He had died long ago at the age of three, when Chris was very young and an unknown chorus girl on Broadway. She had sworn she would not give herself ever again as she had to Jamie; as she had to his father, Howard MacNeil; and as her dream of death misted upward in the vapors from her hot, black coffee, she lifted her glance from the rose and her thoughts as Willie brought juice and set it down before her.

Chris remembered the rats.

"Where's Karl?"

"I am here, Madam!"

He'd come catting in lithely through a door off the pantry. Commanding and yet deferential, he had a fragment of Kleenex pressed to his chin where he'd nicked himself shaving. "Yes?" Thickly muscled and tall, he breathed by the table with glittering eyes, a hawk nose and bald head.

"Hey, Karl, we've got rats in the attic. Better get us some traps."

"There are rats?"

"I just said that."

"But the attic is clean."

"Well, okay, we've got *tidy* rats!"

"No rats."

"Karl, I heard them last night."

"Maybe plumbing," Karl probed; "maybe boards."

"Maybe *rats!* Will you buy the damn traps and quit arguing?"

Bustling away, Karl, said, "Yes! I go now!"

"No not *now*, Karl! The stores are all closed!"

"They are closed!" chided Willie, calling out to him.

But he was gone.

Chris and Willie traded glances, and then, shaking her head,

Willie returned to her tending of the bacon. Chris sipped at her coffee. *Strange. Strange man*, she thought. Like Willie, hard-working; very loyal, very discreet. And yet something about him made her vaguely uneasy. What was it? That subtle air of arrogance? No. Something else. But she couldn't pin it down. The housekeepers had been with her for almost six years, and yet Karl was a mask—a talking, breathing, untranslated hieroglyph running her errands on stilted legs. Behind the mask, though, something moved; she could hear his mechanism ticking like a conscience. The front door creaked open, then shut. "They are closed," muttered Willie.

Chris nibbled at bacon, then returned to her room, where she dressed in her costume sweater and skirt. She glanced in a mirror and solemnly stared at her short red hair, which looked perpetually tousled; at the burst of freckles on the small, scrubbed face; and then crossing her eyes and grinning idiotically, she said, *Oh, hi, little wonderful girl next door! Can I speak to your husband? Your lover? Your pimp? Oh, your pimp's in the poorhouse? Tough!* She stuck out her tongue at herself. Then sagged. *Ah, Christ, what a life!* She picked up her wig box, slouched downstairs and walked out to the piquant, tree-lined street.

For a moment she paused outside the house, breathing in the fresh promise of morning air, the muted everyday sounds of waking life. She turned a wistful look to her right, where, beside the house, a precipitous plunge of old stone steps fell away to M Street far below, while a little beyond were the antique brick rococo turrets and Mediterranean tiled roof of the upper entry to the old Car Barn. *Fun. Fun neighborhood*, she thought. *Dammit, why don't I stay? Buy the house? Start to live?* A deep, booming bell began to toll, the tower clock on the Georgetown University campus. The melancholy resonance shivered on the surface of the mud-brown river and seeped into the actress's tired heart.

She walked toward her work, toward ghastly charade and the straw-stuffed, antic imitation of dust.

As she entered the main front gates of the campus, her depression diminished; then lessened even more as she looked at the row of trailer dressing rooms aligned along the driveway close to the southern perimeter wall; and by 8 A.M. and the day's first shot, she was almost herself: she started an argument over the script.

"Hey, Burke? Take a look at this damned thing, will ya?"

"Oh, you *do* have a script, I see! How nice!" Director Burke Dennings, taut and elfin and with a twitching left eye that gleamed with mischief, surgically shaved a narrow strip from a page of her script with quivering fingers, cackling, "I believe I'll have a bit of munch."

They were standing on the esplanade that fronted the university's main administration building and were knotted in the center of extras, actors and the film's main crew, while here and there a few spectators dotted the lawn, mostly Jesuit faculty. The cameraman, bored, picked up *Daily Variety* as Dennings put the paper in his mouth and giggled, his breath reeking faintly of the morning's first gin.

"Oh, yes, I'm *terribly* glad you've been given a script!"

A sly, frail man in his fifties, he spoke with a charmingly broad British accent so clipped and precise that it lofted even the crudest obscenities to elegance, and when he drank, he seemed always on the verge of a guffaw; seemed constantly struggling to retain his composure.

"Now then, tell me, my baby. What is it? What's wrong?"

The scene in question called for the dean of the mythical college in the script to address a gathering of students in an effort to squelch a threatened sit-in. Chris would then run up the steps to the esplanade, tear the bullhorn away from the dean and then point to the main administration building and shout, "Let's tear it down!"

"It doesn't make any sense," Chris told him.

"Well, it's perfectly plain," Dennings lied.

"Oh, it is? Well, then explain it to me, Burkey-Wurky. Why in freak should they tear down the building? What for? What's your concept?"

"Are you sending me up?"

"No, I'm asking 'what for?' "

"Because it's *there*, love!"

"In the script?"

"No, on the *grounds!"*

"Oh, come on, Burke, it just isn't her. It's not her character at all. She wouldn't do that."

"She would."

"No, she wouldn't."

"Shall we summon the writer? I believe he's in Paris!"

"Hiding?"

"Fucking!"

He'd clipped the word off with impeccable diction, his fox eyes glinting in a face like dough as the word rose crisp to Gothic spires. Chris fell to his shoulders, weak and laughing. "Oh, Burke, you're impossible, dammit!"

"Yes." He said it like Caesar modestly confirming reports of his triple rejection of the crown. "Now then, shall we get on with it?"

Chris didn't hear him. Checking to see if he'd heard the obscenity, she'd darted a furtive, embarrassed glance to a Jesuit in his forties standing amid the cordon of spectators. He had a dark, rugged face. Like a boxer's. Chipped. Something sad about the eyes, something grieving, and yet warm and reassuring as they fastened on hers and as, smiling, he nodded his head. He'd heard it. He glanced at his watch and moved away.

"I say, shall we get on with it?"

Chris turned, disconnected. "Yeah, sure, Burke. Let's do it."

"Thank heaven."

"No, wait!"

"Oh, good Christ!"

She complained about the tag of the scene. She felt that the high point was reached with her line as opposed to her running through the door of the building immediately afterward.

"It adds nothing," said Chris. "It's dumb."

"Yes, it is, love, it is," agreed Burke sincerely. "However, the cutter insists that we do it," he continued, "so there we are. You see?"

"No, I don't."

"No, of course you don't, darling, because you're absolutely right, it *is* stupid. You see, since the scene right after it"—Dennings giggled—"well, since it begins with Jed coming *into* the scene through a door, the cutter feels certain of a nomination if the scene before it ends with you moving *off* through a door."

"Are you kidding?"

"Oh, I agree with you, love. It's simply cunting, puking mad! But now why don't we shoot it and trust me to snip it from the final cut. It should make a rather tasty munch."

Chris laughed. And agreed. Burke glanced toward the cutter, who was known to be a temperamental egotist given to time-wasting argumentation. He was busy with the cameraman. The director breathed a sigh of relief.

Waiting on the lawn at the base of the steps while the lights were warming, Chris looked toward Dennings as he flung an obscenity at a hapless grip and then visibly glowed with satisfaction. He seemed to revel in his eccentricity. Yet at a certain point in his drinking, Chris knew, he could suddenly explode into temper, and if it happened at three or four in the morning, he was likely to telephone people in power and viciously abuse them over trifling provocations. Chris remembered a studio chief whose offense had consisted in remarking mildly at a screening that the cuffs of Dennings's shirt looked slightly frayed, prompting Dennings to awaken him at approximately 3 A.M. to describe him as a "cunting boor" whose father, the founder of the studio, was "more than likely psychotic!" and had "fondled Judy Garland repeatedly" during the filming of *The Wizard of Oz*, then on the following day would pretend to amnesia and subtly radiate with pleasure when those he'd offended described in detail what he had done. Although, if it suited him, he would remember. Chris smiled and shook her head as she remembered him destroying his studio suite of offices in a gin-stoked, mindless rage, and how later, when confronted by the studio's head of production with an itemized bill and Polaroid photos of the wreckage, he'd archly dismissed them as "obvious fakes" since "the damage was far, far worse than that!" Chris did not believe he was an alcoholic or even a hopeless problem drinker, but rather that he drank and behaved outrageously because it was expected of him: he was living up to his legend.

Ah, well, she thought; *I guess it's a kind of immortality.*

She turned, looking over her shoulder for the Jesuit who had smiled when Burke had uttered the obscenity. He was walking in the distance, head lowered despondently, a lone black cloud in search of the rain. She had never liked priests. So assured. So secure. And yet this one . . .

"All ready, Chris?"

"Ready."

"All right, absolute quiet!" the assistant director called out.

"Roll the film," ordered Burke.

"Rolling!"

"Speed!"

"Now *action!*"

Chris ran up the steps while extras cheered and Dennings watched her, wondering what was on her mind. She'd given up the arguments far too quickly. He turned a significant look to the dialogue coach, who immediately padded up to him dutifully and proffered his open script to him like an aging altar boy handing the missal to his priest at solemn Mass.

They had worked with only intermittent sun, and by four, the sky was dark and thick with roiling clouds.

"Burke, we're losing the light," the AD observed worriedly.

"Yes, they're going out all across the fucking world."

On Dennings's instruction the assistant director dismissed the company for the day and now Chris was walking homeward, her eyes on the sidewalk, and feeling very tired. At the corner of Thirty-sixth and O she stopped to sign an autograph for an aging Italian grocery clerk who had hailed her from the doorway of his shop. She wrote her name and "Warm Best Wishes" on a brown paper bag. Waiting for a car to pass before crossing the road at N Street, she glanced diagonally across the street to a Catholic church. Holy Something-or-other. Staffed by Jesuits. John F. Kennedy had married Jackie there, she had heard, and had worshiped there. She tried to imagine it: John F. Kennedy among the votive lights and the pious, wrinkled women; John F. Kennedy with his head bowed down in prayer; *I believe* . . . a détente with the Russians; *I believe, I believe* . . . Apollo IV amid the rattlings of the rosary beads; *I believe in the resurrection and the life ever—*

That. That's it. That's the grabber.

Chris watched as a Gunther beer truck lumbered by on the cobbled street with a sound of quivering, warm, wet promises.

She crossed, and as she walked down O and passed the Holy Trinity grade school auditorium, a priest rushed by from behind her, hands in the pockets of a nylon windbreaker. Young. Very tense. In need of a shave. Up ahead, he took a right, turning into an easement that opened to a courtyard behind the church.

Chris paused by the easement, watching him, curious. He seemed to be heading for a white frame cottage. An old screen door creaked open and still another priest emerged. He nodded curtly toward the young man, and with lowered eyes, he moved quickly toward a door that led into the church. Once again the cottage door was pushed open from within. Another priest. It looked—*Hey, it is! Yeah, the one who was smiling when Burke said "fucking"!* Only now he looked grave as he silently greeted the new arrival, putting his arm around his shoulder in a gesture that was gentle and somehow parental. He led him inside and the screen door closed with a slow, faint squeak.

Chris stared at her shoes. She was puzzled. *What's the drill?* She wondered if Jesuits went to confession.

Faint rumble of thunder. She looked up at the sky. Would it rain? . . . the resurrection and the life ever . . .

Yeah. Yeah, sure. Next Tuesday. Flashes of lightning crackled in the distance. *Don't call us, kid, we'll call you.*

She tugged up her coat collar and slowly moved on.

She hoped it would pour.

A minute later she was home. She made a dash for the bathroom. After that, she walked into the kitchen.

"Hi, Chris, how'd it go?"

Pretty blonde in her twenties sitting at the table. Sharon Spencer. Fresh. From Oregon. For the last three years, she'd been tutor to Regan and social secretary to Chris.

"Oh, the usual crock." Chris sauntered to the table and began to sift messages. "Anything exciting?"

"Do you want to have dinner next week at the White House?"

"Oh, I dunno, Marty; whadda *you* feel like doin'?"

"Eating candy and getting sick."

"Where's Rags?"

"Downstairs in the playroom."

"What doin'?"

"Sculpting. She's making a bird, I think. It's for you."

"Yeah, I need one," Chris murmured. She moved to the stove and poured a cup of hot coffee. "Were you kidding me about that dinner?" she asked.

"No, of course not," answered Sharon. "It's Thursday."

"Big dinner party?"

"No, I gather it's just five or six people."

"Hey, neat-o!"

She was pleased but not really surprised. They courted her company: cabdrivers; poets; professors; kings. What was it they liked about her? Life?

Chris sat at the table. "How'd the lesson go?"

Sharon lit a cigarette, frowning. "Had a bad time with math again."

"Really? That's strange."

"Yeah, I know; it's her favorite subject."

"Oh, well, this 'new math.' Christ, I couldn't make change for the bus if—"

"Hi, Mom!"

Her slim arms outstretched, Chris's young daughter had come bounding through the door toward her mother. Red pigtails. A soft, shining face full of freckles.

"Hi ya, stinkpot!" Beaming, Chris caught her in a bear hug and kissed her pink cheek with smacking ardor; she could not repress the full flood of her love. "Mmum-*mmum-mmum!*" More kisses. Then she held Regan out and probed her face with eager eyes. "So what'djya do today? Anything exciting?"

"Oh, stuff."

"So what *kinda* stuff? Good stuff? Huh?"

"Oh, lemme see." She had her knees against her mother's, swaying gently back and forth. "Well, of course, I studied."

"Uh-huh."

"An' I painted."

"Wha'djya paint?"

"Oh, well, flowers, ya know. Daisies? Only pink. An' then—oh, yeah! This *horse!*" She grew suddenly excited, eyes widening. "This man had a *horse*, ya know, down by the river? We were walking, see, Mom, and then along came this horse, he was *beautiful!* Oh, Mom, ya should've seen him, and the man let me sit on him! *Really!* I mean, practically a minute!"

Chris twinkled at Sharon with secret amusement. "Himself?" she asked, lifting an eyebrow. On moving to Washington for the shooting of the film, the blonde secretary, who was now virtually one of the family, had lived in the house, occupying an extra bedroom upstairs. Until she'd met the "horseman" at a nearby stable, at which point Chris decided that Sharon needed a place to be alone, and had moved her to a suite in an expensive hotel and insisted on paying the bill.

"Yes, himself," Sharon answered with a smile.

"It was a *gray* horse!" added Regan. "Mother, can't we get a horse? I mean, *could* we?"

"We'll see, baby."

"When could I have one?"

"We'll see. Where's the bird you made?"

At first Regan looked blank, then she turned around to Sharon and grinned with a mouth full of braces and shy rebuke. "You told!" she said before turning to her mother and snickering, "It was supposed to be a surprise."

"You mean . . . ?"

"With the long funny nose, like you wanted!"

"Oh, Rags, you're so sweet. Can I see it?"

"No, I still have to paint it. When's dinner, Mom?"

"Hungry?"

"I'm *star*ving."

"Gee, it's not even five. When was lunch?" Chris asked Sharon.

"Oh, twelvish," Sharon answered.

"When are Willie and Karl coming back?"

Chris had given them the afternoon off.

"I think seven," said Sharon.

"Mom, can't we go Hot Shoppe?" Regan pleaded. "Could we?"

Chris lifted her daughter's hand; smiled fondly, kissed it, then answered, "Run upstairs and get dressed and we'll go."

"Oh, I *love* you!"

Regan ran from the room.

"Honey, wear the new dress!" Chris called out after her.

"How would you like to be eleven again?" mused Sharon.

"I dunno."

Reaching for her mail, Chris began sorting through scrawled adulation. "With the brain I've got now? All the memories?"

"Sure."

"No deal."

"Think it over."

Chris dropped the letters and picked up a script with a covering letter from her agent, Edward Jarris, clipped neatly to the front of it. "Thought I told them no scripts for a while."

"You should read it," said Sharon.

"Oh, yeah?"

"Yes, I read it this morning."

"Pretty good?"

"I think it's great."

"And I get to play a nun who discovers she's a lesbian, right?"

"No, you get to play nothing."

"Shit, movies *are* better than ever! What in freak are you talking about, Sharon? What's the grin for?"

"They want you to direct," Sharon exhaled coyly along with the smoke from her cigarette.

"What?"

"Read the letter."

"Oh, my God, Shar, you're kidding!"

Chris pounced on the letter, her eyes snapping up the words in hungry chunks: ". . . new script . . . a triptych . . . studio wants Sir Stephen Moore . . . accepting role provided—"

"I direct his segment!"

Chris flung up her arms, letting loose a hoarse, shrill cry of joy. Then with both her hands she cuddled the letter to her chest. "Oh, Steve, you angel, you remembered!" Filming in Africa, drunk and in camp chairs watching the vermilion and gold end of day. *"Ah, the business is bunk! For the actor it's crap, Steve!" "Oh, I like it." "It's crap! Don't you know where it's at in this business? Directing. Then you've done something, something that's yours; I mean, something that lives!" "Well, then* do *it, love!* Do *it!" "Oh, I've tried, Steve. I've tried; they won't buy it." "Why not?" "Oh, come on, you know why: they don't think I can cut it." "Well, I think you can."*

Warm smile. Warm remembrance. Dear Steve . . .

"Mom, I can't find the dress!" Regan called from the landing.

"In the closet!" Chris answered.

"I looked!"

"I'll be up in a second!" Chris called. She flipped through the pages of the script, and then stopped, looking wilted as she murmured, "I'll bet it's probably crap."

"Oh, I don't think so, Chris! No! I really think it's good!"

"Oh, you thought *Psycho* needed a laugh track."

"Mommy?"

"I'm coming!"

"Got a date, Shar?"

"Yes."

Chris motioned at the mail. "You go on, then. We can catch all this stuff in the morning."

Sharon got up.

"Oh, no, wait," Chris amended. "No, I'm sorry, there's a letter that's got to go out tonight."

"Oh, okay." Sharon reached for her dictation pad.

A whine of impatience. "Moth-therrrr!"

Chris exhaled a sigh, stood up and said, "Back in a minute," but then hesitated, seeing Sharon checking the time on her watch. Chris said, "What?"

"Gee, it's time for me to meditate, Chris."

Chris eyed her narrowly with fond exasperation. In the last six months, she had watched her secretary metamorphose into a "seeker after serenity." It had started in Los Angeles with self-hypnosis, which then yielded to Buddhistic chanting. During the last few weeks that Sharon was quartered in the room upstairs, the house had reeked of incense, and lifeless dronings of *"Nam myoho renge kyo"* ("See, you just keep on chanting that, Chris, just that, and you get your wish, you get everything you want . . .") were heard at unlikely and untimely hours, usually when Chris was studying her lines. "You can turn on the TV," Sharon generously told her employer on one of these occasions. "It's fine. I can chant when there's all *kinds* of noise."

Now it was Transcendental Meditation.

"You really think that kind of stuff is going to do you any good, Shar?"

"It gives me peace of mind," responded Sharon.

"Right," Chris commented tonelessly, and then turned and started away with a murmured *"Nam myoho renge kyo."*

"Keep it up about fifteen or twenty minutes," Sharon called to her. "Maybe for you it would work."

Chris halted and considered a measured response. Then gave it up. She went upstairs to Regan's bedroom, moving immediately to the closet. Regan was standing in the middle of the room staring up at the ceiling.

"So what's doin'?" Chris asked Regan as she hunted in a closet for the dress. It was a pale-blue cotton. She'd bought it the week before, and remembered hanging it in this closet.

"Funny noises," said Regan.

"Yeah, I know. We've got friends."

Regan looked at her. "Huh?"

"Squirrels, honey; squirrels in the attic." Her daughter was squeamish and terrified of rats. Even mice upset her.

The hunt for the dress proved fruitless.

"See, Mom, it's not there."

"Yes, I see. Maybe Willie picked it up with the cleaning."

"It's gone."

"Yeah, well, put on the navy. It's pretty."

After a matinee screening of Shirley Temple in *Wee Willie Winkie* at an art-house cinema in Georgetown, they drove across the river on the Key Bridge to the Hot Shoppe in Rosslyn, Virginia, where Chris ate a salad while Regan had soup, two sourdough rolls, fried chicken, a strawberry shake, and blueberry pie topped with chocolate ice cream. *Where does she put it*, Chris wondered. *In her wrists?* The child was slender as a fleeting hope.

Chris lit a cigarette over her coffee and looked through the window on her right at the spires of Georgetown University before lowering a pensive and moody gaze to the Potomac's deceptively placid surface, which offered no hint of the perilously swift and powerful currents that surged underneath it. Chris shifted her weight a little. In the soft, smoothing light of evening, the river, with its seeming dead calm and stillness, suddenly struck her as something that was planning.

And waiting.

"I enjoyed my dinner, Mom."

Chris turned to Regan's happy smile, and, as so often had happened before, caught a quick, gasping breath as once again she experienced that tugging, unsummoned little ache that she sometimes felt on suddenly seeing Howard's image in her face. It was the angle of the light, she often thought. She dropped her glance to Regan's plate.

"Going to leave that pie?"

Regan lowered her eyes. "Mom, I ate some candy before."

Chris stubbed out her cigarette and smiled.

"Come on, Rags, let's go home."

They were back before seven. Willie and Karl had already returned. Regan made a dash for the basement playroom, eager to finish the sculpture for her mother. Chris headed for the kitchen to pick up the script. She found Willie brewing coffee; coarse; open pot. She looked irritable and sullen.

"Hi, Willie, how'd it go? Have a real nice time?"

"Do not ask." Willie added an eggshell and a pinch of salt to the bubbling contents of the pot. They had gone to a movie, Willie explained. She had wanted to see the Beatles, but Karl had insisted on an art-house film about Mozart. "Terrible," she simmered as she lowered the flame. "That dumbhead!"

"Sorry 'bout that." Chris tucked the script underneath her arm. "Oh, Willie, have you seen that dress that I got for Rags last week? The blue cotton?"

"Yes, I see it in her closet this morning."

"Where'd you put it?"

"It is there."

"You didn't maybe pick it up by mistake with the cleaning?"

"It is there."

"With the cleaning?"

"In the closet."

"No, it isn't. I looked."

About to speak, Willie tightened her lips and scowled. Karl had walked in.

"Good evening, Madam."

He went to the sink for a glass of water.

"Did you set those traps?" asked Chris.

"No rats."

"Did you *set* them?"

"I set them, of course, but the attic is clean."

"Tell me, how was the movie, Karl?"

"Exciting," he said. His tone of voice, like his face, was a resolute blank.

Humming a song made famous by the Beatles, Chris started to leave the kitchen, but then abruptly turned around.

Just one more shot!

"Did you have any trouble getting the traps, Karl?"

His back to her, Karl said, "No, Madam. No trouble."

"At six in the morning?"

"All-night market."

Chris softly slapped a hand against her forehead, stared at Karl's back for a moment, and then turned to leave the kitchen, softly muttering, "Shit!"

After a long and luxurious bath, Chris went to the closet in her bedroom for her robe, and discovered Regan's missing dress. It lay crumpled in a heap on the floor of the closet.

Chris picked it up. The purchase tags were still on it.

What's it doing in here?

Chris tried to think back, then remembered that the day she had purchased the dress she had also bought two or three items for herself.

Must've put 'em all together, she decided.

Chris carried the dress into Regan's bedroom, put it on a hanger and slipped it onto the clothes rack in Regan's closet. Hands on her hips, Chris appraised Regan's wardrobe. *Nice. Nice clothes. Yeah, Rags, look here, not over there at the daddy who never writes or calls.*

As she turned from the closet, Chris stubbed her toe against the base of a bureau. *Oh, Jesus, that smarts!* Lifting her foot and massaging her toe, Chris noticed that the bureau was out of position by about three feet.

No wonder I bumped it. Willie must have vacuumed.

She went down to the study with the script from her agent.

Unlike the massive living room with its large bay windows and view of Key Bridge arching over the Potomac to Virginia's shore, the study had a feeling of whispered density; of secrets between rich uncles: a raised brick fireplace, cherrywood paneling and crisscrossed beams of a sturdy wood that looked as if hewn from some ancient drawbridge. The room's few hints of a time that was present were a modern-looking bar with suede and chrome chairs set around it, and some color-splashed Marimekko pillows on a downy sofa where Chris settled down and stretched out with the script from her agent. Stuck between the pages was his letter. She slipped it out now and read it again. *Faith, Hope and Charity:* a film with three distinct segments, each one with a different cast and director. Hers would be "Hope." She liked the title. Maybe dull, she thought; but refined. *They'll probably change it to something like "Rock Around the Virtues."*

The doorbell chimed. Burke Dennings. A lonely man, he

dropped by often. Chris smiled ruefully, shaking her head, as she heard him rasp an obscenity at Karl, whom he seemed to detest and continually baited.

"Yes, hullo, where's a drink!" he demanded crossly, entering the room and moving to the bar with his glance averted and his hands in the pockets of his wrinkled raincoat.

He sat on a barstool looking irritable, shifty-eyed and vaguely disappointed.

"On the prowl again?" Chris asked.

"What the hell do you mean?" Dennings sniffed.

"You've got that look." She had seen it before when they'd worked on a picture together in Lausanne. On their first night there, at a staid hotel overlooking Lake Geneva, Chris had difficulty sleeping. At a little after 5 A.M., she flounced out of bed and decided to dress and go down to the lobby in search of either coffee or some company. Waiting for an elevator out in the hall, she glanced through a window and saw the director walking stiffly along the lakeside, hands deep in the pockets of his coat against the glacial February cold. By the time she reached the lobby, he was entering the hotel. "Not a hooker in sight!" he snapped bitterly as he hurriedly walked past Chris without even a glance, and then entered an elevator that whooshed him up to his floor and to his room and to bed. When Chris had teasingly mentioned the incident later, the director had grown furious and accused her of promulgating "gross hallucinations" that people were "likely to believe just because you're a star!" He had also referred to her as "simply raving *mad*," but then pointed out soothingly, in an effort to assuage her feelings, that "perhaps" she had seen someone after all, and had simply mistaken him for Dennings. "Not out of the question," he'd offhandedly conceded; "my great-great-grandmother happens to have been Swiss."

Chris moved behind the bar and reminded him of the incident.

"Yeah, *that* look, Burke. How many gin and tonics have you had already?"

"Oh, now, don't be so silly!" snapped Dennings. "It so happens that I've spent the entire evening at a tea, a bloody faculty *tea!*"

Chris folded her arms and leaned them on the bar. "You were *where?*" she said skeptically.

"Oh, yes, go ahead; smirk!"

"You got smashed at a tea with some Jesuits?"

"No, the Jesuits were sober."

"They don't drink?"

"Are you out of your *mind?* They *swilled!* Never seen such capacities in all my *life!*"

"Hey, come on, hold it down, Burke! Regan can hear you!"

"Yes, Regan," said Dennings, lowering his voice to a whisper. "Of course! Now where in Christ is my *drink?*"

Slightly shaking her head in disapproval, Chris straightened up and reached for a bottle and a glass. "Want to tell me what on earth you were doing at a faculty tea?"

"Bloody public relations; something *you* should be doing. I mean, my God, the way we've mucked up their grounds," the director uttered piously. "Oh, yes, go ahead, laugh! Yes, that's all that you're good for, that and showing a bit of bum!"

"I'm just standing here innocently smiling."

"Well, now *someone* had to make a good show."

Chris reached out a hand and lightly ran a finger along a scar above Dennings's left eyelash, the result of a punishing blow by Chuck Darren, the muscular action-adventure star of Dennings's previous film, delivered by the actor on the last day of filming. "It's turning white," Chris said caringly.

Dennings's eyebrows lowered into grimness. "I'll see he never works again at any of the majors. I've already put out the word."

"Oh, come on, Burke. Just for that?"

"The man's a *lunatic*, darling! He's damned well bloody mad and he's dangerous! My God, he's like an old dog who's always peacefully napping in the sun and then one day out of nowhere he jumps up and viciously bites somebody's leg!"

"And of course his putting your lights out had nothing to do with you telling him in front of the cast and crew that his acting was 'a cunting embarrassment somewhere near the level of Sumo wrestling'?"

"Darling, that's crude," Dennings piously rebuked her while accepting a glass of gin and tonic from her hands. "My dear, it's all very well for *me* to say 'cunting,' but not for America's sweetheart. But now tell me, how are you, my little dancing and singing mini-nova?"

Chris answered with a shrug and a despondent look as she leaned over and rested her weight on folded arms atop the bar.

"Come on, tell me, my baby, are you glum?"

"I dunno."

"Tell your uncle."

"Shit, I think I'll have a drink." Chris abruptly straightened up and reached out for a vodka bottle and a glass.

"Oh, yes, excellent! *Splendid* idea! Now, then, what is it, my precious? What's wrong?"

"Ever think about dying?" Chris asked.

Dennings furrowed his brow. "You said 'dying'?"

"Yeah, dying. Ever really *really* think about it, Burke? What it means? What it really means?"

She poured vodka into the glass.

Faintly edgy now, Dennings rasped, "No, love, I don't! I

don't *think* about it, I just *do* it. Why on earth bring up *dying*, for heaven's sakes!"

Chris shrugged and plopped an ice cube into her glass. "I dunno. I was thinking about it this morning. Well, not thinking, exactly; I sort of dreamed it just as I was waking up and it gave me cold shivers, Burke, it hit me hard; what it means. I mean, the *end*, Burke, the really freaking *end*, just like I'd never even *heard* of dying before!" She looked aside and shook her head. "Oh *man*, did that spook me! I felt like I was falling off the freaking planet at a hundred and fifty million miles an hour." Chris lifted the glass to her lips. "I think I'll have this one neat," she murmured. She took a sip.

"Oh, well, rubbish," Dennings sniffed. "Death's a comfort."

Chris lowered the glass. "Not for me."

"Come, you live through the works you leave behind, or through your children."

"Oh, that's bullshit! My children aren't me!"

"Yes, thank heaven. One's entirely enough."

Chris leaned forward, her glass in her hand at waist level and her pixie face tight in a grimace of concern. "I mean, think about it, Burke! Not existing! Not existing forever and forever and—"

"Oh, now stop that! Stop this driveling and think about flaunting your much-adored body-makeup-covered long legs at the faculty tea next week! Perhaps those *priests* can give you comfort!"

Dennings banged down his glass on the bar. "Let's another!"

"You know, I didn't know they drank?"

"Well, you're stupid," the director said grumpily.

Chris eyed him. Was he reaching his point of no return? Or had she in fact touched a hidden nerve?

"Do they go to confession?" she asked.

"Who?"

"Priests."

"How would *I* know!" Dennings erupted.

"Well, didn't you once tell me that you'd studied to be a—"

Dennings slammed his open hand down on the bar, cutting her off as he squalled, "Come on, *where's the bloody drink?*"

"Why don't I get you some coffee?"

"Don't be fatuous, darling! I want a drink!"

"You're getting coffee."

"Oh, come along, ducks," Dennings wheedled in a suddenly gentle voice. "Just one more for the road?"

"The Lincoln Highway?"

"Now that's ugly, love. Truly. Not like you." Looking pouty, Dennings pushed his glass forward. "'The quality of mercy is not strained,'" he intoned; "no, it falleth from heaven like the gentle Gordon's Dry Gin, so come along now, just one and I'll be off and that's a promise."

"A real one?"

"Word of honor and hope to die!"

Chris appraised him, and then, shaking her head, she picked up the bottle of gin. "Yeah, those priests," she said abstractedly while pouring gin into Dennings's glass; "I guess maybe I should ask one or two of them over."

"They'd never leave," Dennings growled, his eyes reddening and suddenly growing even smaller, each one of them a separate, particular hell; "they're fucking plunderers!" Chris picked up the tonic bottle to pour, but Dennings testily waved it off. "No, for heaven's sake, *straight*, can't you ever remember? The third one is *always* straight!" Chris watched him pick up his glass, gulp down the gin, then set the glass back down, and with his head bent, staring into it, he muttered, "Thoughtless bitch!"

Chris eyed him warily. *Yeah, he's starting to blow.* She changed the subject from priests to the offer she'd received to direct.

"Oh, well good," Dennings grunted, still looking down into his glass. "Bravo!"

"To tell the truth, though, it kinda scares me."

Dennings instantly looked up at her, expression now benign and paternal. "Twaddle!" he said. "You see, my baby, the difficult thing about directing is making it *seem* as if the damned thing were difficult. I hadn't a clue my first time out, but here I am, you see. There's no magic involved, love, just bloody hard work and the constant realization from the day you start shooting that you've got a Siberian tiger by the tail."

"Yeah, I know that, Burke, but now that it's real, now that they've offered me my chance, I'm not so sure I could even direct my grandmother across the street. I mean, all of that technical stuff!"

"Oh, now, don't be hysterical! Leave all of that nonsense to your editor, your cinematographer and the script supervisor. Get good ones and, I promise you, they'll have you smiling through. What's important is your handling of the cast, the performances, and at that you'd be *marvelous*, my pretty; you could not only *tell* them what you want, you could *show* them."

Chris looked doubtful. "Oh, well, still," she said.

"Still what?"

"Well, the technical stuff. I mean, I need to understand it."

"Well, for instance. Give your guru an example."

From there, and for almost an hour, Chris probed the acclaimed director to the outermost barricades of minutiae. The technical ins and outs of film directing were available in numerous texts, but reading always tended to fray Chris's patience. So instead, she read people. Naturally inquisitive, she would juice them, she would wring them out. But books were not wring-able. Books were glib. They said "therefore" and "clearly" when it wasn't clear at all, and their circumlocutions could never be challenged; they could never be stopped for a shrewdly disarming, "Hey, now, hold it. I'm dumb. Could I have that again?" Books could never be pinned, or made to wriggle, or dissected.

Books were like Karl.

"Darling, all you really need is a brilliant cutter," Dennings cackled at the end; "I mean a cutter who knows his doors."

He'd grown charming and bubbly, and seemed to have passed the threatened danger point. Until the voice of Karl was heard.

"Beg pardon. You wish something, Madam?"

He was standing attentively at the open door to the study.

"Oh, hullo, Thorndike!" Dennings greeted him, giggling. "Or is it Heinrich?" he asked. "I simply can't seem to keep the name straight."

"It is Karl, sir."

"Yes, of course. I'd forgotten. Tell me, Karl, was it *public* relations that you did for the Gestapo, or was it *community* relations? I believe there's a difference."

Karl replied politely, "Neither one, sir. I am Swiss."

The director guffawed, "Oh, yes, of course, Karl! Right! You're Swiss! And you never went bowling with Goebbels, I suppose!"

"Knock it off, Burke!" Chris scolded.

"Or went flying with Rudolph Hess?" Dennings added.

His manner cool and unperturbed, Karl turned his gaze to Chris and asked her blandly, "Madam wishes?"

"Burke, how about that coffee, huh? Whaddya say?"

"Oh, well, fuck it!" the director declared belligerently, abruptly getting up from the bar and striding out of the room with his head bent forward and his hands clenched into fists. Moments later the front door was heard forcefully slamming shut. Expressionless, Chris turned to Karl and said tonelessly, "Unplug all the phones."

"Yes, Madam. Something else?"

"Oh, well, maybe some decaf."

"I bring it."

"Where's Rags?"

"Down in playroom. I call her?"

"Yeah, it's bedtime. Oh, no, wait a second, Karl! No, never mind. I'm going down there myself." She'd remembered the bird and was heading for the stairs to the basement. "I'll have the decaf when I come back up."

"Yes, Madam. As you wish."

"And for the umpty-eighth time, I apologize for Mr. Dennings."

"I pay no attention."

Chris stopped and turned partway around. "Yes, I know. That's exactly what's driving him nuts."

Turning back around, Chris walked to the entry hall of the house, pulled open the door to the basement staircase and began to descend. "Hi ya, stinky! Whatchya doin' down there? You got that bird done for me yet?"

"Oh, yes, Mom! Come and see! Come on down! It's all finished!"

The playroom was paneled and brightly decorated. Easels. Paintings. A phonograph. Tables for games and a table for sculpting. Red and white bunting left over from a party for the previous tenant's teenage son.

"Oh, honey, that's so great!" Chris exclaimed as Regan grandly handed her the figure. Not quite dry, it resembled a "worry bird" and was painted orange, except for the beak, which was laterally striped in green and white. A tuft of feathers was glued to the head.

"You really like it?" Regan asked, grinning broadly.

"Oh, honey, I do, I really do. Got a name for it?"

Regan shook her head. "No, not yet."

"What's a good one?"

"I dunno," Regan answered, lifting her hands palm upward and shrugging.

Lightly tapping her fingernails against her teeth, Chris furrowed her brow in exaggerated ponder. "Let me see, let me see," she said softly, mulling, then abruptly she lit up and said, "Hey, how about 'Dumbbird'? Huh? Whaddya think? Just plain old 'Dumbbird'!"

Reflexively covering her mouth with a hand to hide the braces on her teeth, Regan snickered and vigorously nodded her head.

"Okay, it's 'Dumbbird' by a landslide!" Chris declared triumphantly as she held up the sculpture in the air. When she lowered it again, she said, "I'm going to leave it here to dry for a while and then I'll put him in my room."

Chris was setting down the bird on a game table a few feet away when she noticed the Ouija board there. She'd forgotten that she had it. As curious about herself as she was about others, she'd originally bought it as a possible means of exposing clues to her subconscious. It hadn't worked, though she'd used it a time or two with Sharon, and one other time with Dennings, who had willfully steered the plastic planchette ("Are you the one moving it, ducky? Are you?") so that all of the "spirit messages" were obscene, and then afterward blamed it on "cunting evil spirits!"

"You been playin' with the Ouija board, Rags, honey?"

"Oh, yeah."

"You know how?"

"Oh, well, sure. Here, I'll show you."

Regan was moving to sit before the board.

"Well, I think you need *two* people, honey."

"No ya don't, Mom; I do it all the time."

Chris was pulling up a chair. "Well, let's both play, okay?"

A hesitation. And then, "Well—okay." The child had her fingertips lightly positioned atop the planchette and as Chris reached out to position hers, it made a swift, sudden move to the position on the board marked NO.

Chris smiled at her slyly. " 'Mother, I'd rather do it myself'? Is that it? You don't want me to play?"

"No, I *do!* Captain Howdy said 'no.' "

"Captain who?"

"Captain Howdy."

"Honey, who's Captain Howdy?"

"Oh, you know: I make questions and he does the answers."

"Oh, yeah?"

"He's very nice."

Chris tried not to frown as she began to feel a dim but prickling concern. Regan had loved her father deeply, yet had never shown the slightest reaction to her parents' divorce. Maybe Regan cried in her room; who knew? But Chris was fearful that her daughter was repressing both anger and grief and that one day the dam would break and her emotions would erupt in some unknowable and harmful form. Chris pursed her lips. A fantasy playmate. It didn't sound healthy. And why the name "Howdy"? For Howard? Her father? *Pretty close.*

"So how come you couldn't even come up with a name for a dum-dum bird, and then you hit me with something like 'Captain Howdy'? Why do you call him that, Rags?"

Regan giggled. " 'Cause that's his *name*, of course."

"Says who?"

"Well, *him*."

"Oh, well, of course."

"Of *course*."

"And what else does he say to you?"

"Stuff."

"What stuff?"

Regan shrugged and looked aside. "I dunno. Just stuff."

"Well, for instance."

Regan turned back and said, "Okay, then, I'll show you. I'll ask him some questions."

"Good idea."

Setting the fingertips of both her hands on the heart-shaped beige plastic planchette, Regan closed her eyes tightly in concentration. "Captain Howdy, don't you think my mom is pretty?" she asked.

Five seconds passed. Then ten.

"Captain Howdy?"

No movement. Chris was surprised. She'd expected her daughter to slide the planchette to the section marked YES. Oh, what now? she fretted. Some unconscious hostility? She blames me for losing her father? I mean, what?

Regan opened her eyes, looking stern. "Captain Howdy, that's not very polite," she chided.

"Honey, maybe he's sleeping," said Chris.

"Do you think?"

"I think *you* should be sleeping."

"Ahhh, Mom!"

Chris stood up. "Yeah, come on, hon. Uppy-uppy! Say good night to Captain Howdy."

"No, I won't. He's a poop," muttered Regan sulkily.

She got up and followed Chris up the stairs.

Chris tucked her into bed and then sat on the bedside. "Honey, Sunday's no work. You want to do somethin'?"

"Sure, Mom. Like what?"

When they'd first come to Washington, Chris had made an effort to find playmates for Regan. She'd uncovered only one, a twelve-year-old girl named Judy. But Judy's family was away for Easter, and Chris was concerned now that Regan might be lonely for companions her age.

Chris shrugged. "Oh, well, *I* don't know," she said. "Somethin'. You want we should drive around town and see the monuments and stuff? Hey, the cherry blossoms, Rags! That's right, they're out early this year! You want to see 'em?"

"Oh, *yeah*, Mom!"

"Well, okay! And then tomorrow night a movie!?"

"Oh, I love you!"

Regan gave her mother a hug and Chris hugged her back with an extra fervor, whispering, "Oh, honey, I love you so."

"You can bring Mr. Dennings if you like."

Chris pulled back from the hug and looked at Regan quizzically "Mr. Dennings?"

"Sure, Mom. It's okay."

"Oh, no, it isn't!" Chris said, chuckling. "Honey, why would I want to bring Mr. Dennings?"

"Well, you like him, don't you?"

"Oh, well, sure I like him, honey. Don't you?"

Looking off, Regan made no answer. Her mother eyed her with concern. "Baby, what's going on?" Chris prodded.

"You're going to marry him, aren't you, Mommy."

It was less a question than a sullen statement of fact.

Chris exploded into a laugh. "Oh, my baby, of *course* not! What on earth are you *talking* about? Mr. Dennings? Where'd you get that idea?"

"But you like him, you said."

"I like pizzas, but I wouldn't ever marry one! Regan, he's a friend, just a crazy old friend!"

"You don't like him like Daddy?"

"I *love* your daddy, honey; I'll always love your daddy. Mr. Dennings comes by here a lot 'cause he's lonely, that's all; he's just a lonesome, goofy friend."

"Well, I heard . . ."

"You heard what? Heard from who?"

Whirling slivers of doubt in the eyes; hesitation; then a shrug of dismissal. "I don't know," Regan sighed. "I just thought."

"Well, it's silly, so forget it."

"Okay."

"Now go to sleep."

"I'm not sleepy. Can I read?"

"Yeah, read that new book I got you."

"Thanks, Mommy."

"Good night, hon. Sleep tight."

"Good night."

Chris blew her a kiss from the door and closed it, then walked down the stairs to her study. *Kids! Where do they get their ideas!* She wondered if Regan had connected Dennings somehow to her filing for divorce. Howard had wanted it. Long separations. Erosion of ego as the husband of a superstar. He'd found someone else. But Regan didn't know that, only that Chris was the one who had filed. *Oh, quit all this amateur psychoanalyzing and try to spend some more time with her. Really!*

In the study, Chris had settled down to read "Hope" when, halfway through it, she heard steps and looked up to see Regan coming toward her sleepily while rubbing a knuckle at the corner of an eye.

"Hey, honey! What's wrong?"

"There's these real funny noises, Mom."

"In your room?"

"Yes, in my room. It's like knocking and I can't go to sleep."

Where the hell are those traps!

"Honey, sleep in my bedroom and I'll see what it is."

Chris led Regan to the master bedroom and was tucking her in when Regan asked, "Can I watch TV for a while till I sleep?"

"Where's your book?"

"I can't find it. Can I watch?"

"Oh, well, I guess so. Sure."

Chris picked up the remote from a bedside table and tuned in a channel. "That loud enough?"

"Yes, Mom. Thanks."

Chris placed the remote on the bed.

"Okay, honey; just watch it till you're sleepy? Okay? Then turn it off."

Chris turned out the light and then went down the hall, where she climbed up the narrow, green-carpeted stairs that led to the attic, opened the door, felt around for the light switch, found it, flicked it on, and then entered the unfinished attic, where she took a few steps and then stopped and slowly glanced all around. Press clippings and correspondence in boxes were neatly stacked on the pinewood floor. She saw nothing else. Except the rat traps. Six of them. Baited. Yet the space looked spotless. Even the air smelled clean and cool. The attic was unheated. No pipes. No radiator. No little holes in the roof for entry. Chris took a step forward.

"There is nothing!" came a voice from behind her.

Chris jumped from her skin. "Oh, good *Jesus!*" she gasped, turning quickly and putting a hand to her fluttering heart. "Jesus *Christ*, Karl, don't *do* that!"

He was standing two steps down on the staircase to the attic.

"Very sorry. But you see, Madam? Everything is clean."

Still a little short of breath, Chris said weakly, "Thanks for sharing that with me, Karl. Yeah, it's clean. Thanks. That's terrific."

"Madam, maybe cat better."

"Cat better for what?"

"To catch rats."

Without waiting for an answer, Karl turned to walk back down the stairs and soon was lost from Chris's sight. For a time she kept staring at the open doorway as she wondered whether Karl had been subtly insolent. She wasn't sure. She turned around again, looking for some cause of the rappings. She lifted her gaze to the angled roof. The street was shaded by enormous trees, most of them gnarled and entangled by vines, and the branches of one of them, a massive basswood tree, lightly touched the front third of the house. Was it squirrels after all? wondered Chris. *Must be. Or maybe even just the branches.* Recent nights had been windy.

"Maybe cat better."

Chris turned around and stared at the doorway again. *Pretty smart-ass, are we Karl?* she reflected. Then in a flash her expression turned pertly mischievous. She went down to Regan's bedroom, picked something up, brought it back to the attic, and then after a minute went back to the bedroom. Regan was sleeping. Chris returned her to her room, tucked her into her bed, then went back to her own bedroom, where she turned off the television and went to sleep.

That night, the house was especially quiet.

Eating her breakfast the following morning, Chris told Karl in an offhand way that during the night she thought she'd heard one of the rat traps springing shut.

"Like to go and take a look?" Chris suggested, sipping coffee and pretending to be engrossed in the *Washington Post*, while, without any comment, Karl went up to the attic to investigate the matter. As he was returning a few minutes later, Chris passed him in the hall on the second floor. His gaze straight ahead, he was stolidly walking without any expression, in his hands the large Mickey Mouse doll whose snout he had pried from one of the traps. As he and Chris passed one another, she heard him mutter, "Someone is funny."

Chris entered her bedroom, and as she slipped off her robe before dressing for work, she murmured softly, "Yeah, maybe cat better . . . *much* better."

When she grinned, her entire face crinkled up.

The filming went smoothly that day. Later in the morning, Sharon came by the set and during breaks between scenes, in her portable dressing room, she and Chris handled items of business: a letter to her agent (she would think about the script); "okay" to the White House; a wire to Howard reminding him to telephone on Regan's birthday; a call to her business manager asking if she could afford to take off a year; and then plans for a dinner party April twenty-third.

Early in the evening, Chris took Regan to a movie, and the following day they drove around to points of interest in Chris's red Jaguar XKE. The Capitol. The Lincoln Memorial. The Cherry Blossoms. A bite to eat. Then across the river to Arlington National Cemetery and the Tomb of the Unknown Soldier, where Regan turned solemn, while later, at the grave of John F. Kennedy, she seemed to grow distant and sad. She stared at the "eternal flame" for a time, and then, mutely reaching up to grip her mother's hand, she said tonelessly, "Mom, why do people have to die?"

The question pierced her mother's soul. *Oh, Rags, you too? You too? Oh, no!* And yet what could she tell her? Lies? No, she couldn't. She looked at her daughter's upturned face, at her eyes misting up with tears. Had Regan sensed her thoughts? She had done it so often before. "Honey, people get tired," she told Regan tenderly.

"Why does God let them?"

Looking down at her daughter, Chris was silent. Puzzled. Disturbed. An atheist, she had never taught Regan religion. She thought it would have been dishonest. "Who's been telling you about God?" she asked.

"Sharon."

"Oh."

She would have to speak to her.

"Mom, why does God *let* us get tired?"

Looking down at the pain in those sensitive eyes, Chris surrendered; couldn't tell her what she really believed. Which was nothing. "Well, after a while God gets lonesome for us, Rags. He wants us back."

Regan folded herself into silence. She stayed totally quiet all during the drive home, her mood persisting all the rest of that day and then, disturbingly, all through Monday.

On Tuesday, Regan's birthday, the spell of strange silence and sadness seemed to break. Chris took her along to the filming, and when the shooting day was over, a huge cake with twelve lighted candles on it was brought out while the film's cast and crew sang "Happy Birthday." Always a kind and gentle man when sober, Dennings had the lights rewarmed and, loudly calling it a "screen test," filmed the scene as Regan blew out the candles and cut the cake, and then promised he would make her a star. Regan seemed cheerful, even gay. But after dinner and the opening of presents, the mood seemed to fade. No word from Howard. Chris placed a call to him in Rome, and was told by a clerk at his hotel that he hadn't been there for several days and that he had left no forwarding number. He was somewhere on a yacht.

Chris made excuses.

Regan nodded, subdued, and shook her head to her mother's

suggestion that they go to the Hot Shoppe for a shake. Without a word, she went down to the basement playroom, where she remained until time for bed.

The following morning when Chris opened her eyes, she found Regan in bed with her, half awake.

"Well, what in the . . . Regan, what are you doing here?" Chris said chuckling.

"Mom, my bed was shaking."

"Oh, you nut!" Chris kissed her and pulled up her covers. "Go to sleep. It's still early."

What looked like morning was the beginning of endless night.

Chapter Two

He stood at the edge of the lonely subway platform, listening for the rumble of a train that would still the ache that was always with him. Like his pulse. Heard only in silence. He shifted his bag to the other hand and stared down the tunnel. Points of light. They stretched into dark like guides to hopelessness.

A cough. He glanced to the left. A gray-stubbled derelict, numb on the ground in a pool of his urine, was sitting up, his yellowed eyes fixed on the priest with the chipped, sad face.

The priest looked away. He would come. He would whine. *Couldjya help an old altar boy, Father? Wouldjya?* The vomit-flaked hand pressing down on the shoulder. The fumbling in his pocket for the holy medal. The reeking of the breath of a thousand confessions with the wine and the garlic and the stale mortal sins belching out all together, and smothering . . . smothering . . .

The priest heard the derelict rising.

Don't come!

Heard a step.

Ah, my God, let me be!

"Hi ya, Faddah."

He winced. Sagged. Couldn't turn. He could not bear to search for Christ again in stench and hollow eyes; for the Christ of pus and bleeding excrement, the Christ who could not be.

In an absent gesture, he felt at his coat sleeve as if for an unseen band of mourning. He dimly remembered another Christ.

"I'm a Cat'lic, Faddah!"

The faint rumbling of an incoming train. Then sounds of stumbling. The priest turned and looked. The bum was staggering, about to faint, and with a blind, sudden rush, the priest got to him; caught him; dragged him to the bench against the wall.

"I'm a Cat'lic," the derelict mumbled. "I'm a Cat'lic."

The priest eased him down; stretched him out; saw his train. He quickly pulled a dollar from out of his wallet and placed it in the pocket of the derelict's jacket. Then decided he might lose it. He plucked out the dollar, stuffed it into a urine-damp trouser pocket, then picked up his bag and boarded the train, sitting in a corner and pretending to sleep until the end of the line, where he climbed up to the street and began the long walk to Fordham University. The dollar had been meant for his cab.

When he reached the residence hall for visitors, he signed his name on the register. *Damien Karras*, he wrote. Then examined it. Something was wrong. Wearily he remembered and added *"S.J.,"* the abbreviation for Society of Jesus. He took a room in Weigel Hall and, after an hour he at last fell asleep.

The following day he attended a meeting of the American Psychiatric Association. As principal speaker, he delivered a paper titled "Psychological Aspects of Spiritual Development," and at the end of the day, he enjoyed a few drinks and a bite to eat with some other psychiatrists. They paid. He left them early. He would have to see his mother.

From a subway stop, he walked to the crumbling brownstone apartment building on Manhattan's East Twenty-First Street. Pausing by the steps that led up to the dark oak door, he eyed the children on the stoop. Unkempt. Ill-clothed. No place to go. He remembered evictions: humiliations: walking home with a seventh-grade sweetheart and encountering his mother as she hopefully rummaged through a city garbage can on the corner of the street. Karras slowly climbed the steps. Smelled an odor like cooking. Like warm, damp, rotted sweetness. He remembered the visits to Mrs. Choirelli, his mother's friend, in her tiny apartment with the eighteen cats. He gripped the banister and climbed, overcome by a sudden, draining weariness that he knew was caused by guilt. He should never have left her. Not alone. On the fourth-floor landing he reached into a pocket for a key and slipped it into the lock: 4C, his mother's apartment. He opened the door as if it were a tender wound.

Her greeting was joyful. A shout. A kiss. She rushed to make coffee. Dark complexion. Stubby, gnarled legs. He sat in the kitchen and listened to her talk, the dingy walls and soiled floor seeping into his bones. The apartment was a hovel. Social Security and every month a few dollars from her brother.

She sat at the table. Mrs. This. Uncle That. Still in immigrant accents. He avoided those eyes that were wells of sorrow, eyes that spent days staring out of a window.

I never should have left her.

She could neither read nor write any English, and so, later, he wrote a few letters for her, and afterward he worked at repairing the tuner on a crackling plastic radio. Her world. The news. Mayor Lindsay.

He went to the bathroom. Yellowing newspaper spread on the tile. Stains of rust in the tub and the sink. On the floor, an old corset. These the seeds of vocation. From these he had fled into love, but now the love had grown cold, and in the night he heard it whistling through the chambers of his heart like a lost and gently crying wind.

At a quarter to eleven, he kissed her good-bye; promised to return just as soon as he could.

He left with the radio tuned to the news.

Once back in his room in Weigel Hall, Karras gave some thought to writing a letter to the Jesuit head of the Maryland province. He'd covered the ground with him once before: request for a transfer to the New York province in order to be closer to his mother; request for a teaching post and relief from his counseling duties. In requesting the latter, he'd cited as a reason "unfitness" for the work.

The Maryland Provincial had taken it up with him during the course of his annual inspection tour of Georgetown University, a function closely paralleling that of an army inspector general in the granting of confidential hearings to those who had grievances or complaints. On the point of Damien Karras's mother, the Provincial had nodded and expressed his sympathy; but the question of the Jesuit's "unfitness," he thought, was contradicted by Karras's record. Still, Karras had pursued it, had sought out Tom Bermingham, the Georgetown University president. *"It's more than psychiatry, Tom. You know that. Some of their problems come down to their vocation, to the meaning of their lives. Tom, it isn't always sex that's involved, it's their faith, and I just can't cut it. It's too much. I need out."*

"What's the problem?"

"Tom, I think I've lost my faith."

Bermingham didn't press him on the reasons for his doubt. For which Karras was grateful. He knew that his answers would have sounded insane. *The need to rend food with the teeth and then defecate. My mother's nine First Fridays. Stinking socks. Thalidomide babies. An item in the paper about a young altar boy waiting at a bus stop; set on by strangers; sprayed with kerosene; ignited.* No. No, too emotional. Vague. Existential. More rooted in logic was the silence of God. In the world there was evil and much of it resulted from doubt, from an honest confusion among men of good will.

Would a reasonable God refuse to end it? Not finally reveal Himself? Not speak?

"Lord, give us a sign . . ."

The raising of Lazarus was dim in the distant past.

No one now living had heard his laughter.

And so why not a sign?

At various times Karras longed to have lived with Christ: to have seen him; to have touched him; to have probed his eyes. *Ah, my God, let me see you! Let me know! Come in dreams!*

The yearning consumed him.

He sat at the desk now with pen above paper. Perhaps it wasn't time that had silenced the Provincial. Perhaps he understood, Karras thought, that finally faith was a matter of love.

Bermingham had promised to consider the requests, to try to influence the Provincial, but thus far nothing had been done. Karras wrote the letter and went to bed.

He sluggishly awakened at 5 A.M., went to the chapel in Weigel Hall to secure a Host for the saying of Mass, then returned to his room. "*'Et clamor meus ad te veniat,'* " he prayed with murmured anguish: " 'And let my cry come unto Thee . . .' " He lifted the Host in consecration with an aching remembrance of the joy it once gave him; felt again, as he did each morning, the pang of an unexpected glimpse from afar and unnoticed of a long-lost love. He broke the Host above the chalice. " 'Peace I leave you. My peace I give you.' " He tucked the Host inside his mouth and swallowed the papery taste of despair. When the Mass was over, he carefully polished the chalice and then placed it in his bag. He rushed for the seven-ten train back to Washington carrying pain in a black valise.

Chapter Three

Early on the morning of April 11, Chris made a telephone call to her doctor in Los Angeles to ask him for a referral to a local psychiatrist for Regan.

"Oh? What's wrong?"

Chris explained. Beginning on the day after Regan's birthday—and following Howard's failure to call—she had noticed a sudden and dramatic change in her daughter's behavior and disposition. Insomnia. Quarrelsome. Fits of temper. Kicked things. Threw things. Screamed. Wouldn't eat. In addition, her energy seemed abnormal. She was constantly moving, touching, turning; tapping; running and jumping about. Doing poorly with schoolwork. Fantasy playmate. Eccentric attention-getting tactics.

"Such as what?" the physician inquired.

Chris started with the rappings. Since the night she'd checked the attic, she'd heard them again on two occasions, and in both of these instances, she'd noticed, Regan was present in the room and the rappings would cease at the moment Chris entered. Secondly, she told him, Regan would "lose" things in the room: a dress; her toothbrush; books; her shoes. She complained about "somebody moving" her furniture. Finally, on the morning following the dinner at the White House, Chris saw Karl in Regan's bedroom pulling a bureau back into place from a spot that was halfway across the room. When Chris had inquired what he was doing, he repeated his former "Someone is funny," and refused to elaborate any further; but shortly thereafter, Chris had found Regan in the kitchen complaining that someone had moved all her furniture during the night when she was sleeping, and this was the incident, Chris explained, that had finally crystallized her suspicions. It was clearly her daughter who was doing it all.

"You mean somnambulism? She's doing it in her sleep?"

"No, Marc, she's doing it when she's awake. To get attention."

Chris mentioned the matter of the shaking bed, which had happened twice more, each time followed by Regan's insistence that she sleep with her mother.

"Well, that could be physical," the internist ventured.

"No, Marc, I didn't say that the bed *was* shaking; what I said was that Regan *said* it was shaking."

"Do you know that it *wasn't?*"

"No, not really."

"Well, it might be clonic spasms," he murmured.

"What was that?"

"Clonic spasm. Any temperature?"

"No. Listen, what do you think?" Chris asked him. "Should I take her to a shrink or what?"

"Chris, you mentioned her schoolwork. How is she doing with her math?"

"Why?"

"How's she doing?" he persisted.

"Just rotten. I mean, *suddenly* rotten."

"I see."

"Why'd you ask?" Chris repeated.

"Well, it's part of the syndrome."

"Syndrome? Syndrome of what?"

"Nothing serious. I'd rather not guess about it over the phone. Got a pencil?"

He wanted to give her the name of a Washington internist.

"Marc, can't you come out here and check her yourself?" She was remembering Jamie and his lingering infection. Chris's doctor at that time had prescribed a new, broad-spectrum antibiotic. Refilling a prescription at a local drugstore, the pharmacist was wary. "I don't want to alarm you, ma'am, but this . . . well, it's quite new on the market, and they've found that in Georgia it's been causing aplastic anemia in young boys." Jamie. Gone. Dead. Ever since, Chris had never trusted doctors. Only Marc, and even that had taken years. "Marc, can't you?"

"No, I can't, but don't worry. This guy I'm recommending is brilliant. He's the best. Now get a pencil."

Hesitation. Then "I've got one. What's the name?"

She wrote it down and then the telephone number.

"Call and have him look her over and then tell him to call me," the internist advised. "And forget the psychiatrist for now."

"Are you sure?"

He delivered a blistering statement regarding the readiness of the general public to recognize psychosomatic illness, while failing to recognize the reverse: that illness of the body was often the cause of seeming illness of the mind. "Now what would you say," he proposed as an instance, "if you were my internist, God forbid, and I told you I had headaches, recurring nightmares, nausea, insomnia and blurring of the vision; and also that I generally felt unglued and was worried to death about my job? Would you say I was neurotic?"

"I'm a bad one to ask, Marc; I *know* you're neurotic."

"Those symptoms I gave you are the same as for brain tumor, Chris. Check the body. That's first. Then we'll see."

Chris telephoned the internist and made an appointment for that afternoon. Her time was her own now. The filming was over, at least for her. Burke Dennings continued, loosely supervising the work of the "second unit," a special crew filming scenes that were of lesser importance, mostly helicopter shots of various exteriors around the city, as well as stunt work and scenes without any of the principal actors. But Dennings wanted every foot of it to be perfect.

The doctor was in Arlington. Samuel Klein. While Regan sat crossly in an examining room, Klein seated her mother in his office and took a brief case history. She told him the trouble. He listened; nodded; made copious notes. When she mentioned the shaking of the bed, he appeared to frown dubiously, but Chris continued:

"Marc seemed to think it was kind of significant that Regan's doing poorly with her math. Now why was that?"

"You mean schoolwork?"

"Yeah, schoolwork, but math in particular. What's it mean?"

"Well, let's wait until I've looked at her, Mrs. MacNeil."

He then excused himself and gave Regan a complete examination that included taking samples of her urine and her blood. The urine was for testing of her liver and kidney functions; the blood for a number of checks: diabetes; thyroid function; red-cell blood count looking for possible anemia and white-cell blood count for exotic diseases of the blood.

When he'd finished, Klein sat and talked to Regan, observing her demeanor, and then returned to his office and started to write a prescription. "She appears to have a hyperkinetic behavior disorder," he said to Chris as he wrote.

"A what?"

"A disorder of the nerves. At least we think it is. We don't know yet exactly how it works, but it's often seen in early adolescence. She shows all the symptoms: the hyperactivity; the temper; her performance in math."

"Yeah, the math. Why the math?"

"It affects concentration." He ripped the prescription from the small blue pad and handed it over to Chris. He said, "This is for Ritalin."

"What?"

"Methylphenidate."

"Oh, yeah, that."

"Ten milligrams, twice a day. I'd recommend one at eight A.M., and the other at two in the afternoon."

Chris was eyeing the prescription.

"What is it? A tranquilizer?"

"A stimulant."

"A stimulant? She's higher'n a kite right *now!*"

"Her condition isn't quite what it seems," explained Klein. "It's a form of overcompensation, an overreaction to depression."

"Depression?"

Klein nodded.

"Depression," Chris repeated, looking aside and at the floor in thought.

"Well, you mentioned her father."

Chris looked up. "Do you think I should take her to see a psychiatrist, Doc?"

"Oh, no. I'd wait and see what happens with the Ritalin. I really think that's the answer. Let's wait two or three weeks."

"So you think it's all nerves."

"I suspect so."

"And those lies she's been telling? This'll stop it?"

His answer puzzled her. He asked her if she'd ever known Regan to swear or use obscenities.

"Funny question. No, never."

"Well, you see, that's quite similar to things like her lying—uncharacteristic, from what you tell me, but in certain disorders of the nerves it can—"

"Wait a minute, hold it," Chris interrupted. "Where'd you ever get the notion that she uses obscenities? I mean, is that what you were saying or did I misunderstand?"

Klein eyed her curiously for a moment before cautiously venturing, "Yes, I'd say that she uses obscenities. Weren't you aware of it?"

"I'm *still* not aware of it! What are you talking about?"

"Well, she let loose quite a string while I was examining her, Mrs. MacNeil."

"Are you kidding me, Doc? Such as what?"

Klein looked evasive. "Well, let's just say that her vocabulary's rather extensive."

"Well, like what? I mean, give me an example!"

Klein shrugged.

"You mean 'shit'? Or 'fuck'?"

Klein relaxed. "Yes, she used those words," he said.

"And what else did she say? I mean, specifically."

"Well, specifically, Mrs. MacNeil, she advised me to keep my goddamn fingers away from her cunt."

Chris gasped with shock. "She used those words?"

"Well, it isn't unusual, Mrs. MacNeil, and I really wouldn't worry about it at all. As I said, it's just a part of the syndrome."

Looking down at her shoes, Chris was shaking her head. "It's just so hard to believe," she said softly.

"Look, I doubt that she even understood what she was saying."

"Yeah, I guess," Chris murmured. "That could be."

"Try the Ritalin," Klein advised her, "and we'll see what develops. And I'd like to take a look at her again in two weeks."

He consulted a calendar pad on his desk. "Let's see; let's make it Wednesday the twenty-seventh. Would that be convenient?"

"Yeah, okay." Subdued and morose, Chris got up from her chair, took the prescription and crumpled it into a pocket of her coat. "Yeah, sure. The twenty-seventh would be fine."

"I'm quite a big fan of yours," Klein told her as he opened the door leading into the hall.

An index fingertip pressed to her lip, head lowered, Chris paused in the doorway, preoccupied. She glanced up at the doctor. "You don't think a psychiatrist, Doc?"

"I don't know. But the best explanation is always the simplest one. Let's wait. Let's wait and see." Klein smiled encouragingly. He said, "Try not to worry."

"How?"

As Chris was driving her home, Regan asked what the doctor had told her.

"He just said you're nervous."

"That's all?"

"That's all."

Chris had decided not to talk about her language.

Burke. She must have picked it up from Burke.

But later Chris spoke to Sharon about it, asking if she'd ever heard Regan use that kind of obscenity.

"Oh, my God, no," said Sharon, slightly taken aback. "No, never. I mean, not even lately. But you know, I think her art teacher made some remark about it."

"You mean recently, Sharon?"

"Last week. But that woman's so prissy. I just figured maybe Regan said 'damn' or 'crap.' You know, something like that."

"Oh, by the way, have you been talking to Rags about religion, Shar?"

Sharon flushed.

"Well, a little; that's all. I mean, it's hard to avoid. Chris, she asks so many questions, and—well . . ." She gave a helpless little shrug. "It's just hard. I mean, how do I answer without telling what I think is a great big lie?"

"Give her multiple choice."

In the days that preceded her scheduled dinner party, Chris was extremely diligent in seeing that Regan took her dosage of Ritalin. By the night of the party, however, she had failed to observe any noticeable improvement. There were subtle signs, in fact, of a gradual deterioration: increased forgetfulness; untidiness; and one complaint of nausea. As for attention-getting tactics, although the familiar ones failed to recur, there appeared to be a new one: reports of a foul, unpleasant "smell" in Regan's bedroom. At Regan's insistence, Chris took a whiff one day and smelled nothing.

"You don't smell it?" Regan asked, looking puzzled.

"You mean, you smell it right now?"

"Oh, well, sure!"

"What's it smell like, baby?"

Regan had wrinkled her nose. "Well, like something burny."

"Oh, yeah?"

Chris had sniffed yet again, this time more deeply.

"Don't you smell it?"

"Oh, yeah, *now* I do. Why don't we open up the window for a while, get some air in."

In fact, Chris had smelled nothing, but had made up her mind that she would temporize, at least until the appointment with the doctor. She was also preoccupied with a number of other concerns. One was arrangements for the dinner party. Another had to do with the script. Although she was still enthusiastic about the prospect of directing, a natural caution had prevented her from making a prompt decision. In the meantime, her agent was calling her daily. She told him that she'd given the script to Dennings for his opinion, and said she hoped he was reading and not consuming it.

The third, and the most important, of Chris's concerns was the failure of two financial ventures: a purchase of convertible debentures through the use of prepaid interest; and an investment in an oil-drilling project in southern Libya. Both had been entered upon for the sheltering of income that would have been subject to enormous taxation. But something even worse had developed: the wells had come up dry and rocketing interest rates had prompted a sell-off in bonds. These were the problems that her gloomy business manager flew into town to discuss. He arrived on Thursday. Chris had him charting and explaining through Friday, when at last she decided on a course of action that the manager thought wise, though he frowned when she then brought up the subject of buying a Ferrari.

"You mean, a new one?"

"Why not? You know, I drove one in a picture once. If we write to the factory, maybe, and remind them, it could be they might give us a deal. Don't you think?"

The manager didn't. And cautioned that he thought such a purchase improvident.

"Ben, I made over eight hundred thou last year and you're telling me I can't buy a freaking *car!* Don't you think that's ridiculous? Where'd the money all go?"

He reminded her that most of her money was in shelters. Then he listed the various drains on her income: federal income tax; her state tax; estimated tax on future income; property taxes; commissions to her agent and to him and to her publicist that added up to twenty percent of her income; another one and a quarter percent to the Motion Picture Welfare Fund; an outlay for wardrobe in tune with the fashion; salaries to Willie and Karl and Sharon and the caretaker of the Los Angeles home; various travel costs; and, finally, her monthly expenses.

"Will you do another picture this year?" he asked her.

Chris shrugged. "I dunno. Do I have to?"

"Yes, I think perhaps you should."

Elbows propped on her knees, Chris held her wistful face cupped in both hands as, eyeing the business manager moodily, she asked him, "What about a Honda?"

He made no reply.

Later that evening, Chris tried to put all of her worries aside; tried to keep herself busy with making preparations for the next night's party.

"Let's serve the curry buffet instead of sit-down," she told Willie and Karl. "We can set up a table at the end of the living room. Right?"

"Very good, Madam," Karl answered quickly.

"So what do you think, Willie? A fresh fruit salad for dessert?"

"Yes, excellent, Madam!" Karl answered.

"Thanks, Willie."

She'd invited an interesting mixture. In addition to Burke ("Show up sober, goddammit!") and the youngish director of the second unit, she expected a senator (and wife); an Apollo astronaut (and wife); two Jesuits from Georgetown; her next-door neighbors; and Mary Jo Perrin and Ellen Cleary.

Mary Jo Perrin was a plump and gray-headed Washington psychic. Chris had met her at the White House dinner and liked her immensely. She'd expected to find her austere and forbidding, but "You're not like that at *all!*" she'd been able to tell her; instead, she was bubbly-warm and unpretentious. Ellen Cleary was a middle-aged State Department secretary who'd worked in the U.S. Embassy in Moscow when Chris toured Russia. She had gone to considerable effort and trouble to rescue Chris from a number of difficulties and encumbrances encountered in the course of her travels, not the least of which had been caused by the redheaded actress's outspokenness. Chris had remembered her with affection over the years, and had looked her up on coming to Washington.

"Hey, Shar, which priests are coming?"

"I'm not sure yet. I invited the president and the dean of the college, but I think that the president's sending an alternate. His secretary called me late this morning and said that he might have to go out of town."

"Who's he sending?" Chris asked with guarded interest.

"Let me see." Sharon rummaged through scraps of notes. "Yes, here it is. It's his assistant, Father Joseph Dyer."

"Oh."

Chris seemed disappointed.

"Where's Rags?" she asked.

"Downstairs."

"You know, maybe you should start to keep your typewriter there; don't you think? I mean, that way you can watch her when you're typing. Okay? I don't like her being alone so much."

"Good idea."

"Okay, later. Go on home, Shar. Meditate. Play with horses."

The planning and preparations at an end, Chris again found herself turning worried thoughts toward Regan. She tried to watch television. Could not concentrate. Felt uneasy. There was a strangeness in the house. Like settling stillness. Weighted dust.

By midnight, all in the house were asleep.

There were no disturbances. That night.

Chapter Four

She greeted her guests in a lime-green hostess costume with long, belled sleeves and pants. Her shoes were comfortable and reflected her hope for the evening.

The first to arrive was the celebrity psychic, Mary Jo Perrin, who came with Robert, her teenage son, and the last was pink-faced Father Dyer. He was young and diminutive, with mischievous eyes behind steel-rimmed spectacles. At the door, he apologized for his lateness. "Couldn't find the right necktie," he told Chris expressionlessly. She stared at him blankly, then burst into laughter. Her daylong depression began to lift.

The drinks did their work. By a quarter to ten, all were scattered about the living room eating their dinners in vibrant knots of conversation.

Chris filled her plate from the steaming buffet and scanned the room for Mrs. Perrin. There. On a sofa with Father Wagner, the Jesuit dean. Chris had spoken to him briefly. He had a bald, freckled scalp and a dry, soft manner. Chris drifted to the sofa and folded to the floor in front of the coffee table as the psychic chuckled with mirth.

"Oh, come on, Mary Jo!" the dean said, smiling, as he lifted a forkful of curry to his mouth.

"Yeah, come on," echoed Chris.

"Oh, hi! Great curry!" said the dean.

"Not too hot?"

"Not at all; it's just right. Mary Jo has been telling me there used to be a Jesuit who was also a medium."

"And he doesn't believe me!" said the psychic with mirth.

"Ah, *distinguo*," corrected the dean. "I just said it was hard to believe."

"You mean *medium* medium?" asked Chris.

"Why, of course," said Mary Jo. "Why, he even used to levitate!"

"Oh, I do that every morning," said the Jesuit quietly.

"You mean he held séances?" Chris asked Mrs. Perrin.

"Well, yes," she answered. "He was very, very famous in the nineteenth century. In fact, he was probably the only spiritualist of his time who wasn't ever convicted of fraud."

"As I said, he wasn't a Jesuit," commented the dean.

"Oh, my, but was he ever!" The psychic laughed. "When he turned twenty-two, he joined the Jesuits and promised not to work anymore as a medium, but they threw him out of France"—she laughed even harder—"right after a séance that he held at the Tuileries. Do you know what he *did?* In the middle of the séance he told the empress she was about to be touched by the hands of a spirit child who was about to fully materialize, and when they suddenly turned all of the lights on"—she guffawed—"they caught him sitting with his naked foot on the empress's *arm!* Now, can you imagine?"

The Jesuit was smiling as he set down his plate. "Don't come looking for discounts any more on indulgences, Mary Jo."

"Oh, come on, every family's got one black sheep."

"We were pushing our quota with the Medici popes."

"Y'know, I had an experience once," Chris began.

But the dean interrupted. "Are you making this a matter of confession?"

Chris smiled and said, "No, I'm not a Catholic."

"Oh, well, neither are the Jesuits," Perrin teased with a smile.

"Dominican slander," retorted the dean. Then to Chris he said, "I'm sorry, my dear. You were saying?"

"Well, just that I thought I saw somebody levitate once. In Bhutan."

She recounted the story.

"Do you think that's possible?" she ended. "I mean, really?"

"Who knows?" replied the Jesuit dean. He shrugged. "Who knows what gravity is. Or matter, when it comes to that."

"Would you like my opinion?" interjected Mrs. Perrin.

"No, Mary Jo," the dean told her. "I've taken a vow of poverty."

"So have I," Chris muttered.

"What was that?" asked the dean, leaning forward.

"Oh, nothing. Say, there's something I've been meaning to ask you. Do you know that little cottage that's back of the church over there?" She pointed in the general direction.

"Holy Trinity?" he asked.

"Yes, right. Well, what goes on in there?"

"Oh, well, that's where they say Black Mass," said Mrs. Perrin.

"Black *who?*"

"Black Mass."

"What's that?"

"She's kidding," said the dean.

"Yes, I know," said Chris, "but I'm dumb. I mean, what's a Black Mass?"

"Oh, well, basically, it's a travesty on the Catholic Mass," explained the dean. "It's connected to devil worship."

"Good grief! You mean, there really is such a thing?"

"I really couldn't say. Although I heard a statistic once about something like possibly fifty thousand Black Masses being said every year in the city of Paris."

"You mean *now?*" marveled Chris.

"It's just something I heard."

"Yes, of course, from the Jesuit secret service," twitted Mrs. Perrin.

"Not at all," said the dean. "My voices told me."

The women laughed.

"You know, back in L.A.," mentioned Chris, "you hear an awful lot of stories about witch cults being around. I've often wondered if it's true."

"Well, as I said, I wouldn't know," said the dean. "But I'll tell you who might—Joe Dyer. Where's Joe?"

The dean looked around.

"Oh, over there," he said, nodding toward the other priest, who was standing at the buffet with his back to them, heaping a second helping onto his plate. "Hey, Joe?"

The young priest turned, his face impassive. "You called, great dean?"

The dean beckoned with his fingers.

"Just a second," answered Dyer, turning back to resume his attack on the curry and salad.

"That's the only leprechaun in the priesthood," said the dean with fondness. He sipped at his wine. "They had a couple of cases of desecration in Holy Trinity last week, and Joe said something about one of them reminding him of some things they used to do at Black Mass, so I expect he knows something about the subject."

"What happened at the church?" asked Mary Jo Perrin.

"Oh, it's really too disgusting," said the dean.

"Come on, we're all through with our dinners."

"No, please. It's too much," he demurred.

"Oh, come on!"

"You mean you can't read my mind, Mary Jo?" he asked her.

"Oh, I could," she responded, smiling, "but I really don't think that I'm worthy to enter *that* Holy of Holies!"

"Well, it really is sick," said the dean.

He described the desecrations. In the first of the incidents, the elderly sacristan of the church had discovered a mound of human excrement on the altar cloth directly before the tabernacle.

"Oh, that really *is* sick." Mrs. Perrin grimaced.

"Well, the other's even worse," the dean remarked; then employed indirection and one or two euphemisms to explain how a massive phallus sculpted in clay had been found glued firmly to a statue of Christ on the left side altar.

"Sick enough?" he concluded.

Chris noticed that the psychic seemed genuinely disturbed as she said, "Oh, that's enough, now. I'm sorry that I asked. Let's change the subject."

"No, I'm fascinated," said Chris.

"Yes, of course. I'm a fascinating human," came a voice.

It was Dyer. A heaping plate of food held up in one hand, he was hovering over Chris as he solemnly intoned, "Listen, give me just a minute, and then I'll be back. I think I've got something going over there with the astronaut."

"Like what?" asked the dean.

Dyer eyed him expressionlessly behind his glasses as he answered, "First missionary on the moon?"

All but Dyer burst into laughter.

His comedic technique relied on deadpan delivery.

"You're just the right size," said Mrs. Perrin. "They could stow you in the nose cone."

"No, not *me*," the young priest corrected her solemnly. "I've been trying to fix it up for Emory," he said to the dean in an aside, then turned back to the women to explain. "That's our dean of discipline on campus. Nobody's up there and that's what he likes. He likes things quiet."

Still deadpan, Dyer glanced across the room at the astronaut. "Excuse me," he said and walked away.

Mrs. Perrin said, "I like him."

"Me too," Chris agreed. Then she turned to the dean. "You haven't told me what goes on in that cottage," she reminded him. "Big secret? Who's that priest I keep seeing there? Sort of dark? Looks like a boxer? Do you know the one I mean?"

The dean nodded, lowering his head. "Father Karras," he said in a lowered tone and with a trace of regret. He put down his wineglass and turned it by the stem. "Had a pretty rough knock last night, poor guy."

"Oh, what?" Chris asked.

"Well, his mother passed away."

Chris felt a mysterious sensation of grief that she couldn't explain. "Oh, I'm so sorry," she said softly.

"He seems to be taking it pretty hard," resumed the Jesuit. "Seems she was living by herself, and I guess she was dead for several days before they found her."

"Oh, how awful," Mrs. Perrin murmured.

"Who found her?" Chris asked, slightly frowning.

"The superintendent of her apartment building. I guess they wouldn't have found her even now except . . . Well, the next-door neighbors complained about her radio going all the time."

"That's so sad," Chris said quietly.

"Excuse me, please, Madam."

Chris looked up at Karl. He was holding a serving tray bearing liqueurs and slender cordial glasses.

"Sure, set it down here, Karl; that'll be fine."

Chris always served liqueurs to her guests herself. It added an intimacy, she felt, that might otherwise be lacking. "Well, let's see now, I'll start with you," she said to the dean and Mrs. Perrin. She served them, then she moved about the room, taking orders and fetching for each of her guests, and by the time she had made the rounds, the various clusters had shifted to new combinations, except for Dyer and the astronaut, who seemed to be getting thicker. "No, I'm really not a priest," Chris heard Dyer say solemnly, his arm on the astronaut's chuckle-heaved shoulder. "I'm actually a terribly avant-garde rabbi."

Chris was standing with Ellen Cleary, reminiscing about Moscow, when she heard a familiar, strident voice ringing angrily through from the kitchen.

Oh, Jesus! Burke!

He was shrieking obscenities at someone.

Chris excused herself and went quickly to the kitchen, where Dennings was railing viciously at Karl while Sharon made futile attempts to hush him.

"Burke!" exclaimed Chris. "Knock it off!"

The director ignored her, and continued to rage, the corners of his mouth flecked foamy with saliva, while Karl leaned mutely against the sink with folded arms and stolid expression, his eyes fixed unwaveringly on Dennings.

"Karl!" Chris snapped. "Will you get out of here? Get *out!* Can't you see how he *is?*"

But the Swiss would not budge until Chris began shoving him toward the door.

"Naa-zi *pig!*" Dennings shouted at Karl's back, then turned genially to Chris and, rubbing his hands together, asked mildly, "Now, then, what's for dessert?"

"Des*sert?*"

Chris thumped her brow with the heel of her hand.

"Well, I'm hungry," Dennings petulantly whined.

Chris turned to Sharon and said, "Feed him! I've got to get Regan up to bed. And for chrissakes, Burke, would you freaking behave yourself? There are priests out there!"

Dennings creased his brow as his eyes grew intense with a sudden and seemingly genuine interest. "Oh, you noticed that too?" he asked without guile. Chris tilted her head up, breathed out, "I'm done!" and strode out of the kitchen.

She went down to check on Regan in the basement playroom, where her daughter had spent the entire day, and discovered her playing with the Ouija board. She seemed sullen; abstracted; remote. *Well, at least she isn't feisty,* Chris reflected, and, hopeful of diverting her, she brought Regan up to the living room and began introducing her to the guests.

"Oh, isn't she darling!" said the wife of the senator.

Regan was strangely well behaved, except with Mrs. Perrin, refusing to speak to her or shake her hand. But the psychic made a joke of it. "Knows I'm a fake," she said, smiling and winking at Chris. But then, with a curious air of scrutiny, she reached forward and gripped Regan's hand with a gentle pressure, as if checking her pulse. Regan quickly shook her off and glared malevolently.

"Oh, dear, she must be very tired," Mrs. Perrin said casually; yet she continued to stare at Regan with a probing fixity and anxiety she couldn't explain.

"She's been feeling kind of sick," Chris murmured in apology. She looked down at Regan. "Haven't you, honey?"

Regan did not answer. She kept her eyes on the floor.

There was no one left for Regan to meet except the senator and Robert, Mrs. Perrin's son, and Chris thought it best to pass them up. She took Regan up to bed and tucked her in.

"Do you think you can sleep?" Chris asked.

"I don't know," Regan answered dreamily. She'd turned on her side and was staring at the wall with a distant expression.

"Would you like me to read to you for a while?"

A shake of the head.

"Okay, then. Try to sleep."

Chris leaned over and kissed her, and then walked to the door and flicked the light switch.

"Night, my baby."

Chris was almost out the door when Regan called out to her very softly: "Mother, what's wrong with me?" So haunted. The tone so despairing and disproportionate to her condition. For a moment Chris felt shaken and confused. But quickly she righted herself. "Well, it's just like I said, Rags; it's nerves. All you need is those pills for a couple of weeks and I know you'll be feeling just fine. Now then, try to go to sleep, hon, okay?"

No response. Chris waited.

"Okay?" she repeated.

"Okay," Regan whispered.

Chris abruptly noticed goose pimples rising on her forearm. She rubbed at it, looking around. *Cheeezus peezus, it gets cold in this room! Where's that draft coming in from?*

She moved to the window and checked along the edges. Found nothing. Turned to Regan. "You warm enough, baby?"

No answer.

Chris moved to the bedside. "You asleep?" she whispered.

Eyes closed. Deep breathing.

Chris tiptoed from the room.

From the hall she heard singing, and as she walked down the stairs, she saw with pleasure that the young Father Dyer was playing the piano near the living-room picture window and was leading a group that had gathered around him in cheerful song.

As she entered the living room, they had just finished singing "Till We Meet Again."

Chris started forward to join the group, but was quickly intercepted by the senator and his wife, who had their coats across their arms and looked edgy.

"Are you leaving so soon?" Chris asked.

"Oh, I'm really so sorry, and my dear, we've had a *marvelous* evening," the senator effused. "But poor Martha's got a headache."

"Oh, I *am* so sorry, but I do feel terrible," moaned the senator's wife. "Will you excuse us, Chris? It's been such a lovely party."

"I'm really sorry you have to go," Chris told them.

As she accompanied the couple to the door, Chris could hear Father Dyer in the background asking, "Does anyone else know the words to 'I'll Bet You're Sorry Now, Tokyo Rose'?" On her way back to the living room, Sharon stepped quietly out from the study.

"Where's Burke?" Chris asked her.

"In there," Sharon answered with a nod toward the study. "He's sleeping it off. Say, what did the senator say to you? Anything?"

"No, they just left."

"Just as well."

"Whaddya mean, Shar? What's harpooning?"

"Oh, well, Burke," Sharon sighed. In a guarded tone, she described an encounter between the senator and Dennings, who had remarked to him, in passing, that there appeared to be "an alien pubic hair floating round in my gin." Then he'd turned to the senator's wife and added in a vaguely accusatory tone, "Never seen it before in my life! Have *you?*"

Chris gasped and then giggled and rolled her eyes as Sharon

went on to describe how the senator's embarrassed reaction had triggered one of Dennings's quixotic rages, in which he'd expressed his "boundless gratitude" for the existence of politicians, since without them to compare to "one couldn't easily distinguish who the *statesmen* were, you see," and when the senator had moved away in an icy huff, the director had turned to Sharon and said proudly, "There, you see? I didn't curse. Don't you agree that I handled the situation demurely?"

Chris couldn't help laughing. "Oh, well, let him sleep. But you'd better stay in there in case he wakes up," she said. "Would you mind?"

"No, of course not."

In the living room, Mary Jo Perrin sat alone in a corner chair. She looked preoccupied. And troubled. Chris started to join her, but changed her mind and headed for Dyer and the piano instead. Dyer broke off his playing of chords and looked up to greet her. "Yes, young lady," he said, "and so what can we offer you today? As it happens, we're running a special on novenas."

Chris chuckled with the others gathered around. "I thought I'd get the scoop on what goes on at Black Mass," she said. "Father Wagner said you were the expert."

The group at the piano fell silent with interest.

"No, not really," said Dyer, lightly touching some chords again. "Why'd you mention Black Mass?"

"Oh, well, some of us were talking before about—well . . . about those things that they found at the church, at Holy Trinity, and—"

"Oh, you mean the desecrations?" Dyer interrupted.

The astronaut broke in. "Hey, someone want to let us on to what you're talkin' about, here? I'm lost."

"Me too," said Ellen Cleary.

Dyer lifted his hands from the piano and looked up at them.

"Well, they found some desecrations at the church down the street," he explained.

"Well, like what?" asked the astronaut.

"Forget it," Father Dyer advised him. "Let's just say some obscenities and leave it at that."

"Father Wagner says you told him it was like at Black Mass," prompted Chris, "and so I wondered what went on at those things."

"Oh, I really don't know all that much," said Dyer. "In fact, most of what I know is what I've heard from another Jeb on campus."

"What's a Jeb?" Chris asked.

"Short for Jesuit. Father Karras, he's our expert on all this sort of stuff."

Chris was suddenly alert. "Oh, the dark-complexioned priest at Holy Trinity?"

"You know him?" Dyer asked her.

"No, I just heard him mentioned, that's all."

"Well, I think he did a paper on it once. You know, just from the psychiatric side."

"Whaddya mean?" asked Chris.

"Whaddya *mean*, whaddya mean?"

"Are you telling me he's a psychiatrist?"

"Oh, well, sure. Gee, I'm sorry. I just assumed that you knew."

"Listen, somebody *tell* me something!" the astronaut demanded good-naturedly. "What *does* go on at Black Mass?"

Dyer shrugged. "Let's just say perversions. Obscenities. Blasphemies. It's an evil parody of the Mass where instead of God they worshiped Satan and sometimes offered human sacrifice."

Ellen Cleary smiled thinly, shook her head and walked away. saying, "This is getting much too creepy for me."

Chris paid her no notice. "But how can you *know* that?" she asked the young Jesuit. "Even if there was such a thing as Black Mass, who's to say what went on there?"

"Well," said Dyer, "I guess they got most of it from the people who were caught and then confessed."

"Oh, come on," said the dean. He had just joined the group unobtrusively. "Those confessions were worthless, Joe. They were tortured."

"No, only the snotty ones," Dyer said blandly.

There was a ripple of vaguely nervous laughter. The dean eyed his watch. "Well, I really should be going," he said to Chris. "I've got the six-o'clock Mass in Dahlgren Chapel."

"I've got the banjo Mass," Dyer beamed. Then his eyes showed shock as they shifted to a point in the room behind Chris, and abruptly he sobered. "Well, now, I think we have a visitor, Mrs. MacNeil," he cautioned, motioning with his head.

Chris turned. And gasped on seeing Regan in her nightgown urinating gushingly onto the rug as, staring up fixedly at the astronaut, she intoned with dead eyes and in a lifeless voice, "You're going to die up there."

"Oh, my baby!" Chris cried out as she rushed with her arms out to her daughter. "Oh, Rags, honey! Come, sweetheart! Come! Let's go upstairs!"

She'd taken Regan by the hand and as she led her away she looked over her shoulder at the ashen astronaut. "Oh, I'm so sorry!" Chris apologized tremulously. "She's been sick, she must be walking in her sleep! She didn't know what she was saying!"

"Gee, maybe we should go," she heard Dyer say to someone.

"No, no, stay!" Chris called back. "It's okay! I'll be back in just a minute!"

Chris paused by the open door to the kitchen, instructing Willie to see to the rug before the stain became indelible, then walked Regan upstairs to her bathroom, bathed her and changed her nightgown. "Honey, why did you say that?" Chris asked her repeatedly, but Regan appeared not to understand and, with her eyes staring vacantly, mumbled soft strings of words without meaning.

Chris tucked her into bed, and almost immediately Regan appeared to fall asleep. Chris waited, listening to her breathing for a time, and then quietly left the room.

At the bottom of the stairs, she encountered Sharon and the young director of the second unit assisting Dennings out of the study. They had called a cab and were going to shepherd him back to his suite at the Georgetown Inn.

"Take it easy," Chris advised as they left the house with Dennings between them and one of his arms draped over each of their shoulders. Barely conscious, he murmured, "Fuck it," and then slipped into the fog and the waiting cab.

Chris returned to the living room, where the guests who still remained expressed their sympathy as she gave them a brief account of Regan's illness. When she mentioned the rappings and the other "attention-getting" phenomena, she noticed that the psychic was staring at her intently. At one point Chris looked at her, expecting her to comment, but Perrin said nothing and Chris continued.

"Does she walk in her sleep quite a bit?" asked Dyer.

"No, tonight's the first time. Or at least, the first time that I know of, so I guess it's this hyperactivity thing. Don't you think?"

"Oh, I really wouldn't know," said the priest. "I've heard sleepwalking's common at puberty, except that—" Here he shrugged and broke off. "I don't know. Guess you'd better ask your doctor."

Throughout the remainder of the discussion, Mrs. Perrin sat

quietly, watching the dance of flames in the living-room fireplace; equally subdued, Chris noticed, was the astronaut, who looked down into his drink with an occasional grunt meant to signify interest and attention. He was scheduled for a flight to the moon within the year.

"Well, I do have that Mass to say," said the dean as he rose to leave. It triggered a general departure. All stood up and expressed their thanks for dinner and the evening.

At the door, Father Dyer took Chris's hand as he earnestly probed her eyes and asked, "Do you think there's a part in one of your movies for a very short priest who can play the piano?"

"Well, if there isn't," Chris said laughing, "then I'll have one written in for you, Father!"

Chris bade him a warm and fond good night.

The last to leave were Mary Jo Perrin and her son. Chris held them at the door with idle chatter. She had the feeling that the psychic had something on her mind but was holding it back. To delay her departure, Chris asked her opinion on Regan's continued use of the Ouija board and her Captain Howdy fixation. "Do you think there's any harm in it?" she asked.

Expecting an airily perfunctory dismissal, Chris was surprised when Mrs. Perrin frowned and looked down at the doorstep. She seemed to be thinking, and still in this posture, she stepped outside and joined her son, who was waiting on the stoop.

When at last she lifted her head, her eyes were in shadow.

"I would take it away from her," she said quietly.

She handed ignition keys to her son. "Bobby, start up the car," she told him. "It's cold."

He took the keys, told Chris shyly that he'd loved her in all her films, and then walked away swiftly toward an old, battered Mustang parked down the street.

His mother's eyes were still in shadow.

"I don't know what you think of me," she said quietly and slowly. "Many people associate me with spiritualism. But that's wrong. Oh, yes, I think I have a gift," she went on, "but it isn't occult. In fact, to me it seems perfectly natural. Being a Catholic, I believe that we all have a foot in two worlds. The one that we're conscious of is in time, but now and then a freak like me gets a flash from the other foot, and that one, I think, is in eternity, where time does not exist and so the future and the past are both the present. So now and again when I'm feeling a tingling in that other foot, I believe that I'm seeing the future. Though who knows," she said. "Maybe not." She shrugged. "Well, whatever. But now the occult . . ." She paused, carefully picking her words. "The occult is something different. I've stayed away from that. I think dabbling with that can be dangerous. And that includes fooling around with a Ouija board."

Until now, Chris had thought her a woman of eminent good sense. And yet something in her manner now was causing Chris to feel a creeping foreboding. She tried to dispel it.

"Oh, come on, Mary Jo," Chris said with a smile. "Don't you know how those Ouija boards work? It isn't anything at all but a person's subconscious, that's all."

"Yes, perhaps," Perrin answered. "Perhaps. It could all be suggestion. But in story after story that I've heard about séances, Ouija boards—*all* of that, Chris—they always seem to be pointing to the opening of a door of some sort. Oh, I know you don't believe in the spirit world, Chris. But I do. And if I'm right, perhaps the bridge between the two worlds is what you yourself just mentioned, the subconscious mind. All I know is that things seem to happen. And, my dear, there are lunatic asylums all over the world filled with people who dabbled in the occult."

"Come on, you're kidding, Mary Jo. I mean, aren't you?"

Silence. Then again the soft voice began droning out of darkness. "There was a family in Bavaria in nineteen twenty-one. I don't remember the name, but they were a family of eleven. You could check it in the newspapers, I suppose. Just a short time following an attempt at a séance, they went out of their minds. All of them. All eleven. They went on a burning spree in their house, and when they'd finished with the furniture, they started on the three-month-old baby of one of the younger daughters. And that is when the neighbors broke in and stopped them.

"The entire family," she ended, "was put in an asylum."

"Oh, man!" Chris breathed as she thought of Captain Howdy, who had now assumed a menacing coloration. Mental illness. Was that it? Something. "I knew I should've taken Rags to see a psychiatrist!"

"Oh, for heaven sakes!" said Mrs. Perrin, stepping forward into the light. "You never mind about me; you just listen to your doctor." There was attempted reassurance in her voice that seemed to Chris to lack conviction. "I'm great at the future," Perrin added with a smile, "but in the present I'm absolutely helpless." She was fumbling in her purse. "Now then, where are my glasses? There, you see? I've mislaid them. Oh, here they are right here." She had found them in a pocket of her coat. "Lovely home," she remarked as she put on the glasses and glanced up at the upper façade of the house. "Gives a feeling of warmth."

"What a flipping relief," said Chris. "For a second there, I thought you were going to tell me the house is haunted!"

Mrs. Perrin glanced down to her, unsmiling.

"Why would I tell you a thing like that?" she asked.

Chris was thinking of a friend, a noted actress in Beverly Hills who had sold her home because of her insistence that it was inhabited by a poltergeist. Grinning wanly, Chris shrugged. "I don't know," she said. "Just kidding."

"It's a good, friendly house," Mrs. Perrin reassured her in an even tone. "I've been here before, you know; many times."

"Have you really?"

"Yes, a friend of mine owned it, an admiral in the navy. I get a letter from him now and then. They've shipped him to sea again, poor dear. I don't know if it's really him that I miss or this house." She smiled. "But then maybe you'll invite me back."

"Mary Jo, I'd *love* to have you back. I mean it. You're a fascinating person. Listen, call me. Will you call me next week?"

"Yes, I would like to hear how your daughter's coming on."

"Got the number?"

"I do."

What was wrong? wondered Chris.

Something in the psychic's tone was off-center.

"Well, good night," said Mrs. Perrin, "and thanks again for a marvelous evening." And before Chris could answer her, the psychic was rapidly walking down the street.

Chris watched her and then slowly closed the front door as a heavy lassitude overcame her. *Quite a night,* she thought; *some night.*

She went to the living room and stood over Willie, who was kneeling by the urine stain. She was brushing up the nap of the rug.

"White vinegar I put on," Willie muttered. "Two times."

"Comin' out?"

"Maybe now. I do not know. We will see."

"No, you can't really tell until it dries."

Yeah, that's brilliant there, punchy. That's a brilliant observation. Judas priest, kid, go to bed!

"C'mon, leave it alone for now, Willie. Get to sleep."

"No, I finish."

"Okay, then. And thanks. Good night."

"Good night, Madam."

Chris started up the stairs with weary steps. "Great curry, there, Willie," she called down. "They all loved it."

"Thank you, Madam."

Chris looked in on Regan and found her still asleep. Then remembered the Ouija board. Should she hide it? Throw it away? *Boy, Perrin's really dingy when it comes to that stuff.* Yet Chris was aware that the fantasy playmate was morbid and unhealthy. *Yeah, maybe I should chuck it.*

Still, she was hesitant. Standing by the bedside and looking at Regan, she remembered an incident when her daughter was three, the night that Howard had decided she was much too old to continue to sleep with her baby bottle, on which she had grown dependent. He'd taken it away from her that night, and Regan had screamed until four in the morning, then behaved hysterically for days. Chris feared a similar reaction now. *Better wait until I talk it all out with a shrink.* Moreover, the Ritalin, she reflected, hadn't had a chance to take effect, so at the last, she decided to wait and see.

Chris retired to her room, settled wearily into bed and almost instantly fell asleep. Then awakened to the sound of Regan screaming. "Mother, come *here!* Come here *quick*, I'm *afraid!*"

"I'm coming, Rags! I'm coming!"

Chris raced down the hall to Regan's bedroom. Whimpering. Crying. A sound of bedsprings rapidly moving up and down.

"Oh, my baby, what's wrong?" Chris exclaimed.

She flicked on the lights.

Good Christ almighty!

Her face stained with tears, contorted with terror, Regan lay taut on her back as she gripped at the sides of her narrow bed. "Mother, why is it *shaking?*" she cried. "Make it *stop!* Oh, I'm *scared!* Make it *stop!* Mother, please make it *stop!*"

The bed's mattress was violently quivering back and forth.

The Edge

In our sleep, pain, which cannot forget, falls drop by drop upon the heart until, in our own despair, against our will, comes wisdom through the awful grace of God.

—*Aeschylus*

Chapter One

They brought her to an ending in a crowded cemetery where the gravestones cried for breath.

The Mass had been lonely as her life. Her brothers from Brooklyn. The grocer on the corner who'd extended her credit. Watching them lower her into the dark of a world without windows, Damien Karras sobbed with a grief he had long misplaced.

"Ah, Dimmy, Dimmy . . ."

An uncle with an arm around his shoulder.

"Never mind, she's in heaven now, Dimmy. She's happy."

Oh, God, let it be! Ah, God! Ah, please! Oh, God, please be!

They waited in the car while he lingered by the grave. He could not bear the thought of her being alone.

Driving to Pennsylvania Station, he listened to his uncles speak of their illnesses in broken, immigrant accents.

". . . emphysema . . . gotta quit smokin' . . . I ohmos' died las' year, you know dat?"

Spasms of rage fought to break from his lips, but he pressed them back and felt ashamed. He looked out the window: they were passing by the Home Relief Station where on Saturday mornings in the dead of winter she would pick up the milk and the sacks of potatoes while he lay in his bed; the Central Park Zoo, where she left him in summer while she begged by the fountain in front of the Plaza. Passing the hotel, Karras burst into sobs, and then choked back the memories, wiped at the wetness of stinging regrets. He wondered why love had waited for this distance, waited for the moment when he need not touch, when the limits of contact and human surrender had dwindled to the size of a printed Mass card tucked in his wallet: *In Memoriam . . .* He knew. This grief was old.

He arrived at Georgetown in time for dinner, but had no appetite. He paced inside his cottage. Jesuit friends came by with condolences. Stayed briefly. Promised prayers.

Shortly after ten, Joe Dyer appeared with a bottle of Scotch. He displayed it proudly: "Chivas Regal!"

"Where'd you get the money for it—out of the poor box?"

"Don't be an asshole, that would be breaking my vow of poverty."

"Where did you get it, then?"

"I stole it."

Karras smiled and shook his head as he fetched a glass and a pewter coffee mug, rinsed them out in his tiny bathroom sink. "I believe you," he said hoarsely.

"Greater faith I have never seen."

Karras felt a stab of familiar pain. He shook it off and returned to Dyer, who was sitting on his cot breaking open the seal on the bottle of Scotch. He sat beside him.

"Would you like to absolve me now or later?" asked Dyer.

"Just pour and we'll absolve each other."

Dyer poured deep into glass and cup. "College presidents shouldn't drink," he murmured. "It sets a bad example. I figure I relieved him of a terrible temptation."

Karras swallowed Scotch, but not the story. He knew the president's ways too well. A man of tact and sensitivity, he always gave through indirection. Dyer had come, he knew, as a friend, but also as the president's personal emissary.

Dyer was good for him; made him laugh; talked about the party and Chris MacNeil; purveyed new anecdotes about the Jesuit Prefect of Discipline. He drank very little but continually replenished Karras's glass, and when he thought he was numb enough for sleep, he got up from the cot and made Karras stretch out, while he sat at the desk and continued to talk until Karras's eyes were closed and his comments were mumbled grunts.

Dyer stood up, undid the laces of Karras's shoes and slipped them off.

"Gonna steal my shoes now?" Karras muttered thickly.

"No, I tell fortunes by reading the creases. Now shut up and go to sleep."

"You're a Jesuit cat burglar."

Dyer laughed lightly and covered him with a coat that he took from a closet. "Listen, someone's got to worry about the bills around this place. All you other guys do is rattle your rosary beads for the winos down on M Street."

Karras made no answer. His breathing was regular and deep. Dyer moved quietly to the door and flicked out the light.

"Stealing is a sin," muttered Karras in the darkness.

"Mea culpa," Dyer said softly.

For a time he waited, then at last decided that Karras was asleep. He left the cottage.

In the middle of the night, Karras awakened in tears. He had dreamed of his mother. Standing at a window high in Manhattan, he'd seen her emerging from a subway kiosk across the street. She stood at the curb with a brown paper shopping bag and was searching for him, calling out his name. Karras waved. She didn't see him. She wandered the street. Buses. Trucks. Unfriendly crowds. She was growing frightened. She returned to the subway and began to descend. Karras grew frantic, ran to the street and began to weep as he called her name; as he could not find her; as he pictured her helpless and bewildered in a maze of tunnels beneath the ground.

He waited for his sobbing to subside, and then fumbled for the Scotch. He sat on the cot and drank in darkness. Wet came the tears. They would not cease. This was like childhood, this grief.

He remembered a telephone call from his uncle:

"Dimmy, da edema, it affected her brain. She don't let a doctor come anywhere near her. Jus' keeps screamin' things. Dimmy, she even talk to da goddamn radio. I figure dat she got ta go Bellevue, Dimmy. A regular hospital won't put up wit' dat. I jus' figure a coupla months an' she's good as new; den we take her out again. Okay? Lissen, Dimmy, we awready done it. Dey give her a shot an' den dey take her in da ambulance dis mornin'. We didn' wanna bodda you, excep' dere is gonna be a hearin' in da court and you gotta sign da papers. What? Private hospital? Who's got da money for dat, Dimmy? You?"

Karras didn't remember falling asleep.

He awakened in torpor, with memory of loss draining blood from his brain. He reeled to the bathroom; showered; shaved; dressed in a cassock. It was five-thirty-five. He unlocked the door to Holy Trinity, put on his vestments and offered up Mass at the left side altar.

"Memento etiam . . . ," he prayed with bleak despair: "Remember thy servant, Mary Karras . . ."

In the tabernacle door he saw the face of the nurse at Bellevue Receiving; heard again the screams from the isolation room.

"You her son?"

"Yes, I'm Damien Karras."

"Well, I wouldn't go in there. She's pitchin' a fit."

He'd looked through the port at the windowless room with the naked lightbulb hanging from the ceiling; padded walls; no furniture save for the cot on which she raved.

". . . grant her, we pray Thee, a place of refreshment, light and peace . . ."

As she saw him and met his gaze, she'd grown suddenly silent; then got out of the bed and slowly moved to the small, round, glass observation port, her expression baffled and hurt.

"Why you do this, Dimmy? Why?"

The eyes had been meeker than a lamb's.

"Agnus Dei . . . ," Karras murmured as he bowed his head and struck his breast with a fist. "Lamb of God, who takest away the sins of the world, grant her rest . . ." Moments later, as he closed his eyes and held up the Host, he saw his mother in the hearing room, her little hands clasped gentle in her lap, her expression docile and confused as the judge explained to her the Bellevue psychiatrist's report.

"Do you understand that, Mary?"

She'd nodded; wouldn't open her mouth; they had taken her dentures.

"Well, what do you say about that, Mary?"

She'd proudly answered him, *"My boy, he speak for me."*

An anguished moan escaped Karras's lips as he bowed his head above the Host. He struck his breast as if it were the years that he wanted to turn back as he murmured, *"Domine, non sum dignus.* Say but the word and my soul shall be healed."

Against all reason, against all knowledge, he prayed there was Someone to hear his prayer.

He did not think so.

After the Mass, he returned to the cottage and tried to sleep.

Without success.

Later in the morning, a youngish priest that he'd never seen before came by unexpectedly. He knocked and looked in through the open door. "You busy? Can I see you for a while?"

In the eyes, the restless burden; in the voice, the tugging plea.

For an instant Karras hated him.

"Come in," he said gently. And inwardly raged at this portion of his being that so frequently rendered him helpless in the face of someone's plea; that he could not control; that lay coiled within him like a length of rope, always ready to fling itself out to rescue at the call of someone else's need. It gave him no peace. Not even in sleep. At the edge of his dreams, there was often a sound like the faint, distant cry of someone in distress, and for minutes after waking, he would feel the anxiety of some duty unfulfilled.

The young priest fumbled; faltered; seemed shy. Karras led him patiently. Offered cigarettes. Instant coffee. Then forced a look of interest as the moody young visitor gradually unfolded a familiar problem: the terrible loneliness of priests.

Of all the anxieties that Karras encountered among the community, this one had lately become the most prevalent. Cut off from their families as well as from women, many of the Jesuits were also fearful of expressing affection for fellow priests; of forming deep and loving friendships.

"Like I'd like to put my arm around another guy's shoulder, but right away I'm scared he's going to think I'm queer. I mean, you hear all these stories about so many latents attracted to the priesthood. So I just don't do it. I won't even go to somebody's room just to listen to records; or to talk; or to smoke. It's not that I'm afraid of *him;* I'm just worried about him getting worried about *me.*"

Karras felt the weight shifting slowly from the young priest and onto him. He let it come; he let him talk. He knew he would return to him again and again to find relief from aloneness, to make Karras his friend, and when he'd realized he had done so without fear and suspicion, perhaps he would go on to make friends among the others.

Growing weary, Karras found himself drifting into private sorrow. He glanced at a plaque that someone had given him the previous Christmas: MY BROTHER HURTS. I SHARE HIS PAIN. I MEET GOD IN HIM. A failed encounter. He blamed himself. He had mapped the streets of his brother's torment, yet never had walked them; or so he believed. He thought that the pain he felt was his own.

At last the visitor looked at his watch. It was time for lunch in the campus refectory. He rose and as he started to leave, he glanced at the cover of a current novel on Karras's desk.

"Oh, you've got *Shadows*," he said.

"Have you read it?" asked Karras.

The young priest shook his head. "No, I haven't. Should I?"

"I don't know. I just finished it and I'm not at all sure that I really understand it," Karras lied. He picked up the book and handed it over. "Want to take it along? You know, I'd really like to hear someone else's opinion."

"Oh, well, sure," said the Jesuit, examining the copy on the inner flap of the dust jacket. "I'll try to get it back to you in a couple of days."

His mood seemed brighter.

As the screen door creaked with the young priest's departure, Karras felt relief. And peace. He picked up his breviary and stepped out to the courtyard, where he slowly paced and said his daily Office prayers.

In the afternoon, he had still another visitor, the elderly pastor of Holy Trinity Church, who took a chair by the desk and offered condolences on the passing of Karras's mother.

"Said a couple of Masses for her, Damien, and one for you as well," he wheezed with a lilting Irish brogue.

"That was thoughtful of you, Father. Thanks so much."

"How old was she?"

"Seventy."

"Ah, well, that's a good old age."

Karras felt a faint flash of anger. *Oh, really?*

He turned his gaze to an altar card that the pastor had carried in with him. One of three employed in the Mass, it was covered in plastic and inscribed with a portion of the prayers that were said by the priest. Karras wondered why the pastor had brought it in. The answer came soon.

"Well, Damien, we've had another one of those things here today. In the church, y'know. Another desecration."

A statue of the Virgin Mary at the left side altar of the church had been painted over and made to look like a harlot, the pastor told him. Then he handed the altar card to Karras. "And then this was found in mid-morning right after you'd gone, y'know, to New York. Was it Saturday? Yes. Yes, it was. Well, take a look at it, will you? I just had a talk with a sergeant of police, and—ah, well, never mind that now. Have a look at this card for me, Damien, now would you?"

As Karras examined the card, the pastor explained that someone had slipped in a typewritten sheet between the original card and its cover. The ersatz text, though containing some strikeovers and various typographical errors, was in fluent and intelligible Latin and described in vivid, erotic detail an imagined homosexual encounter involving Mary Magdalene and the Blessed Virgin Mary.

"That's enough, now, you don't have to read it all," said the pastor, snapping back the card as if fearing that it might be an occasion of sin. "Now that's excellent Latin; I mean, it's got style, a church Latin style. Well, the sergeant says he talked to some fellow, a psychologist, and he says that the person's been doin' all this—well, he could be a priest, y'know, a very sick priest. Could he be right?"

Karras thought for a while. Then nodded. "Yes. Yes, it could. Acting out a rebellion, maybe, in a state of complete somnambulism. I don't know. But it could be. Sure. Maybe so."

"Can you think of any candidates, Damien?"

"I don't get you."

"Well, now, sooner or later they come and see *you*, wouldn't you say? I mean, the sick ones, if there are any, from the campus. Do y'know any *like* that, Damien? I mean with that sort of illness."

"No, I don't, Father."

"No. No, I didn't think you'd tell me."

"No, I wouldn't, but on top of that, Father, somnambulism is a way of resolving any number of possible conflict situations, and the usual form of resolution is symbolic. So I really wouldn't know. And if it is a somnambulist, he'd probably have total posterior amnesia about what he's done, so that even *he* wouldn't have a clue."

"What if you were to tell him?" the pastor asked cagily. He lightly plucked at an earlobe, a habitual gesture, Karras had noticed, whenever he thought he was being wily.

"I know of no one who fits the description," said Karras.

"Yes, I see. Well, it's just as I'd expected." The pastor stood up and started shuffling toward the door. "Y'know what you're like, you people? Like priests!"

As Karras gently chuckled, the pastor returned and dropped the altar card on his desk. "I suppose you could study this thing, don't ya think? Go ahead," he said as he turned and started away again, his shoulders hunched over with age.

"Did they check it for fingerprints?" Karras asked him.

The elderly pastor stopped and looked back. "Oh, I doubt it. After all, it's not a criminal we're after, now, is it? More likely it's only a demented parishioner. What do you think of that, Damien? Do you think that it could be someone in the parish? You know, I'm thinking now maybe that's so. No, it wasn't a priest at all, not at all; it was someone among the parishioners." He was pulling at his earlobe again. "Don't you think?"

"I wouldn't know, Father."

"No. No, I didn't think you'd tell me."

Later that day, Karras was relieved of his duties as counselor and assigned to the Georgetown University Medical School as a lecturer in psychiatry. His orders were to rest.

Chapter Two

Regan lay on her back on Dr. Klein's examining table with her arms and legs bowed outward. Taking her foot in both his hands, Klein flexed it toward her ankle, held it there in tension and then suddenly released it. The foot relaxed into normal position. He repeated the procedure several times but without any variance in the result. He seemed dissatisfied. When Regan abruptly sat up and spat in his face, he instructed a nurse to remain in the room and returned to his office to talk to Chris.

It was April 26. He'd been out of the city both Sunday and Monday and Chris hadn't reached him until this morning to relate the happening at the party and the subsequent shaking of the bed.

"It was actually moving?"

"It was moving."

"For how long?"

"I don't know. Maybe ten, maybe fifteen seconds. I mean, that's all of it I saw. Then she sort of went stiff and wet the bed. Or maybe she'd wet it before. I don't know. But then all of a sudden she was dead asleep and never woke up till the next afternoon."

Klein entered his office thoughtfully.

"Well, what is it?" Chris asked. Her tone was anxious.

When she'd first arrived, he'd reported his suspicion that the shaking of the bed had been caused by a seizure of clonic contractions, an alternating tensing and relaxing of the muscles.

The chronic form of such a condition, he'd told her, was clonus, which often indicated a lesion in the brain.

"Well, the test was negative," he said, then described the procedure, explaining that in clonus the alternate flexing and releasing of the foot would have triggered a run of clonic contractions. But as he sat at his desk, Klein still seemed worried. "Has she ever had a fall?" he asked.

"Like on the head?"

"Well, yes."

"No, not that I know of."

"Childhood diseases?"

"Just the usual: measles and mumps and chicken pox."

"Sleepwalking history?"

"Not until now."

"Now? She was walking in her sleep at the party?"

"Well, yes; I thought I told you. She still doesn't know what she did that night. And there's other stuff, too, that she doesn't remember."

Regan asleep. An overseas telephone call from Howard.

"How's Rags?"

"Thanks a lot for the call on her birthday."

"I was stuck on a yacht. Now for chrissakes, lay off me! I called her the minute I was back in the hotel!"

"Oh, yeah, sure."

"She didn't tell you?"

"You talked to her?"

"Yes. That's why I thought I'd better call you. What the hell's going on with her, Chris?"

"What do you mean?"

"She just called me a 'cocksucker' and hung up the phone."

Recounting the incident to Klein, Chris explained that when Regan had finally awakened, she had no memory whatever of either the telephone call or of what had happened on the night of the dinner.

"Then perhaps she wasn't lying about the moving of the furniture," Klein hypothesized.

"I don't get you."

"Well, she moved it herself, let's say, but perhaps while in a state of automatism. It's like a trance state. The subject doesn't know or remember what he's doing."

"But there's this great big heavy bureau in her room made out of teakwood. It must weigh half a ton. I mean, how could she have moved that?"

"Extraordinary strength is pretty common in pathology."

"Oh, really? How come?"

Klein shrugged. "Who knows. Now, besides what you've told me," he continued, "have you noticed any other bizarre behavior?"

"Well, she's gotten real sloppy."

"Bizarre," Klein repeated.

"Doc, for Regan that's bizarre. Oh, now wait a second! Wait! Yeah, there's this: You remember that Ouija board she's been playing with? Captain Howdy?"

The internist nodded. "The fantasy playmate."

"Well, now she can hear him."

The doctor leaned forward, folding his arms atop the desk, his eyes narrowed, his manner alert. "She can hear him?"

"Yes. Yesterday morning, I could hear her talking to Howdy in her bedroom. I mean, she'd talk, and then seem to wait, as if she were playing with the Ouija board, but when I peeked inside the room, there wasn't any Ouija board there; just Rags; and she was nodding her head, Doc, just like she was agreeing with what he was saying."

"Did she see him?"

"I don't think so. She sort of had her head to the side, the way she does when she listens to records."

The doctor nodded thoughtfully. "Yes. Yes, I see. Any other phenomena like that? Does she see things? Smell things?"

"Yeah, smell," Chris remembered. "She keeps smelling something bad in her bedroom."

"Something burning?"

"Hey, that's right! How'd you know that?"

"Well, it's sometimes the symptom of a type of disturbance in the chemicoelectrical activity of the brain. In the case of your daughter, in the temporal lobe, you see." He put an index finger to the front of his skull. "Up here, in the forward part of the brain. Now it's rare but it does cause bizarre hallucinations and usually just before a convulsion. I suppose that's why it's mistaken for schizophrenia so often; but it *isn't* schizophrenia: it's produced by a lesion in the temporal lobe. So since the test for clonus wasn't conclusive, I think I'd like to give her an EEG—an electroencephalograph. It will show us the pattern of her brain waves. It's a pretty good test of abnormal functioning."

"But you think that's it, huh? Temporal lobe?"

"Well, she does have the syndrome, Mrs. MacNeil. For example, the untidiness; the pugnacity; behavior that's socially embarrassing; the automatism; and of course, the seizures that made the bed shake. Usually, that's followed by either wetting the bed or vomiting, or both, and then sleeping very deeply."

"You want to test her right now?" Chris asked.

"Yes, I think we should do it immediately, but she's going to need sedation. If she moves or jerks it will void the results, so may I give her, say, twenty-five milligrams of Librium?"

"Jesus, do what you have to," a shaken Chris told him.

She accompanied him to the examining room, and when Regan saw him readying the hypodermic, she screamed and filled the air with a torrent of obscenities.

"Oh, honey, it's to *help* you!" Chris pleaded. She held Regan still while Klein administered the injection.

"I'll be back," Klein said, and while a nurse wheeled the EEG apparatus into the room, he left to attend to another patient. When he returned a short time later, the Librium still had not taken effect. Klein seemed surprised. "That was quite a strong dose," he remarked to Chris.

He injected another twenty-five milligrams; left; came back and, finding Regan now tractable and docile, he placed saline-tipped electrodes to her scalp. "We put four on each side," he explained to Chris. "That enables us to take a brain-wave reading from the left and right side of the brain and then compare them. Why? Well, deviations could be significant. For example, I had a patient who used to hallucinate. He'd see things and hear things. Well, I found a discrepancy in comparing the left and right readings of his brain waves and discovered that actually the man was hallucinating on just one side of his head."

"That's wild!" Chris marveled.

"Sure is. The left eye and ear functioned normally; only the right side had visions and heard things. Well, all right, now, let's see," Klein said as he turned on the EEG machine and then pointed to the waves on the fluorescent screen. "Now that's both sides together," he explained. "What I'm looking for now are spiky waves"—he patterned in the air with his index finger—"especially waves of very high amplitude coming at four to eight per second. If they're there, then it's temporal lobe."

He studied the pattern of the brain wave carefully, but discovered no dysrhythmia, no spikes, no flattened domes. And when he switched to comparison readings, the results were negative as well. Klein frowned. He couldn't understand it. He repeated the procedure.

And found no change.

Klein brought in a nurse to attend to Regan and returned to his office with her mother. Chris sat down and said, "Okay, so what's the story?"

Pensive, arms folded across his chest, Klein was sitting on the edge of his desk. "Well, the EEG would have proved that she had it," he said, "but the lack of dysrhythmia doesn't prove to me conclusively that she doesn't. It might be hysteria, but the pattern before and after her convulsion was much too striking."

Chris furrowed her brow. "You know, you keep on saying that, Doc—'convulsion.' What exactly is the name of this disease?"

"Well, it isn't a disease," Klein said somberly and quietly.

"Well then, what do you call it, Doc? I mean, specifically."

"You know it as epilepsy."

"Oh, good Christ!"

"Now, let's hold it," soothed Klein. "I can see that like most of the general public your impression of epilepsy is exaggerated and probably largely mythical."

"Isn't it hereditary?" Chris said, wincing.

"That's one of the myths," Klein told her calmly. "At least, most doctors seem to think so. Look, practically anyone can be made to convulse. You see, most of us are born with a pretty high threshold of resistance to convulsions; some with a low one; so the difference between you and an epileptic is a matter of degree. That's all. Just degree. It is not a disease."

"Then what is it, a freaking hallucination?"

"It's a disorder: a *controllable* disorder. And there are many, many types of it, Mrs. MacNeil. For example, you're sitting here now and for a second you seem to go blank, let's say, and you miss a little bit of what I'm saying. Well, now that's a kind of epilepsy. It's a true epileptic attack."

"Yeah, well, that isn't Regan, Doc. I don't believe it. And how come it's happening just all of a sudden?"

"Look, you're right. I mean we still aren't sure that's what she's got, and I grant you that maybe you were right in the first place; very possibly it's psychosomatic. But I doubt it. And to answer your question, any number of changes in the function of the brain can trigger a convulsion in the epileptic: worry; fatigue; emotional stress; even a particular note on a musical instrument. I had a patient who never used to have a seizure except on a bus when he was a block away from home. Well, we finally discovered what was causing it: flickering light from a white slat fence reflected in the window of the bus. Now at another time of day, or if the bus had been going at a different speed, he wouldn't have convulsed, you see. He had a lesion, a scar in the brain that was caused by some childhood disease. In the case of your daughter, the scar would be forward—up front in the temporal lobe—and when it's hit by a particular electrical impulse of a certain wavelength and periodicity, it triggers a burst of abnormal reactions from deep within a focus in the lobe. Do you see?"

"I'll take your word," Chris sighed, dejected. "But I'll tell you the truth, Doc: I don't understand how her whole personality could have changed."

"In the temporal lobe, that's extremely common, and can last for days or even weeks. It isn't rare to find destructive, even criminal behavior. There's such a big change, in fact, that two or three hundred years ago people with temporal lobe disorders were often considered to be possessed by a devil."

"They were *what?*"

"Taken over by a demon. You know, something like a superstitious version of split personality."

Closing her eyes, Chris lowered her forehead onto a fist. "Listen, tell me something good," she huskily murmured.

"Well, now, don't be alarmed. If it *is* a lesion, in a way she's lucky. Then all we'd have to do is remove the scar."

"Oh, swell."

"Or it could be just pressure on the brain. Look, I'd like to have some X-rays taken of her skull. There's a radiologist here in the building, and perhaps I can get him to take you right away. Shall I call him?"

"Shit, yes; go ahead; let's do it."

Klein called and set it up. They would take her immediately, they told him. He hung up the phone and began writing a prescription. "Room twenty-one on the second floor. Then I'll probably call you tomorrow or Thursday. I'd like a neurologist in on this. In the meantime, I'm taking her off the Ritalin. Let's try her on Librium for a while."

He ripped the prescription sheet from the pad and handed it over. "I'd try to stay close to her, Mrs. MacNeil. In these walking trance states, if that's what it is, it's always possible for her to hurt herself. Is your bedroom close to hers?"

"Yeah, it is."

"That's fine. Ground floor?"

"No, second."

"Big windows in her bedroom?"

"Well, one. What's the deal?"

"Well, I'd try to keep it closed, even have them put a lock on it, maybe. In a trance state, she might fall through it. I once had a—"

"Patient," Chris finished with the trace of a wry, weary smile.

Klein grinned. "I guess I do have a lot of them, don't I?"

"Yeah, a couple."

She propped her face on her hand and leaned pensively forward. "You know, I thought of something else just now."

"And what was that?"

"Well, like after a fit, you were saying that she'd right away fall dead asleep. Like on Saturday night. I mean, didn't you say that?"

"Well, yes." Klein nodded. "Yes, I did."

"Well then, how come those other times when she said that her bed was shaking, she was always wide awake?"

"You didn't tell me that."

"Well, that's how it was. She looked fine. She'd just come to my room and then ask to get in bed with me."

"Any bed-wetting? Vomiting?"

Chris shook her head. "She was fine."

Klein frowned and gently chewed on his lip. "Well, let's look at those X-rays," he finally told her.

Feeling drained and numb, Chris shepherded Regan to the radiologist; stayed at her side while the X-rays were taken; took her home. She'd been strangely mute since the second injection, and Chris made an effort now to engage her.

"Want to play some Monopoly or somethin', sweetheart?"

Slightly shaking her head, Regan stared at her mother with unfocused eyes that seemed to be retracted into infinite remoteness. "I'm feeling real sleepy," she said. The voice belonged to the eyes. Then, turning, she climbed up the stairs to her bedroom.

Worriedly watching her, *Must be the Librium*, Chris reflected.

Then at last she sighed and went into the kitchen. She poured coffee and sat down at the breakfast nook table with Sharon.

"How'd it go?" Sharon asked her.

"Oh, Christ!"

Chris fluttered the prescription slip onto the table. "Better call and get that filled." she said, and then explained what the doctor had told her. "If I'm busy or out, keep a real good eye on her, would you, Shar? Klein told me that—" Dawning. Sudden. "That reminds me."

Chris got up from the table and went up to Regan's bedroom, where she found her asleep underneath her bedcovers. Chris moved to the window, tightened the latch and then stared down below. Facing out from the side of the house, the window directly overlooked the precipitous public staircase that plunged down to M Street far below.

Boy, I'd better call a locksmith right away!

Chris returned to the kitchen and added the chore to the list from which Sharon sat working, gave Willie the dinner menu, returned a call from her agent concerning the film she'd been asked to direct.

"What about the script?" he wanted to know.

"Yeah, it's great, Ed; let's do it. When does it go?"

"Well, your segment's in July, so you'll have to start preparing right away."

"You mean now?"

"I mean now. This isn't acting, Chris. You're involved in a lot of the preproduction. You've got to work with the set designer, the costume designer, the makeup artist, the producer. And you'll have to pick a cameraman and a cutter and block out your shots. C'mon, Chris, you know the drill."

"Oh, shit!" Chris breathed out disconsolately.

"You've got a problem?"

"Yeah, I do, Ed. It's Regan. She's very, very sick"

"Hey, I'm sorry, kid."

"Sure."

"Chris, what is it?"

"They don't know yet. I'm waiting for some tests. Listen, Ed, I can't leave her."

"So who says to leave her?"

"No, you don't understand, Ed. I need to be at home with her. She needs my attention. Look, I just can't explain it, Ed, it's too complicated, so why don't we hold off for a while?"

"We can't. They want to try for the Music Hall over Christmas, Chris, and I think that they're pushing it now."

"Oh, for chrissakes, Ed, they can wait two weeks! Now come on!"

"Look, you've bugged me that you want to direct, and now all of a—"

"Yeah, I know, I know. Yeah, I want it, Ed, I really want it bad, but you'll just have to tell 'em that I need some more time."

"And if I do, we're going to blow it. Now that's my opinion. Look, they don't want you anyway, that's not news. They're just doing this for Moore, and I think if they go back to him now and say she isn't too sure she wants to do it yet, *he'll* have an out. Look, you do what you want. I don't care. There's no money in this thing unless it hits. But if you want it, I'm telling you: I ask for a delay and I think we're going to blow it. Now then, what should I tell them?"

Chris sighed. "Ah, boy!"

"Yeah, I know it's not easy."

"No, it isn't. Okay, listen, Ed, maybe if—" Chris thought. Then shook her head. "Never mind, Ed. They'll just have to wait," she said. "Can't be helped."

"Your decision."

"Let me know what they say."

"Of course. Meantime, sorry about your daughter."

"Thanks, Ed."

"Take care."

"You too."

Chris hung up the phone in a state of depression, lit up a cigarette, then mentioned to Sharon, "I talked to Howard, by the way, did I tell you?"

"Oh, when? Did you tell him about Regan?"

"Yeah, I told him he ought to come see her."

"Is he coming?"

"I don't know. I don't think so," Chris answered.

"You'd think he'd make the effort."

"Yeah, I know." Chris sighed. "But you've got to understand his hang-up, Shar."

"What do you mean?"

"Oh, the whole 'Mr. Chris MacNeil' thing! Rags was a part of it. She was in and he was out. Always me and Rags together on the magazine covers; me and Rags in the layouts; mother and daughter, pixie twins." She moodily tapped ash from her cigarette with a finger. "Ah, nuts, who knows. It's all mixed up, it's a mess. But it's hard to get hacked with him, Shar; I just can't." She reached out for a book by Sharon's elbow. "So what are you reading?"

"Oh, I forgot. That's for you. Mrs. Perrin dropped it by."

"She was here?"

"Yes, this morning. Said she's sorry she missed you and she's going out of town, but she'll call you as soon as she's back."

Chris nodded and glanced at the title of the book: *A Study of Devil Worship and Related Occult Phenomena*. She opened it and found a penned note:

Dear Chris:

I happened by the Georgetown University Library book store and picked this up for you. It has some chapters about Black Mass. You should read it all, however; I think you'll find the other sections particularly interesting. See you soon.

Mary Jo

"Sweet lady," said Chris.

"Yes, she is."

Chris riffled through the pages of the book. "What's the scoop on Black Mass? Pretty hairy?"

"I don't know," answered Sharon. "I haven't read it."

"Did your guru tell you not to?"

Sharon stretched. "Oh, that stuff turns me off."

"Oh, really? And so what happened to your Jesus complex?"

"Oh, come on!"

Chris slid the book across the table to Sharon. "Here, read it and tell me what happens."

"And get nightmares?"

"What do you think you get paid for?"

"Throwing up."

"I can do that for myself," Chris muttered as she picked up the evening paper. "All you have to do is stick your business manager's advice down your throat and you're vomiting blood for a week." Chris abruptly put the paper aside. "Would you turn on the radio, Shar? Get the news."

Sharon had dinner at the house with Chris, and then left for a date. She forgot the book. Chris saw it on the table and thought about reading it, but in the end she felt too weary. She left it on the table and walked upstairs. She looked in on Regan, who was under the covers and apparently sleeping through the night. She then checked the window again. Locked shut. Leaving the room, Chris made sure to leave the door wide open and before getting into bed that night she did the same with her own. She watched part of a television movie, then slept. The next morning the devil worship book had mysteriously vanished from the table. No one noticed.

Chapter Three

The consulting neurologist pinned up the X-rays again and searched for indentations that would look as if the skull had been pounded like copper with a tiny hammer. Dr. Klein stood behind him with folded arms. They had both looked for lesions and collections of fluid; for a possible shifting of the pineal gland. They were probing now for Lückenshadl Skull, the telltale depressions that would indicate chronic intracranial pressure. They did not find it. The date was Thursday, April 28.

The consulting neurologist removed his glasses and carefully tucked them into the left breast pocket of his jacket. "There's just nothing there, Sam. Nothing I can see."

Klein frowned at the floor and shook his head.

"Doesn't figure," he said.

"Want to run another series?"

"I don't think so. I think I'll try an LP."

"Good idea."

"In the meantime, I'd like you to see her."

"How's today?"

"Well, I'm—" Telephone buzzer. "Excuse me." He picked up the telephone. "Yes?"

"Mrs. MacNeil on the phone. Says it's urgent."

"What line?"

"She's on three."

He punched the extension button. "Dr. Klein here."

Chris's voice was distraught and on the brim of hysteria.

"Oh, Christ, Doc, it's Regan! Can you come right away?"

"Well, what's wrong?"

"I don't know, Doc, I just can't describe it! Please come over right away! Come now!"

"I'm on the way!"

He disconnected and buzzed his receptionist. "Susan, tell Dresner to take my appointments." He hung up the phone and started taking off his jacket. "That's her, Dick," he said. "Want to come? It's only just across the bridge."

"I've got an hour, I'd say."

"Okay, let's go."

They were there within minutes, and at the door, where a frightened-looking Sharon greeted them, they heard moans and screams of terror from Regan's bedroom. "I'm Sharon Spencer," she told them. "Come on in. She's upstairs."

Sharon led them to the door of Regan's bedroom, then cracked it open slightly and called in, "Chris, doctors!"

Chris instantly came to the door, her face contorted in a vise of fear. "Oh, my God, come on in!" she said in a quavering voice. "Come on in and take a look at what she's doing!"

"This is Dr.—"

In the middle of the introduction, Klein broke off as he caught sight of Regan. Shrieking hysterically and flailing her arms, her body seemed to fling itself up horizontally into the air above her bed and then be slammed down savagely onto the mattress. It was happening rapidly, again and again.

"Oh, Mother, make him *stop!*" Regan was screeching. "*Stop* him! He's trying to *kill* me! *Stop* him! *Stoooppppppp hiiiiiimmmm-mmmm, Motherrrrrrrrrrrr!*"

"Oh, my baby!" Chris whimpered as she jerked up a fist to

her mouth and bit it. She turned a beseeching look to Klein. "What's *happening*, Doc? What *is* it?"

Klein shook his head, his gaze fixed on Regan as the phenomenon continued. She would lift about a foot each time and then fall with a wrenching of her breath, as if unseen hands had picked her up and thrown her down. Chris pressed both her hands to her mouth, staring wildly as the up-and-down movements abruptly ceased and Regan started twisting feverishly from side to side with her eyes rolled upward into their sockets so that only the whites were exposed. "Oh, he's burning me . . . *burning* me!" she was moaning as her legs began rapidly crossing and uncrossing.

The doctors moved closer, one on either side of the bed, and still twisting and jerking, Regan arched her head back, disclosing a swollen, bulging throat as she muttered incomprehensibly in guttural tone: ". . . nowonmai . . . nowonmai . . ."

Klein reached down to check her pulse.

"Now, let's see what the trouble is, dear," he said gently.

And abruptly he was reeling across the room, staggering backward from the force of a vicious swing of Regan's arm as she suddenly sat up, her face contorted with a hideous rage.

"The sow is *mine!*" she bellowed in a coarse and powerful voice. "She is *mine!* Keep away from her! She is *mine!*"

A yelping laugh gushed up from her throat, and then she fell on her back as if someone had pushed her. She pulled up her nightgown, exposing her genitals. "*Fuck* me! *Fuck* me!" she screamed at the doctors, and with both her hands began masturbating frantically. Moments later Chris ran from the room with a stifled sob right after Regan put her fingers to her lips and licked them.

Riveted, watching in shock, Klein approached the bedside again, this time warily, as Regan appeared to hug herself, her arms folded, her hands caressing them.

"Ah, yes, my pearl . . . ," she crooned in that strangely coarsened voice and with both her eyes closed as if in ecstasy. "My child . . . my flower . . . my pearl . . ." Then again she was twisting from side to side, moaning meaningless syllables over and over, until abruptly she sat up with her eyes staring wide in helpless terror.

She mewed like a cat.

Then barked.

Then neighed.

And then, bending at the waist, started whirling her torso around in rapid, strenuous circles. She gasped for breath. "Oh, *stop* him!" she wept. "Please, *stop* him! It hurts! Make him *stop!* Make him *stop!* I can't *breathe!*"

Klein had seen enough. He fetched his medical bag to the window and quickly began to prepare an injection.

The neurologist remained beside the bed and saw Regan fall backward as if from a shove while her eyes rolled upward into their sockets again, and with her body rolling from side to side, she began to mutter rapidly in guttural tones. The neurologist leaned closer and tried to make it out. Then he saw Klein beckoning and he straightened up and went to him quickly.

"I'm giving her Librium," Klein told him guardedly, holding the syringe to the light of the window. "But you're going to have to hold her."

The neurologist nodded, but seemed preoccupied, inclining his head to the side as if listening to the muttering from the bed.

"What's she saying?" Klein whispered.

"I don't know. Just gibberish. Nonsense syllables." Yet his own explanation seemed to leave him unsatisfied. "She *says* it as if it means something, though. It's got cadence."

Klein nodded toward the bed and the men approached quietly from either side. As they came, the tormented child went rigid, as if in the stiffening grip of tetany, and the doctors, who had stopped at the bedside, turned and looked at each other significantly. Then they looked again to Regan as she started to arch her body upward into an impossible position, bending it backward like a bow until the brow of her head had touched her feet. She was screaming in pain.

The doctors eyed one another with baffled and questioning surmise. And then Klein gave a signal to the neurologist, but before the consultant could seize her, Regan fell limp in a faint and wet the bed.

Klein leaned over and rolled up her eyelid. Checked her pulse. "She'll be out for a while," he murmured. "I think she convulsed. Don't you?"

"Yes, I think so."

"Well, let's take some insurance."

He deftly administered the injection.

"Well, what do you think?" Klein asked as he pressed a circle of sterile tape against the puncture.

"Temporal lobe. Sure, maybe schizophrenia's a possibility, Sam, but the onset's much too sudden. She hasn't any history of it, right?"

"No, she hasn't."

"Neurasthenia?"

Klein shook his head.

"Then hysteria, maybe?"

"I've thought of that," said Klein.

"Of course. Though she'd have to be a freak to get her body twisted up like she did voluntarily, now wouldn't you say?" He shook his head. "No, I think it's pathological, Sam—her strength; the paranoia; the hallucinations. Schizophrenia, okay; those symptoms it covers. But temporal lobe would also cover the convulsions. There's one thing that bothers me, though . . ." He trailed off with a puzzled frown.

"What's that?"

"Well, I'm really not sure but I thought I heard signs of dissociation: 'my pearl' . . . 'my child' . . . 'my flower' . . . 'the sow.' I had the feeling she was talking about herself. Was that your impression too, or am I reading something into it?"

As he mulled the question, Klein stroked his lower lip with a finger, then answered, "Well, frankly, at the time it never occurred to me, but then now that you point it out . . ." He made a sound in his throat, looking thoughtful. "Could be," he said. "Yes. I guess it could." Then he shrugged off the notion. "Well, I'll do an LP right now while she's out and then maybe we'll know something. Sound right?"

The neurologist nodded.

Klein poked around in his medical bag, found a pill and as he tucked it into a pocket, he asked the neurologist, "Can you stay?"

The neurologist checked his watch. "Yeah, sure."

"Let's talk to the mother."

They left the room and entered the hallway.

Their heads lowered, Chris and Sharon were leaning against the balustrade by the staircase. As the doctors approached them, Chris wiped at her nose with a moist and balled-up handkerchief. Her eyes were red and small from crying.

"She's sleeping," Klein told her, "and she's heavily sedated. She'll probably sleep right through until tomorrow."

Gently nodding, Chris responded weakly, "That's good . . . Look, I'm sorry about being such a baby."

"You're doing just fine," Klein assured her. "It's a frightening ordeal. By the way, this is Dr. Richard Coleman."

Chris smiled at him bleakly. "Thanks for coming."

"Dr. Coleman's a neurologist."

"Oh, yeah? And so what do you think?" she asked as she shifted her glance from one of the men to the other.

"Well, we still think it's temporal lobe," Klein answered, "and—"

"Jesus, what in the hell are you *talking* about!" Chris suddenly erupted. "She's been acting like a psycho, like a split personality or something! I mean—" And then, "Oh!" she uttered softly and in pain as abruptly she pulled herself together and lowered her forehead into a hand. "Guess I'm all uptight," she said quietly as she lifted a haggard look to Klein. "I'm so sorry," she said. "You were saying?"

It was the neurologist who answered. "Mrs. MacNeil," he said gently, "there haven't been more than a hundred authenticated cases of split personality in all of medical history. It's a very rare condition. Now I know the temptation is to leap to psychiatry, but any responsible psychiatrist would exhaust the somatic possibilities first. That's the safest procedure."

"Well, okay, then; so what's next?"

"A lumbar tap," said Coleman.

"You mean a spinal?" Chris asked him with a look of distress.

He nodded. "What we missed in the X-rays and the EEG could turn up there. At the least, it would exhaust certain other possibilities. I'd like to do it now, right here, while she's sleeping. I'll give her a local, of course, but it's movement I'm trying to eliminate."

"Listen, how could she jump off the bed like that?" Chris asked, her eyes squinting in incomprehension.

"Well, I think we discussed that before," said Klein. "Pathological states can induce abnormal strength and accelerated motor performance."

"But you said you don't know why."

"Well, it seems to have something to do with motivation," Coleman answered. "But that's about all we know."

"Well, now, what about the spinal?" Klein asked Chris. "Can we go ahead with that?"

Abruptly sagging, Chris stared at the floor. "Go ahead," she said softly. "Do whatever you have to. Just make her well."

"May I use your phone?" asked Klein.

"Yeah, sure. Come on. There's one in the study."

"Oh, incidentally," said Klein as Chris turned around to lead them, "she needs to have her bedding changed."

Quickly moving away, Sharon briskly said, "I'll do it right now."

"Can I make you some coffee?" asked Chris as the doctors followed her down the stairs. "I gave the housekeeping couple the afternoon off, so it'll have to be instant."

They declined.

"I see you haven't fixed that window yet," noted Klein.

"No, we called, though," Chris told him. "They're coming out tomorrow with shutters you can lock."

They entered the study, where Klein called his office and instructed an assistant to deliver the necessary equipment and medication to the house. "And set up the lab for a spinal workup," he instructed. "I'll run it myself right after the tap."

When he'd finished the call, Klein asked Chris what had happened since last he saw Regan.

"Let's see now, last Tuesday"—Chris pondered—"no, on Tuesday there was nothing at all; she went straight up to bed and slept right through until late the next morning, and—oh, no, wait," she amended. "No, she didn't. That's right. Willie mentioned that she'd heard her in the kitchen awfully early. I remember feeling glad that she'd gotten her appetite back. But she went back to bed then, I guess, because she stayed there the rest of the day."

"She was sleeping?" Klein asked her.

"No, I think she was reading. Well, I started feeling a little better about it all. I mean, it looked as if the Librium was just what she needed. She seemed sort of far away, and that bothered me a little, but still it was a pretty big improvement. Then last night, again, nothing," Chris continued. "Then this morning it started. *Boy*, did it start!"

She'd been sitting in the kitchen, Chris recounted, when Regan ran screaming down the stairs to her, cowering defensively behind her chair as she clutched Chris's arms and told her in a high-pitched, frightened voice that Captain Howdy was chasing her; had been pinching her; punching her; shoving her; mouthing obscenities; threatening to kill her. *"There he is!"* she had shrieked at last while pointing to the kitchen door. Then she'd fallen to the floor, her body jerking in spasms, as she gasped and wept and said that Howdy was kicking her. Then suddenly, Chris told the doctors, Regan had stood in the middle of the kitchen with her arms extended and had begun to spin rapidly around "like a top," continuing the movements for almost a minute until she had fallen to the floor in exhaustion.

"And then all of a sudden," Chris finished distressfully, "I saw there was this . . . *hate* in her eyes, this *hate*, and she told me . . . She called me a . . . oh, Jesus!"

Chris burst into convulsive sobbing.

Klein moved to the bar, poured a glass of water from the tap and walked back toward Chris. The sobbing had ceased.

"Oh, shit, where's a cigarette?" she sighed tremulously, wiping at her eyes with the knuckle of a finger.

Klein gave her the water and a small green pill.

"Try this instead," he advised.

"That a tranquilizer?"

"Yes."

"I'll have a double."

"One's enough."

Chris looked away and smiled wanly. "Big spender."

She swallowed the pill and then handed the empty glass to the doctor. "Thanks," she said softly, and then rested her brow on quivering fingertips and gently shook her head. "Yeah, that's when it started," she picked up moodily. "All of that other stuff. It was like she was someone else."

"Like Captain Howdy, perhaps?" asked Coleman.

Chris looked up at him in puzzlement. He was staring so intently. "What do you mean?" she asked.

He shrugged. "I don't know. Just a question."

She turned absent eyes to the fireplace. "I don't know," she said dully. "Just somebody. Somebody else."

There was a moment of silence. Then Coleman stood up. He had another appointment, he told them, and, after some vaguely reassuring statements, said good-bye.

Klein walked him to the door. "You'll check the sugar?" Coleman asked him.

"No, I'm the Rosslyn village idiot."

Coleman smiled thinly. "I'm a little uptight about this myself," he said. He looked away pensively, stroking his lips and his chin with thumb and fingers. "A strange case," he brooded quietly. "*Very* strange." He turned to Klein. "Let me know what you find out."

"You'll be home?"

"Yes, I will. Give a call, okay?"

"Okay."

Coleman waved and left.

When the equipment arrived a short time later, Klein anesthetized Regan's spinal area with Novocain, and as Chris and Sharon watched, he extracted the spinal fluid while keeping a careful watch on the manometer. "Pressure's normal," he murmured. When he'd finished, he went to the window's light to see if the fluid was clear or hazy. It was clear.

He stowed the tubes of fluid in his bag.

"I doubt that she will," Klein said, "but in case she awakens in the middle of the night and creates a disturbance, you might want a nurse here to give her sedation."

"Can't I do it myself?" Chris asked.

"Why not a nurse?"

Chris shrugged. She did not want to mention her distrust of doctors and nurses. "I'd just rather do it myself," she said simply.

"Well, injections are tricky," Klein cautioned. "An air bubble can be very dangerous."

"Oh, I know how to do it," Sharon interjected. "My mother ran a nursing home up in Oregon."

"Oh, would you do that, Shar?" Chris asked her. "Would you stay here tonight?"

"Well, beyond tonight," Klein put in. "She may need intravenous feeding, depending on how she comes along."

"Could you teach me how to do it?" Chris asked him. She was staring at him anxiously. "I need to do it."

Klein nodded and said, "Sure. Sure. Guess I could."

He wrote a prescription for soluble Thorazine and disposable syringes, and gave it to Chris. "Have this filled right away."

Chris handed it to Sharon. "Shar, take care of that for me, would you? Just call and they'll send it. I'd like to go with the doctor while he makes those tests." Chris turned and looked up at the doctor wistfully. "Do you mind?"

Klein noted the tightness around her eyes, the look of helplessness, of confusion. He said, "Sure. Sure, I know how you feel. I feel the same way when I talk to mechanics about my car."

Chris stared at him wordlessly.

They left the house at precisely 6:18 P.M.

In his laboratory in the Rosslyn medical building, Klein ran a number of tests. First he analyzed protein content.

Normal.

Then a count of blood cells.

"Too many red," Klein explained, "means bleeding. And too many white would mean infection." He was looking in particular for a fungus infection that was often the cause of chronic bizarre behavior.

And again drew a blank.

At the last, Klein tested the fluid's sugar content.

"How come?" Chris asked.

"Well," he told her, "the spinal sugar should measure two-thirds of the amount of blood sugar. Anything significantly under that ratio would mean a disease in which the bacteria eat the sugar in the spinal fluid, and if so, it could account for your daughter's symptoms."

But he failed to find it.

Chris folded her arms and shook her head. "Here we are again, folks," she murmured bleakly.

For a while Klein brooded. Then at last he turned and looked to Chris. "Do you keep any drugs in your house?" he asked her.

"Huh?"

"Amphetamines? LSD?"

Chris shook her head and said, "No. Look, I'd tell you. No, there's nothing like that."

Klein nodded, looked down at his shoes, then somberly looked back up at Chris as he told her, "I guess it's time we started looking for a psychiatrist."

Chris was back in the house at exactly 7:21 P.M., and at the door she called out, "Sharon?"

No answer. Sharon wasn't there.

Chris went upstairs to Regan's bedroom and found her still heavily asleep without even a ruffle in her covers. There was an odor of urine in the room, Chris noticed. She looked from the bed to the window. *Cheezus, wide open!* She thought Sharon must have opened it to air out the room. But where was she now? Where did she go? Chris walked over to the window, pulled it down shut and locked it, then went back downstairs just as Willie came through the front door.

"Hi ya, Willie. Any fun today?"

"Shopping, Missus. Movies."

"Where's Karl, Willie?"

Willie made a gesture of dismissal.

"He lets me see Beatles this time. By myself."

"Good work!"

"Yes, Madam."

Willie held up two fingers in a "V for Victory" sign.

The time was 7:35 P.M.

At 8:01, while Chris was in the study on the phone with her agent, she heard the front door coming open and closed again, high-heeled footsteps approaching, then saw Sharon entering the study with several packages in her arms, which she set on the floor. Sharon then flopped down into an overstuffed chair and waited while Chris continued talking.

"Where've you been?" asked Chris when she'd finished.

"Oh, didn't he tell you?"

"Oh, didn't *who* tell me?"

"Burke. Isn't he here?"

"He was here?"

"You mean he wasn't when you got home?"

"Listen, start all over," said Chris.

"Oh, that nut," Sharon chided with a head shake. "I couldn't get the druggist to deliver, so when Burke came around, I thought, fine, he can stay here with Regan while I go get the Thorazine." She shook her head again. "I should have known."

"Yeah, you should've. And so what did you buy?"

"Well, since I thought I had the time, I went and bought a rubber drawsheet for Regan's bed."

"Did you eat?"

"No, I thought I'd fix a sandwich. Would you like one?"

"Good idea."

"So what happened with the tests?" Sharon asked as they walked to the kitchen. "All negative," Chris answered her damply. "I'm going to have to get a shrink."

After sandwiches and coffee, Sharon showed Chris how to give an injection. "The two main things," she explained, "are to make sure that there aren't any air bubbles, and then you make sure that you haven't hit a vein. See, you aspirate a little, like this"—she was demonstrating—"and see if there's blood in the syringe."

For a time, Chris practiced the procedure on a grapefruit, and seemed to grow proficient. Then at 9:28, the front doorbell rang. Willie answered. It was Karl. As he passed through the kitchen, en route to his room, he nodded a good evening and remarked that he'd forgotten to take his key.

"I can't believe it," Chris said to Sharon. "That's the first time he's ever admitted a mistake."

They passed the evening watching television in the study.

At 11:46, Sharon answered the phone, said, "Hold on," and then passed the receiver to Chris, saying, "Chuck."

The young director of the second unit. He sounded grave.

"Have you heard the news yet, Chris?"

"No, what?"

"Well, it's bad."

"Bad?"

"Burke's dead."

He'd been drunk. He had stumbled. He had fallen down the steep flight of steps beside the house to the bottom, where a passing pedestrian on M Street watched as he tumbled into night without end. A broken neck. This bloody, crumpled scene, his last.

As the telephone fell from Chris's fingers, she was silently weeping and then stood up unsteadily. Sharon ran to her and caught her, steadied her, hung up the phone and then led her to the sofa. "Chris, what is it? What's wrong?"

"Burke's dead!"

"Oh, my God, Chris! No! What happened?"

But Chris shook her head. She couldn't speak. She wept.

Then, later, they talked. For hours. Chris drank. Reminisced about Dennings. Now laughed. Now cried. "Ah, my God," she kept sighing. "Poor crazy old Burke . . . poor Burke . . ."

Her dream of death kept coming back to her.

At a little past five in the morning, Chris was standing moodily behind the bar with her elbows propped, her head lowered and her eyes very sad as she waited for Sharon to return from the kitchen with a tray of ice. Then at last she heard her coming. "I still can't believe it," said Sharon as she entered the study.

Chris looked up. Then to the side. And froze.

Gliding spiderlike, rapidly, close behind Sharon, her body arched backward in a bow with her head almost touching her feet, was Regan, her tongue flicking quickly in and out of her mouth while she sibilantly hissed and moved her head very slightly back and forth like a cobra.

Staring numbly, Chris said, "Sharon?"

Sharon stopped. So did Regan. Sharon turned and saw nothing. And then screamed and jumped away as she felt Regan's tongue snaking out at her ankle.

Chris threw a hand to her cheek, her face ashen.

"Call that doctor and get him out of bed! Get him *now!*"

Wherever Sharon moved, Regan would follow.

Chapter Four

Friday, April 29. While Chris waited in the hall outside the bedroom, Dr. Klein and a noted neuropsychiatrist were intently examining Regan, observing her for almost half an hour. Flinging. Whirling. Tearing at the hair and occasionally grimacing and pressing her hands against her ears as if blotting out a sudden and deafening noise. She bellowed obscenities. Screamed in pain. Then at last she flung herself face downward onto the bed and, tucking her legs up under her stomach, she began to moan softly and incoherently.

The psychiatrist motioned Klein to come over to him. "Let's get her tranquilized," he whispered. "Maybe I can talk to her."

The internist nodded and prepared an injection of fifty milligrams of Thorazine. However, when the doctors approached the bed, Regan seemed to sense their presence and quickly turned over, and as the neuropsychiatrist attempted to hold her, she shrieked in malevolent fury. Bit him. Fought him. Held him off. It was only when Karl was called in to assist that they managed to keep Regan sufficiently still for Klein to be able to administer the injection.

The dosage proved inadequate and another fifty milligrams was injected. They waited. And soon Regan grew tractable. Then dreamy. Then stared at the doctors in sudden bewilderment. "Where's Mom? I want Mom!" she said, tearful and frightened.

At a nod from the neuropsychiatrist, Klein left the room.

"Your mother will be here in just a second, dear," the psychiatrist said to Regan soothingly. He sat on the bed and stroked her head. "There, there, it's all right, dear. I'm a doctor."

"I want my mom!"

"Your mom is coming. She's coming. Do you hurt, dear?"

As the tears streamed down her face, Regan nodded.

"Tell me where, dear. Where does it hurt?"

"It hurts every place!" Regan said, sobbing.

"Oh, my baby!"

"Mom!"

Chris ran to the bed and hugged her. Kissed her. Comforted and soothed. Then Chris herself became tearful with happiness. "Oh, you're back, Rags! You're back! It's really you!"

"Oh, Mom, he hurt me!" Regan told her, sniffling. "Please make him stop hurting me! Okay, Mom? Please?"

Chris stared at her, puzzled, then turned to the doctors with a plea and a question in her eyes as she asked them, "What? What is it?"

"She's heavily sedated," the psychiatrist said gently.

"You mean that—"

He quickly cut her off with "We'll see."

He turned to Regan. "Can you tell me what's wrong, dear?"

"I don't *know!*" Regan tearfully answered him. "I don't know! I don't know why he does it! He was always my friend before!"

"Who's that?"

"Captain Howdy! And then after it's like somebody else is inside me! Making me do things!"

"Captain Howdy?"

"I don't know!"

"A person?"

Regan nodded.

"Tell me who?"

"I don't *know!*"

"Well, all right, then; let's try something, Regan. How about if we play a little game?" He was reaching into a jacket pocket and drew out a shining round bauble attached to a silvery length of chain. "Have you ever seen movies where someone gets hypnotized?" he asked.

Wide-eyed, Regan solemnly nodded.

"Well, I'm a hypnotist, Regan. Oh, yes, really! I hypnotize people all the time. I really do! That's, of course, if they let me. Now I think if I hypnotize you, Regan, it will help you get well. Yes, that person inside you will come right out. Would you like to be hypnotized? See, your mother's right here, right beside you."

Regan looked to Chris questioningly.

"Go ahead, honey, do it," Chris urged her. "Try it."

Regan turned to the psychiatrist and nodded. "Okay," she said softly. "But only a little."

The psychiatrist smiled, then quickly glanced to the sound of pottery breaking behind him. A delicate vase had fallen to the floor from the top of a bureau where Klein was now resting his forearm. He looked at his arm and then down at the shards with an air of puzzlement, then stooped to pick them up.

"Never mind, Doc, Willie'll get it," Chris told him.

"Would you please close those shutters for me, Sam?" the psychiatrist asked. "And pull the drapes?"

When the room was dark, the psychiatrist gripped the chain in his fingertips and began to swing the bauble back and forth with an easy movement. He shone a penlight on it. It glowed.

He began to intone the hypnotic ritual: "Now watch this, Regan, keep watching, and soon you'll feel your eyelids growing heavier and heavier . . ."

Within a very short time, Regan seemed to be in a trance.

"Extremely suggestible," the psychiatrist murmured. Then he asked, "Are you comfortable, Regan?"

"Yes," Regan answered in a voice that was soft and whispery.

"How old are you, Regan?"

"Twelve."

"Is there someone inside you?"

"Sometimes."

"When?"

"Different times."

"It's a person?"

"Yes."

"Who is it?"

"I don't know."

"Captain Howdy?"

"I don't know."

"A man?"

"I don't know."

"But he's there."

"Yes, sometimes."

"Now?"

"I don't know."

"If I ask him to tell me, will you let him answer?"

"No!"

"Why not?"

"I'm afraid!"

"Of what?"

"I don't know!"

"If he talks to me, Regan, I think he will leave you. Do you want him to leave you?"

"Yes."

"Let him speak, then. Will you let him speak?"

A long silence. And then finally, "Yes."

"I am speaking to the person inside of Regan now," the psychiatrist said firmly. "If you are there, you too are hypnotized and must answer all my questions." For a moment, he paused to allow the suggestion to enter Regan's bloodstream. Then he repeated it: "If you are there, then you are hypnotized and must answer all my questions. Come forward and answer me now. Are you there?"

Silence. Then something curious happened: Regan's breath turned suddenly foul. It was thick, like a current. The psychiatrist smelled it from two feet away. He shone the penlight on Regan's face and, wide-eyed and shocked, Chris lifted a hand to stifle a gasp as she watched Regan's features contort into a malevolent mask, her lips pulling tautly in opposite directions, and a tumefied tongue lolling wolfishly from her mouth.

"Are you the person in Regan?" asked the psychiatrist.

Regan nodded.

"Who are you?"

"Nowonmai," she answered gutturally.

"That's your name?"

Another nod.

"You're a man?"

She said, "Say."

"Did you answer?"

"Say."

"If that's 'yes,' nod your head."

Regan nodded.

"Are you speaking in a foreign language?"

"Say."

"Where do you come from?"

"Dog."

"You say that you come from a dog?"

"Dogmorfmocion," Regan replied.

The psychiatrist paused, and after thinking it over he decided to attempt another approach. "When I ask you questions now, you will answer by moving your head: a nod for 'yes,' and a shake for 'no.' Do you understand that?"

Regan nodded.

"Did your answers have meaning?" he asked her. *Yes.*

"Are you someone whom Regan has known?" *No.*

"That she knows of?" *No.*

"Are you someone she's invented?" *No.*

"You're real?" *Yes.*

"Part of Regan?" *No.*

"Were you ever a part of Regan?" *No.*

"Do you like her?" *No.*

"Dislike her?" *Yes.*

"Do you hate her?" *Yes.*

"Over something she's done?" *Yes.*

"Do you blame her for her parents' divorce?" *No.*

"Has it something to do with her parents?" *No.*

"With a friend?" *No.*

"But you hate her." *Yes.*

"Are you punishing Regan?" *Yes.*

"You wish to harm her?" *Yes.*

"To kill her?" *Yes.*

"If she died, wouldn't you die too?" *No.*

The answer seemed to disquiet him and he lowered his eyes in thought. The bedsprings squeaked as he shifted his weight. In the smothering stillness, Regan's breathing came raspy as if from a rotted, putrid bellows. Here. Yet far. And sinister.

As he lifted his glance again to that hideous, twisted face, the psychiatrist's eyes gleamed sharply with speculation as he asked, "Is there something she can do that would make you leave her?" *Yes.*

"Can you tell me what it is?" *Yes.*

"Will you tell me?" *No.*

"But—"

Abruptly the psychiatrist gasped in pain as he realized with horrified incredulity that Regan was squeezing his scrotum with a hand that had gripped him like an iron talon. Eyes wide and staring, he struggled to free himself, but he couldn't. "Sam! Sam, help me!" he croaked in agony.

Bedlam.

Chris leaping for the light switch.

Dr. Klein running forward.

Regan with her head back, cackling demonically, then howling like a wolf.

Chris slapped at the light switch, then she turned and saw flickering, grainy black-and-white film of a slow-motion nightmare: Regan and the doctors writhing on the bed in a tangle of shifting arms and legs, in a melee of grimaces, gasps and curses, and the howling and the yelping and that hideous laughter; Regan oinking and grunting like a pig, Regan neighing like a horse, and then the film racing faster with the bedstead shaking and violently quivering from side to side as Regan's eyes rolled upward into their sockets and she wrenched up a keening shriek of terror torn raw and bloody from the base of her spine.

Regan crumpled and fell unconscious.

Something unspeakable left the room.

For a haunted space of time, no one moved. Then slowly and carefully, the doctors untangled themselves. They stood up and stared at Regan, speechless, and then Klein, expressionless, moved to the bed, took Regan's pulse and, satisfied, slowly and gently pulled her blanket up over her, and then nodded to Chris and the psychiatrist. They left the room and went down to the study, where, for a time, no one spoke. Chris was on the sofa, with Klein and the psychiatrist near her in the facing chairs that bracketed the space. The psychiatrist was pensive, pinching at his lip as he stared at the coffee table dully, then finally sighed and looked up at Chris as she turned her burned-out gaze to his. "What the hell is going on?" she asked, in a haggard, vanquished whisper.

"Did you recognize the language she was speaking?"

Chris shook her head.

"Have you any religious beliefs?"

"No, I don't."

"And your daughter?"

"No."

From there the psychiatrist asked a lengthy series of questions relating to Regan's psychological history, and when at last he had finished, he seemed disturbed.

"What is it?" Chris asked him, her white-knuckled fingers clenching and unclenching on the balled-up handkerchief in her fist. "Doc, what has she got?"

The psychiatrist looked evasive. "Well, it's somewhat confusing," he said. "And quite frankly, it would be quite irresponsible for me to attempt a diagnosis after so brief an examination."

"Well, you must have some idea," Chris insisted.

Fingering his brow and looking down, the psychiatrist emitted a sigh, then, relenting, looked up and said, "All right. I know you're quite anxious, so I'll mention a couple of impressions. But they're tentative, okay?"

Chris leaned forward, nodding tensely. "Yeah, okay. So what are they?" Fingers in her lap started fumbling with the handkerchief, telling stitches in the hem like linen rosary beads.

"To begin with," the psychiatrist told her, "it's highly improbable that she's faking. Right, Sam?" Klein was nodding in agreement. "We think so for a number of reasons," the psychiatrist continued. "For example, the abnormal and painful contortions; and most dramatically, I suppose, from the change in her features when we were talking to the so-called person she thinks is inside her. A psychic effect like that is unlikely unless she *believed* in this person. Do you follow?"

"Yeah, I guess," Chris answered; "except one thing I don't understand is where this other person comes from. I mean, you keep hearing about 'split personality' but I've never really known any explanation."

"Well, neither does anyone else. We use concepts like 'consciousness'—'mind'—'personality,' but we don't really know yet what they are. So when I start talking about something like multiple or split personality, all we have are some theories that raise more questions than they give answers. Freud thought that certain ideas and feelings are somehow repressed by the conscious mind, but remain alive in a person's subconscious; remain quite strong, in fact, and continue to seek expression through various psychiatric symptoms. Now when this repressed—or let's call it dissociated material, the word *dissociation* implying a splitting off from the mainstream of consciousness. Are you with me?"

"Yeah, go on."

"All right. Well, when this type of material is sufficiently strong, or where the subject's personality is disorganized and weak, the result can be schizophrenic psychosis. Now that isn't the same," he cautioned, "as dual personality. Schizophrenia means a *shattering* of the personality. But where the dissociated material is strong enough to somehow come glued together, to somehow organize in the individual's subconscious—why, then it's been known, at times, to function independently as a separate personality; in other words, to take over the bodily functions."

"And that's what you think is happening to Regan?"

"Well, that's just one theory. There are several others, some of them involving the notion of escape into unawareness; escape from some conflict or emotional problem. Your daughter hasn't any history of schizophrenia and the EEG didn't show the brain-wave pattern that normally accompanies it. So that leaves us with the general field of hysteria."

"I gave last week," Chris murmured.

The worried psychiatrist smiled thinly. "Hysteria," he continued, "is a form of neurosis in which emotional disturbances are converted into bodily disorders. Now, in certain of its forms, there's dissociation. In psychasthenia, for example, the individual loses consciousness of his actions, but he sees himself act and attributes his actions to someone else. His idea of the second personality is vague, however, and Regan's seems specific. So we come to what Freud used to call the 'conversion' form of hysteria, which grows from unconscious feelings of guilt and the need to be punished. Dissociation is the paramount feature here, even multiple personality. And the syndrome might also include epileptoid-like convulsions, hallucinations and abnormal motor excitement."

Chris had listened intently, her eyes and face scrunched up with the strain of trying to understand. "Well, that does sound a lot like Regan," she said. "Don't you think? Well, except for the guilt part. I mean, what would she have to feel guilty about?"

"Well, a cliché answer might be the divorce. Children often feel that *they* are the ones rejected and sometimes assume the full responsibility for the departure of one of their parents, so in the case of your daughter, that might apply. Here I'm thinking of the symptoms of thanatophobia—a brooding and neurotic depression over the notion of people dying." Chris's stare grew intense. "In children," the psychiatrist continued, "you'll find it accompanied by guilt formation that's related to family stress, very often the fear of the loss of a parent. It produces rage and intense frustration. In addition, the guilt in this type of hysteria needn't be known to the conscious mind. It could even be the guilt that we call 'free-floating,' which means it relates to nothing in particular."

"So this fear of death thing . . ."

"The thanatophobia."

"Yeah, right, what *you* said. Is it something that's inherited?"

Looking slightly aside to avoid betraying his curiosity about the question, the psychiatrist said, "No. No, I don't think so."

Chris lowered her head and shook it. "I just don't get it," she said; "I'm confused." She looked up, gentle furrows lightly lining her brow. "I mean, where does this new personality come in?"

The psychiatrist turned back to her. "Well, again, it's just a guess," he said, "but assuming that it *is* conversion hysteria stemming from guilt, then the second personality is simply the agent who handles the punishing. If Regan herself were to do it, that would mean she would *recognize* her guilt. But she wants to escape that recognition. Therefore, a second personality."

"And that's it? That's what you think she's got?"

"As I said, I don't know." The psychiatrist seemed to be choosing his words as carefully as flat, round stones to skim over a pond. "It's fairly extraordinary for a child of her age to be able to pull together and organize the components of a new personality. And certain—well, there are some other things that are puzzling. Her performance with the Ouija board, for example, would indicate extreme suggestibility; and yet apparently I never really hypnotized her." He shrugged. "Maybe she resisted. But the really striking thing," he noted, "is the new personality's apparent precocity. It isn't a twelve-year-old at all. It's much older. And then there's the language she was speaking . . ." His voice trailed off, as he stared into the fireplace pensively. "There's a similar state, of course," he said, " but we don't know very much about it."

"What is it?"

The psychiatrist turned to her. "Well, it's a form of somnambulism where the subject suddenly manifests knowledge or skills that he's never learned, and where the intention of the second personality is to—" He broke off. "Well, it's terribly complicated," he resumed, "and I've oversimplified outrageously." He had also not completed his statement, for fear of unduly upsetting Chris: the intention of the second personality, he would have said, was the destruction of the first.

"And so what's the bottom line?"

"A bit squiggly. She needs an intensive examination by a team of specialists: two or three weeks of really concentrated study in a clinical atmosphere; someplace like the Barringer Clinic in Dayton."

Chris turned away, looking down.

"It's a problem?" the psychiatrist asked her.

She shook her head and said softly and morosely, "No, I just lost 'Hope,' that's all."

"I didn't get you."

"Long story."

The psychiatrist telephoned the Barringer Clinic. They agreed to take Regan the following day. The doctors left.

Chris swallowed the ache of remembrance of Dennings; thought again about death and the worm and the void and the unspeakable loneliness, the stillness and the silence and the darkness that awaited beneath the sod: no, no movement; no breathing; nothing. *Too much . . . too much.* Chris lowered her head and briefly wept. And then put it away.

Packing for the trip, Chris was standing in her bedroom selecting a camouflaging wig to wear in Dayton when Karl appeared at the open door. There was someone to see her, he told her.

"Who?"

"Detective."

"Detective? And he wants to see *me?*"

"Yes, Madam."

Karl entered and handed Chris a business card. WILLIAM F. KINDERMAN, it announced, LIEUTENANT OF DETECTIVES. The words were printed in an ornate, raised Tudor typeface that might have been selected by a dealer in antiques. Tucked in a corner like a poor relation were the smaller words *Homicide Division*.

Chris looked up at Karl with a tight-eyed suspicion. "Has he got something with him that might be a script? You know, a big manila envelope or something?"

There was no one in the world, Chris had come to discover, who didn't have a novel or a script or a notion for one or both tucked away in a drawer or a mental sock. She seemed to attract them as strongly as priests attracted derelicts and drunks.

Karl shook his head. "No, Madam."

Detective. Was it something to do with Burke?

Chris found him sagging in the entry hall, the brim of his limp and crumpled hat clutched with short fat fingers whose nails had the shine of a recent manicure. Plumpish, in his early sixties, he had jowly cheeks that gleamed of soap. He wore rumpled trousers, cuffed and baggy, beneath an oversized gray tweed overcoat that hung long and loose and old-fashioned. As Chris approached him, the detective told her in a hoarsely emphysematous, whispery voice, "I'd know that face in any lineup, Miss MacNeil."

"Am I *in* one?" Chris asked.

"Oh, my goodness! Oh, no, no! No, of course not! No, it's strictly routine," he assured her. "Look, you're busy? Then tomorrow. Yes, I'll come again tomorrow."

He was turning away as if to leave when Chris said anxiously, "What is it? Is it Burke? Burke Dennings?" The detective's loose and careless ease had somehow tightened the springs of her tension. He turned and came back to her, dolefully staring with moist brown eyes that drooped at the corners and seemed perpetually staring at times gone by. "What a terrible shame," he said. "A shame."

"Was he *killed?*" Chris asked him bluntly. "I mean, you're a homicide cop. Is that why you're here? Burke was killed?"

"No, as I told you, it's routine," the detective repeated. "You know, a man so important, we just couldn't pass it. We couldn't," he repeated with a helpless look and a shrug. "At least one or two questions. Did he fall? Was he pushed?" As he asked, he was listing from side to side with his head and an uplifted hand, palm outward. Then he shrugged and whispered huskily, "Who knows?"

"Was he *robbed?*"

"No, not robbed, Miss MacNeil, never robbed; but then who needs a motive in times like these?" The detective's hands were constantly in motion, like flabby gloves informed by the fingers of a bored puppeteer. "Why, today, for a murderer, a motive is an encumbrance, maybe even a deterrent." He shook his head. "These drugs," he bemoaned. "All these drugs." He tapped at his chest with the tips of his fingers. "Believe me, I'm a father, and when I see what's going on, it breaks my heart. It does. You've got children?"

"Yes, one."

"Son or daughter?"

"A daughter."

"God bless her."

"Look, come on into the study," Chris told him as she turned to lead the way, intensely anxious to hear what it was he had to say about Dennings.

"Miss MacNeil, could I trouble you for something?"

Chris stopped and turned to face him with the dim and weary expectation that he wanted her autograph for his children. It was never for themselves. It was always for their children. "Yeah, sure," she said amiably in an effort to mask her impatience.

The detective gestured with a trace of a grimace. "My stomach," he said. "Do you keep any Calso water, maybe? If it's trouble, never mind."

"No, no trouble at all," Chris answered with a faint, tight smile. "Grab a chair in the study." Chris pointed, then turned and headed for the kitchen. "I think there's a bottle in the fridge," she said.

"No, I'll come to the kitchen," the detective said, following with a gait that bordered on a waddle. "Yes, I hate to be a bother."

"It's no bother."

"No, really, you're busy, I'll come. You've got children?" the detective asked as they walked. "No, that's right," he immediately corrected himself. "Yes, a daughter. You told me. That's right. Just the one. And how old is she?"

"She just turned twelve."

"Ah, then you don't have to worry. No, not yet. Later on, though, watch out." He was shaking his head. "When you see all the sickness day in and day out. Unbelievable! Incredible! Insane! You know, I looked at my wife just a couple of days ago—or maybe weeks, I forget—I said, Mary, the world—the *entire world*"—he had lifted his hands in a global gesture—"is having a massive nervous breakdown."

They had entered the kitchen, where Karl was cleaning and polishing the interior of an oven. He neither turned nor acknowledged their presence.

"This is really so embarrassing," the detective wheezed as Chris opened a refrigerator door; and yet his gaze was on Karl, brushing swiftly and questioningly over the back of the manservant's head like a small, dark bird skimming low above a lake. "I meet a famous motion-picture star," he continued, "and I ask for some Calso water. It's a joke."

Chris had found the bottle and was looking for an opener.

She said, "Ice?"

"Oh, no, plain. Plain is fine."

Chris opened the bottle, found a glass, and poured bubbly Calso water into it.

"You know that film you made called *Angel*?" the detective mentioned with a faint, fond look of reminiscence. "I saw that film six times," he said.

"If you were looking for the murderer, arrest the director."

"Oh, no, no, it was excellent—really—I loved it! Just one little—"

"Come on, we can sit over here," Chris interrupted. She was pointing to the windowed breakfast nook. It had a waxed pine table and seat cushions covered in a flower pattern.

"Yes, of course," the detective replied.

They sat down, and Chris handed him the Calso water.

"Oh, yes, thank you," he said.

"Don't mention it. You were saying?"

"Oh, well, the film—it was lovely, really. So touching. But maybe just one little thing," the detective ventured, "one tiny, almost minuscule flaw. And please believe me, in such matters I am only a layman. Okay? I'm just audience. What do I know? However, it seemed to me the musical score was getting in the way of certain scenes. It was too intrusive." Chris tried not to fidget with impatience as the detective went on earnestly, caught up in the rising ardor of his argument. "It kept on reminding me that this was a movie. You know? Like so many of these fancy camera angles. So distracting. Incidentally, the score—the composer, did he steal it perhaps from Mendelssohn?"

Chris had started drumming her fingertips lightly on the table but now abruptly she stopped. What kind of detective was this? she wondered; and why was he constantly glancing to Karl?

"We don't call that stealing, we call it an homage," said Chris, smiling faintly, "but I'm glad you liked the picture. Better drink that," she added with a nod at the glass of Calso water. "It tends to get flat."

"Yes, of course. I'm so garrulous. Forgive me."

Lifting the glass as if in a toast, the portly detective drained its contents, his little finger arched up in the air demurely. "Ah, good, that's good," he exhaled. As he set down the glass his glance fell fondly on Regan's sculpture of the bird. It was now the centerpiece of the table, its long beak floating mockingly above the salt and pepper shakers. "It's so quaint," he said smiling. "So cute." He looked up at Chris. "And the artist?"

"My daughter."

"Very nice."

"Look, I hate to be—"

"Yes, yes, I know. You're very busy. Listen, one or two questions and we're done. In fact, only one question, that's all, and then I'll be going." He was glancing at his wristwatch as if he were anxious to get away to some important appointment. "Since poor Mr. Dennings," he began, "had completed his filming in this area, we wondered if he might have been visiting someone on the night of the accident. Now other than yourself, of course, did he have any friends in this area?"

"Oh, he was here that night," Chris told him.

"Oh, really?" The detective's eyebrows sickled upward. "Near the time of the accident?" he asked.

"When did it happen?"

"At seven-oh-five P.M."

"Yes, I think so."

"Well, that settles it, then." The detective nodded, twisting in his chair as if preparatory to rising. "He was drunk, he was leaving, he fell down the steps. Yes, that settles it. Definitely. Listen, though, just for the sake of the record, can you tell me approximately what time he left the house?"

With a tilt of her head to the side Chris appraised him with mild wonder. He was pawing at truth like a weary bachelor pinching vegetables and fruit at a market. "I don't know," she replied. "I didn't see him."

The detective looked puzzled. "I don't understand."

"Well, he came and left while I was out. I was over at a doctor's office in Rosslyn."

The detective nodded. "Ah, I see. Yes, of course. But then how do you know he was here?"

"Oh, well, Sharon said—"

"Sharon?" he interrupted.

"Sharon Spencer. She's my secretary."

"Oh."

"She was here when Burke dropped by. She—"

"He came to see *her?*"

"No, he came to see me."

"Yes, go on, please. Forgive me for interrupting."

"My daughter was sick and Sharon left him here while she went to pick up some prescriptions and by the time I got home, Burke was gone."

"And what time was that, please? You remember?"

Chris shrugged and puckered her lips. "Maybe seven-fifteen or so; seven-thirty."

"And what time had you left the house?"

"Six-fifteenish."

"And what time had Miss Spencer left?"

"I don't know."

"Between the time Miss Spencer left and the time you returned, who was here in the house with Mr. Dennings besides your daughter?"

"No one."

"No one? He left alone a sick child?"

Chris nodded, her expression blank.

"No servants?"

"No, Willie and Karl were—"

"Who are they?"

Chris abruptly felt the earth shifting under her feet as the nuzzling interview, she realized, was suddenly a steely interrogation. "Well, Karl's right there." Chris motioned with her head, her glance fixed dully on the manservant's back as he continued to clean and polish the oven. "And Willie's his wife," Chris said. "They're my housekeepers." *Polishing. Polishing. Why?* The oven had been thoroughly cleaned and polished the night before. "They'd taken the afternoon off," Chris continued, "and when I got home they weren't back yet. But then Willie . . ." Chris paused, her eyes still fixed on Karl's back.

"Willie what?" the detective prodded.

Chris turned to him and shrugged. "Oh, well, nothing" she said. She reached for a cigarette. Kinderman lit it. "So then only your daughter would know," he asked, "when Burke Dennings left the house?"

"It was really an accident?"

"Oh, of course. It's routine, Miss MacNeil. Absolutely. Your friend Dennings wasn't robbed and so what would be the motive?"

"Burke could tick people off," Chris said somberly. "Maybe someone at the top of the steps just hauled off and whacked him."

"It's got a name, this kind of bird? I can't think of it. Something." The detective was fingering Regan's sculpture. Noticing Chris's steady stare, he took away his hand, looking vaguely embarrassed. "Forgive me, you're busy. Well, a minute and we're done. Now your daughter—she would know when Mr. Dennings left?"

"No, she wouldn't. She was heavily sedated."

"Ah, a shame, such a shame." The detective's eyelids drooped with concern. "It's serious?" he asked.

"Yes, I'm afraid it is."

"May I ask . . . ?" He had raised his hand in a delicate gesture.

"We still don't know."

"Watch out for drafts," the detective said solemnly. "A draft in the winter when a house is hot is a magic carpet for bacteria. My mother used to say that. Maybe it's folk myth. Maybe. I don't know. But plainly speaking, to me a myth is like a menu in a fancy French restaurant: it's glamorous, complicated camouflage for a fact you wouldn't otherwise swallow, like maybe the lima beans they're constantly giving you whenever you go out and order hamburger steak."

Chris felt herself loosening up. The odd, homey digression had relaxed her. The fuddled-looking, harmless St. Bernard dog had returned.

"That's hers, Miss MacNeil? Your daughter's bedroom?" The detective was pointing up at the ceiling. "The one with that big bay window looking out on those steps?"

Chris nodded. "Yeah, that's Regan's."

"Keep the window closed and she'll get better."

Tense the moment before, Chris now had to struggle to keep from laughing. "Yes, I will," she said; "in fact, it's always closed and shuttered."

"Yes, 'an ounce of prevention,'" the detective quoted sententiously. He was dipping a pudgy hand into the inside pocket of his coat when his gaze fell on Chris's fingertips lightly drumming on the table again. "Ah, yes, you're busy," he said. "Well, we're finished. Just a note for the record—routine—we're all done." From the pocket of his coat he'd extracted a crumpled mimeographed program of a high-school production of *Cyrano de Bergerac* and now he was groping in an outer pocket, retrieving a short yellow stub of a number 2 pencil whose point had the look of having been sharpened with either a knife or the blade of a pair of scissors; then, pressing the play program flat on the table and tamping out the wrinkles, he held the pencil stub over it and wheezed, "Just a name or two, nothing more. Now that's Spencer with a *c*?"

"Yes, a *c*."

"A *c*," the detective repeated, writing the name in a margin of the program. "And the housekeepers? Joseph and Willie . . . ?"

"No, it's Karl and Willie Engstrom."

"Karl. Yes, that's right; Karl Engstrom." He scribbled the names in a dark, thick script. "Now the times I remember," he breathed out huskily while rotating the program in search of white space. "Oh, no, wait! I forgot! Yes, the housekeepers. You said they got home at what time?"

"I didn't say. Karl, what time did you get in last night?" Chris called out to him. The Swiss turned his head, inscrutable. "I am home at exactly nine-thirty."

"Oh, yeah, that's right. You'd forgotten your key." She turned her gaze back to the detective. "I remember I looked at the clock in the kitchen when I heard him ring the doorbell."

"You saw a good film?" the detective asked Karl. "I never go by reviews," he said to Chris in a quiet aside. "It's what the *people* think, the *audience*."

"Paul Scofield in *Lear*," Karl informed the detective.

"Ah, I saw that! It was excellent!"

"I see it at Gemini Theater," Karl continued. "The six-o'clock showing. Then immediately after I take bus from in front of the theater and—"

"Please, that's really not necessary," the detective protested as he held up a hand, palm outward. "No, no, *please!*"

"I don't mind."

"If you insist."

"I get off at Wisconsin Avenue and M Street. Nine-twenty, I think. And then I walk to house."

"Look, you didn't have to tell me," the detective told him, "but anyway, thank you, it was very considerate. By the way, you liked the film?"

"It was good."

"Yes, I thought so too. Exceptional. Well, now . . ." He turned back to Chris and to scribbling on the program. "I've wasted your time, but I have a job. That's the sad yin and yang of it. The whole deal. Oh, well a moment and we're finished," he said reassuringly, then "Tragic . . . tragic . . . ," he added as he jotted down fragments in margins. "Such a talent, Burke Dennings. And a man who knew people, I'm sure: how to handle them. With so many who could make him look good or maybe make him look bad—like the cameraman, the sound man, the composer, not to mention, forgive me, the actors. Please correct me if I'm wrong, but it seems to me nowadays a director of importance has also to be almost a psychologist with the cast. Am I wrong?"

"No, you're not because we're all insecure."

"Even you?"

"*Mostly* me. But Burke was good at that, at keeping up your morale." Chris shrugged diffidently. "But then of course he had one sweetheart of a temper."

The detective repositioned the program. "Ah, well, maybe so with the big shots. People his size." Once again he was scribbling. "But the key is the little people, the people who handle the minor details that if they didn't handle right would be *major* details. Don't you think?"

Chris eyed her fingernails and shook her head. "When Burke let fly," she said, "he never discriminated. But he was only mean when he drank."

"All right, we're finished. We're done." Kinderman was dotting a final *i* when he abruptly remembered something. "Oh, no, wait. The Engstroms. They went and came together?"

"No, Willie went to see a Beatles film," Chris answered just as Karl was turning his head to reply. "She got in a few minutes after I did."

"Oh, well, why did I ask that?" said Kinderman. "It has nothing to do with anything." He folded up the program and tucked it away along with the pencil in the inside pocket of his coat. "Well, that's that," he breathed out with satisfaction. "When I'm back in the office, no doubt I'll remember something that maybe I should have asked. Yes, with me, that always happens. Oh, well, whatever," he said; "I could call you." He stood up and Chris got up with him. "Well, I'm going out of town for a couple of weeks," she said. "It can wait," the detective assured her. "It can wait." He was staring at the sculpture with a smiling fondness. "Ah, so cute, so really cute." He'd leaned over and picked it up and was rubbing his thumb along the sculpted bird's beak, then replaced it on the table and started to leave. “Have you got a good doctor?” the detective asked as Chris accompanied him toward the front door. “I mean for your daughter.” “Well, I’ve sure got enough of them,” Chris said glumly. “Anyway, I’m checking her into a clinic that’s supposed to be great at doing what you do, only with viruses.”

“Let’s hope they’re much better at it, Miss MacNeil. It’s out of town, this clinic?”

“Yes, it is. It’s in Ohio.”

“It’s a good one?”

“We’ll see.”

“Keep her out of the draft.”

They had reached the front door of the house. “Well, I would say that it’s been a pleasure,” the detective said gravely while gripping his hat by the brim with both hands; “but under the circumstances . . .” He bent his head slightly and shook it, then looked back up. “I’m so terribly sorry.”

Her arms folded across her chest, Chris lowered her head and said quietly, “Thank you. Thank you very much.”

Opening the door, the detective stepped outside, put on his hat and turned back to look at Chris. “Well, good luck with your daughter,” he said.

Chris smiled wanly. “Good luck with the world.”

The detective nodded with a warmth and a sadness, then turned to his right and, short of breath, slowly waddled away down the street. Chris watched as he listed toward a waiting squad car that was parked near the corner. He flung up a hand to his hat as a sudden gust of wind sprang sharply from the south and set the bottom of his long, floppy coat to flapping. Chris lowered her gaze and closed the door.

When he’d entered the passenger side of the squad car, Kinderman turned and, looking back at the house, he thought he’d seen movement at Regan's window, a quick, lithe figure moving quickly to the side and out of view. He wasn't sure. He had seen it peripherally and so quickly it was almost subliminal. He kept looking and noticed that the window shutters were open. Odd. Chris had told him they were always closed. For a time the detective continued to watch. No one appeared. With a puzzled frown, the detective looked down and shook his head, and then he opened the glove compartment of the squad car, extracted a penknife and an evidence envelope, and, unclasping the smallest of the blades of the knife, he held his thumb inside the envelope and extracted from under a thumbnail microscopic fragments of green colored clay he'd surreptitiously scraped from Regan's sculpture. Finished, he sealed up the envelope and placed it in the inside pocket of his coat. "Okay," he told his driver, "let's go." They pulled away from the curb, and as they drove down Prospect Street, Kinderman cautioned the driver, "Take it easy," as he noticed the traffic building up ahead. Then lowering his head, he shut his eyes, and gripping the bridge of his nose with weary fingers, he breathed out despondently, "Ah, my God, what a world. What a life."

Later that evening, while Dr. Klein was injecting Regan with fifty milligrams of Sparine to assure her tranquility on the journey to Dayton, Ohio, Kinderman stood brooding in his office with the palms of his hands pressed flat atop his desk as he pored over fragments of baffling data with no other light in the room but the narrow beam of an ancient desk lamp flaring brightly on a clutter of scattered reports. He believed that it helped him to narrow the focus of his concentration. His breathing was adenoidal and heavy in the darkness; his glance flitted here, now there, and then he took a deep breath and shut his eyes. *Mental Clearance Sale!* he instructed himself, as he always did whenever he wished to tidy up his brain for a fresh point of view. *Absolutely*

Everything Must Go! Then he opened his eyes and reexamined the pathologist's report on Dennings:

> . . . tearing of the spinal cord with fractured skull and neck, plus numerous contusions, lacerations and abrasions; stretching of the neck skin; ecchymosis of the neck skin; shearing of platysma, sternomastoid, splenius, trapezius and various smaller muscles of the neck, with fracture of the spine and of the vertebrae and shearing of both the anterior and posterior spinous ligaments . . .

He looked out a window at the dark of the city. The Capitol dome light glowed in signal that the Congress was working late, and once again the detective shut his eyes, recalling his conversation with the District pathologist at 11:55 P.M. on the night of Dennings's death.

"It could have happened in the fall?"

"Oh, well, it's very unlikely. The sternomastoids and the trapezius muscles alone are enough to prevent it. Then you've also got the various articulations of the cervical spine to be overcome as well as the ligaments holding the bones together."

"Speaking plainly, however, is it possible?"

"Yes. The man was drunk and these muscles were doubtless somewhat relaxed. Perhaps if the force of the initial impact were sufficiently powerful and—"

"Falling maybe thirty, forty feet before he hit?"

"Well, yes, that; and if immediately after impact his head got stuck in something—in other words, if there were immediate interference with the normal rotation of the head and body as a unit—well maybe—I say just maybe—you could get this result."

"Could another human being have done it?"

"Yes, but he'd have to be an exceptionally powerful man."

Kinderman had checked Karl Engstrom's story regarding his whereabouts at the time of Dennings's death. The show times matched, as did the schedule that night of a D.C. Transit bus. Moreover, the driver of the bus that Karl had claimed he had boarded near the front of the theater went off duty at Wisconsin and M, where Karl had stated he'd alighted at approximately twenty minutes after nine. A change of drivers had taken place, and the off-duty driver had logged the time of his arrival at the transfer point: precisely nine-eighteen. Yet on Kinderman's desk was a record of a felony charge against Engstrom on August 27, 1963, alleging he had stolen a quantity of narcotics over a period of months from the home of a doctor in Beverly Hills where he and Willie were then employed.

> . . . born April 20, 1921, in Zurich, Switzerland. Married to Willie nee Braun September 7, 1941. Daughter, Elvira, born New York City, January 11, 1943, current address unknown. Defendant . . .

The remainder the detective found baffling:

The doctor, whose testimony was deemed a *sine qua non* for successful prosecution, abruptly—and without explanation—dropped the charges. *Why had he done so?* And as the Engstroms had been hired by Chris MacNeil only two months later, the doctor had given them a favorable reference.

Why would he do so?

Engstrom had certainly pilfered the drugs, and yet a medical examination at the time of the charge had failed to yield the slightest sign that the man was an addict, or even a user.

Why not?

With his eyes still closed, the detective softly recited the beginning of the Lewis Carroll poem "Jabberwocky": "' 'Twas brillig and the slithy toves did gyre and gimble in the wabe . . .'" It was another of Kinderman's mind-clearing tricks, and when he had finished the recitation, he opened his eyes and fixed his gaze on the Capitol rotunda. He was trying to keep his mind a blank, although, as usual, he found the task impossible. Sighing, he glanced at the police psychologist's report on the recent desecrations at Holy Trinity: " . . . *statue* . . . *phallus* . . . *human excrement* . . . *Damien Karras*," he had underscored in red. His breathing slightly whistling in the total silence, he reached for a scholarly work on witchcraft and turned to a page that he had marked with a paper clip:

> Black Mass . . . a form of devil worship, the ritual consisting, in the main, of (1) exhortation (the "sermon") to performance of evil among the community, (2) coition with the demon (reputedly painful, the demon's penis invariably described as "icy cold"), and (3) a variety of desecrations that were largely sexual in nature. For example, communion Hosts of unusual size were prepared (compounded of flour, feces, menstrual blood and pus), which then were slit and used as artificial vaginas with which the priests would ferociously copulate while raving that they were ravishing the Virgin Mother of God or that they were sodomizing Christ. In another instance of such practice, a statue of Christ was inserted deep in a girl's vagina while into her anus was inserted the Host, which the priest then crushed as he shouted blasphemies and sodomized the girl. Life-sized images of Christ and the Virgin Mary also played a frequent role in the ritual. The image of the Virgin, for example—usually painted to give her a dissolute, sluttish appearance—was equipped with breasts which the cultists sucked and also a vagina into which the penis might be inserted. The statues of

> Christ were equipped with a phallus for fellatio by both the men and the women, and also for insertion into the vagina of the women and the anus of the men. Occasionally, rather than an image, a human figure was bound to a cross and made to function in place of the statue, and upon the discharge of his semen it was collected in a blasphemously consecrated chalice and used in the making of the communion host, which was destined to be consecrated on an altar covered with excrement. This—

Kinderman flipped the pages to an underlined paragraph dealing with ritualistic murder, reading it slowly while nibbling at the pad of an index finger, and when he had finished he frowned at the page and shook his head, then lifted a brooding glance to the lamp. He flicked it off and left his office.

He drove to the morgue.

The young attendant at the desk was munching at a ham and cheese sandwich on rye and was brushing the crumbs from a crossword puzzle as Kinderman approached him.

"Dennings," the detective breathed out hoarsely.

The attendant nodded, hastily filled in a five-letter horizontal, then rose with his sandwich and moved down the hall. "Down this way," he said laconically. Kinderman trailed him, hat in hand, following the faint scent of caraway seed and mustard to rows of refrigerated lockers, to the dreamless cabinet used for the filing of sightless eyes.

They halted at locker 32. The expressionless attendant slid it out. He bit at his sandwich, and a fragment of mayonnaise-speckled crust fell lightly to the graying shroud. Kinderman stared, and then, slowly and gently, he pulled back the sheet to expose what he'd seen and yet could not accept: Dennings's head was turned completely around and facing backward.

Chapter Five

Cupped in the warm, green hollow of the Georgetown University campus, Damien Karras jogged alone around an oval, cinder-covered track in khaki shorts and a cotton T-shirt drenched with the cling of healing sweat. Up ahead, on a hillock, the lime-white dome of the astronomical observatory pulsed with the beat of his stride while behind him the medical school fell away with churned-up shards of earth and care. Since release from his duties, he came here daily, lapping the miles and chasing sleep. He had almost caught it; had almost eased the grief that clutched his heart with the grip of a deep tattoo. When he ran until he wanted to fall, exhausted, the grip grew much looser and at times disappeared. For a time.

Twenty laps.

Yes, better. Much better. Two more.

With powerful leg muscles blooded and stinging and rippling with a long and leonine grace, Karras thumped around a turn when he noticed someone sitting on a bench to the side where he'd laid out his towel and his sweatsuit jacket and pants. It was a portly, middle-aged man in a floppy overcoat and a pulpy, crushed felt hat. He seemed to be watching him. Was he? Yes. His stare always following as Karras passed.

The priest accelerated, digging at the final lap with pounding strides and then slowing to a panting, gulping walk as he passed the bench without a glance, both fists pressed light to his throbbing sides. The heave of his muscular chest and shoulders stretched his T-shirt, distorting the stenciled word PHILOSOPHERS inscribed across the front in once-black letters now faded by repeated washings.

The man in the overcoat stood up and began to approach him.

"Father Karras?" Kinderman called to him hoarsely.

The priest turned around and tersely nodded, squinting into sunlight as he waited for the homicide detective to reach him, then beckoned him along as once again he began to move. "Do you mind? I'll cramp," he said pantingly.

"Not at all," the detective answered, nodding with a wincing lack of enthusiasm as he tucked his hands into the pockets of his coat. The walk from the parking lot had tired him.

"Have—have we met?" asked the Jesuit.

"No, Father. No, we haven't. But they said that you looked like a boxer; some priest at the residence hall; I forget." He was tugging out his wallet. "I'm so terrible with names."

"And what's yours?"

"Lieutenant William F. Kinderman, Father." He flashed his identification. "Homicide."

"Really?" Karras scanned the badge and identification card with a shining, boyish interest. Flushed and perspiring, his face had an eager look of innocence as he turned to the detective and said, "What's this about?"

"Hey, you know something, Father?" Kinderman answered with an air of sudden discovery while inspecting the Jesuit's rugged features. "It's really true, you know, you *do* look like a boxer! Excuse me, but that scar there right over your eye?" He was pointing. "Just like Marlon Brando, it looks, in *On the Waterfront*, Father; yes, almost *exactly* Marlon Brando! They gave him a scar"—he was illustrating, pulling at the corner of his eye—"that made his eye look a little bit closed, a little dreamy all the time, a little sad. Well, that's you," he concluded; "Marlon Brando. People tell you that, Father?"

"Do people tell you that you look like Paul Newman?"

"Always. And believe me, inside this body, Mr. Newman is struggling to get out. Too crowded. Inside here is also Clark Gable."

Half smiling, Karras slightly shook his head and looked away.

"Ever done any boxing?" the detective asked him.

"Oh, a little."

"Where? In college? Here in town?"

"No, in New York."

"Ah, I thought so! Golden Gloves! Am I right?"

"You just made captain," Karras told him with a sidelong smile. "Now then, what can I do for you, Lieutenant?"

"Walk slower." The detective pointed to his throat. "Emphysema."

"Oh, I'm sorry. Yeah, sure."

"Do you smoke?"

"Yes, I do."

"You shouldn't."

"Listen, what's this about? Could we get to the point, please, Lieutenant?"

"Yes, of course; I've been digressing. Incidentally, you're busy? I'm not interrupting?"

Karras turned a sidelong look to Kinderman again with a smile of bemusement in his eyes. "Interrupting what?"

"Well, mental prayer, perhaps."

"I think you're going to make captain soon, you know that?"

"Father, pardon me. I missed something?"

Karras shook his head. "I doubt that you ever miss a thing."

"What's your meaning, Father? What?"

Kinderman had halted them and mounted a massive effort at looking befuddled, but seeing the Jesuit's crinkling eyes, he lowered his head and ruefully chuckled. "Ah, well, of course . . . a psychiatrist. Who am I kidding? Look, it's habit with me, Father. *Schmaltz*—that's the Kinderman method. Well, I'll stop and tell you straight what it's all about."

"The desecrations," said Karras.

"So I wasted my schmaltz," the detective said quietly.

"Sorry."

"Never mind, Father; that I deserved. Yes, the things in the church," he confirmed. "That's correct. Only maybe something more than that, Father."

"You mean murder?"

"Yes, kick me again, Father Karras. I enjoy it."

Karras shrugged. "Oh, well, Homicide Division."

"Never mind, Marlon Brando. People tell you for a priest you're a little bit smart-ass?"

"Mea culpa," Karras murmured. Though he was smiling, he felt a regret that perhaps he'd diminished the detective's self-esteem. He hadn't meant to. And now he felt glad of a chance to seem perplexed. "What's the connection?" he said, taking care that he wrinkled his brow; "I don't get it."

Kinderman moved his face in closer to the priest's. "Listen, Father, could we keep this between us? Confidential? Like a matter of confession, so to speak?"

"Yes, of course," Karras answered. "What is it?"

"You know that director who was doing the film here, Father? Burke Dennings?"

"Yes, I've seen him around."

"You've seen him," the detective said, nodding. "And you're also familiar with how he died?"

Karras shrugged. "Well, the papers . . ."

"That's just part of it."

"Oh?"

"Yes, part. Only part. Listen, what do you know about witchcraft?"

Karras grimaced in puzzlement. *"What?"*

"Listen, patience; I am leading up to something."

"I hope so."

"Now then, witchcraft—with this subject you're familiar? From the witching end, Father, not the hunting."

Karras smiled. "Yeah, I once did a paper on it. From the psychiatric end."

"Oh, now really? Oh, that's wonderful! Great! That's a bonus, Father Brando! You could help me a lot more than I thought. Now then, listen . . ." He reached up and gripped the Jesuit's arm as they rounded a turn and approached a bench. "All right, me, I'm a layman and not very well educated. I mean formally, Father. But I read. Look, I know what they say about self-made men, that they're horrible examples of unskilled labor. But as for me—I'll speak plainly—I'm not at all ashamed. Not at all, I'm—" Abruptly he arrested the flow and, looking down, he shook his head. "*Schmaltz*," he moaned. "I can't stop it." He looked up. "Look, forgive me; you're busy."

"Yes, I'm praying."

The Jesuit's delivery being dry and expressionless, the detective abruptly halted their walk. "You're serious?" he asked; and then he answered his own question. "No." He faced forward again and they walked. "Look, I'll come to the point. The desecrations," said Kinderman. "Do they remind you of anything to do with witchcraft?"

"Yeah, maybe. Some rituals used in Black Mass."

"A-plus. And now Dennings—you read how he died?"

"Yes, in a fall down the 'Hitchcock Steps.'"

"Well, I'll tell you, and—*please—confidential!*"

"Of course."

The detective looked suddenly pained as he realized that Karras had no intention of resting on the bench. He stopped and the priest stopped with him.

"Do you mind?" he asked wistfully.

"What?"

"Could we stop? Maybe sit?"

"Oh, sure." They began to move back toward the bench.

"You won't cramp?"

"No, I'm fine now."

"You're sure?"

"Yes, I'm sure."

Kinderman settled his aching bulk on the bench with a sigh of deep content. "Ah, yes, better, much better," he said. "Life is not totally *Darkness at Noon*."

"So okay now: Burke Dennings. What about him?"

The detective stared down at his shoes. "Ah, yes, Dennings, Burke Dennings, Burke Dennings . . ." He looked up and turned his gaze to Karras, who was wiping sweat from his forehead with a corner of his towel. "Burke Dennings, good Father," the detective said evenly and quietly, "was found at the bottom of those steps at exactly five minutes after seven with his head turned completely around and facing backward."

Peppery shouts drifted thinly from the baseball diamond where the varsity team was holding practice. Karras lowered the towel and held the lieutenant's steady gaze. "It didn't happen in the fall?"

Kinderman shrugged. "Sure, it's possible," he said.

"But unlikely," the priest finished broodingly.

"And so what comes to mind in the context of witchcraft?"

Staring off pensively, Karras sat down on the bench next to Kinderman. "That's supposedly how demons broke the necks of witches." He turned to the detective. "Or at least, that's the myth," he said.

"It's a myth?"

"Oh, well, sure," the priest answered, "although people did die that way, I suppose—likely members of a coven who either defected or gave away secrets." He looked off. "I don't know. That's just a guess." He looked back at the detective. "But I know it was a trademark of demonic assassins."

"Exactly, Father Karras! Exactly! I remembered the connection from a murder in London. And that's *now,* I'm talking, Father; I mean, four or five years ago only. I remembered that I read it in the papers."

"Yes, I read that too, but I think it turned out to be a hoax."

"Yes, true. But in this case, at least, you can see some connection, maybe, with that and the things in the church. Maybe somebody crazy, Father; maybe someone with a spite against the Church; some unconscious rebellion, perhaps."

Hunched over, his hands clasped together, the priest turned his head for an appraising stare at the detective. "What are you saying? A sick priest?" he said. "That's your suspicion?"

"Listen, you're the psychiatrist. You tell *me.*"

Karras turned his head, looking off. "Well, of course, the desecrations are clearly pathological," he ruminated, "and if Dennings was murdered—well, I'd guess that the killer's pathological too."

"And perhaps had some knowledge of witchcraft?"

Pensive, Karras nodded. "Yeah, maybe."

"And so who fits the bill, also lives in the neighborhood and also has access in the night to the church?"

Karras turned and held Kinderman's stare; then at the crack

of a bat against ball he turned back to watch a lanky right fielder make a catch. "Sick priest," he murmured. "Maybe so."

"Listen, Father, this is hard for you—please!—I understand. But for priests on the campus here, you're the psychiatrist, right?"

Karras turned to him. "No. I've had a change of assignment."

"Oh, really? In the middle of the year?"

"That's the Order."

"Still, you'd know who was sick at the time and who wasn't, correct? I mean, *this* kind of sickness. You'd *know* that."

"No, not necessarily, Lieutenant. Not at all. It would only be an accident, in fact, if I did. I'm not a psychoanalyst. All I do is counsel. And besides, I know of no one who fits the description."

Kinderman tilted up his jaw. "Ah, yes," he said, "doctor's ethics. If you knew, you wouldn't tell."

"No, I probably wouldn't."

"Incidentally—and I mention it only in passing—this ethic is lately considered illegal. Not to bother you with trivia, Father, but lately a psychiatrist in sunny California, no less, was put in jail for not telling the police what he knew about a patient."

"That a threat?"

"Don't talk paranoid. It's nothing but a casual remark."

Karras stood up and looked down at the detective.

"I could always tell the judge it was a matter of confession," he said wryly, and then added, "Plainly speaking."

The detective stared at him dismally. "Want to go into business, Father?" he asked him, and then stared out at the baseball practice field. "'Father'? What 'Father'?" he wheezed; "you're a Jew who's trying to pass but let me tell you, you've taken it a little bit far."

Getting up from the bench, Karras chuckled.

"Yes, laugh," said the detective as he glared up at Karras moodily. "Go ahead and enjoy, Father; laugh all you want." But then he beamed, looking impishly pleased with himself, as he looked up at Karras and said, "That reminds me. The entrance examination to be a policeman? When I took it, one question on the test was 'What are rabies and what would you do for them?' and someone answered, 'Rabies are Jewish priests and I would do anything that I possibly could for them.'" Kinderman raised up a hand and said, "Honest! It happened! Swear to God!"

Karras smiled warmly at him. "Come on, I'll walk you to your car. Are you parked in the lot?"

The detective looked up at him, reluctant to move. "Then we're finished?" he asked disappointedly.

The priest put a foot on the bench, leaning over with a forearm resting on his knee. "Look, I'm really not covering up," he said. "Really. If I knew of a priest like the one that you're looking for, the least I would do is let you know that there was such a man without giving you his name. Then I guess I'd report it to the Provincial. But I don't know of anyone who even comes close to the man that you're looking for."

"Ah well," said Kinderman, looking down and with his hands again stuffed in the pockets of his coat; "I never thought it was a priest in the first place. Not really." He looked up and gestured with his head toward the lower campus parking lot. "I'm parked over there," he said. He stood up and they started walking, following a path to the main campus buildings. "What I really suspect," the detective continued, "if I said it out loud you would call me crazy. I don't know," he said, shaking his head. "I don't know. All these clubs and these cults where they kill for no reason—it makes you start thinking things. To keep up with the times, these days," he bemoaned, "it seems you have to be a little bit demented." He turned to Karras. "What's that thing on your shirt?" he asked him, motioning his head toward the Jesuit's chest.

"What do you mean?"

"On the T-shirt. The writing there. 'Philosophers.' What's that?"

"Oh, I took a few courses one year," Karras told him, "at Woodstock Seminary in Maryland. I played on the lower class baseball team and we were called the Philosophers."

"Ah, I see. And the upper-class team?"

"Theologians."

Faintly smiling, the detective lowered his gaze to the pathway. "Theologians three, Philosophers two," he mused.

"No, *Philosophers* three, *Theologians* two."

"Yes, of course, that's what I really meant to say."

"Of course."

"Strange things," the detective said broodingly; "so strange. Listen, Father," he said, turning to Karras. "Listen, *doctor.* Am I crazy, or could there be maybe a witch coven here in the District right now? Right now today."

"Oh, come on," Karras scoffed.

"Aha! Then there *could* be!"

" 'Then there could be'? How's that?"

"All right now, Father, *I'll* be the doctor," the detective declared with an air of pouncing as he poked at empty air with an index finger. "You didn't say no, but instead you were smart-ass again. That's defensive. You're afraid you'll look gullible, maybe: a superstitious priest in front of Kinderman the rationalist, the Age of Reason made flesh and now walking beside you! All right, look at me in the eye now and tell me that I'm wrong! Come on, look already! Look! You can't do it!"

Karras turned his head to stare at the detective now with a mounting surmise and respect. "Why, that's very astute," he told him. "Very good!"

"Well, all right, then," said Kinderman. "So I'll ask you again: could there maybe be witch covens here in the District?"

Karras turned his gaze to the pathway, looking thoughtful. "Well, I really wouldn't know," he said, "but there are cities in Europe where Black Masses are said."

"You mean, today?"

"Oh, yeah, today. In fact the center of Satan worship in Europe is in Turin, Italy. Weird."

"Why so?"

"That's where the Burial Shroud of Christ is kept."

"You're talking Satan worship just like the old days, Father? Look, I've read about those things, incidentally, with the sex and the statues and who really knows what. Not meaning to disgust you, by the way, but they did all those things? It's for real?"

"I don't know."

"Just your opinion then, Father. It's okay. I'm not wearing a 'wire.'"

Karras shifted a wan, wry smile to the detective and then turned his gaze back to the pathway. "Well, all right then," he said. "I think it's for real, or let's just say I suspect so, and most of my reasoning's based on pathology. Sure, okay. Black Mass. It happens. But anyone doing those things is a very disturbed human being, and disturbed in a very special way. There's a clinical name for that kind of disturbance, in fact; it's called satanism—meaning people who can't have any sexual pleasure unless it's connected to a blasphemous action. And so I think—"

"You mean 'suspect.'"

"Yes, I suspect that Black Mass was just used as the justification."

"*Is* used."

"Was and is."

"Was and is," the detective echoed dryly. "And the psychiatric name for the disorder in which the person is always having to have the last word?"

"Karrasmania," said the priest with a smile.

"Thank you. This was formerly a lacuna in my vast store of knowledge of the strange and exotic. In the meantime, please forgive me, but the things with the statues of Jesus and Mary?"

"What about them?"

"They're true?"

"Well, I think this might interest you as a policeman." His scholarly interest aroused and stirring, the Jesuit's manner had grown quietly animated. "The records of the Paris police still carry the case of a couple of monks from a nearby monastery—let's see . . ." He scratched the back of his head as he tried to recall. "Yes, maybe the one at Crépy," he said at last. The priest shrugged. "Well, whichever. Some town close by. At any rate, the monks came into an inn and got belligerent about wanting a bed for three—the two of them and a life-sized statue of the Blessed Virgin Mary that they carried in with them."

"Ah, that's shocking," breathed out Kinderman.

"No kidding. But it's a fair indication that what you've been reading is based on fact."

"Well, the sex, maybe so, this I can see; that's a whole other story altogether. Never mind. But the ritual murders now, Father? That's true? Now come on! Using blood from the newborn babies?" The detective was alluding to something else he had read in the book on witchcraft, describing how the unfrocked priest at Black Mass would at times slit the wrist of a newborn infant so that the blood poured into a chalice and later was consecrated and consumed in the form of Holy Communion. "That's just like the stories they used to tell about the Jews," the detective continued. "How they stole Christian babies and drank their blood. Look, forgive me, but *your* people told all those stories."

"If we did, forgive *me*."

"Go and sin no more. You're absolved."

Like the shadow of some pain but briefly remembered, something dark, something sad, flitted swiftly across the priest's blank stare. He turned his head and looked ahead. "Yeah, right."

"You were saying?"

"Well, I really don't know about ritual murder," Karras said; "about that I have no clue. But I do know that a midwife in Switzerland once confessed to the murder of thirty or forty babies for use at Black Mass. Oh, well, maybe she was tortured into saying that," he amended with a shrug. "But she sure as heck told a convincing story. She described how she'd hide a long, thin needle up her sleeve, so that when she was delivering the baby, she'd slip out the needle and stick it through the crown of the baby's head, and then hide the needle again. No marks," Karras said as he turned a glance to Kinderman. "The baby looked stillborn. You've heard of the prejudice European Catholics used to have against midwives? Well, that's how it started."

"Ah, my God!"

"Yes, this century hasn't got a lock on insanity. But—"

"Wait a minute, wait now!" the detective interrupted. "These stories—like you said, they were told by some people who were probably tortured, correct? So they're basically unreliable. They signed the confessions and later, the *machers*, the pious *shmeis* and the haters, they filled in the blanks. I mean, there wasn't any *habeas corpus* then, right? No writ of 'Let My People Go.'"

"Very true, but then a lot of the confessions were voluntary."

"So who would volunteer such things?"

"Doubtless people who were mentally disturbed."

"Ah, *another* reliable source!"

"Oh, well, you're probably right about that too, Lieutenant. I'm just playing devil's advocate."

"You do it so well."

"Look, one thing that we sometimes tend to forget is that people psychotic enough to confess to such things might also be psychotic enough to have done them. For example, the myths about werewolves, let's say. So, okay, they're preposterous: no one can turn himself into a wolf. But what if a person were so disturbed that he not only *thought* that he was a werewolf, but he also *acted* like one?"

"This is theory now, good Father, or fact?"

"Fact. There was a William Stumpf, for example. Or maybe his first name was Karl. I can't remember. Anyway, a German in the sixteenth century. He thought he was a werewolf and murdered maybe twenty or thirty young children."

"You mean, he—quotation marks, Father—confessed it?"

"Yes, he did and I think the confession was valid. When they caught him, he was eating the brains of his two young daughters-in-law."

From the baseball practice field, crisp in the thin, clear April sunlight, came the ghosts of chatter and ball against bat. *"C'mon, Price, let's shag it, let's go, get the lead out!"*

They had come to the parking lot, and for a brief space of time they walked in silence until at last, when they had come to the squad car, the detective turned a mournful, moody look to the priest. "And so what am I looking for, Father?" he asked him.

"A psycho on drugs maybe," Karras answered.

Staring down at the sidewalk, the detective thought it over and then mutely nodded. "Yes, right, Father. Yes. Maybe so." He looked up, his expression now pleasant. "Listen Father, where are you going? Want a ride?"

"No thanks, Lieutenant. It's just a short walk."

"Never mind that! Enjoy!" the detective told him, motioning Karras to get into the backseat of the car. "Then you can tell all your friends you went riding in a police car. I will sign a certificate attesting to it. They will envy you. Come on, now, get in!"

With a nod and a sad half smile, the priest said, "Okay," and slipped into a seat in the back of the car while the detective squirmed into it beside him from the opposite side. "Very good," said the detective, a little short of breath. "And incidentally, good Father, *no* walk is short. No, *none!*" He turned to the policeman at the wheel and said, *"Avanti!"*

"Where to, sir?"

"Thirty-Sixth Street and halfway down Prospect, left side of the street."

As the driver nodded and started backing the squad car out of its parking spot, Karras turned a mildly questioning look to the detective. "How do you know where I live?" he said.

"It's not a Jesuit residence hall? You're not a Jesuit?"

Karras turned his head and stared through the windshield as the squad car slowly headed for the campus front gates. "Yeah, right," he said softly. He had moved his quarters to the residence hall from his Holy Trinity courtyard location just a few days before in the hope it might encourage the men he had counseled to continue to seek his help.

"You like movies, Father Karras?"

"Yes, I do."

"You've seen *Lear* with Paul Scofield?"

"No, I haven't."

"Me, I've seen it. I get passes."

"Good for you."

"I get passes for the very best shows, but Mrs. K., she gets tired very early. She never goes."

"That's too bad."

"Yes, I hate to go alone. You know, afterward I love to talk film; to discuss; to critique."

Silent, Karras nodded, then looked down at his large and powerful hands that he was holding clasped between his legs. Moments passed. And then Kinderman asked in a wistful tone of voice, "Would you like to see a film with me sometime? It's free."

"Yes, I know. You get passes."

"Would you like to?"

"As Elwood P. Dowd says in *Harvey*, 'When?' "

"Oh, I'll call you!" The detective was beaming.

"Okay, do that. I'd like that."

They had exited the campus front gates, taken a right and then left on Prospect Street and had arrived at the residence hall and parked. Karras opened the door on his side partway and, looking back at the detective, said, "Thanks for the ride," got out of the car, shut the car door and, leaning his forearms on the open window jamb, said, "I'm sorry that I couldn't be of very much help."

"No, you were," said the detective. "And thank you. In the meantime, I'll give a call about a film, I really will."

"I'll look forward," said Karras. "Take care, now."

"I will. And you too."

Karras pulled back from the car, straightened up, turned around and was moving away when he heard, "Father, *wait!*"

Karras turned and saw Kinderman emerging from the car and beckoning him to come to him. Karras did, and met Kinderman on the sidewalk. "Listen, Father, I forgot," the detective told him. "It completely slipped my mind about the card. You know, the card with the writing in Latin on it? The one that was found in the church?"

"Yes, the altar card."

"Whatever. It's still around?"

"Yes, I've got it in my room. I was checking out the Latin but I'm finished now. You want it?"

"It could show something. Yes. May I have it?"

"Sure. Hold on and I'll go get it for you now."

"I'm obliged."

While Kinderman leaned back against the squad car and waited, the Jesuit went quickly to his ground-floor room, found the card, placed it inside a manila envelope, came back out to the street and handed the envelope to Kinderman.

"Here you go."

"Father, thank you," said Kinderman as he lifted the envelope to his scrutiny. "There could be some fingerprints, I'm thinking." Then he looked up at Karras with incipient dismay. He said, "*Oy!* You've been handling the card, Kirk Douglas, replaying your role in *Detective Story*? No gloves? Your bare hands."

"I plead guilty."

"And without an explanation," grumbled Kinderman. Shaking his head and eyeing Karras dismally, he added, "Father Brown you are not. Never mind, maybe still we could find something from it." Here he held up the envelope. "Incidentally, you studied this, you say?"

Karras nodded. "Yes, I did."

"And your conclusion? I await with bated breath."

"I couldn't say," Karras told him, "except whatever the motive was—hatred of Catholicism, maybe. Who knows? But what's certain is the guy who did this is deeply disturbed."

"How do you know it was a man?"

Karras shrugged and looked away, his gaze following a passing Gunther beer truck as it rumbled on the cobblestones of the street. "Oh, well, I don't," he said.

"And it couldn't be some teenage lout?"

"No, it couldn't." Karras turned to look at Kinderman again. "It's the Latin," he said.

"The Latin? Oh, you mean on the altar card."

"Yes. The Latin's flawless, Lieutenant, and more than that, it's got a definite style that's extremely individual."

"That's so?"

"That's so. It's as if whoever wrote it can *think* in Latin."

"Can priests?"

"Oh, come on!" Karras scoffed.

"Just answer the question, please, Father Paranoia."

Karras turned his stare back to Kinderman and, after a pause, admitted, "Okay, yes. There comes a point in our training when we do—at least the Jesuits and maybe a couple of the other orders. At Woodstock Seminary in Maryland, our philosophy courses are *taught* in Latin."

"Why is that?"

"For precision of thought. It expresses nuances and subtle distinctions that English can't handle."

"Ah, I see."

Looking suddenly grave, his stare intense, the priest leaned his face in close to the detective's. "Look, Lieutenant, can I tell you who I *really* think did it?"

The detective's eyebrows furrowed with interest.

"Yes, who!"

"The Dominicans. Go pick on them."

Karras smiled, and as he turned and walked away, the detective called after him, "I lied! You look like Sal Mineo!"

Karras turned with a grin and a friendly wave and then opened the door to the residence hall and entered, while outside on the sidewalk the detective stood motionless, speculatively staring as he murmured, "He hums like a tuning fork held under the water." For a few seconds more he continued staring pensively at the residence entry door. And then abruptly he turned and, opening the right front door of the squad car, he slid into the passenger seat, closed the door and told the driver, "Back to headquarters. Hurry. Break laws."

Karras's new quarters in the Jesuit residence hall was sparely furnished: bookshelves built into one wall, a single bed, two comfortable chairs, plus a desk with a straight-backed wooden chair. On the desk was an early photo of his mother, and on the wall above his bed, in silent rebuke, hung a bronze-colored metal crucifix. For Karras, the narrow room was world enough. He cared little for possessions; only that those he had be clean.

He showered, scrubbing briskly, slipped on a white T-shirt and khaki chinos, then ambled to dinner in the priests' refectory, where he spotted pink-cheeked Dyer. Wearing a faded Snoopy sweatshirt, he was sitting alone at a table in a corner. Karras moved to join him.

"Hi, Damien."

"Hey, Joe."

Standing in front of his chair, Karras blessed himself and closed his eyes while inaudibly murmuring a rapid grace, then sat down at the table and spread a napkin on his lap.

"How's the loafer?" Dyer asked him.

"Whaddya mean? I'm working."

"One lecture a week?"

"It's the quality that counts. What's dinner?"

"Can't you smell it?"

Karras grimaced. "Oh hell, is it dog day?"

Knockwurst and sauerkraut.

"It's the quantity that counts," said Dyer; then, as Karras reached out for a pitcher of milk, the young priest quietly warned, "I wouldn't do that," while he buttered a slice of whole wheat bread. "See the bubbles? Saltpeter."

"I need it." As Karras tipped up his glass to fill it, he heard the scrape of a chair as someone pulled it back and joined them at the table.

"Well, I finally read that book," said the newcomer brightly.

Karras glanced up and felt instant dismay, felt the soft crushing weight, press of lead, press of bone, as he recognized the young priest who had come to him recently for counseling, the one who could not make friends.

"Oh, and what did you think of it?" Karras asked as if with interest. He set down the pitcher of milk as if it were the booklet for a broken novena.

The young priest talked and, half an hour later, Dyer was table-hopping, spiking the refectory with laughter. Karras checked his watch. "Want to pick up a jacket and walk across the street?" he asked the young priest. "I like to watch the sunset every night if I can."

Soon they were leaning against a railing at the top of the steps that plunged steeply down to M Street. End of day. The burnished rays of the setting sun flamed glory on the clouds of the western sky before shattering in gold and vermilion dapples on the darkening waters of the river. Once Karras met God in this sight. Long ago. Like a lover forsaken, he still kept the rendezvous.

Drinking it in, the young priest said, "So beautiful. Really."

"Yes, it is."

The campus tower clock boomed out the hour: 7:00 P.M.

At 7:23, Lieutenant Kinderman was pondering a spectrographic analysis showing that the paint from Regan's sculpture matched a scraping of paint from the desecrated statue of the Virgin Mary, and at 8:47, in a slum in the northeast section of the city, an impassive Karl Engstrom emerged from a rat-infested tenement building, walked three blocks south to a bus stop where he waited alone for a minute, expressionless, then clutched at a lamppost with both his hands as he crumpled against it, racked with tears.

At the time, Lieutenant Kinderman was at the movies.

Chapter Six

On Wednesday, May 11, they were back in the house. They put Regan to bed, installed a lock on the shutters and stripped all the mirrors from her bedroom and bathroom.

". . . fewer and fewer lucid moments, and now there's a total blacking out of her consciousness during the fits, I'm afraid. That's new and would seem to eliminate genuine hysteria. In the meantime, a symptom or two in the area of what we call parapsychic phenomena have . . ."

Dr. Klein came by, and Chris attended with Sharon as he drilled them in proper procedures for administering Sustagen feedings to Regan during her periods of coma. He inserted the nasogastric tubing. "First . . ."

Chris forced herself to watch and yet still not see her daughter's face; to grip at the words that the doctor was saying and push away others that she'd heard at the clinic.

"Now you stated 'No religion' here, Mrs. MacNeil. Is that right? No religious education at all?"

"Oh, well, maybe just 'God.' You know, general. Why?"

"Well, for one thing, the content of much of her raving—when it isn't that gibberish she's been spouting—is religiously oriented. Now where do you think she might have gotten that?"

"Well, first give me a for instance."

"Okay, then: 'Jesus and Mary, sixty-nine,' for example."

Klein had guided the tubing into Regan's stomach. "First

you check to see if fluid's gotten into her lungs," he instructed, pinching on the tube in order to clamp off the flow of Sustagen. "If it . . ."

" . . . syndrome of a type of disorder that you rarely ever see anymore, except among primitive cultures. We call it somnambuliform possession. Quite frankly, we don't know much about it except that it starts with some conflict or guilt that eventually leads to the patient's delusion that his body's been invaded by an alien intelligence; a spirit, if you will. In times gone by, when belief in the devil was fairly strong, the possessing entity was usually a demon. In relatively modern cases, however, it's mostly the spirit of someone dead, often someone the patient has known or seen and is able unconsciously to mimic as to the voice and the mannerisms, even the features of the face at rare times."

After a gloomy Dr. Klein had left the house, Chris telephoned her agent in Beverly Hills and announced to him lifelessly that she definitely wouldn't be directing "Hope." Then she called Mrs. Perrin. She was out. Chris hung up the phone with a mounting dread. Who was it who could help her, she desperately wondered. Was there anyone? Anything? What?

". . . Cases where it's spirits of the dead are easier to deal with; you don't find the rages in most of those cases, or the hyperactivity and motor excitement. However, in the other main type of somnambuliform possession, the new personality's always malevolent, always hostile toward the first. Its primary aim, in fact, is to damage and sometimes even kill it."

A set of restraining straps had been delivered to the Prospect Street house and Chris stood watching, wan and spent, while Karl affixed them, first to Regan's bed and then to her wrists. As Chris moved a pillow in an effort to center it under Regan's head, the Swiss straightened up and looked pityingly at the child's ravaged face. "She is going to be well?" he asked.

Chris didn't answer. As Karl was speaking, she had slipped

out an object from under Regan's pillow and was holding it up to her mystified gaze. Then her glance flicked to Karl as she snapped at him sternly, "Karl, who put this crucifix here?"

"The syndrome is only the manifestation of some conflict, of some guilt, so we try to get at it, find out what it is. Well, the best procedure in a case like this is hypnotherapy; however, we can't seem to put her under. So then we took a shot at narcosynthesis, but it looks like another dead end."

"So what's next?"

"Mostly time. We'll just have to keep trying and hoping there's a change. In the meantime, she's going to have to be hospitalized."

Chris found Sharon in the kitchen setting up her typewriter on the table. She had just brought it up from the basement playroom. Willie sliced carrots at the sink for a stew.

With a current of tension and strain in her voice, Chris asked, "Was it you who put the crucifix under her pillow, Shar?"

Sharon looked befuddled. "What do you mean?"

"You didn't?"

"Chris, I don't even know what you're talking about! Look, I told you before, Chris, I told you on the plane, all I've ever said about religion to Rags is stuff like 'God made the world' and maybe things about—"

"Fine, Sharon, fine. I believe you, but—"

"Me, I don't put it!" growled Willie defensively.

"Dammit, *somebody* put it there!" Chris suddenly erupted. Then she wheeled on Karl, who had entered the kitchen and opened the refrigerator door. *"Karl!"* she called out to him sharply.

"Yes, Madam," Karl answered her calmly without turning around. He was folding ice cubes into a face towel.

"Well, I'm asking you one more time," Chris said grittily, her voice cracking and at the edge of shrillness: "Did you put that freaking crucifix under Regan's pillow?"

"No, Madam. Not me. I don't do it," Karl answered as he plopped another ice cube into the towel.

"That fucking cross didn't just walk up there, goddammit!" Chris shrieked as she spun around to Willie and Sharon. *"Now which one of you is lying? Tell me!"*

Karl stopped what he was doing and turned to study Chris. Her sudden rage had stunned the room, and now abruptly she slumped down into a chair, convulsively sobbing into trembling hands. "Oh, I'm sorry, I don't know what I'm doing!" she said tremulously as she wept. "Oh, my God, I don't know!"

While Willie and Karl stood silently watching, Sharon came up behind Chris and started kneading her neck and shoulders with comforting hands. "Hey, okay. It's okay."

Chris wiped at her face with the back of a sleeve. "Yeah, I guess whoever did it"—she found a handkerchief in a pocket and blew her nose, then continued—"Whoever did it was only trying to help."

"Look, I'm telling you again and you'd better believe it, I'm not about to put her into an asylum!"

"Ma'am, it isn't an—"

"I don't care what *you call it! No way! I'm not letting her out of my sight!"*

"I'm so sorry. We all are."

"Yeah, sure. Jesus, eighty-eight doctors and all you can tell me with all of your bullshit is . . . !"

Chris tore the cellophane off a blue packet of Gauloises Blondes, an imported French cigarette, took a few deep puffs and then tamped it out rapidly in an ashtray and went upstairs to look in on Regan. When she opened the door, in the gloom of the bedroom, she made out a male figure by Regan's bedside sitting in a straight-backed wooden chair, his arm outstretched and his hand over Regan's brow. Chris moved closer. It was Karl. When Chris reached the bedside, he neither looked up at her, nor did he speak, but kept his gaze intently on the child's face. There was something in the hand on Regan's brow. What was it? Then she saw it was an improvised ice pack.

Surprised and touched, Chris appraised the stolid Swiss with a look of fondness that she had long ago misplaced; but when he neither moved nor acknowledged her presence, she turned away and quietly left the room. She went down to the kitchen, sat in the breakfast nook, drank coffee and stared off distantly in thought until, on a sudden impulse, she stood up and walked briskly toward the cherrywood paneled study.

"Possession is loosely related to hysteria insofar as the origin of the syndrome is almost always autosuggestive. Your daughter might have known about possession, believed in it, and possibly known about some of its symptoms, so that now her unconscious is producing the syndrome. Follow? Now if that can be firmly established, and you still won't agree to hospitalization, you might want to take a stab at something that I'm going to suggest. It has only an outside chance of a cure, I would think, but still it's a chance."

"Oh, well, name it, for God's sake! What is it?!"

"Have you ever heard of exorcism, Mrs. MacNeil?"

Chris was unfamiliar with the books in the study—they were part of the furnishings that came with the house—and now she was carefully scanning the titles.

"It's a stylized ritual pretty much out of date in which rabbis and priests tried to drive out an evil spirit. It's only the Catholics who haven't discarded it yet, but they keep it pretty much in the closet as sort of an embarrassment, I think. But to someone who really thinks he's possessed, I'd have to say that the ritual's pretty impressive, and it used to work, in fact, although not for the reason they thought; it was purely the force

of suggestion. The victim's belief in possession helped cause it, and in just the same way his belief in the power of the exorcism can make it disappear. It's—I see that you're frowning. Well, of course; I know it sounds far-fetched. So let me tell you something similar that we know to be a fact. It has to do with Australian aborigines. They're convinced that if some wizard thinks a 'death ray' at them from a distance, why, they're definitely going to die. And the fact is that they do! *They just lie down and slowly die! And the only thing that saves them, most times, is a similar form of suggestion: a counteracting 'ray' by another wizard."*

"Are you telling me to take my daughter to a witch doctor?"

"As a last-ditch, desperate measure—well, yes. I suppose that I'm saying exactly that. Take her to a Catholic priest. That's a rather bizarre little piece of advice, I know, and maybe even a little bit dangerous, unless we can definitely ascertain whether or not your daughter knew anything at all about possession, and particularly exorcism, before any of her symptoms came on. Do you think she might have read it somewhere?"

"No."

"Seen a movie about it? Something on the radio? TV?"

"No."

"Read the gospels, maybe? The New Testament?"

"No, she hasn't. Why are you asking?"

"There are quite a few accounts of possession in them and of exorcisms by Christ. The descriptions of the symptoms, in fact, are the same as in possession today, so—"

"Look, it's just no good. Okay? Just forget it! That's all I need is to have her father hear I called in a . . . !"

Chris's fingertips moved from book to book, searching but so far finding nothing until—*Hold it!* Her eyes darted quickly back to a title on the bottom shelf. It was the book about witchcraft that Mary Jo Perrin had sent to her. Chris plucked it out and turned quickly to the table of contents, running her thumbnail slowly down the list until abruptly she stopped and thought,

There! There it is! Soft thrills of surmise rippled through her. Were the doctors at Barringer right after all? Was this it? Had Regan plucked her disorder and her symptoms through autosuggestion from the pages of this book?

The title of a chapter was "States of Possession."

Chris walked to the kitchen where Sharon was seated reading her shorthand from a propped-up notepad while typing a letter. Chris held up the book. "Have you ever read this, Shar?"

Still typing, Sharon asked, "Read what?"

"This book about witchcraft."

Sharon stopped typing, turned her glance to Chris and the book, said, "No, I haven't," and turned back to her work.

"Never seen it? Never put it on a bookshelf in the study?"

"No."

"Where's Willie?"

"At the market."

Chris nodded and stood silently pondering, then went back upstairs to Regan's bedroom, where Karl still kept vigil at her daughter's bedside.

"Karl!"

"Yes, Madam."

Chris held up the book. "By any chance did you find this lying around and then put it with the rest of the books in the study?"

The houseman turned to Chris, expressionless, shifted his gaze to the book and then back to her. "No, Madam," he said; "not me." Then he turned his gaze back to Regan.

Okay then, maybe Willie.

Chris returned to the kitchen, sat down at the table and, opening the book to the chapter on possession, she began to search for anything relevant, anything the doctors at Barringer Clinic thought might have given rise to Regan's symptoms.

And found it.

> Immediately derivative of the prevalent belief in demons was the phenomenon known as possession, a state in which many individuals believed that their physical and mental functions had been invaded and were being controlled by either a demon (most common in the period under discussion) or the spirit of someone dead. There is no period of history or quarter of the globe where this phenomenon has not been reported, and in fairly constant terms, and yet it is still to be adequately explained. Since Traugott Oesterreich's definitive study, first published in 1921, very little has been added to the body of knowledge, the advances of psychiatry notwithstanding.

Chris frowned. Not fully explained? She'd had a different impression from the doctors at Barringer.

> What is known is the following: that various people, at various times, have undergone massive transformations so complete that those around them feel they are dealing with another person. Not only the voice, the mannerisms, facial expressions and characteristic movements are sometimes altered, but the subject himself now thinks of himself as totally distinct from the original person and as having a name—whether human or demonic—and a separate history of its own. In the Malay Archipelago, where possession even now is an everyday, common occurrence, the possessing spirit of someone dead often causes the possessed to mimic its gestures, voice and mannerisms

> so strikingly, that relatives of the deceased will burst into tears. But aside from so-called quasi-possession—those cases that are ultimately reducible to fraud, paranoia and hysteria—the problem has always lain with interpreting the phenomena, the oldest interpretation being the spiritist, an impression that is likely to be strengthened by the fact that the intruding personality may have accomplishments quite foreign to the first. In the demoniacal form of possession, for example, the "demon" may speak in languages unknown to the first personality.

There! Regan's gibberish! An attempt at a language? Chris read on quickly:

> . . . or manifest various parapsychic phenomena, such as telekinesis for example: the movement of objects without application of material force.

The rappings? The flinging up and down on the bed?

> . . . In cases of possession by the dead, there are manifestations such as Oesterreich's account of a monk who, abruptly, while possessed, became a gifted and brilliant dancer although he had never, before his possession, had occasion to dance so much as a step. So impressive, at times, are these manifestations that Jung, the psychiatrist, after studying a case at first hand, could offer only partial explanation for what he was certain could "not have been fraud". . .

Chris frowned. The tone of this was worrisome.

> . . . and William James, the greatest psychologist that America has ever produced, resorted to positing "the plausibility of the spiritualist interpretation of the phenomenon" after closely studying the so-called "Watseka Wonder," a teen-aged girl in Watseka, Illinois, who became indistinguishable in personality from a girl named Mary Roff who had died in a state insane asylum twelve years prior to the possession . . .

Riveted, Chris did not hear the doorbell chime; did not hear Sharon stop typing and go to the door.

> The demoniacal form of possession is usually thought to have had its origin in early Christianity; yet in fact both possession and exorcism pre-date the time of Christ. The ancient Egyptians as well as the earliest civilizations of the Tigris and the Euphrates believed that physical and spiritual disorders were caused by invasion of the body by demons. The following, for example, is the formula for exorcism against maladies of children in ancient Egypt: "Go hence, thou who comest in darkness, whose nose is turned backwards, whose face is upside down. Hast thou come to kiss this child? I will not let thee . . ."

"Chris?"

"Shar, I'm busy."

"There's a homicide detective wants to see you."

"Oh, Christ, Sharon, tell him to—" Abruptly Chris stopped, then looked up and said, "Oh. Yeah, sure, Sharon. Tell him to come in. Let him in." Sharon left and Chris stared at the pages of the book, unseeing, gripped by some formless yet gathering premonition of dread. Sound of a door being closed. Sound of walking this way. A sense of waiting. *Waiting? For what?* Like the vivid dream one can never remember, Chris felt an expectancy that seemed known and yet undefined.

His hat brim crumpled in his hands, he came in with Sharon, wheezing and listing and deferential. "I am really so sorry," Kinderman said as he approached. "Yes, you're busy. I can see that. I'm a bother."

"How's the world?" Chris asked him.

"Very bad. And how's your daughter?"

"No change."

"I'm so sorry." Breathing adenoidally, Kinderman was standing by the table now, his drooping beagle eyes moist with concern. "Look, I wouldn't even bother; I mean, your daughter; it's a worry. God knows, when my little girl Julie was down with the—What, now? What was it? Can't remember. It—"

"Why don't you sit down," Chris cut in.

"Oh, yes, thank you very much," the detective exhaled gratefully while settling his bulk in a chair across from Sharon, who, seemingly oblivious, continued to type.

"Sorry. You were saying?" Chris asked.

"Well, my daughter, she—oh, well, no. Never mind. I get started, I'll be telling you my whole life story, you could maybe make a film of it. No, really! It's incredible! If you only knew *half* the crazy things that used to happen in my family, you would—No. No, never mind. All right, *one!* I'll tell *one!* Like my mother, every Friday she would make for us gefilte fish, all right? Only all week long—*the whole week*—no one gets to take a bath on account of my mother has the carp in the bathtub, it's swimming back and forth, back and forth, because my mother said this cleaned out the poison in its system. I mean, really, who knew! Who knew that carp the whole time are all thinking all these horrible and evil, vindictive thoughts! Oh, well, enough now. Really. Only now and then a laugh just to keep us from crying."

Chris studied him. Waiting.

"Ah, you're reading!" The detective was looking down at the book on witchcraft. "For a film?"

"No, just passing the time."

"Is it good?"

"I just started it."

"Witchcraft," Kinderman murmured, his head angled to the side as he read the book's title at the top of a page.

"So okay now, what's doin'?" Chris asked.

"Yes, I'm sorry. You're busy. I'll finish. As I said, I wouldn't bother you, except . . ."

"Except what?"

Looking suddenly grave, the detective clasped his hands together on the polished pine tabletop. "Well, it seems that Burke—"

"Damn it!" snapped Sharon irritably as she ripped out a letter from the platen of the typewriter, crumpled it up in her hands and then errantly tossed it at a wastepaper basket close to Kinderman's feet. He and Chris had turned their heads to stare at her, and when the secretary saw them, she said, "Oh, I'm so sorry! I didn't even know you were there!"

"You're Miss Fenster?" asked Kinderman.

"Spencer," Sharon corrected him as she slid her chair back and got up to retrieve the balled-up letter from the floor with a murmured "I never said I was Julius Erving."

"Never mind, never mind," the detective told her as, reaching to the floor near his foot, he picked up the crumpled page.

"Oh, thanks." Sharon stopped and went back to her chair.

"Excuse me—you're the secretary?" Kinderman asked her.

"Sharon, this is—" Chris turned to Kinderman. "Sorry," she said to him. "Your name again?"

"Kinderman. William F. Kinderman."

"This is Sharon; Sharon Spencer."

With a courtly tilt and nod of the head, the detective told Sharon, "It's a pleasure." Sharon was now bent forward, eyeing him curiously, her chin resting on folded arms atop the typewriter. "And perhaps you can help me," the detective added.

Her arms still folded, Sharon sat up and said, "Me?"

"Yes, perhaps. On the night of Mr. Dennings's demise, you went out to a drugstore and left him alone in the house, am I correct?"

"Well, not exactly. Regan was here."

"That's my daughter," Chris clarified.

"Spelling?"

"R-e-g-a-n," Chris told him.

"Lovely name," said Kinderman.

"Thank you."

The detective turned back to Sharon. "Now Dennings had come here that night to see Mrs. MacNeil?"

"Yes, that's right."

"He expected her shortly?"

"Yes, I told him I expected her back pretty soon."

"Very good. And you left at what time? You remember?"

"Let's see. I was watching the news, so I guess—oh, no, wait—yes, that's right. I remember being bothered because the pharmacist said the delivery boy had gone home and I said, 'Oh, come on now,' or something about it only being about six-thirty. Then Burke came along just ten, maybe twenty minutes after that."

"So a median," concluded the detective, "would have put him here at six-forty-five. Not so?"

"And so what's this all about?" Chris asked him.

The nebulous tension she'd been feeling had mounted.

"Well, it raises a question, Mrs. MacNeil. To arrive at the house at, say, quarter to seven and leave only twenty minutes later . . ."

Chris shrugged. "Oh, well, that was Burke," she said. "Just like him."

"Was it also like him," Kinderman asked, "to frequent the bars down on M Street?"

"No. Not at all. Not that I know of."

"No, I thought not. I made a little check. And so he wouldn't have had a reason to be at the top of those steps beside your house after leaving here that night. And was it also not his custom to travel by taxi? He wouldn't call a cab from your house when he left?"

"Yes, he would. At least, he always did."

"Then one wonders—not so?—why or how he came to be there that night. And one wonders why taxicab companies do not show a record of calls from this house on that night, except for the one that picked up your Miss Spencer here at precisely six-forty-seven."

Her voice drained of color, Chris said softly, "I don't know."

"No, I doubted that you would," the detective told her. "In the meantime, the matter has now grown somewhat serious."

Chris was breathing shallowly. "In what way?"

"The report of the pathologist," Kinderman recounted, "seems to show that the chance that Dennings died accidentally is still very possible. However . . ."

"Are you saying he was murdered?"

"Well, it seems that the position . . ." Kinderman hesitated. "I'm sorry," he said; "this will be painful."

"Go ahead."

"The position of Dennings's head and a certain shearing of the muscles of the neck would—"

Shutting her eyes, Chris winced and said, "Oh, God!"

"Yes, as I said, it's very painful. I'm so sorry. Really. But you see, this condition—I think we can skip the details, perhaps—it never could happen unless Mr. Dennings had fallen some distance before he hit the steps; for example, maybe twenty, thirty feet before he went rolling down to the bottom. So a clear possibility, plainly speaking, is that maybe . . ." Kinderman turned to Sharon. Arms folded across her chest, she had been listening, mesmerized and wide-eyed. "Well, now, first let me ask you something, Miss Spencer. When you left, he was where, Mr. Dennings? With the child?"

"No, he was down here in the study fixing a drink."

"Might your daughter remember"—he turned to Chris—"if perhaps Mr. Dennings was in her room that night?"

"Why do you ask?"

"Might your daughter remember?"

"How could she? Like I told you, she was heavily sedated and—"

"Yes, yes, you did tell me; that's true; I recall it; but perhaps she awakened."

"No, she didn't," Chris told him.

"She was also sedated when last we spoke?"

"Yes, she was."

"I thought I saw her at her window that day."

"Well, you're mistaken."

"It could be. Perhaps so. I'm not sure."

"Listen, why are you asking all this?"

"Well, a clear possibility, as I was saying, is maybe the deceased was so drunk that he stumbled and fell from the window in your daughter's bedroom. Not so?"

"No way. In the first place that window was always closed, and besides, Burke was *always* drunk, but he never got sloppy. Burke used to *direct* when he was drunk. Now how could he stumble and fall out a window?"

"Were you maybe expecting someone else here that night?"

"Someone else? No, I wasn't."

"Have you friends who drop by without calling?"

"Only Burke."

The detective lowered his head and shook it. "So strange," he breathed out wearily. "Baffling." Then he lifted his glance to Chris. "The deceased comes to visit, stays only twenty minutes without even seeing you, and leaves all alone here a very sick girl? And speaking plainly, as you yourself say, it's not likely he would fall from a window. Besides, a fall wouldn't do to his neck what we found except maybe a chance in a hundred; in a thousand." He motioned with his head at the witchcraft book. "You've read in that book about ritual murder?"

Her chill prescience mounting, Chris quietly said, "No."

"Maybe not in that book," said Kinderman. "However—forgive me; I mention this only so maybe you'll think just a little bit harder—poor Mr. Dennings was discovered with his neck wrenched around in the style of ritual murder by so-called demons, Mrs. MacNeil."

Chris's complexion visibly paled.

"Some lunatic killed Mr. Dennings and—" Kinderman halted. "Something wrong?" he asked. He had noticed a tension in her eyes, her sudden pallor.

"No, nothing's wrong. Go ahead."

"I'm obliged. Now at first, I never told you, to spare you the hurt. And besides, it could technically still be an accident. But me, I don't think so. My hunch? My opinion? I believe he was killed by a powerful man: point one; and the fracturing of his skull—point two—plus the various things I have mentioned would make it very probable—probable, not certain—your director was killed and then *afterward* pushed from your daughter's window. But no one was here *except* your daughter. So then how could this be? Well, it could be one way: if someone came calling between the time Miss Spencer left and the time you returned. Not so? Now I ask you again, please: who might have come?"

Chris lowered her head. "Judas priest, just a second!"

"Yes, I'm sorry. It's painful. And perhaps I'm all wrong. But you'll think now? Who might have come, please?"

Head still lowered, Chris frowned in thought for a time, then looked up. "No, I'm sorry. There's just no one I can think of."

Kinderman turned his glance to Sharon. "Maybe you then, Miss Spencer? Someone comes here to see you?"

"Oh, no, no one."

"Does the horseman know where you work?" Chris asked her.

Kinderman's eyebrows rose. "The horseman?"

"Sharon's boyfriend," Chris explained.

Sharon shook her head. "He's never come here," she said. "And besides, he was in Boston that night at some convention."

"He's a salesman?" asked Kinderman.

"A lawyer."

"Ah." The detective turned back to Chris. "The servants? They have visitors?" he asked.

"No, never. Not at all."

"You expected a package that day? Some delivery?"

"Why?"

"Mr. Dennings was—not to speak ill of the dead—but as you said, in his cups he was somewhat—well, let's call it irascible, and capable, doubtless, of provoking an argument or an anger, and in this case maybe even a rage from perhaps a delivery person who'd come by with a package. So were you expecting something? Dry cleaning, maybe? Groceries? Liquor? A package?"

"I wouldn't know. Karl handles all of that."

"Ah, of course."

"Want to ask him? Go ahead."

The detective sighed morosely. Leaning back from the table, he stuffed his hands into the pockets of his coat as he cast a glum look at the witchcraft book. "Never mind, never mind; it's remote. You've got a daughter very sick, and—well, enough now." He made a gesture of dismissal. "That's it. End of meeting." He stood up. "Thank you for your time," he said to Chris, and then to Sharon, "Very nice to have met you, Miss Spencer."

"Same here," Sharon answered remotely. She was staring into space.

"Baffling," said Kinderman with a head shake. "So strange; so very strange." He was focused on some inner thought. Then he looked at Chris as she rose from her chair. "Well, I'm sorry. I've bothered you for nothing," he said.

"Here, I'll walk you to the door," Chris told him.

Both her expression and her voice were subdued.

"Oh, please don't bother!"

"It's no bother at all."

"If you insist."

"Oh, incidentally," the detective said as he and Chris were moving out of the kitchen, "just a chance in a million, I know, but your daughter—you could ask her if she possibly saw Mr. Dennings in her room that night?"

"Look, he wouldn't have had a reason to be up there in the first place."

"Yes, I know that; I realize that's true; but if certain British doctors never asked, 'What's this fungus?' we wouldn't today have penicillin. Am I right? Please ask. You'll ask?"

"When she's well enough, yes; I'll ask."

"Couldn't hurt."

They had arrived at the home's front door.

"In the meantime . . . ," the detective continued. But he faltered, and, touching two fingertips to his lips, he said gravely, "Look, I hate to be asking you this. Please forgive me."

Expecting some new shock, Chris tensed and felt the prescience tingling again in her bloodstream. She said, "What?"

"For my daughter . . . you could maybe give an autograph?" The detective's cheeks had reddened. After a moment of surprise, Chris almost laughed with relief: at herself and at despair and the human condition.

"Oh, of course! Where's a pen?"

"Right here!" responded Kinderman instantly, whipping out a pen from the pocket of his coat while his other hand dipped into a pocket of his jacket and slipped out a calling card. He handed them to Chris. "She would love it."

"What's her name?" Chris asked, pressing the card against the door as she held the pen poised to write. A weighty hesitation followed as from behind her she heard only wheezing. She glanced around, and in Kinderman's eyes and reddening face she saw the tension of some massive inner struggle.

"I lied," he said finally, his eyes at once desperate and defiant. "The autograph's for me. Write 'To William—William F. Kinderman'—it's spelled on the back."

Chris eyed him with a wan and unexpected affection, checked the spelling of his name and wrote, "William F. Kinderman, I love you! Chris MacNeil," and then gave him the card, which he tucked into his pocket without reading the inscription.

"You're a very nice lady," he said to Chris sheepishly.

"Thanks. You're a very nice man."

He seemed to blush harder. "No, I'm not. I'm a bother." He

was opening the door. "Never mind what I said here today. Forget it. Keep your mind on your daughter. Your *daughter!*"

Chris nodded, her despondency returning as Kinderman stepped out onto a wide and low, black iron-gated stoop. He turned around, and in the daylight was more conscious of the dark sacs beneath the movie star's eyes. He donned his hat. "But you'll ask her?" he reminded, and "I will," she said. "I promise."

"Well, then good-bye. And take care."

"You too."

Chris shut the door and then leaned back against it, closing her eyes, then almost instantly opened them again as she heard the chiming of the doorbell. She turned and opened the door, revealing Kinderman. He grimaced in apology.

"I'm a nuisance. I'm so sorry. I forgot my pen."

Chris looked down and saw the pen still in her hand. She smiled faintly and handed it to the detective.

"And another thing," he said. "Yes, it's pointless, I know that; but I know I won't sleep tonight thinking maybe there's a lunatic loose or a doper if every little point I don't cover. Do you think I could—no, no, it's dumb, it's a—yes; yes, forgive me but I think I really should. Could I maybe have a word with Mr. Engstrom, do you think? It's the deliveries, the question of deliveries."

Chris opened the door wider. "Sure, come in. You can talk to him in the study."

"No, you're busy. You're very kind but enough already. I can talk to him here. This is fine. Here is fine."

He'd leaned back and was resting on the stoop's iron railing.

"If you insist," Chris told him, smiling faintly. "I think he's upstairs with Regan. I'll send him right down."

"I'm obliged."

Chris closed the door and, not long after, Karl opened it. He stepped down to the stoop with his hand on the doorknob, holding the door ajar. Standing tall and erect, he looked directly at Kinderman with eyes that were clear and cool. "Yes?" he asked without expression.

"You have the right to remain silent," Kinderman greeted him, his eyes now steely and locked on Karl's. "If you give up the right to remain silent," he intoned rapidly in a flat and deadly cadence, "anything you say can and will be used against you in a court of law. You have the right to speak with an attorney and to have the attorney present during questioning. If you so desire, and cannot afford one, an attorney will be appointed for you without charge prior to questioning. Do you understand each of these rights I've explained to you?"

Birds twittered softly in the branches of the elder tree beside the house as the traffic sounds of M Street came up to them softly like the humming of bees in a meadow far away.

Karl's gaze never wavered as he answered, "Yes."

"Do you wish to give up the right to remain silent?"

"Yes."

"Do you wish to give up the right to speak to an attorney and have him present during questioning?"

"Yes."

"Did you previously state that on April twenty-eighth, the night of the death of the British director, Burke Dennings, you attended a film that was showing at the Fine Arts theater?"

"I did."

"And at what time did you enter the theater?"

"I do not remember."

"You stated previously you attended the six-o'clock showing. Does that help you to remember?"

"Yes, six-o'clock show. I am remembering."

"And you saw the picture—the *film*—from the beginning?"

"I did."

"And you left at the film's conclusion?"

"I did."

"Not before?"

"No, I see entire film."

"And leaving the theater, you boarded the D.C. Transit bus in front of the theater, debarking at M Street and Wisconsin Avenue at approximately nine-twenty P.M.?"

"Yes."

"And walked home?"

"I walk home."

"And were back in this residence at approximately nine-thirty P.M.?"

"I am back here *exactly* nine-thirty," Karl answered.

"You're sure."

"Yes, I look at my watch. I am positive."

"And you saw the whole film to the very end?"

"Yes, I said that."

"Your answers are being electronically recorded, Mr. Engstrom. Therefore, I want you to be absolutely positive."

"I am."

"You're aware of the altercation between an usher and a drunken patron that happened in the last five minutes of the film?"

"Yes, I remember."

"Can you tell me the cause of it?"

"The man, he was drunk and was making disturbance."

"And what did they do with him finally?"

"Out. They throw him out."

"There was no such disturbance. Are you also aware that during the course of the six-o'clock showing a technical breakdown lasting approximately fifteen minutes caused an interruption in the showing of the film?"

"I am not."

"You recall that the audience booed?"

"No, nothing. No breakdown."

"You're sure?"

"There was nothing."

"There was, as reflected in the log of the projectionist, showing that the film ended not at eight-forty that night, but at approximately eight-fifty-five, which would mean that the earliest bus from the theater would put you at M Street and Wisconsin not at nine-twenty, but nine-forty-five, and that therefore the earliest you could be at the house was approximately five before ten, not nine-thirty, as testified also by Mrs. MacNeil. Would you care now to comment on this puzzling discrepancy?"

Not for a moment had Karl lost his poise and he held it even now as he calmly answered, "No. I would not."

The detective stared at him mutely, then sighed and looked down as he turned off the monitor control that was tucked in the lining of his coat. He held his gaze down for a moment, then looked back up at Karl. "Mr. Engstrom . . . ," he began in a tone that was weary with understanding. "A serious crime may have been committed. You are under suspicion. Mr. Dennings abused you. I have learned that from other sources. And apparently you've lied about your whereabouts at the time of his death. Now it sometimes happens—we're human; why not?—that a man who is married is sometimes someplace where he says that he is not. You will notice I arranged we are talking in private? Away from the others? Away from your wife? I'm not now recording. It's off. You can trust me. If it happens you were out with a woman not your wife on that night, you can tell me, I'll have it checked out, you'll be out of this trouble and your wife, she won't know. Now then tell me, where were you at the time Dennings died?"

Something flickered in the depths of Karl's eyes, but then died as he insisted through narrowed lips, "At movies!"

The detective eyed him steadily, unmoving, with no sound but his wheezing as the seconds ticked by. Then, "You are going to arrest me?" Karl asked in a voice that now subtly quavered.

The detective made no answer but continued to eye him, unblinking, and when Karl seemed again about to speak, the detective abruptly pushed away from the railing, moving toward his parked squad car and driver, with his hands in his pockets as he walked unhurriedly, viewing his surroundings to the left and to the right like an interested visitor to the city. From the stoop, Karl watched, his features stolid and impassive as Kinderman opened the door of the squad car, reached inside to a box of Kleenex affixed to the dashboard, extracted a tissue and blew his nose while staring idly across the river as if considering whether to have lunch at the Marriott Hot Shoppe. Then he entered the squad car without a glance back.

As the car pulled away and rounded the corner of Thirty-Fifth Street, Karl looked at the hand that was not on the doorknob.

It was trembling.

When she heard the sound of the front door closing, Chris was brooding at the bar in the study as she poured herself a vodka over ice. Footsteps. Karl going up the stairs. Chris picked up her glass, took a sip and then slowly moved back toward the kitchen with absent eyes while stirring her drink with an index finger. Something was horribly wrong. Like light leaking under a door into a darkened hallway somewhere out of time, the glow of coming dread had seeped further and further into her consciousness. What lay behind the door?

She feared to open it and look.

She entered the kitchen, sat at the table, sipped at her drink and broodingly remembered, *"I believe he was killed by a powerful man."* She dropped her glance to the book on witchcraft. Something about it or in it. What? And now footsteps tripping lightly downstairs, Sharon returning from Regan's bedroom. Entering. Sitting at the table and cranking fresh stationery into the IBM typewriter's roller. "Pretty creepy," she murmured with her fingertips lightly resting on the keyboard and her eyes on her propped steno notes to the side.

Staring into space, Chris sipped absently at her drink, then set it down and returned her gaze to the cover of the book.

An uneasiness hung in the room.

Her eyes still on her notes, Sharon probed at the silence in a strained, low voice. "They've got an awful lot of hippie joints down around M Street and Wisconsin. Lots of potheads and occultists and stuff. The police call them 'hellhounds.' I wonder if Burke might have—"

"Oh, for shitsakes, Shar!" Chris suddenly erupted. "Just forget about it, would you? I've got all I can think about with Rags! Do you *mind?*"

There was a pause, and then Sharon started typing at a furious tempo while Chris propped her elbows on the tabletop and buried her face in her hands. Abruptly Sharon pushed her chair back with a sound of wood scraping on wood, bolted up and strode out of the kitchen. "Chris, I'm going for a walk!" she said icily.

"Good! And stay the hell away from M Street!" Chris shot back into her hands.

"I will!"

"And N!"

Chris heard the front door being opened, then closed, and,

sighing, she lowered her hands and looked up. Felt a pang of regret. The emotional flurry had siphoned off tension. But not all of it: although fainter, at the edge of her consciousness, there remained that ominous glow. *Shut it out!* Chris took a deep breath and tried to focus on the book. She found her place and, grown impatient, started hastily flipping through its pages, skimming and searching for specific descriptions that would match Regan's symptoms. ". . . demonic possession syndrome . . . case of an eight-year-old girl . . . abnormal . . . four strong men to restrain her from . . ."

Turning a page, Chris froze.

Then sounds: Willie entering the kitchen with groceries.

"Willie?" Chris called out to her tonelessly, her eyes riveted to the book.

"Yes, Madam. I am here," Willie answered. She was setting bags full of groceries down on a white-tiled counter. Dull-eyed and expressionless, her voice flat, and with her slightly trembling fingers holding her place, Chris held up the partly closed witchcraft book, asking, "Willie, was it you put this book in the study?"

Willic came a few steps closer, squinted at the book, briefly nodded, and as she turned and started back toward the groceries, answered, "Yes, Missus. Yes. Yes, I put it."

"Willie, where did you find it?" Chris asked, her voice dead.

"Up in bedroom," Willie answered as she started slipping groceries out of the bags and onto the kitchen counter.

Chris stared fixedly at the pages of the book, now back on the table and open to her place. "*Which* bedroom, Willie?"

"Miss Regan bedroom, Missus. I find it under bed when I am cleaning."

Her voice numb, her eyes wide and fixedly staring, Chris looked up and said, "*When* did you find it?"

"After all go to hospital, Madam; when I vacuum in Regan bedroom."

"Willie, are you absolutely sure?"

"I am sure."

Chris looked down at the pages of the book and for a time did not move, did not blink, did not breathe, as the headlong image of an open window in Regan's bedroom on the night of Dennings's accident rushed at her memory with its talons extended like a bird of prey that knew her name; as she recognized a sight that was so numbingly familiar; as she stared at the right-hand page of the open book where a narrow strip had been shaved from the length of its edge.

Chris jerked up her head. Some commotion in Regan's bedroom: rappings, rapid and loud and with a nightmarish resonance that was massive and yet somehow muffled, like a sledgehammer pounding at a limestone wall deep within some ancient tomb.

Regan screaming in anguish; in terror; imploring!

Karl shouting angrily, fearfully, at Regan!

Chris bolted from the kitchen.

God almighty! What's happening? What!

Frenzied, Chris ran to the staircase, raced up to the second floor, then toward Regan's bedroom when she heard a blow, someone reeling, someone crashing to the floor and her daughter crying, *"No!* Oh, no, *don't!* Oh, no, *please!"* and Karl bellowing! No! No, not Karl! Someone else with a deep bass voice that was threatening and raging!

Chris plunged down the hall and burst into the bedroom, then gasped and stood rooted in paralyzing shock as the rappings boomed massively, shivering through walls; as Karl lay unconscious on the floor near the bureau and as Regan, with her legs propped up and spread wide on a bed that was violently bouncing and shaking, her eyes wide and bulging with terror in a face smeared with blood that was dripping from her nose where the nasogastric tubing had been violently ripped out as she stared at a bone-white crucifix clutched and held poised in the air just above and aimed directly at her vagina. "Oh, please! Oh, no, *please!*" she was shrieking as her hands brought the crucifix closer while seeming to be straining to hold it back.

"You'll do as I *tell* you, filth! You'll *do* it!"

The threatening bellow, the words, came from Regan, in a voice coarse and guttural and bristling with venom, while in an instantaneous flash her expression and features hideously transmuted into those of the feral, demonic personality that had appeared in the course of hypnosis, and as Chris watched, stunned, both the faces and voices interchanged with rapidity:

"No!"

"You'll do it!"

"No! Please, *no!"*

"You *will*, you little bitch, or I will kill you!"

And now the switch back to Regan with her eyes wide and staring as if flinching from the rush of some hideous finality, her mouth agape and shrieking until, again, the demonic personality possessed her, filled her, the room suddenly filling with a stench in the nostrils, with an icy cold that seemed to seep from the walls as the rapping sounds ended and Regan's piercing cry of terror elided into a guttural, yelping laugh of malevolent spite triumphant while she thrust down the crucifix into her vagina, then again and again, as she masturbated with it ferociously while roaring in that deep, coarse, deafening voice, "Now you're *mine*, you bitch, you stinking cow! Yes, let Jesus *fuck* you, *fuck* you *fuck* you!"

Chris stood rooted to the floor in horror, her hands pressing tightly against her cheeks as again the demonic, loud laugh cackled joyously as from Regan's vagina her blood gushed onto white linen sheets, and then abruptly, with a shriek coming raw and clawing from her throat, Chris rushed at the bed, grasping blindly at the crucifix while, her features contorted infernally, Regan flared up at her in fury and, reaching out a hand, clutched Chris's hair and, powerfully yanking her head down, firmly pressed Chris's face against her vagina, smearing it with blood as Regan undulated her pelvis.

"Aahhh, little pig mother!" Regan crooned with a guttural eroticism. "*Lick* me, *lick* me, *lick* me! Aahhhhh!" Then the hand that was holding Chris's head down jerked it upward while the other arm smashed a blow across her chest that sent Chris reeling across the room and crashing to a wall with stunning force while Regan mockingly laughed.

Chris crumpled to the floor in a daze of horror, in a swirling of images, of sounds in the room, as her vision spun, blurring, unfocused, her ears ringing loud with chaotic distortions as she weakly tried to raise herself, pushing up with her hands on the floor, and, faltering, looked toward the bed, toward Regan with her back to her, thrusting the crucifix gently and sensually into her vagina, then out, then in, with that deep, bass voice crooning, "Ahh, there's my sow, yes, my sweet honey piglet, my—"

Chris started crawling painfully toward the bed, her face smeared with blood, her eyes still unfocused, limbs aching, and then cringed, shrinking back in incredulous terror as she thought she saw hazily, as if in an undulating fog, her daughter's head turning slowly and inexorably completely around on a motionless torso until at last Chris was looking directly into the foxlike, angry eyes of Burke Dennings.

"Do you know what she *did*, your cunting daughter?"

Chris screamed until she fainted.

The Abyss

They said, "What sign can you give us to see, so that we may believe."

—John 6:30–31

"You do not believe although you have seen."

—John 6:36–37

Chapter One

She was standing on the Key Bridge walkway, arms atop the parapet, fidgeting, waiting, while homeward-bound traffic stuttered thickly behind her as drivers with everyday cares honked horns and bumpers nudged bumpers with scraping indifference. She had reached Mary Jo. Told her lies.

"Regan's fine. By the way, I've been thinking of another little dinner party. What was the name of that Jesuit psychiatrist again? I thought maybe I'd include him in the . . ."

Laughter floated up from below her: a blue-jeaned young couple in a rented canoe. With a quick, nervous gesture, she flicked ash from her cigarette, the last in her pack, and glanced up the walkway of the bridge toward the District. Someone hurrying toward her: khaki pants and blue sweater; not a priest; not him. She looked down at the river again, at her helplessness swirling in the wake of the bright red canoe. She could make out the name on its side: *Caprice*.

Footsteps: the man in the chinos and sweater coming closer, slowing down as he reached her. Peripherally, she saw him rest a forearm on the top of the parapet and quickly averted her gaze toward Virginia. Another autograph seeker? Or worse?

"Chris MacNeil?"

Flipping her cigarette butt into the river, Chris said coldly, "Keep moving, or, I swear, I'll yell for a cop!"

"Miss MacNeil? I'm Father Karras."

Chris started, then reddened, jerking swiftly around to the chipped, rugged face. "Oh my God! Oh, I'm so sorry!" She was tugging at her sunglasses, flustered, then immediately pushing them back as the sad, dark eyes probed hers.

"I should have told you that I wouldn't be in uniform."

The voice was cradling, stripping her of burden. The priest had clasped his hands together on the parapet, veined Michelangelos, sensitive and large. "I thought it would be much less conspicuous," he continued. "You seemed so concerned about keeping this quiet."

"Guess I should have been concerned about not making such an ass of myself," Chris retorted. "I just thought you were—"

"Human?" Karras finished with a faint, wry smile.

Chris appraised him, and then, nodding and returning the smile, she said, "Yeah. Yeah, I knew that the first time I saw you."

"When was that?"

"On the campus one day while we were filming. Got a cigarette, Father?"

Karras reached into the pocket of his shirt.

"Can you go a nonfilter?"

"Right now I'd smoke rope."

"On my allowance, I frequently do."

Smiling tightly, Chris nodded. "Yeah, right. Vow of poverty," she murmured as she slipped out a cigarette from the packet the priest was holding out to her. Karras reached into a trouser pocket for matches.

"A vow of poverty has its uses," he said.

"Oh yeah? Like what?"

"Makes rope taste better." Again, a half smile as he watched Chris's hand that was holding the cigarette. It was trembling, the cigarette wavering in quick, erratic jumps, and without pausing, he took it from her fingers, put it up to his mouth and, cupping his hands around the match, he lit the cigarette, puffed, and then gave it back to Chris, saying, "Awful lot of breeze from all these cars going by."

Chris looked at him appraisingly, with gratitude, and even with hope. She knew what he'd done. "Thanks, Father" she said, and then she watched as he lit up a Camel for himself. He forgot to cup his hands. As he exhaled, they each leaned an elbow on the parapet.

"Where are you from, Father Karras? I mean, originally."

"New York," he said.

"Me too. Wouldn't ever go back, though. Would you?"

Karras fought down the rise in his throat. "No, I wouldn't." He forced a little smile. "But I don't have to make those decisions."

Chris shook her head and looked aside. "God, I'm dumb," she said. "You're a priest. You have to go where they send you."

"That's right."

"How'd a shrink ever get to be a priest?"

He was anxious to know what the urgent problem was that she'd mentioned when she called him at the residence. She was feeling her way, he sensed—but toward what? He must not prod. It would come. "It's the other way around," he corrected her gently. "The Society—"

"Who?"

"The Society of Jesus. *Jesuit* is short for that."

"Oh, I see."

"The Society sent me through medical school and through psychiatric training."

"Where?"

"Oh, well, Harvard; Johns Hopkins. Places like that."

He was suddenly aware that he wanted to impress her. Why? he wondered; and immediately saw the answer in the slums of his boyhood; in the balconies of theaters on the Lower East Side. Little Dimmy with a movie star.

Chris nodded her head in approval. "Not bad," she said.

"We don't take vows of *mental* poverty."

She sensed an irritation; shrugged; turned front, facing out to the river. "Look, it's just that I don't know you, and . . ." She dragged on the cigarette, long and deep, and then exhaled, crushing out the butt on the parapet and then flipping it out to the river "You're a friend of Father Dyer's, that right?"

"Yes, I am."

"Pretty close?"

"Pretty close."

"Did he talk about the party?"

"At your house?"

"At my house."

"Yes, he said you seemed human."

She missed it; or ignored it. "Did he talk about my daughter?"

"No, I didn't know you had one."

"She's twelve. He didn't mention her?"

"No."

"He didn't tell you what she did?"

"He never mentioned her."

"Priests keep a pretty tight mouth, then; that right?"

"That depends," answered Karras.

"On what?"

"On the priest."

At the fringe of the Jesuit's awareness drifted a warning about women with neurotic attractions to priests, women who desired, unconsciously and under the guise of some other problem, to seduce the unattainable.

"Look, I mean like confession. You're not allowed to talk about it, right?"

"Yes, that's right."

"And outside of confession?" she asked him. "I mean, what if some . . ." Her hands were now agitated; fluttering. "I'm curious. I . . . No. No, I'd really like to know. I mean, what if a person, let's say, was a criminal, like maybe a murderer or something, you know? If he came to you for help, would you have to turn him in?"

Was she seeking instruction? Was she clearing off doubts in the way of conversion? There were people, Karras knew, who approached salvation as if it were at the end of a flimsy bridge overhanging an abyss. "If he came to me for spiritual help, I'd say, no," he answered.

"You wouldn't turn him in?"

"No, I wouldn't. But I'd try to persuade him to turn himself in."

"And how do you go about getting an exorcism?"

There was a pause while Karras stared.

"Beg pardon?" he said at last.

"If a person's possessed by some kind of a demon, how do you go about getting an exorcism?"

Karras looked off, took a breath, then looked back to her. "Oh, well, first you'd have to put him in a time machine and get him back to the sixteenth century."

Puzzled, Chris frowned. "What do you mean?"

"Well, it just doesn't happen anymore."

"Oh, really? Since when?"

"Since when? Since we learned about mental illness and schizophrenia and split personality; all those things that they taught me at Harvard."

"Are you kidding?"

Chris's voice had wavered, sounding helpless, confused, and Karras instantly regretted his flipness. Where had it come from? he wondered. It had leaped to his tongue unbidden.

"Many educated Catholics," he said in a gentler tone, "don't believe in the Devil anymore; and as far as possession is concerned, since the day I joined the Jesuits I've never met a priest who's ever in his life performed an exorcism. Not one."

"Oh, are you really a priest or from Central Casting?" Chris blurted with a suddenly bitter, disappointed sharpness. "I mean, what about all of those stories in the Bible about Christ driving out all those demons?"

Karras answered spontaneously with heat, "Look, if Christ had said those people who were supposedly possessed had schizophrenia, which I imagine they did, they would probably have crucified him three years earlier."

"Oh, really?" Chris put a shaking hand to her sunglasses, deepening her voice in an effort at control. "Well, it happens, Father Karras, that someone very close to me is probably possessed and needs an exorcism. Will you do it?"

To Karras, it suddenly seemed unreal: Key Bridge; motor traffic; across the river, the Hot Shoppe with frozen milk shakes and beside him a movie star asking for an exorcism. As he stared at her, groping for an answer, she slipped off her oversized dark sunglasses and Karras felt a wincing shock at the redness, at the desperate pleading in those haggard eyes. And suddenly realized that the woman was serious. "Father Karras, it's my daughter," she pleaded. "My *daughter!*"

"Then all the more reason," he said to her soothingly, "to forget about getting an exorcism and—"

"Why?" Chris suddenly burst out in a voice that was cracking and strident and distraught. "Tell me *why!* God, I don't under*stand!*"

Karras took hold of her wrist in an effort to calm her. "In the first place," he told her, "it could make things worse."

Incredulous, Chris scrunched up her face and said, *"Worse?"*

"Yes, worse. That's right. Because the ritual of exorcism is dangerously suggestive. It could implant the notion of possession where it didn't exist before, or if it did, it could tend to fortify it."

"But—"

"And secondly," Karras overrode her, "before the Catholic Church approves an exorcism, it conducts an investigation to see if it's warranted, and that takes time. In the meantime, your—"

"Couldn't you do it yourself?" Chris's lower lip was slightly trembling now, her eyes filling up with tears.

"Look, every priest has the power to exorcise, but he has to have Church approval, and frankly, it's rarely ever given, so—"

"Can't you even *look* at her?"

"Well, as a psychiatrist, yes, I could, but—"

"She needs a *priest!*" Chris cried out suddenly, her features contorted with anger and fear. "I've taken her to every goddamn, fucking doctor, psychiatrist in the world and they sent me to *you;* now you send me to *them?*"

"But your—"

"Jesus *Christ*, won't somebody *help me?*"

The heart-stopping shriek bolted raw above the river, sending startled flocks of birds shooting up into the air from its grassy banks with a sound of cawing and a thousand flapping wings. "Oh my God, someone help me!" Chris moaned as, sobbing convulsively, she crumpled to Karras's chest. "Oh, please help me! Please! Please, help!"

The Jesuit looked down at her, and then lifted up comforting hands to her head as the riders in traffic-locked automobiles glanced out windows to watch them with passing disinterest.

"It's all right," Karras told her. He wanted only to calm her; to stem her hysteria. *"My daughter?"* No, it was *Chris* who needed psychiatric help, he believed. "It's all right. I'll go see her," he told her. "I'll see her right now. Come on, let's go."

With that sense of unreality still lingering, Karras let her lead him to the house in silence and with thoughts of his next day's lecture at the Georgetown Medical School. He had yet to prepare his notes.

As they climbed the front stoop, Karras glanced at his watch. It was ten before six. He looked down the street at the Jesuit residence hall as he realized he would now miss dinner. "Father Karras?" The priest turned to look at Chris. About to turn her key in the front door lock, she had hesitated and turned to him. "Do you think you should be wearing your priest clothes?" she said.

Karras eyed her with a pity that he tried to conceal. Her face and her voice: how helplessly childlike they were. "Too dangerous," he told her.

"Okay."

Chris turned back and started opening the door, and it was then that Karras felt it: a chill, tugging warning. It scraped through his bloodstream like particles of ice.

"Father Karras?"

He looked up. Chris had entered.

For a hesitant moment the priest stood unmoving; then slowly and deliberately, as if he had made a decision to do so, he went forward, stepping into the house with an odd sense of ending.

Karras heard commotion. Upstairs. A deep, booming voice was thundering obscenities, threatening in anger and in hate and frustration. Taken aback, he turned to Chris with a look of wonderment. She was staring at him mutely. Then she moved on ahead. He followed her upstairs and along a hall to where Karl was standing with his head bent low over folded arms just opposite the door to Regan's bedroom. At this close range, the voice from the bedroom was so loud that it almost seemed amplified electronically. As Karl looked up at their approach, the priest saw bafflement and fright in his eyes as in an awed and cracking voice he said to Chris, "It wants no straps."

Chris turned to Karras. "I'll be back in a second," she told him, the words coming dully from a worn-out soul. Karras watched her as she turned and walked away down the hall and then into her bedroom. She left the door open behind her.

Karras turned his glance to Karl. The houseman was staring at him intently. "You are priest?" he asked.

Karras nodded, then looked quickly back to Regan's bedroom door. The raging voice had been abruptly displaced by the long, strident lowing of some animal that might have been a steer. Something prodding at Karras's hand. He looked down. "That's her," Chris was saying; "that's Regan." She was handing him a photograph and he took it. Young girl. Very pretty. Sweet smile.

"That was taken four months ago," Chris said dreamily. She took back the photo and motioned with her head at the bedroom door. "Now you go and take a look at her now." Chris leaned back against the wall beside Karl, and with her eyes cast down, her arms folded across her chest, she said hopelessly and quietly, "I'll wait here."

"Who's in there with her?" Karras asked.

Chris looked up at him, expressionless. "No one."

The priest held her haunted gaze and then turned with a frown to the bedroom door, and as he grasped the doorknob, the sounds from within abruptly ceased. In the ticking silence, Karras hesitated, then slowly entered the room, almost flinching backward at the pungent stench of moldering excrement that hit his face and his nostrils like a palpable blast. Reining in his revulsion, he closed the door and then his eyes locked, stunned, on the thing that was Regan, on the creature that was lying on its back on the bed, head propped against a pillow while eyes bulging wide in their hollow sockets shone with mad cunning and burning intelligence, with interest and with spite, as they fixed upon his; as they watched him intently, seething in a face shaped into a skeletal mask of unthinkable malevolence. Karras shifted his gaze to the tangled and thickly matted hair; to the wasted arms and legs and distended stomach jutting up so grotesquely; then back to the eyes: they were watching him . . . pinning him . . . shifting now to follow as he moved to a desk and chair near the large bay window. Karras fought to sound calm, even warm and friendly. "Hello, Regan," he said. He picked up the chair and took it over by the bed. "I'm a friend of your mother's," he said, "and she tells me that you're very, very sick." Karras sat down. "Do you think you'd like to tell me what's wrong?" he asked. "I'd like to help you."

Regan's eyes gleamed fiercely, unblinking, as a yellowish saliva dribbled down from a corner of her mouth to her chin, to her lips stretched taut into a feral grin of bow-mouthed mockery.

"Well, well, well," she gloated sardonically and hairs prickled up on the back of Karras's neck at a voice that was deep and thick with menace and power. "So it's you . . . they sent *you!*" she continued as if pleased. "Well, we've nothing to fear from you at all."

"Yes, that's right," Karras answered; "I'm your friend and I'd like to help you."

"You might loosen these straps, then," Regan croaked. She had tugged up her wrists so that now Karras noticed they were bound with a double set of leather restraining straps.

"Are the straps uncomfortable for you?"

"Extremely. They're a nuisance. An *infernal* nuisance."

The eyes glinted slyly with secret amusement.

Karras saw the scratch marks on Regan's face; the cuts on her lips where apparently she'd bitten them. "I'm afraid you might hurt yourself, Regan," he told her.

"I'm not Regan," she rumbled, still with that taut and hideous grin that Karras now guessed was her permanent expression. How incongruous the braces on her teeth looked, he thought. "Oh, I see," he said, nodding. "Well, then, maybe we should introduce ourselves. I'm Damien Karras. Who are you?"

"I'm the Devil!"

"Ah, good." Karras nodded approvingly. "Now we can talk."

"A little chat?"

"If you wish."

"Yes, I would like that," Regan said, drooling a little from a corner of her mouth. "However, you will find that I cannot talk freely while bound with these straps. As you know, I've spent much of my time in Rome and I'm accustomed to gesturing, Karras. Now then, kindly undo the straps."

What precocity of language and thought, reflected Karras. He leaned forward in his chair with a mixture of amazement and professional interest. "You say you're the Devil?" he asked.

"I assure you."

"Then why don't you just make the straps disappear?"

"Come, that's much too vulgar a display of power. After all, I'm a prince! 'The Prince of This World,' as some very strange person said of me once. Can't quite remember who." A low chuckle. Then, "I much prefer persuasion, Karras; togetherness; community involvement. Moreover, if I loosen the straps myself, I deny you the opportunity of performing a charitable act."

Incredible! thought Karras. "But a charitable act," he parried, "is a virtue and that's what the Devil would want to prevent; so in fact I'd be *helping* you now if I *didn't* undo the straps. Unless, of course"—Karras shrugged—"unless of course you really *aren't* the devil, and in that case I probably *would* undo them."

"How very foxy of you, Karras. If only dear Herod were here to enjoy this."

Karras stared with narrowed eyes and an even deeper interest. Was she punning on Christ's calling Herod "that fox"? "Which Herod?" he asked. "There were two. Are you talking about the King of Judea?"

"No, I am talking about the tetrarch of Galilee!" Regan shot back at Karras in a voice raised to blast him with scorching contempt; then abruptly she was grinning again as she quietly cajoled in that soft and sinister voice, "There, you see how these damnable straps have upset me? Undo them. Undo them and I'll tell you the future."

"Very tempting."

"My forte."

"But then how do I know you really *can* read the future?"

"Because I'm the Devil, you ass!"

"Yes, you say so, but you won't give me proof."

"You have no faith."

Karras stiffened. Paused. "No faith in *what?*"

"Why in *me*, my dear Karras; in *me!*" Something mocking and malicious danced hidden in those eyes. "All these proofs, all these signs in the sky!"

Karras barely had a grip on his composure as he answered, "Well, now, something very simple might do. For example, the Devil knows everything, correct?"

"No, in fact I know *almost* everything, Karras. There, you see? They keep saying that I'm proud. I am not. Now then, what are you up to, sly fox? Spit it out!"

"Well, I thought we might test the extent of your knowledge."

"Very well, then. How's this? The largest lake in South America," the Regan-thing japed, her eyes bulging with mocking glee, "is Lake Titicaca in Peru! Will that do it?"

"No, I'll have to ask something only the Devil would know."

"Ah, I see. Such as what?"

"Where is Regan?"

"She is here."

"Where is 'here'?"

"In the piglet."

"Let me see her."

"Why, Karras? Do you want to fuck her? Loose these straps and I will let you go at it!"

"I want to see if you're telling me the truth. Let me see her."

"Very succulent cunt," Regan leered, her furred and lolling tongue licking spittle across dry, cracked lips. "But a poor conversationalist, my friend. I strongly advise you to stay with me."

"Well, it's obvious you don't know where she is"—Karras shrugged—"so apparently you aren't the Devil."

"I *am!*" Regan bellowed with a sudden jerk forward, her face contorting with rage. Karras shivered as the terrifying voice boomed and crackled off the walls of the room. "I *am!*"

"Well, then, let me see Regan. That would prove it."

"There are much better ways! I will show you! I will read your mind!" the Regan creature seethed furiously. "Think of a number between one and one hundred!"

"No, that wouldn't prove a thing. I would have to see Regan."

Abruptly it chuckled, leaning back against the headboard.

"No, nothing would prove anything at all to you, Karras. That is why I love all reasonable men. How splendid! How splendid indeed! In the meantime, we shall try to keep you properly beguiled. After all, now, we would not wish to lose you."

"Who is 'we'?" Karras probed with a quick, alert interest.

"We are quite a little group in the piglet," came the answer. "Ah, yes, quite a little multitude. Later I may see about discreet introductions. In the meantime, I am suffering from a maddening itch that I cannot reach. Would you loosen one strap for a moment? Just one?"

"No, just tell me where it itches and I'll scratch it."

"Ah, sly, very sly!"

"Show me Regan and perhaps I'll undo one strap," offered Karras. "That's providing she's—"

Abruptly the priest flinched in shock as he found himself staring into eyes filled with terror and a mouth gaping wide in a soundless shriek for help; but then quickly the Regan identity vanished in a blurringly rapid remolding of features as, "For pity's sakes, won't you kindly remove these cunting straps?" asked a wheedling voice in a clipped British accent just before, in a flash, the demonic personality returned. "Couldjya help an old altar boy, Faddah?" it croaked, and then it threw back its head in wild and high-pitched laughter.

Stunned, Karras leaned back, as he felt the glacial hands at the back of his neck again, more palpable now, and more clearly something more than suggestion.

The Regan-thing broke off its laughter and fixed him with taunting eyes. "Feeling icy hands? Oh, incidentally, your mother is in here with us, Karras. Would you like to leave a message? I will see that she gets it." Mocking laughter. And then suddenly Karras was leaping out of his chair as he dodged a projectile stream of vomit. It caught a portion of his sweater and one of his hands.

His face drained of color, the priest looked down at the bed; at Regan cackling with glee as his hand dripped vomit onto the rug. "If that's true," he said numbly, "then you must know my mother's first name."

"Oh, I do."

"Well, what is it?"

The Regan-thing hissed at him, mad eyes gleaming, and the head gently undulating from side to side like a cobra's.

"What is it?" Karras repeated.

With her eyes rolling upward into their sockets, Regan lowed like a steer in an angry bellow that pierced the shutters and shivered through the glass of the large bay window. For a time Karras watched as the bellowing continued; then he looked at his hand and walked out of the room.

Chris pushed herself quickly away from the wall as she glanced with distress at the Jesuit's sweater. "What happened? Did she vomit?"

"Got a towel?" Karras asked her.

"There's a bathroom right there!" Chris said hurriedly, pointing at a hallway door. "Karl, go in and take a look at her!" she instructed over her shoulder as she followed the priest to the bathroom. "I'm so sorry!" she exclaimed.

The Jesuit moved to the washbasin.

"Have you got her on tranquilizers?" he asked.

Chris turned on the water taps and answered, "Yes, Librium. Here, take off that sweater and then you can wash."

"What dosage?" Karras asked as he tugged at the sweater with his clean left hand.

"Here, I'll help you." Chris pulled at the sweater from the bottom. "Well, today she's had four hundred milligrams, Father."

"Four *hundred?*"

Chris had the sweater pulled up to his chest. "Yeah, that's how we got her into those straps. It took all of us together to—"

"You gave your daughter four hundred milligrams *at once?*"

"She's so strong you can't believe it. Get your arms up, Father."

"Okay."

He raised them and Chris pulled the sweater up and off, pulled back the shower curtain and tossed the sweater into the bathtub. "I'll have Willie get it cleaned for you, Father." She dejectedly sat down on the edge of the bathtub and slipped a pink towel off a towel bar, her hand inadvertently covering the word *Regan* embroidered in navy blue script. "I'm so sorry," she said.

"Never mind. It doesn't matter." Karras unbuttoned the right sleeve of his starched white shirt and rolled it up, exposing a matting of fine brown hairs on a thickly muscled forearm as he asked, "Is she taking any nourishment at all?" He held his hand underneath the hot-water tap to rinse away the vomit.

"No, Father. Just Sustagen when she's been sleeping. But she ripped out the tubing."

"Ripped it out? When?"

"Today."

Disturbed, Karras soaped and rinsed his hands, and after a thoughtful pause he said gravely, "Your daughter really needs to be in a hospital."

Chris lowered her head. "I just can't do that, Father," she said in a soft, flat, toneless voice.

"Why can't you"

"I just can't," Chris repeated in a husky, dead whisper. "She . . . she's done something, Father, and I can't take the risk of someone else finding out. Not a doctor . . . not a nurse . . . not anyone."

Frowning, Karras turned off the water taps. *"What if a person, let's say, was a criminal."* Troubled, he looked down at the washbasin, gripping its sides. "Who's been giving her the Sustagen? the Librium? her medicines?"

"We are. Her doctor showed us how."

"You need prescriptions."

"Well, you could do some of that, couldn't you, Father?"

His thoughts now spinning, Karras turned to her, his hands upraised, as he met Chris's haunted, vanquished gaze. He nodded toward the towel in her hands, and said, "Please."

Chris stared at him blankly and said, "What?"

"The towel, please," Karras said softly.

"Oh, I'm sorry!" Very quickly, Chris fumbled it out to him, and as the Jesuit dried his hands, she asked him with a tightly searching expectancy, "So now, Father, what's it look like? Do you think she's possessed?"

"Look, how much do you know about possession?"

"Just a little that I've read and some things that some doctors told me."

"What doctors?"

"At Barringer Clinic."

"I see," said Karras, gently nodding his head. He had folded the towel and was carefully draping it back onto the towel bar as he asked, "Miss MacNeil, are you a Catholic?"

"No, I'm not."

"And your daughter?"

"Not her either."

"What religion, then?"

"None."

Karras stared at her speculatively.

"Why did you come to me, then?" he asked.

"Because I was desperate!" Chris blurted in a quavering voice.

"I thought you said psychiatrists advised you to come to me."

"Oh, I don't know *what* I was saying! I've been practically out of my head!"

Karras turned and, folding his arms and leaning his weight against the washbasin's white marble counter, he looked down at Chris and told her with a carefully tempered intensity, "Look, the only thing I care about is doing what's best for your daughter. But I'll tell you right now that if you're looking for an exorcism as an autosuggestive cure, you'd be much better off if you *had* Central Casting, Miss MacNeil, because Catholic Church authorities aren't going to buy it and you've wasted precious time."

Karras felt his hands trembling slightly.

What's wrong with me? he wondered. *What's happening?*

"Incidentally, it's *Mrs.* MacNeil," Chris corrected him tartly.

Karras gentled his tone. "My apologies. Look, whether it's a demon or a mental disorder, I'll do everything I possibly can to help your daughter. But I've got to have the truth, the whole truth. It's important. It's important for Regan. Mrs. MacNeil, right now I'm groping. I'm completely overwhelmed by what I've just seen and heard in your daughter's bedroom. Now why don't we both get out of this bathroom and go downstairs where we can talk." With a faint, warm smile of reassurance, Karras reached out his hand to help Chris up. "I could use a cup of coffee."

"I could use a 'Sea and Ski' on the rocks."

While Karl and Sharon looked after Regan, Karras and Chris sat in the study, she on the sofa and Karras in a chair beside the fireplace as Chris went through the history of Regan's illness, though she carefully withheld any mention of phenomena relating to Dennings. The priest listened, saying little: an occasional question, a nod or a frown, as Chris admitted that at first she'd considered an exorcism as shock treatment. "But now I don't know," she said. Shaking her head, she looked down at her freckled, clasped fingers subtly twitching in her lap. "I don't know." She lifted a helpless look to the priest. "What do *you* think, Father Karras?"

Lowering his head, the priest took in a breath, shook his head and said quietly, "I don't know, either. Compulsive behavior produced by guilt, perhaps, put together with split personality."

"What?" Chris looked appalled. "Father, how can you say that after all you've just seen up there!"

Karras looked up at her. "If you've seen as many patients in psychiatric wards as I have, you can say it very easily," he said. "Come on, now! Possession by demons? Okay, listen: Let's assume it's a fact and that it sometimes happens. But your daughter doesn't say she's a demon; she insists she's the *Devil himself*, and that's the same thing as saying you're Napoleon Bonaparte!"

"Then explain all those rappings and things."

"I haven't heard them."

"Well, they heard them at Barringer, Father, so it wasn't just here in the house."

"Maybe so, but we'd hardly need a devil to explain them."

"So explain them!"

"Well, psychokinesis, maybe."

"What?"

"You've heard of poltergeist phenomena, haven't you?"

"Ghosts throwing dishes and acting like assholes?"

"It's not that uncommon and usually happens around an emotionally disturbed adolescent. Apparently, extreme inner tension of the mind can sometimes trigger some unknown energy that seems to move objects around at a distance. But there's nothing supernatural about it. Same with Regan's abnormal strength—in pathology, that's common. Call it mind over matter, if you like, but in any case it happens outside of possession."

Chris looked away, slightly shaking her head. "Boy, isn't this beautiful?" she said with weary irony. "Here I am an atheist and here you are a priest and—"

"The best explanation for any phenomenon," Karras gently

cut in, "is always the simplest one available that accommodates all the facts."

"Oh, really?" Chris retorted, in her red-veined eyes a look of pleading and despair and confusion. "Well, maybe I'm dumb, Father Karras, but telling me some unknown gizmo in somebody's head throws dishes at a wall seems to me even dumber! So what *is* it? Can you tell me what it is? And what's 'split personality,' anyway? You *say* it. I *hear* it. What *is* it? Am I really that stupid? Will you tell me what it is in a way I can finally get it through my head?"

"Look, there's no one who pretends to understand it. All we know is that it happens, and anything beyond the phenomenon itself is just pure speculation. But think of it this way, if you like."

"Yeah, go ahead."

"The human brain contains something like seventeen billion cells, and when we look at them we see that they handle approximately a hundred million sensations that are bombarding your brain every second, and your brain not only integrates all of these messages, they do it efficiently—they do it without ever stumbling or getting in each other's way. Now then, how could they do that without some form of communication? Well, they couldn't, so apparently each of these cells has a consciousness, maybe, of its own. Are you with me?"

Chris nodded. "Yeah, a little."

"Good. Now imagine that the human body is a gigantic ocean liner, and that all of your brain cells are the crew. Now one of these crew cells is up on the bridge. He's the captain. But he never knows *precisely* what the rest of the crew belowdecks is doing; all he knows is that the ship keeps running smoothly and the job's getting done. Now the captain is you—it's your waking consciousness. And what happens in dual personality—*maybe*—

is that one of those crew cells down belowdecks comes up on the bridge and takes over command of the ship. In other words, mutiny. Does that help you understand it?"

Chris was staring in unblinking incredulity. "Father, that's so far out of sight that I think it's almost easier to believe in the flipping Devil!"

"I—"

"Look, I don't know about all of these theories and stuff," Chris overrode him in a low, intense voice; "but I'll tell you something, Father: you show me Regan's identical twin—same face, same voice, same smell, same everything down to the way she dots her *i's*—and still I'd know in a second that it wasn't really her! I'd just know it, I'd know it in my gut, and I'm telling you *that thing upstairs is not my daughter!* Now you tell me what to do," she said, her voice slowly rising and quivering with tightly held emotion. "You tell me that you know for a fact there's nothing wrong with my daughter except in her head; that you know for a *fact* that she doesn't need an exorcism and that you're absolutely sure it wouldn't help her! Go ahead! You tell me that, Father! *You tell me!*"

At the end, it was almost a scream.

Karras looked aside, and for long, pensive seconds, he was still. Then he turned a probing glance back to Chris. "Does Regan have a low-pitched voice?" he asked her quietly. "I mean, normally."

"No. In fact, I'd say it's very light."

"Would you consider her precocious?"

"Not at all."

"Her IQ?"

"About average."

"Reading habits?"

"Nancy Drew and comic books, mostly."

"And her style of speech right now: how much different would you say it is from normal?"

"Completely. She's never used half of those words."

"I don't mean the *content* of her speech; I mean the *style*."

"Style?"

"The way she puts words together."

Chris's eyebrows lowered. "I'm still not really sure what you mean."

"Do you have any letters she's written? Compositions? A recording of her voice would be—"

"Yes. Yes, there's a tape of her talking to her father. She was making it to send to him as a letter but she never got it finished. You want it?"

"Yes, I do. And I'll also need her medical records, especially the file from Barringer."

Chris looked aside and shook her head. "Oh, Father, I've *been* that route and I—"

"Yes. Yes, I know, but I'll have to see the records for myself."

"So you're still against an exorcism?"

"No. I'm only against the chance of doing your daughter more harm than good."

"But you're talking now strictly as a psychiatrist, right?"

"No, I'm talking now also as a priest. If I go to the Chancery Office, or wherever it is I have to go to get permission for an exorcism, the first thing I'd have to have is a pretty substantial indication that your daughter's condition isn't a purely psychiatric problem, plus evidence that the Church would accept as signs of possession."

"Like what?"

"I don't know. I'll have to go and look it up."

"Are you kidding? I thought you were supposed to be an expert."

"There *aren't* any experts. You probably know more about

demonic possession right now than most priests. Now, how soon can you get me those Barringer records?"

"I'll charter a plane if I have to!"

"And that tape?"

Chris stood up. "I'll go see if I can find it."

"And just one other thing."

"What?"

"That book that you mentioned with the section on possession: do you think you can remember now if Regan might have read it *prior* to the onset of the illness?"

Looking down, Chris concentrated. "Gee, I seem to remember her reading *some*thing the day before the shi—before the trouble really started, but I really can't be sure. But she did read it, I think. I mean, I'm sure. *Pretty* sure."

"I'd like to see it."

Chris started away. "Sure, I'll get it for you, Father. And the tape. It's in the basement, I think. I'll go and look."

Karras nodded absently, staring at a pattern in an Oriental area rug, and then after many minutes he got up and walked slowly to the entry hall, where, with his hands in the pockets of his trousers, he stood motionless in the darkness as if in some other dimension as he listened to the grunting of a pig from upstairs, then the yelping of a jackal, and then hiccupping and snakelike hissing.

"Oh, you're there! I went looking in the study."

Karras turned to see Chris flicking on the entry hall lights. "Are you leaving?" she asked as she came forward with the witchcraft book and Regan's tape-recorded letter to her father.

"Yes, I've got to. I've got a lecture to prepare for tomorrow."

"Oh? Where?"

"At the med school," Karras answered, accepting the book and the tape from Chris's hands. "I'll try to get by here sometime tomorrow afternoon or evening. In the meantime, if anything urgent develops, you be sure that you call me, no matter what time. I'll leave word at the switchboard to let you ring through. Listen, how are you fixed for medication?"

"We're okay. They're all on refillable prescriptions."

"You won't call your doctor in again?"

The actress lowered her head. "I can't," she said barely above a whisper; "I just can't."

"You know, I'm not a GP," Karras cautioned.

"It's okay."

Chris still hadn't looked up and Karras studied her intently and with concern. He could almost hear her anxiety pulsing and throbbing. "Well, now, sooner or later," he said to her gently, "I'm going to have to tell one of my superiors what I'm up to, most especially if I'm going to be coming by here at various unusual hours of the night."

Chris looked up at him, worriedly frowning.

"Do you have to? I mean, tell them?"

"Well, if I don't, don't you think it might look a bit odd?"

Chris looked down again, nodding. "Yeah, I see what you mean," she said wanly.

"Do you mind? I'll tell them only what I have to. And don't worry, it won't get around."

She lifted a helpless, tormented face to the strong, sad eyes. Saw the strength. Saw the pain. "Okay," she said weakly.

She trusted the pain.

"We'll be talking," Karras told her.

He started outside, but then hung in the doorway, head down with the back of a fist to his lips, as if thinking; and then he looked up at Chris. "Did your daughter know a priest was coming over here tonight?"

"No, nobody knew but me."

"Did you know that my mother had died just recently?"

"Yes. I'm very sorry."

"Is Regan aware of it?"

"Why?"

"Is she aware of it?"

"No, not at all. Why do you ask?"

Karras shrugged. "It's not important," he said; "I just wondered." He examined Chris's features with a faint look of worry. "Are you getting any sleep?"

"Oh, well, some."

"Get pills, then. Are you taking any Librium?"

"Yes."

"How much?"

"Ten milligrams, twice a day."

"Make it twenty. In the meantime, try to keep away from your daughter. The more you're exposed to her present behavior, the greater the chance of some permanent damage being done to your feelings about her. Stay clear. And slow down. You'd be no help to Regan with a nervous breakdown."

Her head and eyes lowered, Chris nodded despondently.

"Now go to bed," Karras told her. "Will you please go to bed right now?"

"Yeah, okay," Chris said softly; "I promise." She looked up at him with warmth and the trace of a smile. "Good night, Father Karras. And thanks. Thanks so much."

For a moment Karras studied her clinically again, then said, "Okay, now, good night," and then, turning, he moved quickly away. Chris stood watching from the doorway. As he crossed the street, it occurred to her that he'd probably missed his dinner, and then she worried that he might be cold: he was rolling his shirt sleeve down. As he was passing the 1789 Restaurant, he dropped something, possibly the witchcraft book or the tape of Regan's voice. He stooped to retrieve it, and at the corner of Thirty-Sixth Street and P, he turned left and vanished from her sight. Chris abruptly was aware of a feeling of lightness.

She didn't see Kinderman sitting alone in an unmarked car.

Half an hour later, Damien Karras hurried back to his room in the Jesuit residence hall with a number of books and periodicals taken from the shelves of the Georgetown campus library. Hastily, he dumped them on top of his desk and then rummaged through drawers for a package of cigarettes, and then, finding a half-empty pack of stale Camels, he lit one, drew on it deeply and held the smoke in his lungs as his mind went to Regan. Hysteria, he thought; that had to be it. He exhaled the smoke, hooked his thumbs in his belt and looked down at the books. He had Oesterreich's *Possession;* Huxley's *The Devils of Loudun; Parapraxis in the Haizman Case of Sigmund Freud;* McCasland's *Demon Possession and Exorcism in Early Christianity in the Light of Modern Views of Mental Illness;* and extracts from psychiatric journals of Freud's "A Neurosis of Demoniacal Possession in the 17th Century," and "The Demonology of Modern Psychiatry."

"Couldjya help an old altar boy, Faddah?"

The Jesuit felt at his brow, and then looked at a sticky sweat on his fingers. Then he noticed that he'd left his door open. He crossed the room and closed it, and then went to a shelf for his red-bound copy of *The Roman Ritual*, a compendium of rites and prayers. Clamping the cigarette between his lips, he squinted through smoke as he turned to the "General Rules" for exorcists, looking for the signs of demonic possession. He first skimmed it and then started to read more slowly:

> . . . The exorcist should not believe too readily that a person is possessed by an evil spirit; but he ought to ascertain the signs by which a person possessed can be

> distinguished from one who is suffering from some illness, especially one of a psychological nature. Signs of possession may be the following: ability to speak with some facility in a strange language or to understand it when spoken by another; the faculty of divulging future and hidden events; display of powers which are beyond the subject's age and natural condition; and various other conditions which, when taken together as a whole, build up the evidence.

For a time Karras pondered, then he leaned against the bookshelf and read the remainder of the instructions. When he had finished, he found himself glancing back up at instruction number 8:

> Some reveal a crime which has been committed.

A light knocking at the door. "Damien?"

Karras looked up and said, "Come in."

It was Dyer. "Hey, Chris MacNeil has been trying to reach you," he said as he entered the room. "Did she ever get hold of you?"

"When? You mean, tonight?"

"No, this early afternoon."

"Oh, yes, Joe. Thanks. Yes, I spoke to her."

"Good. I just wanted to be sure you got the message."

The pixieish priest was prowling the room as if searching for something. "What do you need, Joe?" Karras asked.

"Got any lemon drops? I've looked all through the hall but nobody's got any and *man* do I crave one, maybe two," Dyer broodingly uttered, still prowling. "I once spent a year hearing children's confessions, and I wound up a lemon-drop junkie.

The little shitheads keep *breathing* it on you along with all that pot and between the two I've come to think it's addictive." Dyer lifted the lid of a pipe-tobacco humidor half filled with pistachio nuts. "What are these?" he asked. "Dead Mexican jumping beans?"

Karras turned to his bookshelves, looking for a title. "Listen, Joe, I'm sort of busy right now and—"

"Hey, isn't that Chris really nice?" interrupted Dyer, flopping down on Karras's cot and stretching out full-length with his hands clasped comfortably behind his head. "Neat lady. Have you met her? I mean, seen her in person?"

"We've talked," answered Karras as he plucked out a green-bound volume titled *Satan*, a collection of articles and Catholic position papers by various French theologians. He carried it back with him toward his desk. "Now then—"

"Plain. Down-to-earth. Unaffected," Dyer ruminated obliviously while staring up at the room's high ceiling. "She can help us with my plan for when we both quit the priesthood."

Karras looked at Dyer sharply. "*Who's* quitting the priesthood?"

"Gays. In droves. Basic black has gone out."

Karras shook his head in bemused disapproval as he set down the books on his desk. "Hey, come on, Joe," Karras chided him, "take it to some lounge act in Vegas. Come on, scoot! I've got a lecture to prepare for tomorrow."

"First we go to Chris MacNeil," the young priest persisted, "with this notion that I've got for a screenplay based on the life of Saint Ignatius Loyola that for now I'm calling *Brave Jesuits Marching.*"

Tamping out his cigarette in an ashtray, Karras lifted his head to Dyer with a scowl. "Would you get your ass out of here, Joe? I've got some heavy work to do."

"So who's stopping you?"

"You!" Karras had started to unbutton his shirt. "I'm going to jump in the shower and when I come back in here I expect you to be gone."

"Oh, well," grumbled Dyer reluctantly as he rose and swung his legs around so that he was sitting on the side of the bed. "Didn't see you at dinner, by the way. Where'd you eat?"

"I didn't."

"That's foolish. Why diet when you only wear frocks?"

"Is there a tape recorder here in the hall?"

"There isn't even a lemon drop here in the hall. Use the language lab."

"Who's got a key? Father President?"

"No. Father Janitor. You need it tonight?"

"Yes, I do," Karras answered as he draped his shirt on the back of the desk chair. "Where do I find him?"

"Want me to get it for you, Damien?"

"Would you, Joe? I'm really in a bind."

Dyer stood up.

"No sweat!"

Karras showered and then dressed in a T-shirt and trousers. Sitting down to his desk, he discovered a carton of Camel nonfilters, and beside it a key that was labeled LANGUAGE LAB and another tagged REFECTORY REFRIGERATOR. Appended to the latter was a note: *Better you than the rats and Dominican cat burglars.* Karras smiled at the signature: *The Lemon Drop Kid.* He put the note aside, then unfastened his wristwatch and placed it in front of him on the desk. The time was 10:58 P.M.

He read. First, Freud; then McCasland; parts of *Satan*; parts of Oesterreich's exhaustive study, and at a little after 4 A.M., he had finished and was rubbing at his face and at his eyes: they were smarting and smoke was hanging thick in the air while the ashtray on Karras's desk was mounded high with ashes and the twisted butts of cigarettes. He stood up and walked wearily to a window, slid it open, gulped in the coolness of moist early morning air and then stood there thinking about Regan. Yes, she had the physical syndrome of possession. About that he had no doubt. In case after case, irrespective of geography or period of history, the symptoms of possession were substantially a constant. Some of them Regan had not evidenced as yet: stigmata or the desire for repugnant foods, or insensitivity to pain as well as frequently loud and irrepressible hiccupping; but some others she had clearly manifested: the involuntary motor excitement; foul breath; furred tongue; the wasting away of the bodily frame; the distended stomach; the irritations of the skin and mucous membrane; and most significantly present were the basic symptoms of the hard core of cases that Oesterreich had characterized as "genuine" possession: the striking change in the voice and in the features, plus the manifestation of a new personality.

Through the window, Karras stared darkly up the street. Through the branches of trees he could see the MacNeil house and the large bay window of Regan's bedroom. From his readings he had learned that when possession was voluntary, as with mediums, the new personality was often benign. *Like Tia*, brooded Karras, the spirit of a woman who'd possessed a man, a sculptor, intermittently and for only an hour or so at a time, until a friend of the sculptor fell desperately in love with Tia and pleaded with the sculptor to permit her to permanently remain in possession of his body. *But in Regan, there's no Tia*, the priest reflected grimly, for the seemingly "invading personality" was malevolent and typical of cases of demonic possession where the new personality sought the destruction of the body of its host.

And frequently achieved it.

Moodily the Jesuit walked back to his desk, picked up a

package of cigarettes and lit one. *So okay, she's got the physical syndrome of demonic possession. Now how do you cure it?* He fanned out the match. *That depends on what caused it.* He sat on the edge of his desk and reflected on the case of the nuns at the convent of Lille in early-seventeenth-century France. Allegedly possessed, they had "confessed" to their exorcists that while helpless in the state of possession, they had regularly attended Satanic orgies at which they had varied their erotic fare: Mondays and Tuesdays, heterosexual copulation; Thursdays, sodomy, fellatio and cunnilingus with homosexual partners; Saturday, bestiality with domestic animals and dragons. And *dragons?* The Jesuit ruefully shook his head. As with Lille, he thought the causes of many possessions were a mixture of fraud and mythomania, with still others caused by mental illness: paranoia; schizophrenia; neurasthenia; psychasthenia; and this was the reason, he knew, that the Church had for years recommended that the exorcist work with a psychiatrist or neurologist present during the rite. Yet not every possession had a cause so clear. Many had led Oesterreich to characterize possession as a separate disorder all its own; to dismiss the explanatory "split personality" label of psychiatry as no more than an equally occult substitution for the concepts "demon" and "spirit of the dead."

Karras rubbed the side of an index finger in the crease beside his nose. The indications from Barringer, Chris had told him, were that Regan's disorder might be caused by suggestion; by something that was somehow related to hysteria. And Karras thought it likely so. He believed the majority of the cases he had studied had been caused by precisely these two factors. *For one thing, it mostly hits women. For another, all those outbreaks of possession epidemics. And then those exorcists . . .* Karras frowned. The exorcists themselves at times became the victims of possession, as had happened in 1634 at the Ursuline Convent of nuns at

Loudun, France. Of the four Jesuit exorcists sent there to deal with an epidemic of possession, three—Fathers Lucas, Lactance and Tranquille—not only became seemingly possessed, but died soon after of apparent cardiac arrest caused by unrelenting hyper-psychomotor activity—the constant cursing and bellowing in rage, the unceasing fits of thrashing about in their beds—while the fourth, Père Surin, who at the time of the possessions was thirty-three years of age and one of Europe's foremost intellectuals, became insane and was sequestered in a mental institution for the subsequent twenty-five years of his life. Karras broodily nodded. If Regan's disorder was rooted in hysteria and the onset of the symptoms of possession was the product of suggestion, then the only likely source of the suggestion was the chapter on possession in the witchcraft book. He pored over its pages. Had Regan read it? Were there striking similarities between any of its details and Regan's behavior? He found some correlations:

. . . The case of an eight-year-old girl who was described in the chapter as "bellowing like a bull in a thunderous, deep bass voice." *Regan lowing like a steer.*

. . . The case of Helene Smith, who'd been treated by the great psychologist Flournoy; his description of the changing of her voice and her features with "lightning rapidity" into those of a variety of personalities. *She did that with me. The personality who spoke with a British accent. Quick change. Instantaneous.*

. . . A case in South Africa, reported firsthand by the noted ethnologist Junod; his description of a woman who'd vanished from her dwelling one night to be found on the following morning "tied to the top" of a very tall tree by "fine lianas," and then afterward "gliding down the tree, head down, while hissing and rapidly flicking her tongue in and out like a snake. She hung there suspended, for a time, and proceeded to speak in a language that no one had ever heard." *Regan gliding like a snake when she was following Sharon. The gibberish. An attempt at an "unknown language"?*

. . . The case of Joseph and Thiebaut Burner, aged eight and ten; a description of them "lying on their backs and suddenly whirling like tops with the utmost rapidity." *Sounds either totally made up or greatly exaggerated, but pretty close to Regan whirling like a dervish.*

There were other similarities, still other reasons for suspecting suggestion: a mention of abnormal strength and obscenity of speech, plus the accounts of possession in the gospels, which perhaps were the basis, speculated Karras, of the curiously religious content of Regan's ravings at the Barringer Clinic. Moreover, in the chapter there was mention of the onset of possession in stages: ". . . The first, infestation, consists of an attack through the victim's surroundings: noises, odors, the displacement of objects without visible cause; and the second, obsession, is a personal attack on the subject designed to instill terror through the kind of injury that a person might inflict on another through blows and kicks." *The rappings. The flingings. The attacks by Captain Howdy.*

All right, maybe . . . maybe she read it, Karras thought. But he wasn't convinced. *No, not at all!* And even Chris. She had seemed so uncertain about it.

Karras walked to the window again. *What's the answer, then? Genuine possession? A demon?* He looked down and shook his head. *Oh, come on! No way!* But paranormal happenings? *Sure. Why not?* Too many competent observers had reported them. Doctors. Psychiatrists. Men like Junod. *But the problem is how do you* interpret *the phenomena?* He thought back to Oesterreich's mention of a shaman of the Altai in Siberia who had deliberately invited possession as a means of performing a "magical act." Examined in a clinic just prior to performing the act of levitation, his pulse rate had spurted to one hundred, and then, afterward, leaped to an amazing two hundred while there were also marked changes in his bodily temperature and respiration. *So his paranormal action was tied to physiology! It was caused by some bodily energy or force!* But as proof of possession, Karras had learned, the Church wanted clear and exterior verifiable phenomena that suggested . . . He'd forgotten the wording, but tracing a finger down the page of the *Satan* book lying on his desk, Karras found it: ". . . verifiable exterior phenomena which suggest the idea that they are due to the extraordinary intervention of an intelligent cause other than man." Was that the case with the shaman? *No, not necessarily. And what of Regan? Is that the case with her?*

Karras turned to a passage he had bracketed in pencil in his copy of *The Roman Ritual:* "The exorcist will simply be careful that none of the patient's manifestations are left unaccounted for." Karras thoughtfully nodded. *Okay, then. Let's see.* Pacing, he ran through the manifestations of Regan's disorder along with their possible explanations. He ticked them off mentally, one by one:

The startling change in Regan's features.

Partly her illness and partly undernourishment, although mostly, he concluded, it was due to physiognomy being an expression of one's psychic constitution.

The startling change in Regan's voice.

He had yet to hear her "real" voice, Karras thought. And even if that had been light, as reported by her mother, constant shrieking would thicken the vocal cords with a consequent deepening of the voice, the only problem here being the unexplained booming volume of that voice, for even with a thickening of the cords this would seem to be physiologically impossible. And yet, he considered, in states of anxiety or pathology, displays of paranormal strength in excess of muscular potential were known to be a commonplace. Might not vocal cords and voice box be subject to the same mysterious effect?

Regan's suddenly extended vocabulary and knowledge.

Cryptomnesia: buried recollections of words and data she had once been exposed to, even in infancy, perhaps. In somnambulists—and frequently in people at the point of death—the buried data often came to the surface with almost photographic fidelity.

Regan's recognition of him as a priest.

A good guess. If she *had* read the chapter on possession, she might have expected a visit by a priest. And according to Jung, the unconscious awareness and sensitivity of hysterical patients could sometimes be fifty times greater than normal, which Jung thought accounted for seemingly authentic "thought-reading" via table-tapping by mediums, for what the medium's unconscious was actually "reading" were the tremors and vibrations created in the table by the hands of the person whose thoughts were supposedly being read. The tremors formed a pattern of letters or numbers. Thus Regan might conceivably have "read" his identity merely from his manner or even from the scent of holy oils on his hands.

Regan's knowledge of the death of his mother.

Another good guess. He was forty-six.

"Couldjya help an old altar boy, Faddah?"

Textbooks in use in Catholic seminaries accepted telepathy as both a reality and a natural phenomenon.

Regan's precocity of intellect.

This was by far the most difficult of all to explain. But in the course of personally observing a case of multiple personality involving alleged occult phenomena, the psychiatrist Jung had concluded that in states of hysterical somnambulism not only were unconscious perceptions of the senses heightened, but also the functioning of the intellect, for the new personality in the case in question seemed clearly more intelligent than the first. And yet did merely reporting the phenomenon explain it?

He abruptly stopped pacing and hovered by his desk, brought up short, as it suddenly dawned upon him that Regan's pun on Herod was even more complicated than at first it had appeared, for when the Pharisees told Christ of Herod's threats, the Jesuit remembered, Christ had answered: "Go and tell that fox that I cast out devils!"

Karras glanced at the tape of Regan's voice, and then wearily sat down at the desk, where he lit another cigarette and blew out a ragged cone of bluish-gray smoke as he thought once again of the Burner boys and of the case of the eight-year-old girl who had manifested symptoms of full-blown possession. What book had *this* girl read that had enabled her unconscious mind to simulate the symptoms of possession to such perfection? And how did the unconscious of victims in China communicate the symptoms to the various unconscious minds of people possessed in Siberia, in Germany, in Africa and everywhere else in every culture and period of time, so that the symptoms were always the same?

"Incidentally, your mother is in here with us, Karras."

The Jesuit was staring straight ahead, unseeing, wisps of smoke from the cigarette held between his fingers wafting up into life and then instant death like mistaken recognitions and one's memory of dreams. He looked down at the left-hand bottom drawer of his desk, holding silent and still for several moments before at last leaning over, pulling open the drawer and extracting a faded English language exercise book for an adult education course. His mother's. He set it on the desk, waited and then thumbed through the pages with a tender care. At first letters of the alphabet, over and over. Then simple exercises:

LESSON VI
MY COMPLETE ADDRESS

Between the pages, an attempt at a letter:

Dear Djmmy,
I have been waiting

Then another beginning. Incomplete. He looked away. Saw her eyes at the window . . . waiting . . .

" 'Domine, non sum dignus.' "

The eyes became Regan's.

" 'Speak but the word . . .' "

Karras glanced again at the tape of Regan's voice.

He left the room and took the tape to a campus language lab, found a tape recorder and sat down, carefully threaded the tape to an empty reel, clamped on earphones, turned a switch to the on position and then, exhausted and intense, he leaned forward and listened. For a time, only tape hiss. Squeaking of the mechanism. Suddenly, a thumping sound of activation. Noises. "Hello?" Then a whining feedback. Chris MacNeil, her tone hushed, in the background: "Not so close to the microphone, honey. Hold it back." "Like this?" "No, more." "Like this?" "Yeah, okay. Go ahead now, just talk." Giggling. The microphone bumping a table. Then the sweet, clear voice of Regan MacNeil:

"Hello, Daddy? This is me. Ummm . . ." Giggling; then a whispered aside: "Mom, I can't tell what to say!" "Oh, just tell him how you are, honey. Tell about all of the things you've been doing." More giggling. "Umm, Daddy . . . Well, ya see . . . I mean, I hope you can *hear* me okay, and, umm—well, now, let's see. Umm, well, first we're— No, wait! See, first we're in Washington, Daddy, ya know? It's where the president lives, and this house—ya know, Daddy?—it's— Darn! Daddy, wait, now; I better start over. See, Daddy, there's . . ."

Karras heard the rest only dimly and as if from afar and through the roaring of blood in his ears, as through his being there swelled an overwhelming intuition:

The thing that I saw in that room wasn't Regan!

Karras returned to the Jesuit residence hall, where he found an unoccupied cubicle and said his Mass before the early morning rush. As he lifted the Host in consecration, it trembled in his fingers with a hope that he dared not hope, that he fought with every particle and fiber of his will. "'For this—is—My Body,'" he intoned with a whispered intensity.

No, it's bread! It's nothing but bread!

He dared not love again and lose. That loss was too great, that pain too keen. The cause of his skepticism and his doubts, his attempts to eliminate natural causes in the case of Regan's seeming possession, was the fiery intensity of his yearning to be able to believe. He bowed his head and placed the consecrated Host in his mouth, where in a moment it would stick in the dryness of his throat. And of his faith.

After Mass, he skipped breakfast, making notes for his lecture, then met with his class at the Georgetown University Medical School, where he managed to thread hoarsely through the ill-prepared lecture: ". . . and in considering the symptoms of manic mood disorders, you will . . ."

"Daddy, this is me . . . this is me . . ."

But who was "me"?

Karras dismissed the class early and returned to his room,

where he immediately sat at his desk and intently reexamined the Church's position on the paranormal signs of demonic possession. *Was I being too hard-nosed?* he wondered. He scrutinized the high points in *Satan:* "Telepathy . . . natural phenomenon . . . even telekinesis, the movement of objects from a distance . . . our forefathers . . . science . . . nowadays we must be more cautious, the seeming paranormal evidence notwithstanding." As he came to what followed, Karras slowed down the pace of his reading: "All conversations held with the patient must be carefully analyzed, for if they present the same system of association of ideas and of logicogrammatical habits that he exhibits in his normal state, the possession must then be held suspect."

Karras gently shook his head. *Doesn't cut it.* He glanced to the plate on the facing page. A demon. His gaze flicked down idly to the caption: "Pazuzu." Karras shut his eyes and envisioned the death of the exorcist, Father Tranquille: the final agonies: the bellowing and the hissing and the vomiting, the hurlings to the ground from his bed by his "demons," who were furious because soon he would be dead and beyond their torment. *And then Lucas! My God! Father Lucas!* Lucas kneeling at the dying Tranquille's bedside, praying, and, at the moment of his death, Lucas instantly assuming the identity of Tranquille's demons and viciously kicking at the still-warm corpse, at the shattered, clawed body strongly reeking of excrement and vomit, while four strong men were attempting to restrain him, for he did not stop, it was reported, until the corpse had been carried from the room. Could it be? wondered Karras. Could the only hope for Regan be the ritual of exorcism? Must he open up that locker of aches? He could not shake it or leave it untested. He must know. And yet how? Karras opened his eyes. ". . . conversations with the patient must be carefully . . ." Yes. Yes, why not? If discovery that Regan's speech patterns and that of the "demon" turned out to be markedly different, that would leave possession open as a possibility, whereas if the patterns were the same, it would have to be ruled out.

Karras stood up and paced the room. *What else? What else? Something quick. She—Wait a minute!* Karras stopped in his tracks, staring down in thought. *That chapter in the book on witchcraft. Had it mentioned . . . ? Yes! Yes, it had!* It had stated that demons invariably reacted with fury when confronted with the consecrated Host or with holy relics or even . . . Karras lifted his head and stared ahead with a sudden realization: *And with holy water! Right! That could nail it one way or the other!* He feverishly rummaged through his black valise. He was looking for a holy-water vial.

Willie admitted him to the house, and in the entry he glanced up toward Regan's bedroom. Shouts. Obscenities. And yet not in the deep, coarse voice of the demon. Much lighter. Raspy. A broad British . . . *Yes!* It was the manifestation that had fleetingly appeared when Karras had last seen Regan.

Karras looked at a waiting Willie. She was staring in puzzlement at the round Roman collar, at the priestly robes.

"Where's Mrs. MacNeil, please?"

Willie motioned him upstairs.

"Thank you."

Karras moved to the staircase. Climbed. Saw Chris in the hall. She was sitting in a chair near Regan's bedroom, head lowered, her arms folded across her chest. As the Jesuit approached, she heard the swishing of his robes, turned and saw him and quickly stood up. "Hello, Father."

Karras frowned. There were bluish sacs beneath her eyes. "Did you sleep?" he asked with concern.

"Oh, a little."

Karras shook his head in admonishment. "Chris."

"Well, I couldn't," Chris told him, motioning with her head at the door to Regan's bedroom. "She's been doing that all night."

"Any vomiting?"

"No." Chris took hold of the sleeve of his cassock as if to lead him away. "C'mon, let's go downstairs where we can—"

"No, I'd like to see her," Karras said firmly.

"Right now?"

Something's wrong here, Karras reflected. Chris looked tense. Afraid. "Why not?" he asked.

She glanced furtively at Regan's bedroom door. From within shrieked the hoarse, mad British voice: "Damned Naa-zi! Nazi bastard!" Chris looked down and aside. "Go ahead," she said softly. "Go on in."

"Got a tape recorder here in the house? You know, a little one; a portable?" asked Karras.

Chris looked up. "Yeah, we do, Father. Why?"

"Could you have it brought up to the room with a blank reel of tape, please?"

Abruptly, Chris frowned with incipient alarm. "What for? Hey, wait a minute, now. You mean, you want to tape Regan?"

"It's important."

"No way, Father! Absolutely not!"

"Look, I need to make comparisons of patterns of speech," Karras said to her earnestly. "It could prove to the Church authorities that your daughter is really possessed!"

They both turned to the suddenly loud sound of an excoriating stream of obscenities directed at Karl as the houseman opened Regan's bedroom door and emerged with a laundry sack filled with soiled diapers and bedding. His face ashen, he closed the door behind him, muting the continuing tirade.

"Get a fresh one on her, Karl?" Chris asked.

The manservant's fearful glance went from Karras, then to Chris. "They are on," he said tersely. He turned and walked quickly down the hallway to the staircase. Chris listened to his thumping, quick steps going down, and when the sounds had dwindled into silence, Chris turned to Karras, and with her shoulders slumping, looking downcast, she said quietly and submissively, "Okay, Father. I'll have it sent up."

And abruptly she was hurrying away down the hall.

Karras watched her. What was she hiding? he wondered. Something. Then noticing the sudden silence within, he moved to the bedroom door, opened it, entered, closed the door behind him quietly, and turned front. And stared. At the horror; at the emaciated, skeletal thing on the bed that was watching intently with mocking eyes that were filled with cunning and with hate and, most unsettling of all, with a posture of towering authority.

Karras moved slowly to the foot of the bed, where he stopped and then listened to the quiet rumbling of diarrhetic voiding into plastic pants.

"Why, hello, Karras!" Regan greeted him cordially.

"Hello," the priest answered calmly. "Tell me, how are you feeling?"

"At the moment, very happy to see you. Yes. Very glad." And now a long, furred tongue lolled out of the mouth while the eyes appraised Karras with naked insolence. "Flying your colors, I see. Very good." Another rumbling. "You don't mind a bit of stink, do you, Karras?"

"Not at all."

"What a liar!"

"Does lying bother you?"

"Mildly."

"But the Devil *likes* liars."

"Only good ones, my dear Karras; only good ones. Moreover, who told you I'm the Devil?"

"Didn't *you?*"

"Oh, I might have. I might. I'm not well. By the way, did you believe me?"

"Oh, I did."

"Then my apologies in case I misled you. In fact, I'm just a poor struggling demon. *A* devil. A subtle distinction, but one not entirely lost upon Our Father in Hell. Nasty term, that—Hell. I've been mentioning we ought to think of changing it to the Scottish Dimension, but he never seems to listen. You won't mention my slip of the tongue to him, Karras, now will you? Eh? When you see him?"

"See him? Is he here?"

"In the piglet? No such luck. We're just a poor little family of wandering souls. By the way, you don't blame us for being here, do you? After all, we have no place to go. No home."

"And how long are you planning to stay?"

Face contorted in sudden rage, Regan jerked up from the pillow as she shouted in fury, *"Until the piglet dies!"* and then as suddenly, she settled back onto her pillows with a thick-lipped, drooling grin, saying, "Incidentally, what an excellent day for an exorcism."

The book! She must have read that in the book!

The sardonic eyes were staring piercingly.

"Do begin it soon, Karras. Very soon."

"You would like that?"

"Intensely."

"But wouldn't that drive you out of Regan?"

"It would bring us together."

"You and Regan?"

"You and *us*, my dear morsel. You and *us*."

Karras stared. At the back of his neck, he felt hands, icy cold and lightly touching. And then abruptly they were gone. Caused by fear? wondered Karras. Fear of *what?*

"Yes, you'll join our little family," Regan continued. "You see, the trouble with signs in the sky is that, once having seen them, one has no excuse. Have you noticed how few miracles one hears about lately? Not *our* fault, dear Karras. *We try!*"

Karras jerked around his head at a sudden loud banging sound. A bureau drawer had popped open, sliding out its entire length, and the priest felt a quick-rising thrill as he watched it abruptly bang shut. *There it is! A verifiable, paranormal event!* And then as suddenly, the emotion dropped away like a rotted chunk of bark from an ancient tree as the priest remembered psychokinesis and its various natural explanations. Hearing a low, sustained chuckling, he turned back to Regan. She was grinning. "How pleasant to chat with you, Karras," she told him in that guttural voice; "I feel free. Like a wanton, I spread my great wings. In fact, even my telling you this will serve only to increase your damnation, my doctor, my dear and inglorious physician."

"You did that? You made the dresser drawer move just now?"

The creature called Regan wasn't listening. It had glanced toward the door, to the sound of someone rapidly approaching down the hall, and now its features turned to those of the other personality that had once before appeared. "Damned butchering bastard!" it shrieked in that hoarse, British-accented voice. "Cunting *Hun!*"

Through the door came Karl, moving swiftly with the tape recorder. Eyes averted from the bed, he handed it to Karras and then, ashen-faced, rapidly retreated from the room.

"*Out*, Himmler! Out of my sight! Go and visit your club-footed daughter! Bring her *sauerkraut!* Sauerkraut and *heroin*, Thorndike! She will *love* it! She will—!"

Karl had slammed the door shut behind him, and now abruptly the thing within Regan turned cordial. "Oh, yes, hullo hullo hullo! What's up?" it said cheerily as it watched Karras setting down the tape recorder on a small round end table next to the bed. "Are we going to record something, Padre? How fun! Oh, I *do* love to playact, you know! Oh, yes, immensely!"

"Oh, good!" responded Karras, pushing down on the tape recorder's red RECORD button with his index finger, causing a tiny red light to come on. "I'm Damien Karras, by the way. And who are you?"

"Are you asking for my credits now, ducks?" it said with a giggle. "Oh, well, I did play Puck in the junior class play." It glanced around. "Where's a drink, incidentally? I'm parched."

"If you'll tell me your name, I'll try to find one."

"Yes, of course," it said, giggling again. "And then drink it all yourself, I suppose."

"Why not tell me your name?" Karras asked.

"Fucking plunderer!"

With this, the British-accented identity vanished and was instantly replaced by the demonic Regan. "And so what are we doing now, Karras? Oh, I see. We're recording. How quaint."

Karras pulled up a chair beside the bed and sat down.

"Do you mind?" he said.

"Not at all. Read your Milton and you'll see that I *like* infernal engines. They block out all those damned silly messages from '*him.*'"

"Who is 'him'?"

The creature loudly broke wind. "There's your answer."

Abruptly a powerful stench assailed Karras. It was an odor like . . .

"Sauerkraut, Karras? Have you noticed?"

It does *smell like sauerkraut*, the Jesuit marveled. It seemed to be coming from the bed, from Regan's body, and then it was gone, replaced by the putrid stench of before. Karras frowned. *Did I imagine it? Autosuggestion?* "Who's the person I was speaking to before?" Karras asked.

"Merely one of the family."

"A demon?"

"You give far too much credit. The word *demon* means 'wise one.' He is stupid."

The Jesuit grew tautly alert. "Oh, really? In what language does *demon* mean 'wise one'?" he asked.

"Why, in Greek."

"You speak Greek?"

"Very fluently."

One of the signs! Karras thought with excitement. *Speaking in an unknown tongue!* It was more than he'd hoped for. *"Pos egnokas hoti piesbyteros eimi?"* he asked quickly in classical Greek.

"I am not in the mood now, Karras."

"Oh, I see. Then you really can't—"

"I *said*, I am *not in the mood!*"

Karras looked aside, then back and asked amiably, "Was it you who made the drawer come sliding out?"

"Oh, most assuredly, Karras."

Karras nodded. "Most impressive. You must be a very, very powerful demon."

"Oh, I am, my dear morsel; I am. Incidentally, do you like it that at times I sound exactly like my older brother Screwtape?" A burst of high-pitched guffaws and raucous laughter. Karras waited for it to subside. "Yes, I do find that interesting," he said; "but in the meantime, the drawer trick?"

"What about it?"

"It's incredible! I was wondering if you'd do it again."

"In time."

"Why not now?"

"Why, we must give you *some* reason for doubt! Yes, just enough to assure the final outcome." The demonic personality chuckled maliciously. "Ah, how novel to attack through the truth! Yes, 'surprised by joy,' indeed!"

Karras stared, icy fingers once again touching lightly at the back of his neck. Why the fear again? he wondered. Why?

Hideously grinning, Regan said, "Because of me."

Karras stared, feeling wonder again, and then promptly chipped it down: *In this state, she just might be telepathic.*

"Can you tell me what I'm thinking now, devil?"

"My dear Karras, your thoughts are too dull to entertain."

"Oh, then you *can't* read my mind. That what you're saying?"

Regan looked away, her hand pinching distractedly at her bedsheet, idly lifting and then lowering a tiny linen cone. "You may have it as you wish," she then said dully; "as you wish."

Then silence. Karras listened to the squeaking of the tape-recorder mechanism, Regan's fluttery and whistling, heavy breathing. Thinking he needed more of a sampling of her speech in this state, he leaned forward, hunching over, as if with keen interest. "You're such a fascinating person," he said warmly.

Regan turned to him, sneering. "You mock!"

"Oh, no, really! I would love to know more about your background. You've never told me who you are, for example."

"Are you *deaf*? I *have* told you! I'm a devil!"

"Yes, I know, but *which* devil? What's your name?"

"Ah, now what's in a name, Karras? Really! But all right, call me Howdy if that makes you more comfortable."

"Ah, I see! You're Captain Howdy, Regan's friend!"

"Her very *close* friend, Karras."

"Oh, really? But then why do you torment her?"

"*Because* I am her friend! The piglet likes it!"

"That doesn't make any sense, Captain Howdy. Why on earth would Regan like to be tormented?"

"Ask *her!*"

"Would you allow her to answer?"

"I would not!"

"Well, then what would be the point in my asking?"

"None!" The eyes glinted with mockery and spite.

"Who's the person I was speaking to earlier?" asked Karras.

"Come, you've asked me that before."

"Yes, I know, but you never gave an answer."

"Just another good friend of the sweet honey piglet."

"May I speak to this person?"

"No. He is busy with your mother. She is sucking his cock to the *bristles*, Karras! to the *root!*" Low and deep chuckling; and then, "Marvelous tongue. Soft lips."

Karras felt a rage sweeping through him, and then realized with a start that his anger was directed not at Regan, but at the demon! The *demon!* He tightly gripped calm by its shoulders, breathed deeply and then, standing up, he slipped a slender glass vial from a pocket and uncorked it.

Regan stared at it warily. "What's that in your hand?" she rasped, drawing back rigidly, her eyes apprehensive.

"Don't you know? Why it's holy water, devil!" answered Karras, and as Regan immediately began whimpering and straining against her straps, he began shooting sprinkles of the vial's content at her. "Oh, it burns! It burns!" Regan cried out gutturally, as she thrashed about, writhing in terror and in pain. "Stop it, stop it, priest bastard!" she wailed. "Stop iiiiiiitttttttttt!"

Staring blankly, both Karras's body and soul seemed to sag. He stopped sprinkling and his arm and the vial dropped slowly and listlessly to his side. *Hysteria. Suggestion. She* did *read the book!* He glanced at the tape recorder, and then lowered his head and shook it. *Why bother?* But now he noticed the silence, so airless, so deep, and he looked up at Regan and instantly his eyebrows lowered and bunched together in perplexity. *What's this?* he thought. *What's going on?* The demonic personality had vanished and in its place were other features, which were similar, and yet different, with the eyes now rolled upward into their sockets so that only the whites balefully showed. Lips moving. A feverish gibberish. Karras came around to the side of the bed and leaned over to listen. *It's nothing, just nonsense syllables,* he thought; *and yet it's got cadence, like a language. Could it possibly be?* Karras wondered. Hoped. He felt a fluttering of wings in his chest. Swiftly gripped them. Held them still. *Come on, don't be an idiot, Damien!*

And yet . . .

He checked the tape recorder's volume monitor, dialed up the amplification knob and was listening intently with his ear held low above Regan's lips when abruptly the gibberish ceased and was replaced by heavy breathing, raspy and deep. Something new. No. *Someone* new. Karras drew himself up and looked down at Regan in quiet wonder. Whites of eyes. Eyelids fluttering. "Who are you?" he asked.

"Nowonmai," something answered him in pain and in a groaning whisper. "Nowonmai. Nowonmai." The cracking, breathy voice seemed to come from afar, from some dark, cloistered space at the edge of the worlds, beyond time, beyond hope, beyond even the comfort of resignation and despair.

Karras frowned. "Is that your name?"

The lips moved. Fevered syllables. Slow. Unintelligible.

And then abruptly they ceased.

"Are you able to understand me?" asked Karras.

Silence. Only breathing, long and deep. The sound of sleep in a hospital respirator. Karras waited. Hoped for more.

Nothing came.

Karras picked up the tape recorder, gave Regan a last, searching look and then left the room and went downstairs.

He found Chris in the kitchen sitting somberly over coffee at the table with Sharon. As they saw him approach, the two women looked up at him with a questioning, anxious expectancy. "Better go check on Regan," Chris said quietly to Sharon.

"Yeah, sure." Sharon took a final sip of coffee, gave Karras a little smile of acknowledgment and left. Karras watched her and when she was gone he sat down at the table.

Anxiously searching his eyes, Chris asked, "So what's doin'?" About to answer, Karras hesitated as Karl entered quietly from the pantry and went over to the sink to scrub pots.

"It's okay," Chris said softly. "Go ahead, Father Karras. And so what happened upstairs? What do you think?"

Karras clasped his hands together on the table. "There were two personalities," he said; "one that I hadn't ever seen before and another that I once might have gotten a glimpse of. Adult male. Sounds British. Is that anyone you know?"

"Is that important?"

Once again Karras noticed that certain sudden tension in Chris's face. "Yes, I think so," he said. "Yes, it's important."

Chris looked down at the blue porcelain creamer on the table. Then, "Yeah," she said; "I knew him."

"Knew?"

Chris looked up and said quietly, "Burke Dennings."

"The director?"

"Yes."

"The director who—"

"Yes."

Pondering her answer, Karras looked down at her hands. Chris's left index finger was slightly twitching.

"Are you sure you don't want coffee or anything, Father?"

Karras looked up. "No, I'm okay" he said. "I'm fine," and

then, resting folded arms on the table, he leaned forward. "And so, was Regan acquainted with him?" he asked.

"You mean Burke?"

"Yes, Dennings."

"Well—"

A sudden sound, a loud clattering. Startled, Chris flinched, then saw that Karl had dropped a roasting pan to the floor, and as he stooped to retrieve it, as he picked it up, he dropped it yet again.

"God almighty, Karl!"

"Sorry, Madam! Sorry!"

"Go on, get out of here, Karl! Take a break! Go see a movie or something!"

"No, Madam, maybe better if—"

"Karl, I mean it!" Chris snapped at him edgily. "Get out! Just get out of this house for a while! We've *all* got to start getting out of here! Now *go!*"

"Yes, you go!" echoed Willie as she entered and snatched away the pan from Karl's grasp. She pushed him irritably toward the pantry.

Karl briefly eyed Karras and Chris and then left.

"Sorry, Father," Chris murmured. She reached for a cigarette. "He's had to take an awful lot lately."

"You were right," said Karras gently. He picked up a packet of matches. "You should *all* make an effort to get out of the house." He lit her cigarette, fanned out the match and placed it in an ashtray as he added, "You too."

"Yeah, I know. And so this Burke thing—whatever—I mean, what did it say?" Chris was eyeing the priest intently.

Karras shrugged. "Just obscenities."

"That's all?"

The priest caught the faint pulse of fear in her tone. "Pretty much," he responded. Then he lowered his voice. "Incidentally, does Karl have a daughter?"

"A daughter? No, not that I know of. Or if he does, he's never mentioned it."

"You're sure?"

Chris turned to Willie, who was scouring at the sink. "Say, you don't have a daughter, do you, Willie?"

Willie kept stolidly scouring as she answered, "Yes, Madam, but she die long before."

"Oh, I'm sorry, Willie."

"Thank you."

Chris turned back to Karras. "That's the first I ever heard of her," she whispered. "Why'd you ask? How'd you know?"

"Regan mentioned it."

Chris stared at him incredulously, and whispered, *"What?"*

"She did. Has she ever shown signs before of having—well—ESP?"

"ESP, Father?"

"Yes."

Hesitant, Chris looked aside with a frown. "I don't know. I'm not sure. I mean, there have been lots of times when she seems to be thinking the same things that *I'm* thinking, but doesn't that happen with people who are close?"

Karras nodded and said, "Yes. Yes, it does. Now this other personality, the third one that I mentioned—that's the one that showed up when she was hypnotized?"

"Talks gibberish?"

"Talks gibberish. Who is it?"

"I don't know."

"It's not familiar at all?"

"No, not at all."

"Have you sent for Regan's medical records?"

"They'll be here this afternoon. They're coming straight to you, Father. That's the only way I could get them loose, and even at that I had to raise hell."

"Yes, I thought there might be trouble."

"There was. But they're coming."

"Good."

Folding her arms across her chest, Chris leaned back in her chair and stared at Karras gravely. "Okay, Father, so where are we now? What's the bottom line?"

"Well, your daughter—"

"No, you know what I mean," Chris interrupted. "I mean, what about getting permission for an exorcism?"

Karras cast his eyes down and gently shook his head. "I'm just not very hopeful I could sell it to the Bishop."

"What do you mean, 'not very hopeful'? How come."

Karras dipped into a pocket, extracted the holy-water vial and held it out to Chris. "See this?" he asked.

"What about it?"

"I told Regan it was holy water," Karras said softly, "and when I started to sprinkle it on her, she reacted very violently."

"Oh, well, that's good, Father. Isn't it?"

"No. This really isn't holy water. It's just ordinary tap water."

"So? So what's the difference, Father?"

"Holy water's blessed."

"Oh, well, I'm happy for it, Father! I really am!" Chris shot back with a rising frustration and annoyance. "And so maybe some demons are dumb!"

"You really believe there's a demon inside her?"

"I believe that there's *something* inside of her that's trying to kill her and whether it knows piss from Seven-Up doesn't seem to have very much to do with it, don't you think so, Father Karras? I mean, sorry, but you asked my opinion!" Chris irritably tamped out her cigarette in the ashtray. "And so what are you telling me now—no exorcism?"

"Look, I've only just begun to dig into this," Karras retorted, beginning to match Chris's heat. "But the Church has criteria that have to be met and they have to be met for very good reasons, like not doing more harm than good, as well as trying to keep clear of the superstitious garbage that people keep pinning on us year after year! I give you 'levitating priests,' for example, and statues of the Blessed Mother that supposedly cry blood on Good Fridays and feast days! Now I think I can live without contributing to that!"

"Would you like a little Librium, Father?"

"I'm sorry, but you asked my opinion."

"I think I pretty much got it."

Karras reached for the cigarette pack.

"Me too," Chris said.

Karras extended the pack. Chris took one, then Karras, who lit them both and together they dragged and then exhaled smoke with audible sighs of relief at the return of calm and peace.

"I'm so sorry," said Karras, looking down at the table.

"Yeah, those nonfilter cigarettes'll kill ya."

After that there was quiet as Chris looked off to the side and through a floor-to-ceiling window at Key Bridge traffic. Then a sound of something softly and intermittently thumping. Chris turned and saw Karras staring down at the cigarette pack as he slowly kept turning it end over end. Abruptly he looked up and met Chris's moist and demanding stare. "Okay, listen," he said; "I'm going to give you the signs that the Church might accept before authorizing a formal rite of exorcism."

"Yeah, good. I want to hear them."

"One is speaking in a language that the subject has never known before; never studied. That one I'm working on. We'll see. After that there's clairvoyance, although nowadays it might be ruled out as just telepathy or ESP."

"You *believe* in that stuff?"

Karras studied her, the grimace of disbelief, the frown. She was serious, he decided. "It's undeniable these days," he told her, "although, as I said, it isn't at all supernatural."

"Good *grief*, Charlie Brown!"

"Oh, so you do have a skeptical side."

"What other symptoms?"

"Well, the last that the Church might accept is—quote—'powers beyond her ability and age.' That's a catchall; it means anything inexplicably paranormal or occult."

"Oh, really? Well, then, what about those poundings in the wall and the way she was flying up and down off the bed?"

"By themselves, they mean nothing."

"Well, then, what about those things on her skin?"

"What things?"

"I didn't tell you?"

"Tell me what?"

"Oh, well, it happened at Barringer Clinic," Chris explained. "There were—well . . ." She traced a finger on her chest. "You know, like writing? Just letters. They'd show up on her chest, then disappear. Just like that."

Karras frowned. "You said 'letters.' Not words?"

"No, no words. Just an *M* once or twice. Then an *L*."

"And you *saw* this?" Karras asked her.

"Well, no. But they told me."

"*Who* told you?"

"Shit, the doctors at the clinic!" Chris said irritably. Then, "Okay, sorry," she said. "Look, you'll see it in the records. It's for real."

"But it, too, could be a natural phenomenon."

"Where? In Transylvania?" Chris erupted again, incredulous.

Karras shook his head. "Look, I've come across cases of that in the journals and the Bishop could bring it up against us. There was one, I remember, where a prison psychiatrist reported that a patient of his—an inmate—could go into a self-induced state of trance and make the signs of the zodiac appear on his skin." He made a gesture at his chest. "Made the skin raise up."

"Boy, miracles sure don't come easy with you, do they?"

"What can I tell you? Look, there was once an experiment in which the subject was hypnotized, put into trance; and then surgical incisions were made in each arm. He was told his left arm was going to bleed, but that the right arm wouldn't. Well, the left arm bled and the right arm didn't."

"Whoa!"

"Yes, whoa! The power of the mind controlled the blood flow. How? Who knows. But it happens. So in cases of stigmata—like the one with that prisoner I mentioned, or maybe even with Regan—the unconscious mind is controlling the differential of blood flow to the skin, sending more to the parts that it wants raised up. And so then you have letters, or images, maybe even words. It's mysterious, but hardly supernatural."

"You're a real tough case, Father Karras, do you know that?"

"I'm not the one who sets the rules."

"Well, you've sure got your heart into enforcing them."

Pensive, the priest lowered his head and touched the end of a thumb to his lips; then he dropped it and looked up at Chris. "Listen, maybe this will help you to understand," he said slowly and gently. "The Church—not me; the Church—once published a warning to would-be exorcists. I read it last night. What it said was that most of the people who think they're possessed or are *thought* to be possessed—and now I'm quoting word for word—'are far more in need of a doctor than of a priest.' Now can you guess when that warning was issued?"

"No, when?"

"The year fifteen eighty-three."

Chris stared in surprise at first, and then, lowering her gaze, she murmured, "Yeah, that sure was one hell of a year." She heard the priest getting up from his chair. "Let me wait and check the records from the clinic," he told her, "and in the meantime I'll be taking Regan's letter to her father tape plus the tape I just made to the Georgetown University Institute of Languages and Linguistics. It could be this gibberish is some kind of a language. I doubt it. But it's possible. In the meantime, there's a lot that could be riding on comparing Regan's pattern of speech in her normal state with what I just recorded. If they're the same, you'll know for sure that she isn't possessed."

"And what then?" Chris asked him.

The priest probed her eyes. They were swirling with turbulence. *My God*, Karras thought, *she's worried that her daughter* isn't *possessed!* His nagging sense of some even deeper problem, something hidden, had returned. "Could I borrow your car for a while?" he asked.

Chris looked bleakly aside. "You could borrow my *life* for a while. Just get it back by Thursday. You never know; I might need it."

With an ache, Karras stared at the bowed and defenseless head. He yearned to be able to take Chris's hand and assure her that all would be well. But he couldn't. He didn't believe it.

Chris stood up. "I'll go get you the keys."

She drifted away like a hopeless prayer.

Karras walked back to his room at the residence hall where he left Chris's tape recorder, collected the tape of Regan's voice, then went back across the street to Chris's parked car. As he was settling into the driver's seat, he heard Karl Engstrom calling out from the doorway of Chris's house: "Father Karras!" Karras looked. Karl was rushing down the stoop. He was pulling on a black leather jacket and waving. "Father Karras! Just a moment, please!" he called as he trotted up to Chris's car.

Karras leaned over and cranked down the window on the passenger side, where Karl stooped down to look in at Karras and ask, "You are going which way, Father Karras?"

"DuPont Circle."

"Ah, yes, good! You could drop me, please, Father? You would mind?"

"Glad to do it, Karl. Get in."

"I appreciate it, Father!"

Karl got into the car and closed the door. Karras started up the engine. "Mrs. MacNeil is quite right, Karl," he said. "Do you good to get out."

"Yes, I think so. I go to see a film, Father."

"Perfect."

Karras put the car in gear and pulled away.

For a time they drove in silence; Karras preoccupied, searching for answers. *Possession? Impossible! The holy water!*

But still . . .

"Karl, you knew Mr. Dennings pretty well?"

Sitting stiffly erect and staring stoically straight ahead through the windshield, Karl said, "Yes. Yes, I know him."

"When Regan—I mean, when she appears to be Dennings—do you get the impression that she actually *is?*"

A weighted silence.

And then a flat and expressionless "I do."

Karras nodded and murmured, "I see."

After that, there was no more conversation until they reached DuPont Circle, where they came to a traffic signal and stopped. Karl opened his door. "I get off here, Father Karras."

"Really? Here?"

"Yes, from here I take bus." He climbed out of the car and with a hand gripping the edge of the open door, he leaned down and said, "Thank you, Father Karras. Very much."

"Are you sure I can't take you all the way? I've got time."

"No, no, Father! This is good! Very good!"

"Well, okay. Enjoy the movie."

"I will, Father! Thank you!"

Karl closed the car door and stepped onto a safety island, where he waited for a traffic light to go green, and as Karras pulled away he stood stoically watching the bright red Jaguar coupe until at last it disappeared around the bend onto Massachusetts Avenue. Karl looked at the traffic light. It had changed and he ran for a bus that was now pulling into a bus stop. He boarded, took a transfer, changed buses and then finally debarked at a northeast tenement section of the city, where he walked three blocks and then entered a crumbling apartment building. At the bottom of a gloomy staircase, he paused, smelling acrid aromas from efficiency kitchens, heard from somewhere upstairs the soft crying of a baby as a roach scuttled quickly from out of a baseboard in erratic, zigzagging darts, and in that moment, the sturdy, stoic houseman's entire being seemed to crumple and to sag; but then, gathering himself, he moved forward to a staircase, put a hand on the banister and started slowly climbing the creaking and groaning old wooden stairs. To his ears each footfall had the sound of a rebuke.

On the second floor, Karl walked to a door in a murky wing, and for a moment he stood there, a hand on the door frame. He glanced at the wall: peeling paint; graffiti; *Petey and Charlotte* in a penciled scrawl, and, below it, a date and a drawing of a heart that was bisected by a thin, jagged line of cracking plaster. Karl pushed the buzzer and waited, head down. From within the apartment, a squeaking of bedsprings. Low muttering. Then someone approaching with a sound that was irregular—the dragging clump of an orthopedic shoe—and abruptly the door jerked partly open, the chain of a safety latch rattling to its limit as a woman in a stained pink paisley slip scowled out through the aperture, a cigarette dangling from the corner of her mouth.

"Oh, it's you," she said throatily. She unloosed the chain.

Karl met the eyes that were shifting hardness, that were haggard wells of pain and blame; glimpsed briefly the dissolute bending of the lips and the ravaged face of a youth and a beauty buried alive in a thousand motel rooms, in a thousand awakenings from restless sleep with a stifled cry at remembered grace.

"C'mon, tell 'im ta fuck off!"

A coarse male voice from within the apartment.

Slurred. The boyfriend.

The girl turned her head. "Shut up, asshole, it's Pop!" she scolded, and then turned back to Karl. "Listen, he's drunk, Pop. Ya better not come in."

Karl nodded.

The girl's hollow eyes shifted down to his hand as it reached to a back trouser pocket for a wallet. "How's Mama?" she asked him, dragging on her cigarette, her eyes fixed now on the hands dipping into the wallet, the hands counting out ten-dollar bills.

"She is fine." Karl nodded tersely. "Your mother is fine."

As he handed her the money, the girl began coughing rackingly. She threw up a hand to her mouth. "Fuckin' cigarettes!" she chokingly complained; "I've gotta quit, goddammit!" Karl stared at the puncture scabs on her arm, felt the ten-dollar bills being slipped from his fingers.

"Thanks, Pop."

"Jesus, hurry it up!" growled the boyfriend from within.

"Listen, Pop, we better cut this kinda short. Okay? Ya know how he gets sometimes."

"Elvira . . . !" Karl had suddenly reached through the opening in the door and grasped her wrist. "There is clinic in New York now!" he whispered to her pleadingly as she grimaced and struggled to break free from Karl's grip. "Pop, let go!"

"I will send you! They will help you! You don't go to jail! It is—"

"Jesus, come *on*, Pop!" Elvira screeched as she wrenched herself free.

"No, no, please!"

His daughter slammed shut the door.

Standing silent and motionless in the dank, graffitied tomb of his hopes, the Swiss manservant stared without sight for long moments until at last he slowly lowered his head in grief.

From within the apartment he could hear a muffled conversation that ended with a cynical, ringing woman's laugh. It was followed by a spate of coughing. Karl turned away.

And felt a sudden stab of shock.

"Perhaps we could talk now," said Kinderman breathily, hands in the pockets of his coat, his eyes sad. "Yes, I think that perhaps we could now have a talk."

Chapter Two

Karras threaded tape to an empty reel on a table in the office of Frank Miranda, the rotund, silver-haired director of the Institute of Languages and Linguistics. Having edited sections of both his tapes onto separate reels, Karras started the tape recorder, and the two men listened with headphones to the fevered voice croaking gibberish. When it ended, Karras slipped the headphones onto his shoulders and asked, "Frank, what *is* that? Could it possibly be a language?"

His earphones off as well, Miranda was sitting on the edge of his desk, his arms folded as he stared at the floor and frowned in puzzlement. "I don't know," he said, shaking his head. "Pretty weird." He glanced up at Karras. "Where'd you get that?"

"I'm working on a case of dual personality."

"You're kidding me! A priest?"

"I can't say."

"Yes, of course. I understand."

"Well, what about it, Frank? You'll do it?"

Staring off thoughtfully, Miranda gently lifted off his tortoiseshell reading glasses, absently folding and then slipping them into the slim lapel pocket of his seersucker jacket. "No, it isn't any language that *I've* ever heard of," he said. "However . . ." Slightly frowning, he glanced up at Karras. "Want to play it again?"

Karras rewound the tape, replayed it, turned off the recorder and said, "Any ideas?"

"Well, I must say, it does have the cadence of speech."

A sudden quickening of hope arose in the Jesuit, brightening his eyes for an instant, and then dimming as he reflexively fought down the hope.

"But I don't recognize it, Father," the director continued. "Is it ancient or modern?" he asked.

"I don't know."

"Well, why not leave it with me, Father? I'll check it much more thoroughly with some of the boys. Maybe one of them will know what it is."

"Could you please make a copy of it, Frank? I'd like to keep the original myself."

"Oh, well, sure."

"In the meantime, I've got another tape. Got the time?"

"Yes, of course. A tape of what?"

"Let me ask you something first."

"Sure, what is it?"

"Frank, what if I were to give you samples of ordinary speech by what are apparently two different people. Could you tell by semantic analysis whether just one person might have been capable of both modes of speech?"

"Oh, I think so. Yeah. Oh, well, sure. A 'type-token' ratio, I suppose, would be as good a way as any to work that out, and with samples of a thousand words or more, you could just check the frequency of occurrence of the various parts of speech."

"And would you call that conclusive?"

"Pretty much. You see, that sort of test would discount any change in the basic vocabulary. It's not the words but the *expression* of the words; the style. We call it 'index of diversity.' Very baffling to the layman, which, of course, is what we want." The director smiled wryly. Then he nodded at the tape in Karras's hands. "And so this other person's voice is on that one?"

"Not exactly."

"Not exactly?"

"The voices and the words on both tapes came out of the mouth of one and the same person."

The director's eyebrows rose. "The *same* person?"

"Yes. As I said, it was a case of dual personality. Could you compare them against one another for me, Frank? I mean, the voices sound totally different, but I'd still like to see what a comparative analysis would show."

The director looked intrigued, even pleased. He said, "Fascinating! Yes. Yes, we'll run the analysis. I'm thinking maybe now I'll give it to Paul, he's my top instructor. Brilliant mind. I think he dreams in Indian 'code talk.' "

"Another favor. It's a big one."

"What?"

"I'd prefer it if you did the comparison yourself."

"Oh?"

"Yes. And as quickly as possible. Please?"

The director read the urgency in Karras's voice and in his eyes. "Okay," he said, nodding. "I'll get on it."

Returning to his room in the Jesuit residence hall, Karras found a message slip under his door: Regan's records from Barringer Clinic had arrived. Karras hurried to reception, signed for the package, then returned to his room, sat down at his desk and started avidly reading, but at the end, as he read the conclusion of the clinic's psychiatric team, his mood of hopeful anticipation had slipped into one of disappointment and defeat: ". . . indications of guilt obsession with ensuing hysterical-somnambulistic . . ." Needing to read no more, Karras stopped, propped his elbows on the desk and, with a sigh, slowly lowered his face into his hands. *Don't give up. Room for doubt. Interpretation.* But in the matter of Regan's skin stigmata, which, according to the records, had recurred again repeatedly while Regan had been under observation at Barringer, the clinic's summary analysis had noted that Regan had hyperreactive skin and could herself have produced the mysterious letters by tracing them on her flesh with a finger a short time prior to their appearance, by a process known as dermatographia, a theory buttressed by the fact that as soon as Regan's hands had been immobilized by restraining straps, the mysterious phenomena ceased.

Karras lifted his head and eyed the telephone. Frank. Was there really any point now in running a comparison of the voices on the tapes? Call him off? *Yes, I should*, the priest concluded. He picked up the receiver. Dialed. No answer. He left word for the institute director to call, and then, exhausted, he stood up and walked slowly to his bathroom, where he splashed cold water onto his face. *"The exorcist will simply be careful that none of the patient's manifestations are left unexplained."* Karras worriedly looked up at himself in the mirror. Had he missed something? *What? The sauerkraut odor?* He turned and slipped a towel off the rack and wiped his face. No, autosuggestion would explain that, he recalled, as well as reports that, in certain instances, the mentally ill seemed able to unconsciously direct their bodies to emit a variety of odors.

Karras wiped his hands. The poundings. The opening and closing of the drawer. Was that psychokinesis? Really? *"You believe in that stuff?"* Becoming suddenly aware that he wasn't thinking clearly, Karras set the damp towel back on its bar. *Tired. Too tired.* Yet the core of his being refused to give up, to surrender this child to sinuous theories and speculations, to the blood-drenched history of betrayals of the human mind.

He left the residence hall and walked swiftly up Prospect

Street to the gray stone walls of Georgetown University's Lauinger Library, entered and searched through the *Guide to Periodical Literature*, running a finger down subjects beginning with a *P,* and after finding what it was that he'd been looking for, he sat down at a long, oaken reading table with a scientific journal containing an article about poltergeist phenomena, written by the eminent German psychiatrist Dr. Hans Bender. *No doubt about it*, the Jesuit concluded when he'd finished reading the article: having for many years been thoroughly documented, filmed and observed in psychiatric clinics, psychokinetic phenomena were real. *But!* In none of the cases reported in the article was there any connection to demonic possession; rather, the favorite hypothesis explaining the phenomenon was "mind-directed energy" unconsciously produced and usually—and significantly, Karras noted—by adolescents in stages of "extremely high inner tension, rage and frustration."

Karras lightly rubbed his knuckles into the corners of his moist and tired eyes, and, still feeling remiss, he ran back through Regan's symptoms, touching each like a schoolboy making sure that he taps every slat as he walks along a white picket fence. Karras wondered which one he had missed.

The answer, he wearily concluded, was none.

He walked back to the MacNeil house, where Willie admitted him and led him to the door of the study. It was closed. Willie knocked. "Father Karras," she announced, and from within Karras heard a subdued "Come in."

Karras entered and closed the door behind him. Standing with her back to him, Chris had an elbow propped on the bar top and her forehead lowered into a hand. Without turning, she greeted him, "Hello, Father," in a voice that was husky, yet soft and despairing.

Concerned, the priest went to her side. "You okay?"

"Yeah, I'm fine, Father. Really."

Karras frowned, his worry deepening: Chris's voice had held tension, and the hand that was obscuring her face was trembling. Lowering her arm, she turned and looked up at Karras, revealing a haggard-eyed, tearstained face. "So what's doin'?" she said. "What's new?"

Karras studied her before answering, "Well, the latest is I've looked at the records from Barringer Clinic and—"

"Yes?" Chris interjected tensely.

"Well, I believe . . ."

"You believe what, Father Karras? What?"

"Well, my honest opinion right now is that Regan can best be helped by intensive psychiatric care."

Chris stared at Karras mutely and with her eyes a little wider as she very slowly shook her head back and forth. "No way!"

"Where's her father?" Karras asked her.

"In Europe."

"Have you told him what's happening?"

"No."

"Well, I think it would help if he were here."

"Listen, nothing's going to help except something out of *sight!*" Chris erupted in a voice that was loud and quavery.

"I believe you should send for him."

"Why?"

"It would—"

"I've asked you to drive a demon *out*, goddammit, not ask another one *in!*" Chris cried out, her features contorted in anguish. "What happened to the exorcism all of a sudden?"

"Look—"

"What in the hell do I want with *Howard?*"

"We can talk about that later when—"

"Talk about it *now*, goddammit! What the hell good is *Howard* right now?"

"Well, there's a strong probability that Regan's disorder is rooted in a guilt over—"

"Guilt over *what?*" Chris squalled, her eyes wild.

"It could—"

"Over the *divorce?* All that psychiatric *bullshit?*"

"Now—"

"Regan feels guilty because she *killed Burke Dennings!*" Chris shrieked, her hands lifted in fists pressed against her temples. "She *killed* him! She killed him and they'll put her away; they're going to put her away! Oh, my God, oh, my . . ."

Karras caught her up as she crumpled, sobbing, and guided her toward the sofa. "It's all right," he kept telling her softly, "it's all right . . ."

"No, they'll put . . . her away," Chris kept sobbing. "They'll put . . . put . . . !"

"It's all right."

Karras eased Chris down and helped her to stretch out on the sofa, then he sat on its edge and took her hand in both of his. Racing thoughts now. Of Kinderman. Of Dennings. Chris sobbing. Unreality. "All right . . . it's all right . . . take it easy . . . it's all going to be okay . . ."

Soon the crying subsided and he helped her sit up. He brought her water and a box of tissues that he'd found on a shelf behind the bar and then he sat down beside her.

"Oh, I'm glad," Chris said, sniffling and blowing her nose.

"You're *glad?*"

"Yeah, I'm glad I got it out."

"Oh, well, yes—yes—yes, that's good."

And now again the weight pressed heavily down on the Jesuit's shoulders. *No more! Say no more!* he tried warning himself, yet "Do you want to tell me more?" he asked Chris gently.

Chris nodded mutely, and then, weakly, she said, "Yes. Yes, I do." She wiped at an eye and began to speak haltingly and in spasms: of Kinderman; of the narrow strips torn from the edges of the witchcraft book and of her certainty that Dennings had been up in Regan's bedroom on the night he had died; of Regan's abnormally great strength and of the Dennings personality Chris thought she had seen with its head turned around and facing backward. Finished, depleted, she waited for Karras's reaction, and just as he was about to tell her his mind, he looked into her eyes and her beseeching expression, and instead said, "You can't be really *sure* that she did it."

"But Burke's head turned around? The things it says?"

"You'd hit your own head pretty hard against a wall," Karras answered. "You were also in shock. You imagined it."

Holding Karras's gaze with dead eyes, Chris said quietly, "No. Burke told me that she did it. She pushed him out the window and she killed him."

Momentarily stunned, the priest stared at her blankly, but then gathered himself. "Your daughter's mind is deranged," he said, "and so her statements mean nothing."

Chris lowered her head and shook it. "I don't know," she said barely audibly. "I don't know if I'm doing what's right. I think she did it and so maybe she could kill someone else. I don't know." She turned a hopeless, hollow stare back to Karras and in a throaty, husky whisper asked him, "What should I do?"

Karras inwardly sagged. The weight was now set in concrete, and, in drying, it had shaped itself to his back. "You've already done what you should do," he said. "You've told someone, Chris. You've told *me*. So now just leave it up to me to decide what's best to do. Will you do that, please? Just leave it to me."

Wiping at an eye with the back of her hand, Chris nodded, and said, "Yeah. Yeah, well, sure. That would be best." Trying to muster a smile, she added weakly, "Thanks, Father. Thank you so much."

"Feeling better now?"

"Yes."

"Then will you do me a favor?"

"Sure, anything. What?"

"Go out and see a movie."

For a moment Chris stared blankly, and then she smiled and shook her head. "No, I hate 'em."

"Then go visit a friend."

Chris looked at him warmly. "Got a friend right here."

"You bet. Now get some rest, please. Will you promise?"

"Yes, I promise."

Karras had a thought, another question. "You think Dennings brought the book upstairs," he asked, "or was it already there?"

"I believe it was there."

Looking slightly aside, Karras nodded his head. "I see," he said quietly. Then abruptly he stood up. "Well, okay. You need the car back, by the way?"

"No, you can keep it."

"All right, then. I'll be back to you later."

Lowering her head, Chris said softly, "Okay."

Karras left the house and walked out onto the street with thoughts that raced and tumbled recklessly in his mind. Regan killing Dennings? What madness! He envisioned her shoving him out through her bedroom window to hurtle down those long and steep stone steps, turning over and over and flailing helplessly until his world came to a sudden stop. *Impossible!* thought Karras. *No!* And yet Chris's near conviction it was so!

Her hysteria! *And that's exactly what it is!* the priest tried telling himself. *It's nothing more than hysterical imagining!* And yet . . .

Karras chased after certainties like fallen leaves in a wind.

As he was passing the precipitous steps beside the house, Karras heard a sound from below, by the river, and he stopped and looked down toward the C&O Canal. A harmonica. Someone playing "Red River Valley," since boyhood the Jesuit's favorite song. He stood and listened until a traffic light changed down below and the melancholy melody was crushed and overwhelmed by the sound of auto traffic starting up again on M Street, rudely shattered by a world that was now, of this moment, and in torment, dripping blood on exhaust fumes as it cried out for help. Staring down the steps unseeingly, Karras thrust his hands into his pockets, as once again he thought feverishly about the plight of Chris MacNeil and of Regan and of Lucas aiming kicks at the dead Tranquille. He must do something. What? Could he hope to outguess the clinicians at Barringer? *"Oh, are you really a priest or from Central Casting!"* Karras absently nodded, remembering the case of possession of a Frenchman named Achille who, like Regan, had called himself a devil, and like Regan his disorder had been rooted in guilt, in Achille's case remorse over marital infidelity. The great psychologist Janet had effected a cure by hypnotically suggesting the presence of the wife, who appeared to Achille's hallucinated eyes and solemnly forgave him. Karras nodded. Yes, suggestion *could* work for Regan. Although not through hypnosis. They had tried that at Barringer. The counteracting suggestion for Regan, he believed, was what her mother had insisted on all along. It was the ritual of exorcism. Regan knew what it was and its intended effect. *Her reaction to the holy water. She got that from a chapter in that book and in that chapter there were also descriptions of successful exorcisms. It could work! It really could!* But then how to get permission from the Chancery

Office? How to build up a case without mention of Dennings? Karras could not lie to the Bishop. And so what facts did he have that could possibly convince him? His temples beginning to pulse with headache, Karras lifted a hand to his brow. He knew he needed sleep. But he couldn't. Not now. *What facts?* The tapes at the Institute? What would Frank find? Was there anything he *could* find? No. But who knew? Regan hadn't known holy water from tap water. *Sure. But if supposedly she's able to read my mind, why is it that she didn't know the difference between them?* Karras again put a hand to his forehead. The headache. Confusion. *Come on, kid! Somebody's* dying! *Wake* up!

Once back in his room, Karras telephoned the Institute. No Frank. Pensive, he set down the receiver. *Holy water. Tap water. Something.* He opened up the Ritual to "Instructions to Exorcists": ". . . evil spirits . . . deceptive answers . . . so it might appear that the afflicted one is in no way possessed." Was that it? Karras wondered? But then instantly he bridled with impatience at the thought. *What in the hell are you talking about?* What *"evil spirit?"*

He slammed shut the book and then reread the medical records, scanning through them in a hurried, fevered search for anything that might help him make the case for an exorcism. *Here's one. No history of hysteria. That's something. But weak. There's something else here*, he remembered*; some discrepancy. What was it?* And then he recalled it. *Not much. Still, it's something.* He telephoned Chris MacNeil. She sounded groggy.

"Hi, Father."

"Were you sleeping? I'm sorry."

"No, it's okay, Father. Really. So what's up?"

"Chris, where can I find this . . . ?" Karras ran a finger down the records. Stopped. "Doctor Klein," he said; "Samuel Klein."

"Doctor Klein? Oh, he's across the bridge. In Rosslyn."

"In the medical building?"

"Yeah, right. What's the matter?"

"Please call him and tell him Doctor Karras will be by and that I'd like to take a look at Regan's EEG. Tell him *Doctor* Karras."

"Got it."

When he'd hung up the phone, Karras snapped off his collar and got out of his clerical robe and black trousers, changing quickly into khaki pants and a sweatshirt, and over these he wore his priest's black raincoat; but then examining himself in a mirror, Karras frowned and thought, *Priests and policemen!* They had identifying auras they couldn't hide. Karras slipped off the raincoat, then his shoes, and got into the only ones he owned that were not black, a pair of scuffed white Tretorn tennis shoes.

In Chris's car, he drove quickly toward Rosslyn. As he waited on M Street for the light to change at Key Bridge, he glanced to his left through the windshield and saw Karl getting out of a black sedan parked in front of the Dixie Liquor Store.

The driver of the car was Kinderman.

The light changed. Karras gunned the car forward, turning onto the bridge, then looked back through the mirror. Had they seen him? He didn't think so. But what were they doing together? Had it something to do with Regan? he worried. With Regan and . . . ?

Forget it! One thing at a time!

He parked at the medical building and went upstairs to Dr. Klein's suite of offices. The doctor was busy, but a nurse handed Karras the EEG and very soon he was standing in a cubicle scrolling through the long narrow band of graphed paper slipping slowly through his fingers.

Klein hurried in, his glance briefly brushing over Karras's dress. "You're Doctor Karras?"

"Yes."

"Sam Klein. Pleased to meet you."

As they shook hands, Klein asked, "How's the girl?"

"Progressing."

"Glad to hear it." Karras looked back to the graph and Klein joined him in scanning it, tracing his finger over patterns of waves. "There, you see? It's very regular. No fluctuations whatsoever," Klein noted.

"Yes, I see that. Curious."

"Curious? How so?"

"Well, presuming that we're dealing with hysteria."

"What do you mean?"

"No, I suppose it isn't very well known," Karras answered, as he kept pulling paper through his hands in a steady flow, "but a Belgian named Iteka discovered that hysterics seemed to cause some rather odd fluctuations in the graph, a very minuscule but always identical pattern. I've been looking for it here and I don't see it."

Klein grunted noncommittally. "How about that."

Karras stopped scrolling and looked up at him. "She was certainly disordered when you ran this graph; is that right?"

"Yes, I'd say so. Yes. Yes, she was."

"Well then, isn't it curious that she tested so perfectly? Even subjects in a normal state of mind can influence their brain waves at least within the normal range, and as Regan was disturbed at the time, wouldn't it seem there'd be *some* fluctuations. If—"

"Doctor, Mrs. Simmons is getting impatient," a nurse interrupted, cracking open the door.

"Okay, I'm coming," Klein told her. As the nurse hurried off, he took a step toward the hallway but then turned with his hand gripping the edge of the door. "Speaking of hysteria," he commented dryly. "Sorry. Got to run."

He closed the door behind him. Karras heard his footsteps heading down the hall, the opening of a door, then "Well now, how are we feeling today, Mrs. . . ." The closing of the door shut off the rest. Karras went back to his study of the graph, and when he'd finished, he folded it up and banded it, then returned it to the nurse in Reception. *Something.* It was something he could use with the Bishop as an argument that Regan was not a hysteric and therefore conceivably could be possessed. And yet the EEG had posed still another mystery: why no fluctuations, none at all?

Karras drove back toward Chris's house, but at a stop sign at the corner of Prospect and Thirty-Fifth he froze behind the wheel: sitting in the driver's seat of a car that was parked between Karras and the Jesuit residence hall was Kinderman, his elbow out the window as he fixedly stared straight ahead. Karras took a right before the homicide detective could see him. He quickly found a space, parked and locked the car, and then walked around the corner as if heading for the residence hall. *Is he watching the house?* Karras worried. The specter of Dennings rose up again to haunt him. Was it possible that Kinderman thought Regan had . . . ?

Easy, boy! Easy! Slow down!

He walked up beside the car and leaned his head through the window on the passenger side. "Hello, Lieutenant," he said pleasantly. "Come to visit me or just goofing off for a while?"

The detective turned quickly, looking surprised, and then he flashed a beaming smile. "Why, Father Karras! So *there* you are! So nice to see you!"

Off key, Karras thought. *What's he up to? Don't let him know that you're worried! Play it light!* "Don't you know you'll get a ticket?" Karras pointed to a sign. "Weekdays, no parking between four and six."

"Never mind," growled Kinderman. "I'm talking to a priest. Every meter maid in Georgetown is a Catholic."

"How've you been?"

"Speaking plainly, Father Karras, only so-so. And yourself?"

"Can't complain. Did you ever solve that case?"

"Which one?"

"You know, the movie director?"

"Oh, that one." The detective made a gesture of dismissal. "Don't ask! Listen, what are you doing tonight? Are you busy? I've got passes for the Biograph. It's *Othello*."

"That depends on who's in it."

"Who's in it? John Wayne, Othello, and Desdemona, Doris Day. You're happy? This is freebies, Father Marlon Annoyingly Particular! This is William F. Shakespeare! Doesn't matter who's starring, who's not! Now, you're coming?"

"I'm afraid I'll have to pass. I'm snowed under."

"I can see that," the detective said dolefully as he searched the Jesuit's face. "You're keeping late hours? You look terrible."

"I *always* look terrible."

"Only now more than usual. Come on now! Get away for one night! You'll enjoy!"

Karras decided to test; to touch a nerve. "Are you sure that's what's playing?" he asked. His eyes were probing steadily into the detective's. "I could have sworn there was a Chris MacNeil film at the Biograph."

The detective missed a beat, and then said quickly, "No, you're wrong. It's *Othello*."

"Oh. And so what brings you to the neighborhood?"

"You! I came only to invite you to the film!"

"Yes, it's easier to drive than to pick up a phone, I suppose."

The detective's eyebrows lifted in a dismally unconvincing stab at looking innocent. "Your telephone was busy."

The Jesuit stared at him silently and gravely.

"So what's wrong?" asked Kinderman. "What?"

Karras reached a hand inside the car, lifted Kinderman's eyelid and examined the eye. "I don't know," he said, frowning. "You look terrible. You could be coming down with a case of mythomania."

"I don't know what that means. Is it serious?"

"Yes, but not fatal."

"What is it? The suspense is now driving me crazy!"

"Look it up," Karras told him.

"Listen, don't be so snotty. You should render unto Caesar just a little now and then. I'm the law. I could have you deported, you know that?"

"What for?"

"A psychiatrist shouldn't piss people off, plus also the *goyim*, plainly speaking, would love it. You're a nuisance to them, Father. No, really, you embarrass them. Who needs it? a priest who wears sweatshirts and sneakers!"

Smiling faintly, Karras nodded. "Got to go. Take care." He tapped a hand on the window frame twice in farewell, and then turned and walked slowly toward the entry of the residence.

"See an analyst!" the detective called after him hoarsely. Then his warm look yielded to one of deep concern. He glanced up through his windshield at the house, then started the engine and drove up the street. Passing Karras, he honked his horn and waved. Karras waved back, and when Kinderman's car turned the corner at Thirty-Sixth Street, he stopped and stood motionless for a time, rubbing gently at his brow with a trembling hand. Could she really have done it? Could Regan have murdered Burke Dennings so horribly? With feverish eyes, Karras turned and looked up at Regan's window, thinking, *What in God's name is in that house?* And how much longer before Kinderman demanded to see Regan? Had a chance to see the Dennings personality? To hear it? How much longer before Regan would be institutionalized? Or die?

He had to build the exorcism case for the Chancery.

He walked quickly across the street to the Chris MacNeil house, rang the doorbell and waited for Willie to let him in.

"Missiz taking little nap now," she said.

Karras nodded. "Good. That's good." He walked by her and then upstairs to Regan's bedroom. He was seeking a knowledge he must clutch by the heart.

He entered and saw Karl in a chair by the window. Silent and present as a dense, dark wood, he was sitting with folded arms and with his stare pinned steadily on Regan.

Karras walked up beside the bed and looked down. The whites of the eyes like milky fog; the murmurings, incantations from some other world. Karras slowly leaned over and began to unfasten one of Regan's restraining straps.

"No, Father! *No!"*

Karl rushed to the bedside and vigorously yanked back the Jesuit's arm. "Very bad, Father! Strong! It is strong!"

In Karl's eyes there was a fear that Karras recognized as genuine. And now he knew that Regan's extraordinary strength was a fact. She could have done it. Could have twisted Dennings's neck around. *Come on, Karras! Hurry! Find some evidence! Think!*

And then a voice from beneath him. On the bed.

"Ich möchte Sie etwas fragen, Herr Engstrom!"

With a stab of discovery and surging hope, Karras jerked around his head and looked down at the bed to see Regan's demonic visage grinning at Karl. *"Tanzt Ihre Tochter gern?"* it taunted, and then burst into mocking laughter. German. It had asked if Karl's club-footed daughter liked to dance! Excited, Karras turned to Karl and saw that his cheeks were flushing crimson. Hands clenched into white-knuckled fists, he was glaring at Regan with fury as the laughter continued.

"Karl, you'd better step outside," Karras cautioned him.

The Swiss shook his head. "No, I stay!"

"You will go, please," the Jesuit said firmly, his gaze holding Karl's implacably until, after a moment or two more of resistance, the houseman turned and hurried out of the room. When the door closed, the laughter abruptly ceased, to be replaced by that thick and airless silence.

Karras turned his gaze to the bed. The demon was watching him. It looked pleased. "So you're back," it croaked. "I'm surprised. I would think that embarrassment over the holy water might have discouraged you from ever returning. But then I forget that a priest has no shame."

Karras took a few breaths as he forced himself to concentrate, to think clearly. He knew that the language test for possession required intelligent conversation as proof that whatever was said was not traceable to buried linguistic recollections. *Easy! Slow down! Remember that girl?* A Parisian teenage servant, allegedly possessed, while in delirium had quietly babbled a language that finally was recognized to be Syriac. Karras forced himself to think of the excitement it had caused, of how finally it was learned that the girl had at one time been employed in a boardinghouse where one of the lodgers was a student of theology who, on the eve of examinations, would pace in his room and walk up and down stairs while reciting his Syriac lessons aloud. And the girl had overheard them.

Take it easy. Don't get burned.

"Sprechen Sie deutsch?" asked Karras.

"More games?"

"Sprechen Sie deutsch?" the Jesuit repeated, his pulse still throbbing with that distant hope.

"Natürlich," the demon answered, leering. "*Mirabile dictu*, wouldn't you agree?"

The Jesuit's heart leaped up. Not only German, but Latin! And in context! *"Quod nomen mihi est?"* he asked quickly: what is my name?

"Karras."

And now the priest rushed on with excitement.

"Ubi sum?" Where am I?

"In cubiculo." In a room.

"Et ubi est cubiculum?" And where is the room?

"In domo." In a house.

"Ubi est Burke Dennings?" Where is Burke Dennings?

"Mortuus." He is dead.

"Quomodo mortuus est?" How did he die?

"Inventus est capite reverso." He was found with his head turned around.

"Quis occidit eum?" Who killed him?

"Regan."

"Quomodo ea occidit ilium? Dic mihi exacte!" How did she kill him? Tell me in detail!

"Ah, well, that's sufficient excitement for now," said the demon with a grin. "Yes, sufficient altogether, I would think. Though of course it will occur to you, I suppose—I mean, you being you—that while you were asking your questions in Latin, you were mentally formulating *answers* in Latin." It laughed. "All unconscious, of course. Yes, whatever would we do without unconsciousness, Karras? Do you see what I'm driving at? I cannot speak Latin at all! I read your mind! I merely plucked the responses from your head!"

Karras felt an instant dismay as his certainty crumbled; felt tantalized and frustrated now by the nagging doubt that had been planted in his brain.

The demon chuckled. "Yes, I knew that would occur to you, Karras," it croaked. "That is why I'm so fond of you, dear morsel; yes, that is why I cherish all reasonable men."

The demon's head tilted back in a wild spate of laughter.

The Jesuit's mind raced rapidly, desperately, formulating questions to which no single answer was correct, but rather many. *But maybe I'd think of them all!* he realized. *Then ask a question that you don't know the answer to!* he reasoned. He could check the answer later to see if it was correct.

He waited for the laughter to ebb and then spoke:

"Quam profundus est imus Oceanus Indicus?" What is the depth of the Indian Ocean at its deepest point?

The demon's eyes glittered. *"La plume de ma tante."*

"Responde Latine."

"Bon jour! Bonne nuit!"

"Quam—"

Karras broke off as the eyes rolled upward into their sockets and the gibberish entity appeared. Impatient and frustrated, Karras demanded, "Let me speak to the demon again!"

No answer. Only the breathing from an alien shore.

"Quis es tu?" he snapped hoarsely in a fraying voice.

Only silence. The breathing.

"Let me speak to Burke Dennings!"

A hiccup. Sputtery breathing. A hiccup.

"Let me speak to Burke Dennings!"

The hiccupping, regular and wrenching, continued. Karras lowered his head and shook it, then trudged to an overstuffed chair where he sat, leaned back and closed his eyes. Tense. Tormented. And waiting . . .

Time passed. Karras drowsed. Then jerked his head up. *Stay awake!* And then with blinking, heavy lids, he looked over at Regan. Not hiccupping now. Eyes closed. Was she asleep?

He stood up, walked over to the bed, reached down and felt Regan's pulse, then, stooping over, he examined her lips. They were parched. He straightened up and waited a little time, and then at last he left the room and went down to the kitchen in search of Sharon. He found her at the table eating soup and a sandwich. "Can I fix you something to eat, Father Karras?" she asked him. "You must be hungry."

"No, I'm not," Karras answered. "Thanks." Sitting down, he reached over and picked up a pencil and pad by Sharon's typewriter. "She's been hiccupping," he told her. "Have you had any Compazine prescribed?"

"Yes, we've got some."

He was writing on the pad. "Then tonight give her half of a twenty-five-milligram suppository."

"Okay."

"She's beginning to dehydrate," Karras continued, "so I'm switching her to intravenous feedings. First thing in the morning, call a medical-supply house and have them deliver these right away." He slid the pad across the table to Sharon. "In the meantime, she's sleeping, so you could start her on a Sustagen feeding."

Sharon nodded. "Right. I will." Spooning soup, she turned the pad around and looked at the list. Karras watched her. Then he frowned in concentration. "You're her tutor?" he said.

"Yes, that's right."

"Have you taught her any Latin?"

"Latin? No, I don't know any Latin. Why?"

"Any German?"

"Only French."

"What level? *La plume de ma tante?*"

"Pretty much."

"But no German or Latin."

"No."

"But the Engstroms—don't they sometimes speak German?"

"Oh, well, sure."

"Around Regan?"

Standing up, Sharon shrugged. "Oh, well, sometimes, I suppose." She started toward the kitchen sink with her plates as she added, "As a matter of fact, I'm pretty sure."

"Have you ever studied Latin?" Karras asked her.

Sharon giggled as she answered, "Me, Latin? No, I haven't."

"But you'd recognize the general sound?"

"Yeah, I guess."

She rinsed the soup bowl and put it in the rack.

"Has she ever spoken Latin in your presence?"

"Regan?"

"Yes. Since her illness."

"No, never."

"Any language at all?"

Sharon turned off the faucet, looking thoughtful. "Well, I might have imagined it, I guess, but . . ."

"But what?"

"Well, I think . . ." Sharon frowned. "Well, I could have sworn I heard her talking in Russian once."

Karras stared, his throat dry. "Do you speak it?" he asked.

"Oh, well, so-so. I took two years of it in college, that's all."

Karras sagged. *Then Regan* did *pick the Latin from my brain!* Staring bleakly, he lowered his brow into his hand and into doubt: *Telepathy more common in states of great tension*: *speaking always in a language known to someone in the room*: *". . . thinks the same things I'm thinking . . ."*: *"Bon jour . . ."*: *"La plume de ma tante . . ."*: *"Bonne nuit . . ."* With thoughts such as these, Karras sadly watched blood turning back into wine.

What to do? *Get some sleep. Then come back and try again . . .*

try again . . . He stood up and looked blearily at Sharon. She was leaning with her back against the sink, her arms folded, as she pensively and curiously watched him. "I'm going over to the residence," he told her. "As soon as Regan's awake, I'd like a call."

"Yes, I'll call you."

"And the Compazine. Okay? You won't forget?"

She shook her head. "No, I'll take care of it right away."

Karras nodded and with his hands in hip pockets, he looked down, trying to think of what he might have forgotten to tell Sharon. Always something to be done; always something overlooked when even everything was done.

"Father, what's going on?" he heard the secretary asking him somberly. "What is it? What's really going on with Rags?"

Karras lifted up eyes that were haunted and seared. "I don't know," he said emptily; "I really don't know."

He turned and walked out of the kitchen.

As he passed through the entry hall, Karras heard footsteps coming up rapidly behind him. "Father Karras!"

Karras turned and saw Karl with his sweater.

"Very sorry," said the houseman as he handed it over. "I was thinking to finish much before. But I forget."

He handed the sweater to Karras. The vomit stains were gone and it had a sweet smell. "That was thoughtful of you, Karl," the priest said to him gently. "Thank you."

"Thank *you*, Father Karras," said Karl with a tremor in his voice, his eyes full. "Thank you for your helping Miss Regan." Then averting his head, self-conscious, Karl turned and walked swiftly away.

As Karras watched him, he remembered him in Kinderman's car. Why? More mystery now; more confusion. Wearily, Karras turned around and opened the door. It was night. Despairing, he stepped out of darkness into darkness.

He crossed to the residence, groping toward sleep, but decided to stop by Dyer's room. He knocked on the door, heard "Advance and be proselytized!" from within, and, entering, found Dyer typing on his IBM Selectric. Karras flopped down on the edge of Dyer's cot as the younger Jesuit continued to type.

"Hey, Joe!"

"Yeah, I'm listening. What is it?"

"Do you happen to know of anyone who's done a formal exorcism?"

"Joe Louis, Max Schmeling, June twenty-second, 1938."

"Joe, get serious."

"No, *you* get serious. Exorcism? Are you kidding me?"

Karras made no answer and for moments he watched expressionlessly as Dyer continued to type, until at last he got up and walked to the door. "Yeah, Joe," he said, "I was kidding."

"I thought so."

"See ya round the campus."

"Find funnier jokes."

Karras walked down the hall and as he entered his room he looked down and saw a pink message slip on the floor. He picked it up. From Frank. A home number. "Please call . . ."

Karras picked up the telephone and requested that a call be put through to the Institute director's number, and as he waited, he looked down at his free hand, the right one. It was trembling with desperate hope.

"Hello?" Piping voice. A young boy.

"May I speak to your father, please."

"Yes. Just a minute." Phone clattering. Then quickly picked up. Still the boy. "Who is this?"

"Father Karras."

"Father Karits?"

"Karras. Father Karras . . ."

Down went the phone again.

Karras lifted the tremulous hand, lightly touching his fingertips to his brow.

Phone noise.

"Father Karras?"

"Yes, hello, Frank. I've been trying to reach you."

"Oh, I'm sorry. I've been working on your tapes at the house."

"Are you finished?"

"Yes, I am. By the way, this is pretty weird stuff."

"Yes, I know," said Karras as he strained to flatten the tension in his voice. "So what's the story so far? What have you found?"

"Well, this 'type-token' ratio, first . . ."

"Yes, Frank?"

"Now I didn't have enough of a sampling to be absolutely accurate, you understand, but I'd say it's pretty close, or at least it's as close as you can get with these things. Well, at any rate, the two different voices on the tapes, I would say, are probably separate personalities."

"Probably?"

"Well, I wouldn't want to swear to it in court; in fact, the variance is really pretty minimal."

"Minimal . . . ," Karras repeated dully. *Well, there goes the ball game.* "And what about the gibberish?" he asked. "Is it any kind of language?"

Frank chuckled.

"What's funny?" asked the Jesuit moodily.

"Was this really some sneaky psychological testing, Father?"

"What do you mean?"

"Well, I guess you got your tapes mixed around or something. It's—"

"Frank, is it a language or not?" cut in Karras.

"Oh, I'd say it was a language, all right."

Dumbfounded, Karras stiffened. "Are you kidding?"

"No, I'm not."

"What's the language?"

"It's English."

For a moment, Karras stared blankly, and when he spoke there was an edge to his voice. "Frank, we seem to have a very poor connection; or would you like to let me in on the joke?"

"Got your tape recorder there?"

It was sitting on his desk. "Yes, I do."

"Has it got a reverse-play position?"

"Why?"

"Has it *got* one?"

"Just a second." Irritable, Karras set down the phone and took the top off the tape recorder to check it. "Yes, it's got one. Frank, what's this all about?"

"Put your tape on the machine and play it backward."

"What?"

"You've got gremlins." Frank chuckled good-naturedly. "Look, play it and I'll talk to you tomorrow. Good night, Father."

"Night, Frank."

"Have fun."

"Yeah, right."

Karras hung up. He looked baffled. He hunted up the gibberish tape and placed it into the recorder. First he ran it forward and nodded his head. No mistake. It was gibberish.

He let it run through to the end and then played it in reverse. He heard his voice speaking backward. And then Regan's demon voice: *Marin marin karras let us be let us . . .*

English! Senseless! But still English!

How on earth could she do that? Karras marveled.

He listened to it all, rewound the tape and played it through again. And again. And then realized that the order of speech was inverted. He stopped the tape, rewound it, and with a pencil and a writing tablet at hand, he sat down at the desk and began to play the tape from the beginning while transcribing the words, working laboriously and long with almost constant stops and starts of the tape recorder. When finally it was done, he made another transcription on a second sheet of paper, reversing the order of the words. Then he leaned back and read it:

> . . . danger. Not yet. [unintelligible] will die. Little time. Now the [unintelligible]. Let her die. No, no, sweet! It is sweet in the body! I feel! There is [unintelligible]. Better [unintelligible] than the void. I fear the priest. Give us time. Fear the priest! He is [unintelligible]. No, not this one: the [unintelligible], the one who [unintelligible]. He is ill. Ah, the blood, feel the blood, how it [sings?].

Karras asked on the tape, "Who are you?" with the answer:

> I am no one. I am no one.

Then Karras: "Is that your name?" And the answer:

> I have no name. I am no one. Many. Let us be. Let us warm in the body. Do not [unintelligible] from the body into void, into [unintelligible]. Leave us. Leave us. Let us be. Karras. Merrin. Merrin.

Again and again Karras read his transcription over, haunted by its tone, by the feeling that more than one person was speaking, until finally repetition itself dulled the words into commonness and he set down the transcription and rubbed at his face, at his eyes, at his thoughts. Not an unknown language. And writing backward with facility was hardly paranormal or even unusual. But *speaking* backward: adjusting and altering the phonetics so that playing them backward would make them intelligible; wasn't such performance beyond the reach of even a hyperstimulated intellect, the accelerated unconscious referred to by Jung? No, something . . . something at the rim of memory. Then he remembered. He went to his shelves for a book: Jung's *Psychology and Pathology of So-called Occult Phenomena.* Something similar here, he was thinking as he rapidly searched through the pages of the book. What was it?

He found it: an account of an experiment with automatic writing in which the unconscious of the subject seemed able to answer his questions with anagrams. *Anagrams!*

He propped the book open on the desk, leaned over and read an account of a portion of the experiment:

3RD DAY

What is man? *Tefi hasl esble lies.*
Is that an anagram? *Yes.*
How many words does it contain? *Five.*
What is the first word? *See.*
What is the second word? *Eeeee.*
See? Shall I interpret it myself? *Try to!*

The subject found this solution: *"The life is less able."* He was astonished at this intellectual pronouncement, which seemed to him to prove the existence of an intelligence independent of his own. He therefore went on to ask:

Who are you? *Clelia.*
Are you a woman? *Yes.*
Have you lived on earth? *No.*
Will you come to life? *Yes.*
When? *In six years.*
Why are you conversing with me? *E if Clelia el.*

The subject interpreted this answer as an anagram for "I, Clelia, feel."

4TH DAY

Am I the one who answers the questions? *Yes.*
Is Clelia there? *No.*
Who is there, then? *Nobody.*
Does Clelia exist at all? *No.*
Then who was I talking to yesterday? *With nobody.*

Karras stopped reading and shook his head. There was nothing paranormal here, he thought, only proof of the limitless abilities of the mind. He reached for a cigarette, sat down and lit it. *"I am no one. Many."* Where did it come from, Karras wondered, this eerie content of Regan's speech? From the same place Clelia had come from? Emergent personalities?

"Merrin . . . Merrin . . ." "Ah, the blood . . ." "He is ill . . ."

His eyes haunted, Karras glanced at his copy of *Satan* and moodily leafed to the opening inscription: *"Let not the dragon be my leader . . ."* Closing his eyes as he exhaled smoke, Karras lifted a fist to his mouth as he coughed, and, aware of his throat feeling raw and inflamed, he crushed out the cigarette in an ashtray. Exhausted, he slowly and awkwardly got up, flicked out the room light, shuttered his window blinds, kicked off his shoes and collapsed facedown on his narrow cot. Fevered fragments spun and tumbled through his mind: Regan. Kinderman. Dennings. What to do? He must help! He had to help! But how? Try the Bishop with what little he had? He did not think so. He could never convincingly argue the case.

He thought of undressing, of getting under the covers.

Too tired. This burden. He wanted to be free.

". . . Let us be!"

As he began the slow drift into granite sleep, Karras's lips moved almost imperceptibly, forming the soundless words "Let me be." And then suddenly he was lifting his head, awakened by adenoidal breathing and the soft sound of cellophane being crinkled, and opening his eyes he saw a stranger in his room, a slightly overweight, middle-aged, freckle-faced priest with thin strands of red hair that were combed straight back on a balding head. Sitting in an overstuffed corner chair, he was watching Karras and tearing off the seal from a packet of Gauloises cigarettes. The priest smiled. "Oh, well, hello."

Karras swung his legs around and sat up.

"Yeah, hello and good-bye," Karras growled. "Who are you and what the fuck are you doing in my room?"

"Look, I'm sorry, but when I knocked and you didn't answer, I saw the door was unlocked so I just thought I'd come in and wait. And then there you were!" The priest gestured to a pair of crutches tilted and leaned against the wall near the chair. "I couldn't wait for very long in the hall, you see; I can stand for so long but then at some point I just have to sit. I do hope you'll forgive me. I'm Ed Lucas, by the way. Your Father President suggested that I see you."

Slightly frowning, Karras tilted his head to the side.

"You said 'Lucas'?"

"Yes, it's Lucas all the time," said the priest, his grin displaying long and nicotine-stained teeth. He'd extracted a cigarette from the packet and was slipping a hand into his pocket for a lighter. "Mind if I smoke?"

"No, go ahead. I'm a smoker."

"Oh, well, yes," Lucas said as he glanced at a crush of cigarette butts in an ashtray on the end table next to his chair. The priest held out the cigarette packet to Karras. "Try a Gauloise?"

"Thanks, no. Look, you said that Tom Bermingham sent you?"

"Good old Tom. Yeah, we're 'buds.' We were in the same high school class at Regis, and after that we did our Tertianship together at St. Andrews on Hudson. Yes, Tom recommended that I see you, so I took a Greyhound from New York. I'm at Fordham."

Karras's mood abruptly lifted. He said, "Oh, New York! Is this about my request for reassignment?"

"Reassignment? No, I know nothing at all about that. It's a personal matter," said the priest.

Karras's shoulders slumped with his hopes. "Well, okay then," he said in a tone more subdued. He stood up and walked over to the straight-backed wooden chair behind his desk, turned it around, sat down and began to measure Lucas with a clinically appraising eye. To Karras, from this closer vantage, the priest's black suit looked rumpled and baggy, even seedy. There was dandruff on the shoulders. The priest had pulled a cigarette out of its package and now he lit it with the leaping, tall flame of a Zippo lighter that he seemed to have produced unnoticed from a pocket, like a magician's sleight-of-hand, and then blew out a stream of moody bluish gray smoke, which he watched with what looked like a deep satisfaction as he drawled, "Ah, there's just nothing like a Gauloise for the nerves!"

"Are you nervous, Ed?"

"A little."

"Well, okay, then let's get to it. Go ahead and lay it out for me, Ed. How can I help you?"

Lucas studied Karras with a look of concern. "You look exhausted," he said. "Perhaps it's best if we meet up tomorrow. What do you say?" Then he quickly added, "Yes! Yes, most definitely tomorrow! Could you hand those to me, please?"

He had reached out a hand to the crutches.

"No, no, no!" Karras told him. "I'm fine, Ed! Just fine!"

Leaning forward with his hands clasped together between his knees, Karras scanned the priest's face as he told him, "Procrastination is what we often call 'resistance.' "

Lucas lifted an eyebrow, in his eyes a faint hint of what might have been bemusement. "Oh, is that so?"

"Yes, it's so."

Karras lowered his gaze to Lucas's legs.

"Does that depress you?" he asked.

"What do you mean? Oh, my legs! Oh, well sometimes, I suppose."

"Congenital?"

"No. No, it happened in a fall."

For a moment Karras studied his visitor's face. That faint, secret smile. Had he seen it yet again? "That's too bad," Karras murmured sympathetically.

"Oh, well, that's the world we've inherited, not so?" reacted Lucas, the Gauloise cigarette still dangling from a corner of his mouth. He took it from his lips between two fingers and lamented amid an exhale of smoke, "Ah, well."

"So okay, Ed, let's get to it. Okay? You didn't come here all the way from New York to play dodgeball with me, that's for sure, so let's open up now. Tell me everything. Okay? Open up."

Lucas gently shook his head and looked aside. "Oh, well, it's such a long story," he began, but then he had to put a fist to his mouth as a new spell of coughing racked him.

"Want a drink?" Karras asked.

His eyes watering, the priest shook his head. "No, no, I'm fine," he said chokingly, "Really!" as the spasm seemed to pass. He looked down and brushed cigarette ash from the front of his jacket. "Filthy habit!" he grumbled as Karras noticed now what looked to be a soft-boiled egg stain on the black clergy shirt the priest wore beneath his jacket.

"Okay, what's the problem?" Karras asked.

Lucas lifted his gaze to him and said, "You."

Karras blinked. He said, "Me?"

"Yes, Damien, you. Tom's terribly worried about you."

Karras stared at Lucas steadily now with the beginning of realization, for in his eyes and in his voice there was a deep compassion. "Ed, what do you do up at Fordham?" Karras asked.

"I counsel," said the priest.

"You counsel."

"Yes, Damien. I'm a psychiatrist."

Karras stared. "A psychiatrist," he echoed blankly.

Lucas looked aside. "Oh, well, now where do I begin?" he breathed out reluctantly. "I'm not sure. It's so tricky. *Very* tricky. Ah, well then, let's see what we can do," he said softly, leaning over and tamping out his Gauloise in the ashtray. "But then again you're a pro," he said, looking up, "and at times it's best to put things on the table straightaway." The priest began coughing into his fist again. "Damn! I'm so sorry! Really!" The coughing ended, Lucas eyed Karras somberly. "Look, it's all this crazy business with you and the MacNeils."

Karras reacted with surprise. "The MacNeils?" he marveled. "Listen, how could you possibly know about that? There's no way that Tom would ever let that out. No, no way. It would be harmful to the family."

"There are sources."

"What sources? Such as who? Such as what?"

"Does it matter?" said the priest. "No, not at all. All that matters is your health and your emotional stability, both of which are clearly already in danger, and this thing with the MacNeils will only stress it all the more, so the Provincial is ordering you to break it off. Break it off for your own sake, Karras, as well as for the good of the Order!" The priest's bushy eyebrows had gathered inward, almost touching, and he'd lowered his head so that his stare and his visage seemed threatening. "Break it off!" he warned, "before it leads to some greater catastrophe; before things get even worse, *much* worse! We don't want any more desecrations now, Damien, do we?"

Karras stared at his visitor in bafflement, and then shock.

"The desecrations? Ed, what are you talking about? What does my mental health have to do with *them?*"

Lucas leaned back in his chair. "Oh, come on!" he scoffed cynically. "You join the Jesuits and leave your poor mother to die all alone and in abject poverty? And so who would someone hate for all of that unconsciously if not the Catholic Church!" Here, the priest leaned forward again, hunching over as he hissed, "Don't be obtuse! *Stay away from the MacNeils!*"

His eyes tight, his head angled in surmise, Karras rose and stared down at the priest, demanding huskily, "Who in the hell are you, pal? *Who are you?*"

The soft ringing of the telephone on Karras's desk drew a swift, alarmed glance from Father Lucas. "Watch out for Sharon!" he warned Karras sharply, and then abruptly the phone was ringing loudly so that Karras awakened and realized he'd been dreaming. Groggy, he got up from his cot, stumbled over to a light switch, flicked it on, and then moved to the desk and picked up the phone. It was Sharon. What time was it? he asked her. A little after three. Could he come to the house right away? *Ah, God!* Karras inwardly groaned, and yet, "Yes," he said. Yes. He would come. And once again he felt trapped; smothered; enmeshed.

He lurched into his white-tiled bathroom where he splashed cold water on his face and, drying off, he suddenly remembered Father Lucas and the dream. What did it mean? Perhaps nothing. He would think about it later. When about to leave his room, at the door Karras stopped, turned around and came back for a black woolen sweater, pulling it over his head, and as he tugged it down, he abruptly stopped, numbly staring at the end table by the corner chair. Taking a breath and then a slow step forward, he reached down to the ashtray, picked up a cigarette butt and then stood motionless for a time as he held it up to his stunned surmise. It was a Gauloise. Racing thoughts. Suppositions. A coldness. Then an urgency: *"Watch out for Sharon!"* Karras placed the Gauloise butt back into the ashtray, hurried from his room and down the hall and then out onto Prospect Street, where the air was thin and still and damp. He passed the steps, crossed over to the opposite side diagonally and found Sharon watching and waiting for him at the MacNeil house's open front door. Looking frightened and bewildered, one hand held a flashlight while a hand at her neck held together the edges of a blanket that was draped around her shoulders. "Sorry, Father," she huskily whispered as the Jesuit entered the house, "but I thought you ought to see this."

"See what?"

Sharon soundlessly closed the door. "I'll have to show you," she whispered. "Let's be quiet, now. I don't want to wake up Chris. She shouldn't see this." She beckoned and Karras followed her, tiptoeing quietly up the stairs to Regan's bedroom. Entering, the Jesuit felt chilled. The room was icy. Frowning, he turned a questioning look to Sharon, and she nodded her head and whispered, "Yes, Father. Yes. The heat's on." They turned and stared at Regan, at the whites of her eyes glowing eerily in dim lamplight. She seemed to be in a coma. Heavy breathing. Motionless. The nasogastric tubing was in place and the Sustagen was slowly seeping into her body.

Sharon moved quietly toward the bedside. Karras followed, still staggered by the cold. When they were standing by the bed, he saw beads of perspiration on Regan's forehead; glanced down and saw her wrists gripped firmly in the leather restraining straps. Sharon bent over the bed, gently pulling the top of Regan's pink and white pajama top wide apart, and an overwhelming pity hit Karras at the sight of the wasted chest, the protruding ribs where one might count the remaining weeks or days of her life. He felt Sharon's haunted stare upon him. "I don't know if it's stopped," she whispered. "But watch: just keep looking at her chest."

Sharon turned on the flashlight and shone it on Regan's bare chest, and the Jesuit, puzzled, followed her gaze. Then silence. Regan's slightly whistling breathing. Watching. The cold. Then the Jesuit's brows knitted tightly together as he saw something happening to the skin of Regan's chest: a faint redness, but in sharp definition. He peered down closer.

"There, it's coming!" Sharon whispered sharply.

Abruptly the gooseflesh on Karras's arms was not from the icy cold in the room, but from what he was seeing on Regan's chest; from the bas-relief script rising up in clear letters of raised and blood-red skin. Two words:

help me

Her wide stare riveted to the words, Sharon's breath came frosty as she whispered, "That's her handwriting, Father."

At 9:00 that morning, Karras went to the president of Georgetown University and asked for permission to seek an exorcism. He received it, and immediately afterward went to the Bishop of the diocese, who listened with grave attention to all that Karras had to say. "You're convinced that it's genuine?" the Bishop asked finally.

"Well, I've made a prudent judgment that it meets the conditions set forth in the *Ritual*," Karras answered evasively. He still did not dare to believe. Not his mind but his heart had tugged him to this moment: pity and the hope for a cure through suggestion.

"You would want to do the exorcism yourself?"

Karras felt elation; saw the door swinging open to fields, to escape from the crushing weight of caring and that meeting each twilight with the ghost of his faith. And yet, "Yes, Your Grace," he answered.

"How's your health?"

"My health is fine, Your Grace."

"Have you ever been involved with this sort of thing before?"

"No, I haven't."

"Well, we'll see. It might be best to have a man with experience. There aren't too many these days but perhaps someone back from the foreign missions. Let me see who's around. In the meantime, I'll call you as soon as we know."

When Karras had left him, the Bishop called the president of Georgetown University, and they talked about Karras for the second time that day.

"Well, he does know the background," said the president at a point in their conversation. "I doubt there's any danger in just having him assist. In any case, there should be a psychiatrist present."

"And what about the exorcist? Any ideas? I'm a blank."

"Well, now, Lankester Merrin's around."

"Merrin? I had a notion he was over in Iraq. I think I read he was working on a dig around Nineveh."

"Yes, down below Mosul. That's right. But he finished and came back around three or four months ago, Mike. He's at Woodstock."

"Teaching?"

"No, he's working on another book."

"God help us! Don't you think he's too old, though? How's his health?"

"Well, it must be all right or he wouldn't still be running around digging up tombs, don't you think?"

"Yes, I suppose so."

"And besides, he's had experience, Mike."

"I didn't know that."

"Well, at least that's the word."

"And when was that? This experience, I mean."

"Oh, maybe ten or twelve years ago, I think, in Africa. Supposedly the exorcism lasted for months. I heard it damn near killed him."

"Well, in that case, I doubt that he'd want to do another one."

"We do what we're told here, Mike. All the rebels are over there with you seculars."

"Thanks for reminding me."

"Well, what do you think?"

"Look, I'll leave it up to you and the Provincial."

Early that quietly waiting evening, a young scholastic preparing for the priesthood wandered the grounds of Woodstock

Seminary in Maryland. He was searching for a slender, gray-haired old Jesuit. He found him on a pathway, strolling through a grove. He handed him a telegram. His manner serene, the old priest thanked him and then turned to renew his contemplation, to continue his walk through a nature that he loved. Now and then he would pause to hear the song of a robin, to watch a bright butterfly hover on a branch. He did not open and read the telegram. He knew what it said. He had read it in the dust of the temples of Nineveh. He was ready.

He continued his farewells.

"And let my cry come unto thee . . ."

He who abides in love, abides in God,
and God in him . . .

—*Saint John*

Chapter One

In the breathing dark of his quiet office, Kinderman brooded above his desk. He adjusted the desk-lamp beam a fraction. Below him were records, transcripts, exhibits; police files; crime lab reports; scribbled notes. In a pensive mood, he had carefully fashioned them into a collage in the shape of a rose, as if to belie the ugly conclusion to which they had led him; that he could not accept.

Engstrom was innocent. At the time of Dennings's death, he had been visiting his daughter, supplying her with money for the purchase of drugs. He had lied about his whereabouts that night in order to protect her and to shield her mother, who believed Elvira to be dead and past all harm and degradation.

It was not from Karl that Kinderman had learned this. On the night of their encounter in Elvira's hallway, the houseman had kept obdurately silent. It was only when Kinderman apprised the daughter of her father's involvement in the Dennings case that she volunteered the truth. There were witnesses to confirm it. Engstrom was innocent. Innocent and silent concerning events that involved the MacNeils.

Kinderman frowned at the collage: something was wrong with the composition. He shifted a petal point—the corner of a deposition—a trifle lower and to the right.

Roses. Elvira. He had warned her grimly that failure to

check herself into a clinic within two weeks would result in his dogging her trail with warrants until he had evidence to effect her arrest. Yet he did not believe she would go. There were times when he stared at the law unblinkingly as he would the noonday sun in the hope it would temporarily blind him while some quarry made its escape. Engstrom was innocent. What remained? Gently wheezing, the detective shifted his weight and, closing his eyes, he imagined he was soaking in a sudsy hot bath. *Mental Closeout Sale!* he bannered at himself: *Moving to New Conclusions! Everything Must Go!* Then, *Positively!* he added sternly, and with that the detective opened his eyes and examined afresh the bewildering data.

Item: The death of director Burke Dennings seemed somehow linked to the desecrations at Holy Trinity. Both involved witchcraft and the unknown desecrator could easily be Dennings's murderer.

Item: An expert on witchcraft, a Jesuit priest, had been seen making visits to the home of the MacNeils.

Item: The typewritten sheet of paper containing the text of the blasphemous altar card discovered at Holy Trinity had been checked for latent fingerprints. Impressions had been found on both sides. Some had been made by Damien Karras. But still another set had been found that, from their size, were adjudged to be those of a person with very small hands, quite possibly a child.

Item: The typing on the altar card had been analyzed and compared with the typed impressions on the unfinished letter that Sharon Spencer had pulled from her typewriter, crumpled up and tossed at a wastepaper basket, missing it, while Kinderman had been questioning Chris. He had picked it up and smuggled it out of the house. The typing on this letter and the typing on the altar card sheet had been done on the same machine.

According to the report, however, the touch of the typists differed. The person who had typed the blasphemous text had a touch far heavier than Sharon Spencer's. Since the typing of the former, moreover, had not been "hunt and peck" but skillfully accomplished, it suggested that the unknown typist of the altar card text was a person of extraordinary strength.

Item: Burke Dennings—if his death was not an accident—had been killed by a person of extraordinary strength.

Item: Engstrom was no longer a suspect.

Item: A check of domestic airline reservations disclosed that Chris MacNeil had taken her daughter to Dayton, Ohio. Kinderman had known that the daughter was ill and was being taken to a clinic. But the clinic in Dayton would have to be Barringer. Kinderman had checked and the clinic confirmed that the daughter had been in for observation. Though the clinic refused to state the nature of the illness, it was obviously a serious mental disorder.

Item: Serious mental disorders at times caused extraordinary strength.

Kinderman sighed, closed his eyes and shook his head. He was back to the same conclusion. Then he opened his eyes and stared at the center of the paper rose: a faded old copy of a national newsmagazine. On the cover were Chris and Regan. He studied the daughter: the sweet, freckled face and the ribboned ponytails, the missing front tooth in the grin. He looked out a window into darkness, where a drizzling rain had begun to fall.

He went down to the garage, got into the unmarked black sedan and then drove through rain-slick, shining streets to Georgetown, where he parked on the eastern side of Prospect Street and for minutes sat silently staring up at Regan's window. Should he knock at the door and demand to see her? Lowering his head, he rubbed at his brow. *William F. Kinderman, you are sick!* he thought. *You are ill! Go home! Take medicine! Sleep! Get better!* He looked up at the window again and ruefully shook his head. To this place had his haunted logic led him. He shifted his gaze as a cab pulled up to the house. He started his engine and turned on the windshield wipers in time to see a tall old man stepping out of the cab. He paid the driver, then turned and stood motionless under a misty streetlamp's glow, staring up at a window of the house like a melancholy traveler frozen in time. As the cab pulled away and rounded the corner of Thirty-Sixth Street, Kinderman quickly pulled out to follow. As he turned the corner, he blinked his headlights, signaling the taxi to stop, while inside the MacNeil house at that moment Karras and Karl were pinning Regan's emaciated arms while Sharon injected her with Librium, bringing the total amount injected in the last two hours to four hundred milligrams, a dosage, Karras knew, that was staggering; but after a lull of many hours, the demonic personality had awakened in a fit of fury so frenzied that Regan's debilitated system could not for very long endure it.

Karras was exhausted. After his visit to the Chancery Office that morning, he returned to the house to tell Chris what had happened, and after setting up an intravenous feeding for Regan, he'd gone back to his room in the Jesuit residence hall, where he fell facedown and limp onto his bed and instantly into a profound and deep sleep. But after barely two hours, the strident ringing of his telephone had wrenched him awake. Sharon. Regan was still unconscious and her pulse had been gradually slipping lower. Karras had then rushed to the house with his medical bag and pinched Regan's Achilles tendon, looking for reaction to pain. There was none. He pressed down hard on one of her fingernails. Again, there was no reaction. Karras grew alarmed: though he knew that in hysteria and in certain states of trance there was sometimes an insensitivity to pain, he now feared coma, a state from which Regan might so very easily slip into death. He checked her blood pressure: ninety over sixty; then her pulse rate: sixty. He had waited in the room then, and checked her again every fifteen minutes for an hour and a half before he was satisfied that both her blood pressure and pulse rate had stabilized, meaning Regan was not in shock but rather in a state of stupor. Sharon was instructed to continue to check Regan's pulse every hour. Then Karras had returned to his room and his sleep. But now again a ringing telephone awakened him. The exorcist, the Chancery Office told him, would be Lankester Merrin, with Karras to assist.

The news had stunned him. Merrin! the philosopher-paleontologist! the soaring, staggering intellect! His books had stirred ferment in the Church, for they interpreted his faith in terms of matter that was still evolving and destined to be spirit that at the end of time would join with Christ, the "Omega Point."

Karras had immediately telephoned Chris to give her the news, but found that she'd heard from the Bishop directly that Merrin would arrive the next day. "I told the Bishop he could stay at the house," Chris said. "It'll just be a day or so, won't it?" Before answering, Karras had paused, then said quietly, "I don't know." And then, pausing again, he said, "You mustn't expect too much." "If it works, you mean," Chris had answered. Her tone had been subdued. "I didn't mean to imply that it wouldn't," the priest reassured her. "I just meant that it might take time." "How long?" "It varies." Karras knew that an exorcism could take weeks, even months; knew that frequently it failed altogether. He expected the latter; expected that the burden, barring cure through suggestion, would fall once again, and at the last, upon him. "It can take a few days or weeks," he'd then told her, and she'd answered him numbly, "How long has she got, Father Karras?"

When he'd hung up the phone, he'd felt heavy, tormented; stretched out on his bed, he thought of Merrin. *Merrin!* An excitement and a hope had seeped into him, although a sinking disquiet had followed. He himself had been the natural choice for exorcist, and yet the Bishop had passed him over. Why? Because Merrin had done this before? As he'd closed his eyes, he'd recalled that exorcists were selected on the basis of "piety" and "high moral qualities"; that a passage in the gospel of Matthew related that Christ, when asked by his disciples the cause of their failure in an effort at exorcism, had answered, "Because of your little faith." The Provincial had known about his problem, as had also Tom Bermingham, the Georgetown president. Had either of them mentioned it to the Bishop?

Here Karras had turned over on his bed, despondent; feeling somehow unworthy; incompetent; rejected. It stung. Unreasonably, it stung. Then, finally, sleep flowed into his emptiness, filling in the niches and cracks in his heart.

Then again the waking ring of his telephone, Chris calling to inform him of Regan's sudden frenzy. Back at the house, he checked Regan's pulse. It was strong. He gave her Librium, then gave it again. And again. Finally, he made his way to the kitchen, slumping down at the breakfast table with Chris. She was reading a book, one of Merrin's that she'd ordered delivered to the house. "Way over my head," she told Karras softly; and yet she looked touched and deeply moved. "But there's some of it so beautiful—so great." She flipped back through pages to a passage she had marked, and handed the book across the table to Karras.

"Here, take a look. Ever read it?"

"I dunno. Let me see."

Karras took the book and began to read:

We have familiar experience of the order, the constancy, the perpetual renovation of the material world which surrounds us. Frail and transitory as is every part of it, restless and migratory as are its elements, still it abides. It is bound together by a law of permanence, and though it is ever dying, it is ever coming to life again. Dissolution does but give birth to fresh modes of organization, and one death is the parent of a thousand lives. Each hour, as it comes, is but a testimony how fleeting, yet how secure, how certain, is the great whole. It is like an image on the waters, which is ever the same, though the waters ever flow. The sun sinks to rise again; the day is swallowed up in the gloom of night, to be born out of it, as fresh as if it had never been quenched. Spring passes into summer, and through summer and autumn into winter, only the more surely, by its own ultimate return, to triumph over that grave towards which it resolutely hastened from its first hour. We mourn the blossoms of May because they are to wither; but we know that May is one day to have its revenge upon November, by the revolution of that solemn circle which never stops—which teaches us in our height of hope, ever to be sober, and in our depth of desolation, never to despair.

"Yes, it's beautiful," Karras said softly, and as he poured a cup of coffee for himself, the raging of the demon from upstairs grew louder.

"Bastard . . . scum . . . pious hypocrite!"

"She used to put a rose on my plate . . . in the morning . . . before I'd go to work," Chris said distantly.

Karras looked up with a question in his eyes, and Chris answered it: "Regan," she told him.

She looked down. "Yeah, that's right. I forget."

"Forget what?"

"I forget that you've never met her."

She blew her nose and dabbed at her eyes.

"Want some brandy in that coffee?"

"Thanks, no."

"Coffee's flat," Chris whispered tremulously. "I think I will get some brandy. Excuse me." She stood up and left the kitchen.

Karras sat alone and sipped bleakly at his coffee. He felt warm in the sweater that he wore beneath his cassock; felt weak in his failure to have given Chris comfort. Then a memory of childhood shimmered up sadly, a memory of Reggie, his mongrel dog, growing skeletal and dazed in a box in a run-down tenement apartment; Reggie shivering with fever and vomiting while Karras tried covering him with towels, tried to make him drink warm milk, until a neighbor came by, looked at Reggie and, shaking his head, said, "Your dog has distemper. He needed shots right away." Then dismissal from school one afternoon . . . to the street . . . in columns of twos to the corner . . . his mother there to meet him . . . unexpected . . . looking sad . . . and then pressing a shiny half-dollar piece into his hand . . . elation . . . so much money! . . . then her voice, soft and tender, "Reggie die . . ."

He looked down at the steaming, bitter blackness in his cup and felt his hands bare of comfort or of cure.

". . . pious bastard!"

The demon. Still raging.

"Your dog needed shots right away."

Karras immediately got up and returned to Regan's bedroom, where he held her while Sharon administered a Librium injection that brought the total dosage up to five hundred milligrams. As Sharon swabbed the needle puncture, preparing to slap a Band-Aid onto it, Karras was staring down at Regan in puzzlement, for the frenzied obscenities spewing from her mouth seemed directed at no one in the room, but rather at someone unseen—or not present.

He dismissed it. "I'll be back," he told Sharon.

Concerned about Chris, he went down to the kitchen, where again he found her sitting alone at the table. She was pouring brandy into her coffee. "Are you sure you wouldn't like some, Father?" she asked him.

Shaking his head, he came over to the table, where he sat down wearily and lowered his face into his hands on propped elbows; heard the porcelain clicks of a spoon stirring coffee. "Have you talked to her father?" he asked.

"Yes, he called," Chris said. "He wanted to talk to Rags."

"And what did you tell him?"

"I told him she was out at a party."

Silence. Karras heard no more clicks. He looked up and saw Chris staring up at the ceiling. And then he noticed it too: the shouting of obscenities above had ceased.

"I guess the Librium took hold," he said gratefully.

Chiming of the doorbell. Karras glanced toward the sound, then at Chris, who met his look of surmise with a questioning, apprehensive lifting of an eyebrow. Kinderman?

Seconds ticked by as they sat and listened. No one was coming to answer; Willie was resting in her room and Sharon and Karl were still upstairs. Tense, Chris abruptly got up from the table and went to the living room, where, kneeling on a sofa, she parted a curtain and peered furtively through the window at her caller. No, not Kinderman. *Thank God!* It was a tall old man in a threadbare black raincoat and black felt hat, his head bowed patiently in the rain as at his side he was gripping a black valise. For an instant, a silvery buckle gleamed in streetlamp glow as the bag shifted slightly in his grip. *Who on earth is that?*

Another doorbell chime.

Puzzled, Chris got down off the sofa and walked to the entry hall. She opened the front door slightly, squinting out into darkness as a fine mist of rain brushed across her eyes. The man's hat brim obscured his face. "Yes, hello; can I help you?"

"Mrs. MacNeil?" came a voice from the shadows, gentle and refined, yet as full as a harvest.

As the stranger reached up to remove his hat, Chris was nodding her head, and then suddenly she was looking into eyes that overwhelmed her: that shone with intelligence and kindly understanding, with serenity that poured from them into her being like the waters of a warm and healing river whose source was both in him and yet somehow beyond him; whose flow was contained and yet headlong and endless.

"I'm Father Lankester Merrin," he said.

For a moment Chris stared blankly at the lean and ascetic face, at the sculptured cheekbones polished like soapstone; then quickly she flung wide the door. "Oh my gosh, please come *in!* Oh, come *in!* Gee, I'm . . . *Honestly!* I don't know where my . . ."

He entered and she closed the door.

"I mean, I didn't expect you until tomorrow!" Chris finished.

"Yes, I know," she heard him saying.

As she turned around to face him, she saw him standing with his head angled sideways, glancing upward, as if he were listening—no, more like *feeling*, she thought—for some presence out of sight; for some distant vibration that was known and familiar. Puzzled, Chris studied him. His skin seemed weathered by a sun that shone elsewhere, somewhere remote from her time and her place.

What's he doing?

"Can I take that bag for you, Father?"

"It's all right," he said softly. Still feeling. Still probing. "It's like part of my arm: very old . . . very battered." He looked down with a warm, tired smile in his eyes. "I'm accustomed to the weight. Is Father Karras here?"

"Yes, he is. He's in the kitchen. Have you had any dinner, Father Merrin?"

Merrin did not answer. Instead, he flicked his glance upward at the sound of a door being opened. "Yes, I had some on the train."

"Are you sure you wouldn't like something else?"

No answer. Then the sound of the door being closed. Merrin's warm gaze came back to Chris. "No, thank you," he said. "You're very kind."

Still flustered, "Gee, all of this rain," Chris babbled. "If I'd known you were coming, I could have met you at the station."

"It's all right."

"Did you have to wait long for a cab?"

"A few minutes."

"I'll take that, Father!"

Karl. He'd descended the stairs very quickly and now slipped the bag from the priest's easy grip and took it down the hall.

"We've put a bed in the study for you, Father." Chris was fidgeting. "It's really very comfortable and I thought you'd like the privacy. I'll show you where it is." She'd started moving, then stopped. "Or would you like to say hello to Father Karras?"

"I should like to see your daughter first."

"Right now, you mean, Father?" Chris said doubtfully.

Merrin glanced upward again with that air of distant attentiveness. "Yes, now," he said. "I think now."

"Gee, I'm sure she's asleep."

"I think not."

"Well, if—"

Suddenly, Chris flinched at a sound from above, at the voice of the demon. Booming and yet muffled, croaking, like an amplified premature burial, it called out "Merriiiiinnnnnn!" And then the massive and shiveringly hollow jolt of a single sledgehammer blow against the bedroom wall.

"God almighty!" Chris breathed out as she clutched a pale hand against her chest. Stunned, she looked at Merrin. The priest hadn't moved. He was still staring upward, intense and yet serene, and in his eyes there was not even a hint of surprise. It was more, Chris thought, like recognition.

Another blow shook the walls.

"Merriiiiinnnnnnnnnn!"

The Jesuit moved slowly forward, oblivious of Chris, who was gaping in wonder; of Karl, stepping lithe and incredulous from the study; of Karras, emerging bewildered from the kitchen while the nightmarish poundings and croakings continued. Merrin went calmly up the staircase, a slender hand like alabaster sliding upward on the banister. Karras came up beside Chris, and together they watched from below as Merrin entered Regan's bedroom and closed the door behind him. For a time there was silence. Then abruptly the demon laughed hideously and Merrin swiftly exited the room, closed the door, then moved quickly down the hall while behind him the bedroom door opened again and Sharon poked her head out, staring after him with an odd expression on her face.

Merrin descended the staircase rapidly and put out his hand to the waiting Karras.

"Father Karras!"

"Hello, Father."

Merrin had clasped Karras's hand in both of his; he was squeezing it, searching the younger priest's face with a look of gravity and concern, while upstairs the hideous laughter turned to vicious obscenities directed at Merrin. "You look terribly tired," Merrin said. "Are you tired?"

"No."

"Good. Do you have your raincoat here with you?"

"No, I don't."

"Well, then here, take mine," said the gray-haired Jesuit, unbuttoning the rain-sprinkled coat. "I should like you to go to the residence, Damien, and gather up a cassock for myself, two surplices, a purple stole, some holy water and two copies of *The Roman Ritual*, the large one." He handed his raincoat to the puzzled Karras. "I believe we should begin."

Karras frowned. "You mean now? Right away?"

"Yes, I think so."

"Don't you want to hear the background of the case first?"

"Why?"

Karras realized that he had no answer. He averted his gaze from those disconcerting eyes. "Right, Father," he said. He was slipping on the raincoat and turning away. "I'll go and get them."

Karl made a dash across the room, got ahead of Karras and pulled the front door open for him. They exchanged brief glances, and then Karras stepped out into the rainy night. Merrin glanced back to Chris. "I should have asked you. You don't mind if we begin right away?"

She'd been watching him, glowing with relief at the sense of decision and direction and command sweeping into the house like sun-drenched day. "No, I'm glad," she said gratefully. "But you must be so tired, Father Merrin."

The old priest saw her anxious gaze flicking upward toward the raging of the demon. "Would you like a cup of coffee?" she was asking in a voice that was insistent and faintly pleading. "It's hot and fresh-made. Wouldn't you like some?"

Merrin saw the hands lightly clasping and unclasping; the

deep caverns of her eyes. "Yes, I would," he said warmly. "Thank you." Something heavy had been gently brushed aside; told to wait. "If you're sure it's no trouble."

Chris led him to the kitchen and soon he was leaning against the stove with a mug of black coffee in his hands. Chris picked up a liquor bottle. "Want some brandy in it, Father?" she asked him.

Merrin bent his head and looked down into his coffee mug without expression. "Well, the doctors say I shouldn't," he said, "but thank God, my will is weak."

Chris blinked and stared blankly, unsure of his meaning, until she saw the smile in his eyes as he lifted his head and held out his mug. "Yes, thank you, I will."

With a smile, Chris poured the liquor. "What a lovely name you have," Merrin told her as she did so. "Chris MacNeil. It's not a stage name?"

Trickling brandy into her coffee, Chris shook her head. "No, I'm really not Sadie Glutz."

"Thank God for *that*," murmured Merrin with lowered eyes.

With a gentle, warm smile, Chris sat down. "And what's Lankester, Father? So unusual. Were you named after someone?"

"I think perhaps a cargo ship," Merrin murmured as he stared off absently. Lifting the coffee mug to his lips, he sipped, then reflected, "Or a bridge. Yes, I suppose it was a bridge." Turning his gaze to Chris, he looked ruefully amused. "But now 'Damien,' " he said; "how I wish I had a name like that. So lovely."

"Where does that come from, Father? That name?"

"It was the name of a priest who devoted his life to taking care of the lepers on the island of Molokai. He finally caught the disease himself." Merrin looking aside. "Lovely name," he said again. "I believe that with a first name like Damien, I might even be content with the last name Glutz."

Chris chuckled. She unwound. Felt easier. And for minutes, she and Merrin spoke of homely things, little things. Finally, Sharon appeared in the kitchen, and only then did Merrin move to leave. It was as if he had been waiting for her arrival, for immediately he carried his mug to the sink, rinsed it out and placed it carefully in the dish rack. "That was good; that was just what I wanted," he said.

Chris got up and said, "I'll take you to your room." Merrin thanked her and followed her to the door of the study, where she told him, "If there's anything you need, Father, just let me know."

He put his hand on her shoulder and as he squeezed it lightly and reassuringly, Chris felt a warmth and a power flowing into her, as well as a feeling of peace and an odd sense of something that felt like—What? she wondered. Safety? Yes, something like that. "You're very kind," she said. His eyes smiled. He said, "Thank you." He removed his hand and as he watched her walk away a sudden tightening of pain seemed to clutch at his face. He entered the study and closed the door. From a pocket of his trousers, he slipped out a tin marked *Bayer Aspirin*, opened it, extracted a nitroglycerin pill and placed it carefully under his tongue.

Entering the kitchen, Chris paused by the door and looked over at Sharon. She was standing by the stove, the palm of her hand against the percolator as she waited for the coffee to reheat. Looking troubled, she was staring into space. Concerned, Chris walked over to her and said softly, "Hey, honey, why don't you get yourself a little bit of rest?"

For a moment, no response. Then Sharon turned and stared blankly at Chris. "I'm sorry. Did you say something?"

Chris studied the tightness in her face, the distant look. "What happened up there, Sharon?" she asked.

"Happened where?"

"When Father Merrin walked into Regan's bedroom."

"Oh, yes . . ." Slightly frowning, Sharon shifted her faraway gaze to a point in space between doubt and remembrance. "Yes. It was funny."

"Funny?"

"Strange. They only . . ." She paused. "Well, they only just stared at each other for a while, and then Regan—that thing—it said . . ."

"What?"

"It said, 'This time, you're going to lose.' "

Chris stared at her, waiting. "And then?"

"That was it," Sharon answered. "He turned around and walked out of the room."

"And how did he look?" Chris asked her.

"Funny."

"Oh, Christ, Sharon, think of some other word!" Chris snapped and was about to say something else when she noticed that Sharon had angled her head up and a little to the side, abstracted, as if she were listening. Following her gaze, Chris heard it too: the silence; the sudden cessation of the raging of the demon; yet something more . . . something else . . . and growing.

The women flicked sidelong stares at each other.

"You feel it too?" Sharon asked.

Chris nodded. Something in the house. A tension. A gradual pulsing and thickening of the air, like opposing energies slowly building. The lilting of the door chimes sounded unreal.

Sharon turned away. "I'll get it."

She walked to the entry hall and opened the door. It was Karras. He was carrying a cardboard laundry box.

"Father Merrin's in the study," Sharon told him.

"Thanks."

Karras moved quickly to the study, tapped lightly and cursorily at the door and then entered with the box. "Sorry, Father," he was saying, "I had a little—"

Karras stopped short. Merrin, in trousers and T-shirt, was kneeling in prayer beside the rented bed, his forehead bent low to his tightly clasped hands, and for a moment Karras stood rooted, as if he had casually rounded a corner and suddenly encountered his boyhood self with an altar boy's cassock draped over an arm and hurrying by without a glance of recognition.

Karras shifted his eyes to the open laundry box, to the speckles of rain on starch. He moved to the sofa, where he soundlessly laid out the contents of the box, and when he'd finished, he took off the raincoat and draped it carefully over a chair. Glancing back toward Merrin, he saw the priest blessing himself and he hastily looked away. He reached down for the larger of the white cotton surplices and had begun to put it on over his cassock when he heard Merrin rising and coming toward him. Tugging down his surplice. Karras turned to face him as the old priest stopped in front of the sofa, his eyes brushing tenderly over the contents of the laundry box.

Karras reached for a sweater. "I thought you might wear this under your cassock, Father," he said as he handed it over. "Her room gets extremely cold at times."

Looking down at the sweater, Merrin touched it with his fingertips. "That was thoughtful of you, Damien. Thank you."

Karras picked up Merrin's cassock from the sofa and as he watched him pull the sweater down over his head, only then, and very suddenly, while watching this homely, prosaic action, did he fully feel the staggering impact of the man; of the moment; of a thickening stillness in the house, crushing down on him, choking off breath and his sense of a world that was solid and real. He came back to full awareness with the feeling of the cassock being tugged from his hands. Merrin. He was slipping it on. "You're familiar with the rules concerning exorcism, Damien?"

"I am."

Merrin began buttoning up the cassock. "Especially important is the warning to avoid conversations with the demon."

The demon! thought Karras.

He'd said it so matter-of-factly. It jarred him.

"We may ask what is relevant," Merrin continued. "But anything beyond that is dangerous. Extremely." He lifted the surplice from Karras's hands and began to slip it over the cassock. "Especially, do not listen to anything he says. The demon is a liar. He will lie to confuse us; but he will also mix lies with the truth to attack us. The attack is psychological, Damien. And powerful. Do not listen. Remember that. Do not listen."

As Karras handed him the stole, the exorcist added, "Is there anything at all you would like to ask me now, Damien?"

Karras shook his head. "No. But I think it might be helpful if I gave you some background on the different personalities that Regan has manifested. So far, there seem to be three."

While slipping the stole around his shoulders, Merrin said quietly, "There is only one." Then he reached for the copies of *The Roman Ritual* and gave one to Karras. "We will skip the Litany of the Saints. You have the holy water, Damien?"

Karras slipped the slender, cork-tipped vial from his pocket. Merrin took it, then nodded serenely toward the door. "If you will lead, please, Damien."

Upstairs, by the door to Regan's bedroom, Sharon and Chris stood waiting. Tense. Bundled in heavy sweaters and jackets, they turned at the sound of a door coming open and looked below to see Merrin, with Karras behind him, approaching the staircase in solemn procession. How striking they looked, Chris thought: Merrin so tall, and Karras with the dark of that rock-chipped face above the innocent, altar-boy white of the surplice. She watched them steadily ascending the stairs, and although her reason said they had no unearthly powers, still she felt deeply and strangely moved as something whispered to her soul that perhaps they did. She felt her heart begin to beat faster.

At the door of the room, the Jesuits stopped. Karras frowned at the sweater and jacket Chris wore. "You're coming in?"

"You think I shouldn't?"

"Please don't," Karras urged her. "Don't. You'd be making a mistake."

Chris turned questioningly to Merrin.

"Father Karras knows best," said the exorcist quietly.

Chris looked to Karras again. Dropped her head. "Okay," she said despondently. She leaned her back against the wall. "I'll wait out here."

"What is your daughter's middle name?" Merrin asked.

"It's Teresa."

"What a lovely name," the old priest said warmly. He held Chris's gaze for a moment, reassuringly, and when he turned his head and looked at the door to Regan's bedroom, Chris again felt that tension, that thickening of coiled darkness behind it. In the bedroom.

Beyond that door.

Merrin nodded. "All right," he said softly.

Karras opened the door, and almost reeled back from the blast of stench and icy cold. In a corner of the room, bundled up in a faded green sheepskin hunting jacket, Karl sat huddled in a chair. He turned expectantly to Karras, who had quickly flicked his glance to the demon in the bed. Its gleaming eyes stared beyond him to the hall. They were fixed on Merrin.

Karras moved forward to the foot of the bed while Merrin,

tall and erect, walked slowly to the side, where he stopped and stared down into hate. And now a smothering stillness hung over the room. Then Regan licked a wolfish, blackened tongue across her cracked and swollen lips. It sounded like a hand smoothing crumpled parchment. "Well, proud scum!" the demonic voice croaked. "At last! At last you've come!"

The old priest lifted his hand and traced the sign of the cross above the bed, and then repeated the gesture toward all in the room. Turning back, he plucked the cap from the vial of holy water.

"Ah, yes! The holy urine now!" the demonic voice rasped. "The semen of the saints!"

Merrin lifted up the vial and the demonic face grew livid and contorted as the voice seethed, "Ah, *will* you, bastard? *Will* you?"

Merrin started shooting holy water sprinkles, and the demon jerked its head up, the mouth and the neck muscles trembling with rage. "Yes, sprinkle! Sprinkle, Merrin! Drench us! Drown us in your sweat! Your sweat is sanctified, Saint Merrin! Bend and fart out clouds of incense! Bend and show us the holy rump that we may worship and adore it, Merrin! *Kiss* it! Make—"

"Be silent!"

The words were flung forth like thunderbolts. Karras flinched and jerked his head around in wonder at Merrin, now staring commandingly at Regan. And the demon was silent. Was returning his stare.

But the eyes were now hesitant. Blinking. Wary.

Merrin capped the holy-water vial routinely and returned it to Karras. The psychiatrist slipped it into his pocket and watched as Merrin kneeled down beside the bed and closed his eyes in murmured prayer. " 'Our Father . . .' " he began.

Regan spat and hit Merrin in the face with a yellowish glob of mucus. It oozed slowly down the exorcist's cheek.

" '. . . Thy kingdom come . . .' " His head still bowed, Merrin continued the prayer without a pause while his hand plucked a handkerchief out of his pocket and unhurriedly wiped away the spittle. " '. . . and lead us not into temptation,' " he ended mildly.

" 'But deliver us from evil,' " responded Karras.

He looked up briefly. Regan's eyes were rolling upward into their sockets until only the white of the sclera was exposed. Karras felt uneasy. Felt something in the room congealing. He returned to his text to follow Merrin's prayer:

" 'God and Father of our Lord Jesus Christ, I appeal to your holy name, humbly begging your kindness, that you may graciously grant me help against this unclean spirit now tormenting this creature of yours; through Christ our Lord.' "

"Amen," responded Karras.

Now Merrin stood up and prayed reverently: " 'God, Creator and defender of the human race, look down in pity on this your servant, Regan Teresa MacNeil, now trapped in the coils of man's ancient enemy, sworn foe of our race, who . . .' "

Karras glanced up as he heard Regan hissing, saw her sitting erect with the whites of her eyes exposed, while her tongue flicked in and out rapidly, her head weaving slowly back and forth like a cobra's, and once again he had that feeling of disquiet. He looked down at his text.

" 'Save your servant,' " prayed Merrin, standing and reading from the *Ritual*.

" 'Who trusts in you, my God,' " answered Karras.

" 'Let her find in you, Lord, a fortified tower.' "

" 'In the face of the enemy.' "

As Merrin continued with the next line—"Let the enemy have no power over her"—Karras heard a gasp from Sharon behind him, and turning quickly around, he saw her looking stupefied at the bed. Puzzled, he looked back. And was electrified.

The front of the bed was rising up off the floor!

Karras stared incredulously, transfixed. Four inches. Half a foot. A foot. Then the back legs began to come up.

"Gott in Himmel!" Karl whispered in fear. But Karras did not hear him or see him make the sign of the cross on himself as the back of the bed lifted level with the front.

It's not happening! he thought.

The bed drifted upward another foot and then hovered there, bobbing and listing gently as if it were floating on a stagnant lake.

"Father Karras?"

Regan undulating and hissing.

"Father Karras?"

Karras turned. The exorcist was eyeing him serenely, and now motioned his head toward the copy of the *Ritual* in Karras's hands. "The response, please, Damien."

Karras looked blank and uncomprehending, unaware that Sharon had run out of the room.

" 'Let the enemy have no power over her,' " Merrin repeated.

Hastily, Karras glanced back at the text and with a pounding heart breathed out the response: " 'And the son of iniquity be powerless to harm her.' "

" 'Lord, hear my prayer,' " continued Merrin.

" 'And let my cry come unto Thee.' "

" 'The Lord be with you.' "

" 'And with your spirit.' "

Merrin embarked upon a lengthy prayer and Karras again returned his gaze to the bed, to his hopes of his God and the supernatural hovering low in the empty air. An elation thrilled up through his being. *It's there! There it is! Right in front of me!* He looked suddenly around at the sound of the door coming open and Sharon rushing in with Chris, who stopped, unbelieving, and gasped, *"Jesus Christ!"*

" 'Almighty Father, everlasting God . . .' "

The exorcist reached up his hand in a workaday manner and traced the sign of the cross, unhurriedly, three times on Regan's brow while continuing to read from the text of the *Ritual:*

" '. . . who sent your only begotten Son into the world to crush that roaring lion . . .' "

The hissing ceased and from the taut-stretched O of Regan's mouth came the nerve-shredding lowing of a steer.

" '. . . snatch from ruination and from the clutches of the noonday devil this human being made in your image, and . . .' "

The lowing grew louder, tearing at flesh and shivering through bone.

" 'God and Lord of all creation . . .' " Merrin routinely reached up his hand and pressed a portion of the stole to Regan's neck while continuing to pray: " '. . . by whose might Satan was made to fall from heaven like lightning, strike terror into the beast now laying waste your vineyard . . .' "

The bellowing ceased, and at first there ensued a ringing silence, and then a thick and putrid greenish vomit began to pump from Regan's mouth in slow and regular spurts that oozed over her lip and flowed in thin waves onto Merrin's hand. But he did not move it. " 'Let your mighty hand cast out this cruel demon from Regan Teresa MacNeil, who . . .' "

Karras was dimly aware of a door being opened, of Chris bolting from the room.

" 'Drive out this persecutor of the innocent . . .' "

The bed began to rock lazily, then to pitch, and then suddenly it was violently dipping and yawing, and with the vomit still pumping from Regan's mouth, Merrin calmly made adjustments and kept the stole firmly to her neck.

" 'Fill your servants with courage to manfully oppose that reprobate dragon lest he despise those who put their trust in you, and . . .' "

Abruptly, the movements subsided and as Karras watched, mesmerized, the bed drifted featherlike and slowly to the floor, where it settled on the rug with a cushioned thud.

" 'Lord, grant that this . . .' "

Numb, Karras shifted his gaze. Merrin's hand. He could not see it. It was buried under mounded, steaming vomit.

"Damien?"

Karras glanced up.

" 'Lord, hear my prayer,' " said the exorcist gently.

Karras turned. " 'And let my cry come unto Thee.' "

Merrin lifted off the stole, took a slight step backward and then jolted the room with the lash of his voice as he commanded, " 'I cast you out, unclean spirit, along with every power of the enemy! every specter from hell! every savage companion!' " Merrin's hand, at his side, dripped vomit to the rug. " 'It is Christ who commands you, who once stilled the wind and the sea and the storm! Who . . .' "

Regan stopped vomiting and sat silent and unmoving, the whites of her eyes gleaming balefully at Merrin. From the foot of the bed, Karras watched her intently as his shock and excitement began to fade, as his mind began feverishly to thresh, to poke its fingers, unbidden, compulsively, deep into corners of logical doubt: poltergeists; psychokinetic action; adolescent tensions and mind-directed force. He frowned as he remembered something. He moved to the side of the bed, leaned over, reached down to grasp Regan's wrist. And found what he'd feared. Like the shaman in Siberia, Regan's pulse was racing at an unbelievable speed. The fact drained him suddenly of sun, and, glancing at his watch, Karras counted the heartbeats, now, like arguments against his life.

" 'It is He who commands you, He who flung you headlong from the heights of heaven!' "

Merrin's powerful adjuration pounded off the rim of Karras's consciousness in resonant, inexorable blows as the pulse came faster now. And faster. Karras looked at Regan. Still silent. Unmoving. Into icy air, thin mists of vapor wafted from the vomit like a reeking offering. Then the hair on Karras's arms began prickling up as, with nightmare slowness, a fraction at a time, Regan's head was turning, swiveling like a manikin's, and creaking with the sound of some rusted mechanism, until the dread and glaring whites of those ghastly eyes were fixed on his.

" 'And therefore, tremble in fear, now, Satan . . .' "

The head turned slowly back toward Merrin.

" '. . . you corrupter of justice! you begetter of death! you betrayer of the nations! you robber of life! you . . .' "

Karras glanced warily around as the lights in the room began flickering, and dimming, and then faded to an eerie, pulsing amber. Karras shivered. The room was getting even colder.

" '. . . you prince of murderers! you inventor of every obscenity! you enemy of the human race! you . . .' "

A muffled pounding jolted the room. Then another. Then steadily, shuddering through walls, through the floor, through the ceiling, splintering, and throbbing at a ponderous rate like the beating of a heart that was massive and diseased.

" 'Depart, you monster! Your place is in solitude! Your abode is in a nest of vipers! Get down and crawl with them! It is God himself who commands you! The blood of . . .' "

The poundings grew louder, began to come ominously faster and faster.

" 'I adjure you, ancient serpent . . .' "

And faster . . .

" '. . . by the judge of the living and the dead, by your Creator, by the Creator of all the universe, to . . .' "

Sharon cried out, pressing her fists against her ears as the poundings grew deafening and now suddenly accelerated and leaped to a terrifying tempo.

Regan's pulse was astonishing. It hammered at a speed too rapid to gauge. Across the bed, Merrin reached out calmly and with the end of his thumb traced the sign of the cross on Regan's vomit-covered chest. The words of his prayer were swallowed up in the poundings.

Karras felt the pulse rate suddenly drop, and as Merrin prayed and traced the sign of the cross on Regan's brow, the nightmarish poundings abruptly ceased.

" 'O God of heaven and earth, God of the angels and archangels . . .' " Karras could now hear Merrin praying as the pulse kept dropping, dropping . . .

"Prideful bastard, Merrin! Scum! You will lose! She will die! The *pig will die!*"

The flickering haze had grown gradually brighter and the demon had returned to rage hatefully at Merrin. "Profligate peacock! Ancient heretic who dares to believe that the universe will one day become Christ! I adjure you, turn and look on me! Yes, look on me, you scum*!*" The demon jerked forward and spat in Merrin's face, croaking afterward, "*Thus* does your master cure the blind!"

" 'God and Lord of all creation . . .' " prayed Merrin, reaching placidly for his handkerchief and wiping away the spittle.

"Now follow his teaching, Merrin! *Do* it! Put your sanctified cock in the piglet's mouth and *cleanse* it, *swab* it with the wrinkled relic and she will be *cured*, Saint Merrin! Yes, a *miracle!* A—"

" '. . . deliver this servant of . . .' "

"*Hypocrite!* You care nothing at *all* for the pig. You care *nothing!* You have *made her a contest between us!*"

" '. . . I humbly . . .' "

"Liar! Lying bastard! Tell us, where is your humility, Merrin? In the desert? in the ruins? in the tombs where you fled to escape your fellowman? to escape from your inferiors, from the halt and the lame of mind? Do you speak to *men*, you pious vomit? . . ."

" '. . . deliver . . .' "

"Your abode is in a nest of peacocks, Merrin! Your place is within yourself! Go back to the mountaintop and speak to your only equal!"

Merrin continued with the prayers, unheeding, as the torrent of abuse raged on. "Do you hunger, Saint Merrin? Here, I give you both nectar and ambrosia, I give to you the daily bread of your God!" croaked the demon mockingly as Regan excreted diarrhetically. "For *this* is my body! Now consecrate *that*, Saint Merrin!"

Repelled, Karras focused his attention on the text as Merrin read a passage from Saint Luke:

> . . . "My name is Legion," answered the man, for many demons had entered into him. And they begged Jesus not to command them to depart into the abyss. Now a herd of swine was there, feeding on the mountain-side. And the demons kept entreating Jesus to let them enter into them. And he gave them leave. And the demons came out from the man and entered into the swine, and the herd rushed down the cliff and into the lake and were drowned. And . . .

"Willie, I bring you good news!" croaked the demon. Karras glanced up and saw Willie near the door, stopping short with an armload of towels and sheets. "I bring you tidings of redemption!" it gloated. "Elvira is *alive!* She *lives!* She is . . ."

Willie stared in shock and now Karl turned and shouted at her, "*No,* Willie! *No!*"

". . . a *drug* addict, Willie, a hopeless—"

"Willie, do not listen!" cried Karl.

"Shall I tell you where she lives?"

"Do not listen! Do not listen!" Karl was rushing Willie out of the room.

"Go and visit her on *Mother's* Day, Willie! Surprise her! Go and—"

Abruptly the demon broke off and fixed its eyes on Karras. He had again checked Regan's pulse and, finding it strong enough to give her more Librium, he was moving to Sharon to instruct her to prepare another injection. "Karras, do you want her?" leered the demon. "She is yours! Yes, the stable whore is yours! You may ride her as you wish! Why, she fantasizes nightly concerning you, Karras! Yes, you and your long, thick, priestly cock!"

Sharon crimsoned and kept her eyes averted as Karras told her it was safe to give Regan the Librium. "And a Compazine suppository in case there's more vomiting," he added.

Sharon nodded at the floor and started stiffly away. As she walked by the bed with her head still lowered, Regan croaked at her, *"Slut!"* and then jerked up and hit her face with a flung bolt of vomit, and while Sharon stood paralyzed and in shock, the Dennings personality appeared, rasping, "Stable whore! Cunt!"

Sharon bolted from the room.

The Dennings personality now grimaced with distaste, glanced around and asked, "Would someone crack a *window* open, please? It bloody *stinks* in this room! It's simply—no no no, don't!" it then amended. "No, for *heaven's* sake, don't, or someone *else* might wind up bloody well dead!" And then it cackled, winked monstrously at Karras and vanished.

" 'It is He who expels you . . .' "

"Oh, does he, Merrin? Does he?"

The demonic entity had returned and Merrin continued the adjurations, the applications of the stole and the constant tracings of the sign of the cross while the entity lashed him again obscenely.

Too long, Karras worried: the fit was continuing far too long.

"Now the sow comes! The mother of the piglet!"

Karras turned and saw Chris coming toward him with a swab and a disposable syringe. She kept her head down as the demon hurled abuse, and Karras went to her, frowning.

"Sharon's changing her clothes," Chris explained, "and Karl's—"

Karras cut her short with a brusque "All right," and together they approached the bed.

"Ah, yes, come see your handiwork, sow-mother! Come!"

Chris tried not to listen, not to look, while Karras pinned Regan's unresisting arms.

"See the puke! See the murderous bitch!" the demon raged. "Are you pleased? It is *you* who has done it! Yes, *you* with your career before *anything*, your career before your *husband*, before *her*, before . . ."

Karras glanced around. Chris stood paralyzed. "Go ahead!" he told her firmly. "Don't listen! Go ahead!"

". . . your *divorce!* Go to priests, will you? Priests will not help! The piglet is *mad!* Don't you understand that? You have driven her to madness and to murder and . . ."

"I *can't!*" Face contorted, Chris was staring at the quivering syringe in her trembling hand. She shook her head. "I can't do it!"

Karras plucked the syringe from her fingers. "All right, swab it! Swab the arm! Over here!"

". . . in her *coffin*, you bitch, by . . ."

"Don't listen!" Karras cautioned Chris again, and at this the demonic entity jerked its head around, its red-laced eyes bulging fury. "And *you*, Karras! Yes! About *you*!"

Chris swabbed Regan's arm. "Now, get out!" Karras ordered as he poked the hypodermic needle into wasted flesh.

Chris fled from the room.

"Yes, we *know* of your kindness to *mothers*, dear Karras!" croaked the demon. The Jesuit blenched and for a moment did not move. Then slowly he drew out the needle and looked into the whites of Regan's eyes as out of her mouth came a slow, lilting singing in a sweet, clear voice like that of a very young choirboy, " *'Tantum ergo sacramentum veneremur cernui . . .'* "

It was a hymn sung at Catholic benediction. Karras stood bloodlessly as it continued. Weird and chilling, the singing was a vacuum into which Karras felt the horror of the evening rushing with a horrible clarity. He looked up and saw Merrin with a towel in his hands. With weary, tender movements he wiped away the vomit from Regan's face and neck.

" *'. . . et antiquum documentum . . .'* "

The singing. *Whose voice?* wondered Karras. And then fragments: *Dennings . . . The window* . . . Drained, he saw Sharon come back into the room and take the towel from Merrin's hands. "I'll finish that, Father," she told him. "I'm all right now. I'd like to change her and get her cleaned up before I give her the Compazine. Okay? Could you both wait outside for a while?"

The priests left the room, stepping into the warmth and the dimness of the hall, where they both leaned wearily against the wall, their heads down and arms folded as they listened to the eerie, muffled singing from within. It was Karras who at last broke their silence. "You—you said earlier, Father, there was only one entity we're dealing with."

"Yes."

The hushed tones, the lowered heads, were confessional.

"All the others are but forms of attack," continued Merrin. "There is one . . . only one. It is a demon." There was a silence. Then Merrin stated simply, "I know you doubt this. But this demon I have met once before. And he is powerful, Damien. Powerful."

A silence. Then Karras spoke again.

"We say the demon cannot touch the victim's will."

"Yes, that is so. There is no sin."

"Then what would be the *purpose* of possession? What's the point?"

"Who can know?" answered Merrin. "Who can really hope to know? And yet I think the demon's target is not the possessed; it is us . . . the observers . . . every person in this house. And I think—I think the point is to make us despair; to reject our own humanity, Damien: to see ourselves as ultimately bestial, vile and putrescent; without dignity; ugly; unworthy. And there lies the heart of it, perhaps: in unworthiness. For I think belief in God is not a matter of reason at all; I think it finally is a matter of love: of accepting the possibility that God could ever love us."

Merrin paused, then continued more slowly and with an air of introspection: "Again, who really knows. But it is clear—at least to me—that the demon knows where to strike. Oh, yes, he knows. Long ago I despaired of ever loving my neighbor. Certain people . . . repelled me. And so how could I love them? I thought. It tormented me, Damien; it led me to despair of myself and from that, very soon, to despair of my God. My faith was shattered."

Surprised, Karras turned and looked at Merrin with interest. "And what happened?" he asked.

"Ah, well . . . at last I realized that God would never ask of me that which I know to be psychologically impossible; that the love which He asked was in my *will* and not meant to be felt as emotion. No. Not at all. He was asking that I *act* with love; that I *do* unto others; and that I should do it unto those who repelled me, I believe, was a greater act of love than any other." Merrin lowered his head and spoke even more softly. "I know that all of this must seem very obvious to you, Damien. I know. But at the time I could not see it. Strange blindness. How many husbands and wives," Merrin uttered sadly, "must believe they have fallen out of love because their hearts no longer race at the sight of their beloveds. Ah, dear God!" He shook his head. And then he nodded. "There it lies, I think, Damien . . . possession; not in wars, as some tend to believe; not so much; and very rarely in extraordinary interventions such as here . . . this girl . . . this poor child. No, I tend to see possession most often in the little things, Damien: in the senseless, petty spites and misunderstandings; the cruel and cutting word that leaps unbidden to the tongue between friends. Between lovers. Between husbands and wives. Enough of these and we have no need of Satan to manage our wars; these we manage for ourselves . . . for ourselves."

The lilting singing in the bedroom could still be heard, drawing Merrin to look up at the door with a distant stare. "And yet even from this—from evil—there will finally come good in some way; in some way that we may never understand or even see." Merrin paused. "Perhaps evil is the crucible of goodness," he brooded. "And perhaps even Satan—Satan, in spite of himself—somehow serves to work out the will of God."

Merrin said no more, and for a time they stood in silence while Karras reflected; until another objection came to his mind. "Once the demon's driven out," he asked, "what's to keep it from coming back in?"

"I don't know," Merrin answered. "And yet it never seems to happen. No, never." Merrin put a hand to his face, pinching tightly at the corners of his eyes. " 'Damien' . . . what a wonderful name," he murmured. Karras heard exhaustion in his voice. And something else. Some anxiety. Something like repression of pain.

Abruptly, Merrin pushed himself away from the wall, and with his face still hidden in his hand, he excused himself and hurried down the hall to a bathroom. What was wrong? wondered Karras. He felt a sudden envy and admiration for the exorcist's strong and simple faith. Then he turned toward the door. The singing. It had stopped. Had the night at last ended?

Some minutes later, Sharon came out of the bedroom with a foul-smelling bundle of bedding and clothing. "She's sleeping now," she said, and then she looked away quickly and moved off down the hall.

Karras took a deep breath and reentered the bedroom. Felt the cold. Smelled the stench. He walked slowly to the bedside. Regan. Asleep. At last. And at last, Karras thought, he could rest. He reached down, gripped Regan's thin wrist and then, lifting his other arm, he stared at the sweep-second hand of his watch.

"Why you do dis to me, Dimmy?"

The Jesuit's heart froze over.

"Why you do dis?"

Karras did not move, did not breathe, did not dare to glance over to that sorrowful voice to see whether those eyes were really there. Eyes accusing. Eyes lonely. His mother's. His *mother's!*

"You leave me to be priest, Dimmy; send me institution . . ."

Don't look!

"Now you chase me away?"

It's not her!

"Why you do dis?"

His head throbbing, his heart in his throat, Karras shut his eyes tightly as the voice grew imploring, grew frightened and tearful. "You always good boy, Dimmy. Please! I am 'fraid! Please no chase me outside, Dimmy! *Please!*"

You're not my mother!

"Outside *nothing!* Only dark, Dimmy! Lonely!"

"You're not my mother!" Karras vehemently whispered.

"Dimmy, *please!*"

"You're not my mother!" Karras shouted in agony.

"Oh, for *heaven's* sake, Karras!"

The Dennings personality had appeared.

"Look, it simply isn't fair to drive us out of here!" it wheedled. "Look now, speaking for myself it's only justice I should be here. I admit it. But the bitch destroyed my body and I think it only right that I ought to be allowed to stay in hers, don't you think? Oh, for *Christ's* sake *look* at me, Karras, now would you? Come along! I mean, it isn't very often I get out to speak my piece. Just turn around now. I won't bite you or spew vomit or anything else of that boorish sort. This is me, now."

Karras opened his eyes and saw the Dennings personality.

"There, that's better," it continued. "Look, she killed me. Not our *inn*keeper, Karras—*she!* Oh, yes, indeed!" It was nodding affirmation. *"She!* I was minding my business at the bar, you see, when I thought I heard her moaning from upstairs in her bedroom. Well, now, I *had* to see what ailed her, after all, so up I went and don't you know she bloody took me by the *throat*, the little cunt!" The voice was whiny now; pathetic. "Christ, I've never in my *life* seen such strength! Began screaming that I was diddling her mother or some such or that I caused the divorce. It wasn't clear. But I tell you, love, *she pushed me out the bloody fucking window!"* The voice cracking now and high-pitched. "She fucking killed me! All right? Now you think it bloody fair to throw me out of her? I mean, *really*, Karras! *Do* you?"

Karras swallowed, then spoke hoarsely. "Well, if you're really Burke Dennings—"

"I keep telling you I *am!* Are you cunting *deaf?*"

"Well, if you are, then tell me how did your head get turned around?"

"Bloody Jesuit!" it cursed beneath its breath

"What was that?"

It shifted its gaze around evasively. "Oh, well, the head thing. Freaky thing, that. Yes. Very freaky."

"How did it happen?"

It turned away. "Oh, well, frankly, who gives a good damn? Front or back, it's all sixes and sevens, you know; twiddles and twaddles."

Looking down, Karras picked up Regan's wrist again and glanced at his watch as he counted her pulse rate.

"Dimmy, please! Please no make me be all alone!"

His mother.

"If instead of be priest, you was doctor, I live in nice house, Dimmy, not wit' da cockroach, not all by myself in da lousy apartment!"

His eyes on his watch, Karras strained to block it all out, as once again he heard the sound of weeping. "Dimmy, *please!*"

"You're not my mother!"

"Oh, won't you face the truth?" It was the demon. Seething. "You believe what Merrin tells you, you fool? You believe him to be holy and good? Well, he is *not!* He is proud and unworthy! I will prove it to you, Karras! I will prove it by *killing the piglet!* She will die and neither you nor Merrin's God will save her! She will die from Merrin's pride and your incompetence! *Bungler! You should not have given her the Librium!*"

Stunned, Karras looked up into eyes that were shining with triumph and with piercing spite, then looked down at his wristwatch again. "Noticing her pulse, are we, Karras? Are we?"

Karras frowned worriedly. The pulse beat was rapid and . . .

"Feeble?" croaked the demon. "Ah, yes. For the moment, just a bit. Just a trifle."

Karras let go of Regan's wrist, fetched his medical bag hurriedly to the bedside, plucked out a stethoscope and pressed the resonator to Regan's chest as the demon rasped, "Listen, Karras! Listen! Listen well!"

Karras listened and grew even more concerned: Regan's heart tones sounded distant and inefficient.

"I will not let her sleep!"

Chilled, Karras flicked his glance up to the demon.

"Yes, Karras!" it croaked. "She will not sleep! Do you hear? *I will not let the piglet sleep!*"

As the demon put its head back in gloating laughter, Karras stared numbly. He did not hear Merrin come back into the room until the exorcist was standing beside him and intently and worriedly studying Regan's face. "What is it?" Merrin asked.

"The demon," Karras answered him dully; "it said it wouldn't let her sleep." He turned a vanquished stare up to Merrin. "Her heart's begun to work inefficiently, Father. If she doesn't get rest pretty soon, she'll die of cardiac exhaustion."

Merrin frowned, his expression grave. "Can't you give her drugs?" he asked. "Some medicine to make her sleep?"

"No, that's dangerous. She might go into coma." Karras turned his gaze to Regan. She was clucking like a hen in a barnyard. "If her blood pressure drops any more . . ."

The priest's voice trailed off.

"What can be done?" Merrin asked.

"Nothing," Karras answered. "Nothing." His anxious gaze

returned to Merrin. "But I don't know," he said. "I can't be sure. I mean, maybe there've been some recent new advances. I'm going to call in a cardiac specialist!"

Merrin nodded, and said, "Yes. That would be good."

He watched as Karras closed the bedroom door behind him, and then added very softly, "And I will pray."

Karras found Chris keeping vigil in the kitchen and from the room off the pantry he heard Willie sobbing, heard Karl's consoling voice as he explained the urgent need for consultation while carefully not divulging the full extent of Regan's danger. Chris gave him permission, and Karras telephoned a friend, a noted specialist at the Georgetown University Medical School, awakening him from sleep and then briefing him tersely.

"Be right there," said the specialist.

In less than half an hour he arrived at the house, where, once in Regan's bedroom, he reacted to the cold and the stench and Regan's condition with bewilderment, horror and compassion. When he'd entered the room, Regan was quietly croaking gibberish, and while he examined her, she alternately sang and made animal noises. Then Dennings appeared.

"Oh, it's terrible," it whined at the specialist. "Just awful! Oh, I do hope there's something you can do! Is there something? We'll have no place to go, you see, otherwise, and all because . . . Oh, *damn* the stubborn devil!" As the specialist stared with wide eyes while taking Regan's blood pressure, Dennings looked to Karras and complained, "What the hell are you doing! Can't you see the little bitch should be in hospital? She belongs in a madhouse, Karras! Now you *know* that! For heaven's sakes, why can't we stop all this cunting mumbo-jumbo! If she dies, you know, the fault will be yours! Yes, all yours! I mean, just because God's self-anointed second son is being stubborn doesn't mean that *you* have to behave like a snot! You're a doctor! You should know better, Karras! Now come along, dear heart, have compassion. There's just a *terrible* shortage of housing these days!"

And now back came the demon, howling like a wolf. Expressionless, the specialist undid the sphygmomanometer wrapping and, still a little wide-eyed and bewildered, he nodded at Karras. He was finished.

They went out into the hall, where the specialist looked back at the bedroom door before turning back to Karras and asking, "What the hell is going on in there, Father?"

The Jesuit averted his glance. "I can't say," he said softly.

"You can't or you won't?"

Karras turned his gaze back to him.

"Maybe both," he said. "So what's the story with her heart?"

The specialist's manner was somber. "She's got to stop that activity. To sleep . . . to sleep before her blood pressure drops."

"Is there anything *I* can do, Mike?"

"Pray."

As the specialist walked away, Karras watched him, his every artery and nerve begging rest, begging hope, begging miracles, even though he felt certain that there would be none. And then shutting his eyes, he winced as he remembered, *"You should not have given her the Librium!"* He put a fist to his mouth as his throat made a soft, convulsive sound of regret and stinging self-recrimination. He took a deep breath, then another, and then, opening his eyes and moving forward, he pushed open the door to Regan's bedroom with a hand less heavy than his soul.

Merrin stood by the bedside, watching while Regan neighed shrilly like a horse. He heard Karras enter and turned to look at him inquiringly, and Karras somberly shook his head. Merrin nodded. There was sadness in his face; then acceptance; and as he turned back to Regan, there was grim resolve.

Merrin knelt by the bed. "Our Father . . . ," he began.

Regan splattered him with dark, stinking bile, and then croaked, "You will *lose!* She will *die!* She will *die!*"

Karras picked up his copy of *The Roman Ritual*. Opened it. Looked up and stared at Regan.

" 'Save your servant,' " prayed Merrin.

" 'In the face of the enemy.' "

Go to sleep, Regan! Sleep! shouted Karras's will.

But Regan did not sleep.

Not by dawn.

Not by noon.

Not by nightfall.

And not even by Sunday, when her pulse rate was one hundred and forty and ever threadier, while the fits continued unremittingly, and while Karras and Merrin kept repeating the ritual, never sleeping, Karras feverishly groping for remedies: a restraining sheet to hold Regan's movements to a minimum; keeping everyone out of the bedroom for a time to see if lack of provocation might terminate the fits. Neither method was successful. And Regan's shouting was as draining as her movements. Yet the blood pressure held. *But how much longer?* Karras agonized. *Ah, God, don't let her die!* The aching prayer of his mind was repeated so often it was almost a litany.

Don't let her die! Let her sleep! Let her sleep!

At approximately 7 P.M. that Sunday, Karras sat mutely next to Merrin in the bedroom, exhausted and racked by the demon's scathing attacks: his lack of faith; his medical incompetence; his flight from his mother in search of status. And Regan! Regan! *His* fault!

"You should not have given her the Librium!"

The priests had just finished a cycle of the ritual and were resting, listening to Regan singing "Panis Angelicus" in that same sweet choirboy's voice. They rarely left the room; Karras once to change clothes and to shower. But in the cold it was easier to stay wakeful, even in the stench that since early morning had altered in character to the gorge-raising odor of decayed, rotted flesh.

Staring feverishly at Regan with reddened eyes, Karras thought he heard a sound. Something creaking. Then again each time Karras blinked. And then he realized it was coming from his own crusted eyelids. He turned his head to look at Merrin. Through the hours, the elderly exorcist had said very little: now and then a homely story of his boyhood. Reminiscences. Little things. A story about a duck he once owned named Clancy. Karras was profoundly worried about him. His age. The lack of sleep. The demon's verbal assaults. After Merrin closed his eyes and let his chin rest on his chest, Karras glanced around at Regan, and then wearily stood up and trudged over to the bed, where he checked her pulse and then began to take a blood pressure reading. As he wrapped the black sphygmomanometer cloth around her arm, he blinked repeatedly to clear away a blurring of his vision.

"Today Muddir Day, Dimmy."

For a moment, the priest could not move as he felt his heart being wrenched from his chest; and then slowly, very slowly, he looked into eyes that didn't seem to be Regan's anymore, but rather eyes that were sadly rebuking. His mother's.

"I not good to you? Why you leave me to die all alone, Dimmy? Why? Why you—"

"Damien!"

Merrin's hand was clutching tightly at Karras's arm. "Please go and rest for a little now, Damien."

"Dimmy, *please!*"

"Do not listen, Damien! Go! Go now!"

With a lump rising dry to his throat, Karras turned and left the bedroom, and for a time he stood in the hallway, weak and irresolute. Coffee? He craved it. But a shower even more. But when he'd left the MacNeil house and returned to his room in the residence hall, it took only one look at his bed for Karras to change his priorities. *Forget the shower, man! Sleep! Half an hour!* As he reached for the telephone to ask Reception to give him a wake-up call, it rang.

"Yes, hello," Karras answered hoarsely.

"Someone here to see you, Father Karras: a Mr. Kinderman."

Karras briefly held his breath, and then he exhaled in resignation. "Okay, tell him I'll be out in just a minute," he said weakly. As he hung up the telephone, Karras saw a carton of nonfilter Camel cigarettes on his desk. A note from Dyer was attached.

> *A key to the Playboy Club has been found on*
> *the chapel kneeler in front of the votive lights.*
> *Is it yours? You can claim it at Reception.*
>
> *Joe*

With a fond expression, Karras set down the note, quickly dressed in fresh clothing and walked out of the room and to Reception, where Kinderman was standing at the telephone switchboard counter, delicately rearranging the composition of a vase full of flowers. As he turned and saw Karras, he was holding the stem of a pink camellia.

"Ah, Father! Father Karras!" Kinderman greeted him cheerfully, his expression quickly changing to concern when he saw the exhaustion in the Jesuit's face. He replaced the camellia and came forward to meet him. "You look awful!" he said. "What's the matter? That's what comes of all this *schlepp*ing around the track? Give it up, Father, you're going to die anyway. Listen, come!" He gripped Karras by the elbow and an upper arm and propelled him toward the exit to the street. "You've got a minute?" he asked as they passed through the door.

"Just barely," Karras murmured. "What is it?"

"A little talk. I need advice, nothing more; just advice."

"What about?"

"In just a minute. For now we'll just walk. We'll take air. We'll enjoy." He hooked his arm through the Jesuit's and guided him diagonally to the other side of the street. "Ah, now, *look* at that! Beautiful! Gorgeous!" He was pointing to the sun sinking low on the Potomac, and in the stillness sudden laughter rang out, and then the talking-all-together of Georgetown undergraduates in front of a drinking hall near the corner of Thirty-Sixth Street. One punched another one hard on the arm, and the two began amicably wrestling. "Ah, college . . . ," breathed out Kinderman ruefully as he glanced at the lively gathering of young men. "I never went . . . but I wish . . ." Turning his gaze back to Karras, he frowned with concern. "I mean, seriously, you really look bad," he said. "What's the matter? You've been sick?"

When would Kinderman come to the point? Karras wondered.

"No, just busy," the Jesuit answered.

"Slow it down, then," wheezed Kinderman. "Slow. You saw the Bolshoi Ballet, incidentally, at the Watergate?"

"No."

"No, me neither. But I wish. They're so graceful . . . so cute!"

They had come to the Car Barn's low stone wall, where the view of the sunset was unimpeded, and they stopped, Karras resting a forearm on top of the wall and turning his glance from the sunset to Kinderman.

"Okay, what's on your mind?" Karras asked him.

"Ah, well, Father," said Kinderman, sighing. He turned, then, hunching forward with his hands clasped on top of the wall as he moodily stared across the river and said, "I'm afraid I've got a problem."

"Professional?"

"Well, partly; only partly."

"What is it?"

"Well, mostly it's—" Kinderman hesitated, then continued: "Well, mostly it's ethical, you could say, Father Karras. A question—" His voice trailing off, the detective turned around and, leaning his back against the wall, he looked down at the sidewalk and frowned. "There's just no one I could talk to about it; not my captain in particular, you see. I just couldn't. I couldn't tell him. So I thought . . ." Here, abruptly, the detective's eyes lit up. "I had an aunt—you should hear this; it's funny. She was terrified—*terrified*—for years of my uncle. The poor woman, she never dared to say a word to him—*never!*—much less to ever raise her voice. So whenever she got mad at him for something, right away, she'd run quick to the closet in her bedroom, and then there in the dark—you won't believe this!—in the dark, by herself, with all the clothes hanging up and the moths, she would curse—she would *curse!*—at my uncle and tell him what she thought of him for maybe twenty minutes! Really! I mean, *yelling!* She'd come out, she'd feel better, she'd go kiss him on the cheek. Now what is that, Father Karras? That's good therapy or not!"

"It's very good," Karras answered with a wan, bleak smile. "And I'm your closet now? Is that what you're saying?"

"In a way," the detective answered gravely. "But more serious. And the closet must speak."

"Got a cigarette?"

Kinderman stared at Karras blankly, incredulous.

"A condition like mine and I would *smoke?*"

"No, you wouldn't," Karras murmured as he turned to face the river and clasped his hands atop the wall. It was to make them stop trembling.

"Some doctor! God forbid I should be sick in some jungle and instead of Albert Schweitzer, there is with me only *you!* You cure warts still with frogs, Doctor Karras?"

"It's toads," Karras answered, subdued.

Kinderman frowned. "You're not smiling jaunty jolly today, Father Karras. Something's wrong. Now what is it? Come on, tell me."

Karras lowered his head and was silent. Then, "Okay," he said softly. "Ask the closet whatever you want."

Sighing, the detective faced out to the river. "I was saying . . . ," he began. He scratched his brow with a thumbnail, then continued: "I was saying—well, let's say I'm working on a case, Father Karras. It's a homicide."

"Dennings?"

"No, you wouldn't be familiar with it, Father. It's something purely hypothetical."

"Got it."

"Like a ritual witchcraft murder, this looks," the detective continued broodingly, picking his words very carefully and slowly. "And let us say that in this house—this hypothetical house—there are living five people, and that one must be the killer." With his hand, he made flat, chopping motions of emphasis. "Now I *know* this. I *know* this—I know this for a *fact.*" Then he paused, slowly exhaling breath. "But then the problem—all the evidence—well, it points to a child, Father Karras; a little girl maybe ten, twelve years old . . . just a baby; she could maybe be my daughter. Yes, I know: sounds fantastic . . . ridiculous . . . but true. Now there comes to this house, Father Karras, a very famous Catholic priest, and this case being purely hypothetical, Father, I learn through my also hypothetical genius that this priest has once cured a very special type illness. An illness which is mental, by the way, a fact I mention just in passing for your interest."

Karras mournfully lowered his head and nodded. "Yes, go on," he said bleakly. "What else?"

"What else? A great deal. It also seems that there is . . . well, satanism involved in this illness, plus also strength . . . yes, incredible strength. And this . . . hypothetical girl, let us say, then, could so easily twist a man's head around." Head lowered, the detective was nodding now. "Yes . . . yes, she could. And so the question . . ." Breaking off, the detective grimaced thoughtfully, then went on: "You see . . . you see, the girl is not responsible, Father. She's insane, Father, totally demented and also just a child, Father Karras! A *child!* And yet the illness that she has . . . it could be dangerous. She could kill someone else. Who's to know?" Once again the detective turned and squinted out across the river. "It's a problem," he said quietly and morosely. "What to do? Hypothetically, I mean. Just forget it? Forget it and hope she gets"—Kinderman paused—"gets well?" He reached for a handkerchief and blew his nose. "Oh, well, I just don't know. I don't know. It's a terrible decision," he said as he searched for a clean, unused section of the handkerchief. "Yes, it's awful. Just awful. Horrific. And I hate to be the one who has to make it." He again blew his nose, lightly dabbed at a nostril, then stuffed the damp handkerchief back into a pocket. "Father, what would be right in such a case?" he asked, turning back to Karras. "Hypothetically, I mean. What do you believe would be the right thing to do?"

For an instant, Karras throbbed with a surge of rebellion,

with a dull, weary anger at the piling on of weight upon weight. He let it ebb away into calm, and firmly meeting the detective's gaze, he answered softly, "I would put it in the hands of a higher authority."

"I believe it is there at this moment."

"Yes. And I would leave it there, Lieutenant."

For some moments their gazes stayed locked. Then Kinderman nodded, saying, "Yes, Father. Yes. Yes, I thought you would say that." He turned to again observe the sunset. "So beautiful," he said. "And so what makes us think such a thing has beauty while the Leaning Tower of Pisa does not. Also lizards and armadillos. Another mystery." He tugged back his sleeve for a look at his wristwatch. "Ah, well, I have to go. Any minute, Mrs. K. will be *schreiing* that the dinner is cold." He turned back to Karras. "Thank you, Father. I feel better . . . much better. Oh, incidentally, you could maybe do a favor? Give a message? If by chance you should ever meet a man last name Engstrom, please tell him—well, just say to him, 'Elvira is in a clinic. She's all right.' He'll understand. Would you do that? I mean, if by some crazy chance you should meet him."

Faintly puzzled, Karras answered, "I will."

"Look, we couldn't make a film some night, Father?"

Karras cast his eyes down and, nodding, murmured, "Soon."

"You're like a rabbi when he mentions the Messiah: always 'Soon.' Listen, do me yet another favor please, would you?" Glancing up, Karras saw that the detective looked gravely concerned. "Stop this running round the track for a little. Just walk. Okay, Father? Slow it down. Could you do that for me, please?"

Karras smiled faintly and said, "I will."

Hands in the pockets of his coat, the detective looked down at the sidewalk in resignation. "Yes, I know," he said, nodding. "Soon. Always soon." As he started away, he stopped, reached up a hand to the Jesuit's shoulder and squeezed, saying, "Elia Kazan, your director, sends regards."

For a time, Karras watched him as he listed down the street; watched with fondness and with wonder at the heart's labyrinthine turnings and improbable redemptions. He looked up at the clouds washed in pink above the river, then beyond to the west, where they drifted at the edge of the world, glowing faintly like a promise remembered. There'd been a time when he often saw God in such sights, felt His breath in the tinting of clouds, as now the lines of a poem he'd once loved returned to haunt him:

Glory be to God for dappled things,
For skies of couple-color as a brindled cow;
For rose-moles all in stipple upon trout that swim;
Fresh-fire-coal chestnut falls; finches' wings . . .
He fathers forth whose beauty is past change.
Praise Him.

Karras pressed the side of a fist against his lips and looked down against the sadness and the pain of loss welling up from his throat toward the corners of his eyes as he thought of a line from a psalm that once filled him with joy. *"Oh, Lord,"* he remembered achingly, *"I have loved the beauty of Thy house."*

Karras waited. Dared not risk another glance at the sunset.

Instead, he looked up at Regan's window.

Sharon let him in and told him nothing had changed. She was carrying a bundle of foul-smelling laundry. She excused herself. "I've got to get this into the washing machine."

Karras watched her. Thought of coffee. But now he heard the demon croaking viciously at Merrin. He started toward the staircase, but then stopped as he remembered the message he was supposed to give Karl. Where was he? He turned to ask Sharon and glimpsed her disappearing down the basement steps. He went looking for the houseman in the kitchen. He wasn't there. Only Chris. Her elbows propped and hands cupped at her temples, she was sitting at the breakfast table looking down at . . . What was it? Karras quietly moved closer. Stopped. A photo album. Scraps of paper. Pasted photos. Chris hadn't seen him.

"Excuse me, please," Karras said softly. "Is Karl in his room?"

Chris looked up at him wanly and shook her head. "He's on an errand," she answered huskily and softly. Karras heard her sniffle. Then "There's coffee there, Father," Chris murmured. "It ought to perc in just a minute."

As Karras glanced over at the percolator light, he heard Chris getting up from the table, and when he turned he saw her moving quickly past him with her face averted. He heard a quavery "Excuse me," and in a moment Chris had exited the kitchen. Karras looked down at the photo album. Candid shots. A young girl. Very pretty. With a pang, Karras realized he was looking at Regan: here, blowing out candles on a whipped-creamy birthday cake; here, sitting on a lakefront dock in shorts and a T-shirt, waving gaily at the camera. Something was stenciled on the front of the T-shirt: CAMP . . . He could not make it out. On the opposite page a ruled sheet of paper bore the script of a child:

> If instead of just clay
> I could take all the prettiest things
> Like a rainbow,
> Or clouds or the way a bird sings,
> Maybe then, dearest Mommy,
> If I put them all together,
> I could really make a sculpture of you.

Below the poem: I LOVE YOU! HAPPY MOTHER'S DAY! The signature, in pencil, was *Rags*.

Karras shut his eyes. He could not bear this chance meeting. He turned away wearily and waited for the coffee to brew. With lowered head, he gripped the counter and again closed his eyes. *Shut it out!* he thought; *shut it all out!* But he could not, and as he listened to the thumping and bubbling of the percolating coffee, his hands began trembling again as compassion swelled suddenly and blindly into rage at disease and at pain, at the suffering of children and the frailty of the body and the monstrous and outrageous corruption of death.

"If instead of just clay . . ."

The rage ebbed away to sorrow and helpless frustration.

". . . all the prettiest things . . ."

He could not wait for coffee. He must go. He must do something. Help someone. Try. He left the kitchen and as he came to the living room, he looked through the open door and saw Chris on the sofa, sobbing convulsively, while Sharon tried comforting her. He looked away and walked up the stairs, heard the demon roaring frenziedly at Merrin. ". . . would have *lost!* You would have *lost* and you knew it! You *scum*, Merrin! *Bastard!* Come *back!* Come and . . ."

Karras blocked it out.

". . . or the way a bird sings."

As he entered Regan's bedroom, Karras realized he had forgotten to put on his sweater. Slightly shivering from the cold, he turned his gaze to Regan. Her head was sideways and a little turned away from him as the demonic voice continued to rage.

He went slowly to his chair and picked up a blanket, and only then, in his exhaustion, did he notice Merrin's absence. Moments later, remembering that he needed to check Regan's blood pressure, Karras wearily got up again, and was shambling toward her when abruptly he pulled up in shock. Limp and disjointed, Merrin lay sprawled facedown on the floor beside the bed. Karras knelt, turned him over, and seeing the bluish coloration of his face, he quickly felt for a pulse and in a wrenching, stabbing instant of anguish, Karras realized that Merrin was dead.

"Saintly flatulence! *Die*, will you? *Die?* Karras, *heal* him!" raged the demon. "Bring him back and let us finish, let us . . ."

Heart failure. Coronary artery. "Ah, God!" Karras groaned in a whisper. "God, *no!*" He shut his eyes and shook his head in disbelief, in despair, and then, abruptly, with a surge of grief, he dug his thumb with savage force into Merrin's pale wrist as if to squeeze from its sinews the lost beat of life.

". . . pious . . ."

Karras sagged back and took a breath. Then he saw the tiny pills scattered loose on the floor. He picked one up and with aching recognition saw that Merrin had known. Nitroglycerin. He'd known. His eyes red and brimming, Karras looked at Merrin's face. *". . . go and rest for a little now, Damien."*

"Even *worms* will not eat your corruption, you . . . !"

Hearing the words of the demon, Karras looked up and began visibly trembling with an uncontrollable, murderous fury.

Do not listen!

". . . homosexual . . ."

Do not listen! Do not listen!

A vein stood out angrily throbbing on Karras's forehead, and as he picked up Merrin's hands and started tenderly to place them in the form of a cross on his chest, he heard the demon croak, "Now put his *cock* in his hands!" as a glob of putrid spittle hit the dead priest's eye. "The last rites!" mocked the demon. It put back its head and laughed wildly.

Karras stared numbly at the spittle. Did not move. Could

not hear above the roaring of his blood. And then slowly, in quivering, side-angling jerks, he looked up with a face that was a purpling snarl, an electrifying spasm of hatred and rage. *"You son of a bitch!"* Karras seethed in a burning whisper, and though he did not move, he seemed to be uncoiling, the sinews of his neck pulling taut like cables. The demon stopped laughing and eyed him with malevolence. "You were losing!" Karras taunted. "You're a loser! You've *always* been a loser!" Regan splattered him with vomit. He ignored it. "Yes, you're very good with children!" he said through gritted teeth. "Little girls! Well, come on! Let's see you try something bigger! Come on!" He had his hands out like great, fleshy hooks, slowly beckoning, inviting. "Come on! Come on, loser! Try *me!* Leave the girl and take *me!* Come into *me!*"

The next instant Karras's upper body jerked sharply upright with his head bent back and facing up to the ceiling, and then convulsively down and forward again, with the Jesuit's features twitching and contorting into a mask of unthinkable hatred and rage, while in strong, spasmodic jerks, as if pushing against some unseen resistance, the Jesuit's large and powerful hands were reaching out to clutch the throat of a screaming Regan MacNeil.

Chris and Sharon heard the sounds. They were in the study. Chris sat at the bar while Sharon was behind it, mixing them a drink, when both the women glanced up at the ceiling as they heard a commotion in Regan's bedroom: Regan screaming in terror and then Karras's voice fiercely shouting, *"No!"* And then stumblings. Sharp bumps against furniture. Against a wall. Chris knocked her drink over as she flinched at a violent crashing sound, a sound of breaking glass, and in an instant she and Sharon were racing up the stairs to the door of Regan's bedroom where, bursting in, they saw the shutters of the window on the floor, ripped off their hinges! And the window! The glass had been totally shattered!

Alarmed, they rushed forward toward the window, and as they did, Chris saw Merrin on the floor by the bed. She gasped, standing rooted in shock, and then she ran to him, kneeling beside him. "Oh, my God!" she whimpered. "Sharon! Shar, come here! Quick, come—"

Sharon's scream of horror cut her off. Chris looked up bloodlessly, gaping, and saw Sharon at the window staring down at the steps with both hands to her cheeks.

"Shar, what is it?"

"It's Karras! Father Karras!" Sharon cried out hysterically, racing from the room. Her face ashen, Chris got up and moved quickly to the window. Looked below. And felt her heart dropping out of her body. At the bottom of the steps on M Street, Karras lay crumpled and bloody as a crowd began gathering around him.

A hand to her cheek as she stared down in horror, Chris tried to move her lips. To speak. She couldn't.

"Mother?"

A small, wan voice calling tearfully behind her. Chris partly turned her head, her eyes wide, not quite daring to believe what she had heard. Then the voice came again. Regan's. "Mother, what's happening? Come here! I'm afraid, Mom! Oh, please, Mom! Please! Please come here!"

Chris had turned and seen the tears of confusion, and suddenly she was racing to the bed, weeping, "Rags! Oh, my baby, my baby! Oh, Rags! It's really you! It's really you!"

Downstairs, Sharon lunged from the house and ran frantically to the Jesuit residence hall, where she urgently asked to see Dyer. He came quickly to Reception. She told him. He stared at her in shock. "Called an ambulance?" he asked her.

"Oh my God! No, I didn't! I didn't think!"

Swiftly Dyer gave instructions to the switchboard operator, then he raced from the hall along with Sharon. Crossed the street. Raced down the steps.

"Let me through, please! Coming through!" As he pushed his way through the bystanders, Dyer heard murmurs of the litany of indifference. "What happened?" "Some guy fell down the steps." "Yeah, he must've been drunk. See the vomit?" "Come on, sweeties, we're going to be late."

At last Dyer broke through, and for a heart-stopping instant he felt frozen in a timeless dimension of grief, in a space where the air was too painful to breathe. Karras lay crumpled and twisted, on his back, with his head in the center of a growing pool of blood. His jaw slack, an odd shine in his eyes, he'd been fixedly staring upward as if at the patiently waiting stars of some beckoning, mysterious horizon. But now his eyes shifted over to Dyer. Seemed to glow with an elation. Of completion. Of something like triumph.

And then with some plea. Something urgent.

"Come on, back now! Move it back!" A policeman. Dyer knelt and put a light, tender hand like a caress against the bruised, gashed face. So many cuts. A bloody ribbon trickled down from the mouth. "Damien . . ." Dyer paused to still the quaver in his throat, as in Karras's eyes he saw that faint, eager shine; the warm plea.

Leaning over, Dyer asked, "Can you talk?"

Slowly Karras reached his hand to Dyer's wrist. He clutched it and gave it a squeeze.

Fighting back the tears, Dyer leaned down closer and, putting his mouth next to Karras's ear, he asked softly, "Do you want to make your confession now, Damien?"

A squeeze.

"Are you sorry for all of the sins of your life and for having offended Almighty God?"

The hand slowly releasing; and then a squeeze.

Leaning back upright, Dyer slowly traced the sign of the cross over Karras as he emotionally recited the words of absolution: *"Ego te absolvo . . ."*

An enormous tear rolled down from a corner of Karras's eye, and now Dyer felt his wrist being squeezed even harder, continuously, as he finished the absolution: *". . . in nomine Patris, et Filii, et Spiritus Sancti. Amen."*

Dyer leaned over again with his mouth next to Karras's ear. Waited. Forced the swelling from his throat. And then he murmured, "Are you . . . ?" Dyer stopped short. The pressure on his wrist had abruptly slackened. He pulled back his head and saw the eyes filled with peace; and with something else: something like joy at the end of heart's longing. The eyes were still staring. But at nothing in this world. Nothing here.

Slowly and tenderly, Dyer slid the eyelids down. He heard the ambulance wail from afar. He began to say, "Good-bye," but could not finish. He lowered his head and wept.

The ambulance arrived. They put Karras on a stretcher, and as they were loading him aboard, Dyer climbed in and sat beside the intern. He reached over and took Karras's hand.

"There's nothing you can do for him now, Father," said the intern in a kindly voice. "Don't make it harder on yourself. Don't come."

His gaze holding on that chipped, torn face, Dyer slowly shook his head and said quietly, "No. I'm coming."

The intern looked up to the ambulance rear door, where the patiently waiting driver was standing and looking in with his eyebrows raised in a question. The intern mutely nodded and the rear door was raised and locked shut.

From the sidewalk, Sharon watched numbly as the ambulance slowly drove away. She heard murmurs from the bystanders.

"What happened?"

"Oh, well, who the hell knows."

The wail of the ambulance siren lifted shrill into night above the river. Then abruptly it ceased.

The driver had remembered that time no longer mattered.

Epilogue

Thin June sunlight streamed through the window of Chris's bedroom as she folded a blouse on top of the contents of a suitcase on her bed and then closed it. She moved quickly toward the door. "Okay, that's all of it," she told Karl, and as the Swiss came forward to lock the suitcase, Chris went out into the hall and toward Regan's bedroom. "Hey, Rags, how ya comin'?" she called out.

It was now six weeks since the deaths of the priests. Since the shock, since the closed investigation by Kinderman. And still there were no answers. There were only haunting speculations and frequent awakenings from sleep in tears. Merrin's death had been caused by coronary artery disease, but as for Karras . . . "Baffling," Lieutenant Kinderman had breathed out emphysematously. "No. Not the girl," he'd decided. She hadn't done it: she'd been firmly secured by restraining straps. Therefore, Karras had ripped away the shutters, leaping through the window to deliberate death. But why? An attempt to escape something horrible? Kinderman had quickly ruled that out, for had he wished to escape, the priest could have gone out the door. Nor was Karras in any case a man who would run. But then why the fatal leap?

For Kinderman, the answer began to take shape in a statement by Dyer making mention of Karras's emotional conflicts: his guilt about his mother; her death; his problem of faith; and when Kinderman added to these the continuous lack of sleep for several days; to the concern and the guilt over Regan's imminent death; to the demonic attacks in the form of his mother, and then, finally, the shock of Merrin's death, he sadly concluded that, shattered by guilts he could no longer endure, the Jesuit psychiatrist's mind had snapped. Moreover, in the course of investigating the mysterious death of Burke Dennings, the detective had learned from his readings on possession that exorcists themselves had at times become possessed, and in circumstances much the same as had been present here: strong feelings of guilt and the need to be punished, these added to the power of autosuggestion. Karras had been ripe. Although Dyer had refused to accept it. Again and again he returned to the house during Regan's convalescence to talk to Chris, asking over and over if Regan was now able to recall what had happened in the bedroom that night, but the answer was always a head shake or a no, and finally the case was closed.

Chris poked her head into Regan's bedroom. With two stuffed animals in her clutch, she was staring down with a child's discontent at the packed and open suitcase on her bed. They were catching an afternoon flight to Los Angeles, leaving Sharon and the Engstroms to close up the house, and then Karl to drive the red Jaguar cross-country back home. "How are you coming with your packing, honey?" Chris asked. Regan tilted her face up to her. A little wan. A little gaunt. A little dark beneath the eyes. "There's not enough room in this thing!" she said, frowning and with her lips in a pout.

"Well, you can't take it all, now, sweetheart. Come on, leave it and Willie will bring all the rest. Come on, baby. Gots to hurry or we'll miss our plane."

"Okay, Mom."

"That's my baby."

Chris left her and went quickly down the stairs. As she got to the bottom, the door chimes rang and she went to the door and pulled it open.

"Hi, Chris." It was a long-faced Father Dyer. "Just came by to say so long," he said.

"Come on in. I was just going to call you."

"No, that's okay, Chris; I know you're in a hurry."

She took his hand and drew him in. "Oh, come on! I was just about to have a cup of coffee. Have one with me."

"Well, if you're sure . . ."

She said that she was, and they went to the kitchen, where they sat at the table, drank coffee and spoke pleasantries, while Sharon and the Engstroms bustled back and forth. Chris spoke of Merrin: how awed and surprised she had been at seeing the notables and foreign dignitaries at his funeral; then for moments they were silent together while Dyer stared down into his cup and into sadness. Chris read his thought. "She still can't remember," she said gently. "I'm sorry."

Still downcast, the Jesuit nodded. Chris glanced to her breakfast plate. Nervous and excited, she hadn't eaten. The rose was still there. She picked it up and pensively twisted it, rolling it back and forth by the stem. "And he never even knew her," she murmured. Then she held the rose still and flicked her eyes up at Dyer. He was staring at her intently. "What do you think really happened?" he asked Chris softly. "I mean, as a nonbeliever. Do you think she was really possessed?"

Chris pondered, looking down as she absently toyed with the rose again. "I don't know, Father Dyer. I just don't. You come to God and you have to figure if there is one, then he must need a million years' sleep every night or else he tends to get irritable.

Know what I mean? He never talks. But when it comes to the Devil . . ." She looked up at Dyer. "Well, the Devil's something else. I could buy that; in fact, maybe I do. You know why? Because the creep keeps doing commercials."

Dyer stared at her with fondness for a moment, then said quietly, "But if all of the evil in the world makes you think that there might be a devil, Chris, how do you account for all of the good?"

Chris held Dyer's steady gaze. The words had made her squint and frown in thought until at last she looked aside and gently nodded her head. "Never thought of that," she murmured. "Good point." The sadness and shock of Karras's death had settled on her mood like a melancholy haze, but she tried now to focus on this modest invitation to hope and to light by remembering what Dyer had said to her once as he had walked her to her car at the Jesuit cemetery on campus after Karras's burial there. *"Can you come to the house for a while?" she'd asked him. "Oh, I'd like to, but I can't miss the feast," he'd replied.* She'd looked puzzled and so he'd explained, *"When a Jesuit dies, we have a feast of celebration. For him it's a beginning."*

"You said he had a problem with his faith."

Dyer nodded.

Chris lowered her head a bit and shook it. "I can't believe that," she answered abstractedly. "I've never seen such strong faith before in my life."

"Car is here now, Madam!"

Snapped out of her reverie, Chris called out, "Okay, Karl! We're coming!" She and Dyer stood up. "No, you stay, Father. I'm just going upstairs to get Rags."

Dyer nodded absently. "Okay." He was thinking of Karras's puzzling shout of "No!" and then the sound of running steps overheard before his leap through the window. There was something there, he thought. What was it? Both Chris's and Sharon's recollections had been vague. But now Dyer thought again of that mysterious look of joy in Karras's eyes. And something else, he now remembered: a fiercely shining glint of . . . what? He didn't know; but he thought it was something like victory. Like triumph. Inexplicably, the thought seemed to lift him. He felt lighter. He walked to the entry hall, hands in his pockets, and then leaned in the open doorway watching Karl help the driver stow luggage in the trunk of the limo. Dyer wiped his brow—it was humid and hot. He turned his glance to the sound of footsteps coming downstairs, Chris and Regan, hand in hand. They came toward him. Chris kissed his cheek, then held her hand to it as tenderly she probed the priest's sad eyes.

"It's all right, Chris. I've got this feeling it's all right."

Chris said, "Good." She looked down at Regan. "Honey, this is Father Dyer," she said. "Say hello."

"Pleased to meet you, Father Dyer."

"And I'm so very pleased to meet you too."

Chris checked her wristwatch.

"Gotta get going now, Father."

"It's been peachy. Oh, no, wait! I almost forgot!" The priest reached into a pocket of his coat and extracted something. "This was his," he said.

Chris looked down at the holy medal and chain that was cupped in Dyer's open and upraised hand. "Saint Christopher. I thought you might like to have it."

For long, silent moments Chris stared down at the medal thoughtfully, her brow lightly furrowed as if debating some decision; then, slowly, she reached out a hand, took the medal, slipped it into a pocket of her coat and said to Dyer, "Thanks,

Father. Yeah. Yeah, I would." Then "Come on, honey," she said to Regan, but as she reached out to take her daughter's hand, Chris saw that she was frowning and squinting up fixedly at the Jesuit's round Roman collar as if at sudden remembrance of forgotten concern. Then suddenly she reached up her arms to the priest. Surprised, the young Jesuit leaned over, and with her hands on his shoulders Regan kissed his cheek, and then, dropping her arms, she looked off with a frown of puzzlement, as if she were wondering why she had done so.

Her eyes abruptly moist, Chris briefly looked away, then, taking Regan's hand, she said softly and huskily, "Oh, well, we've *really* gotta go now. Come on, honey. Say good-bye to Father Dyer."

"Bye, Father."

Smiling, Dyer wiggled the fingers of a hand in farewell and said, "Good-bye. Safe journey home."

"Father, I'll call you from L.A.," Chris said over her shoulder. It would only be later that she would wonder what he actually meant by "home."

"You take care now."

"You too."

Dyer watched them move away. As a driver opened a door for them, Chris turned and waved, then blew a kiss. Dyer waved back and watched her climb into the back of the limo, next to Regan. As the car pulled away from the curb, Regan stared at Dyer hauntingly through the rear window until the car turned a corner and was gone from his sight.

Dyer turned and looked left as from across the street he heard a squealing of brakes: a police car. Climbing out of it was Kinderman, who walked quickly around the front of the car and then waved as he hurried toward Dyer, calling, "I came to say good-bye."

"You just missed them."

Crestfallen, the detective stopped dead in his tracks.

"Really? They're gone?"

Dyer nodded.

Kinderman turned to look down Prospect Street regretfully, turned back, lowered his head and shook it. *"Oy!"* he murmured. Then he glanced up at Dyer. He walked up to him and somberly asked, "How's the girl?"

"She seemed fine. Really fine."

"Ah, that's good. That's really all that's important." Lifting an arm, the detective glanced at his wristwatch. "Well, back to business," he said; "back to work. Bye, now, Father." He turned away and took a step toward the squad car, but stopping, he turned his head to stare speculatively at the priest. "You go to films, Father Dyer? You like them?"

"Oh, well, sure."

Kinderman turned back and moved closer to Dyer. "I get passes," he said weightily. "In fact, I've got passes for the Biograph tomorrow night. You'd like to go?"

"What's playing?"

"Wuthering Heights."

"Who's in it?"

"Who's in it?" The detective's eyebrows bunched together in a scowl as he gruffly answered, "Heathcliff, Sonny Bono and in the role Catherine Earnshaw, Cher. Are you coming or not?"

"I've seen it."

The detective stared at the Jesuit limply, then looked away and murmured ruefully, "Another one!" Then he turned back to Dyer with a smile and, stepping up to the sidewalk, he hooked an arm through the priest's and started walking him slowly up the street. "I'm reminded of a line in the film *Casablanca*," he said fondly. "At the end Humphrey Bogart says to

Claude Rains: 'Louie—I think this is the beginning of a beautiful friendship.' "

"You know, you *look* a little bit like Bogart."

"You noticed."

In forgetting, they were trying to remember.

Author's Note

I have taken a few liberties with the current geography of Georgetown University, notably with respect to the location of the Institute of Languages and Linguistics. Moreover, the house on Prospect Street does not exist, nor does the Jesuit residence hall in the location in which I have described it. Finally, the fragment of prose attributed to Lankester Merrin is not my creation, but is taken from a sermon of Cardinal John Henry Newman titled "The Second Spring."

THE EXORCIST